WAITING GAME

NEW YORK STARS: TWO

G. A. MAZURKE

Photograph: Michelle Lancaster

Model: Chad Hurst

Illustration: Chelsea Chira

Cover Design: RBA Designs

Editing: Anne-Geneviève Ducharme-Audran

Proofreading: Norma's Nook & Cynthia Mejia

To the animals of our hearts who honored us with the rest of their lives…
Mine was called Trever.
My heart fur baby.
I miss you more than words can say.
And to Triskelle, who is forever memorialized as Mia's chapter heading, you are irreplaceable and loved by two girls whose pillows miss your imprint.
<3

PLEASE READ: FOREWORD & TRIGGER WARNINGS

HEY LOVELIES!

Welcome to the second novel in the New York Stars' series.

This is a complete standalone and requires no other reading to enjoy this book.

Cole is a total smut slut and he lurrves being a part of Facebook groups where he can catch some good recs. 'The Smuthood' is a real Facebook book group that rocks - go join and find your people like he did: https://www.facebook.com/groups/346663333653640 :D

The Sarajevo 1984, Olympic gold medal-winning, figure-skating routine '*Boléro*' by Jayne Torvill and Christopher Dean is featured in this story. You can see it for yourself here: https://olympics.com/en/video/torvill-and-dean-s-legendary-bolero-performance-music-mondays/

I also reference S.H.I.T - the team text chat. Thank you to Kerri Lynn Keizer for that suggestion in my Diva reader group competition! (Bubble Butt Buddies by Kimberly Litto was a very close contender. ;) So thank you, haha.)

Writing this book brought out my Canadian pride. *And I'm British!* But some of these characters **are** from Canada, so you will find dates and, perhaps, cultural references that seem foreign to you because they are… They are Canadian! For example, July 1st is Canada Day and their Thanksgiving is held on the second Monday in October. Regardless, I hope you will follow me down this path, with maple leaves shining in your eyes and maple syrup running through your veins!

Cole's mother is a Brit and, as a result, he calls her 'mum.' This isn't a typo. :)

GLOSSARY:

Bébé: baby

Cibole: (colloquialism) fuck = derivative of ciboire which is the chalice used during Eucharist.

Tabarnak: (colloquialism) fuck = derivative of the tabernacle which is the ornamented box in which Communion hosts and wine are kept.

Minou: kitten

TRIGGERS:

Parental death

References to animal neglect (not involving the main characters)

References to grief in relation to the passing of a beloved pet

Loss of spouse to cancer (not involving Cole and Mia)

You should also know that none of the NHL team names match the ones in my league.

Don't forget when **WAITING GAME** reaches 1000 reviews, head to my reader group for a bonus scene! www.facebook.com/groups/SerenaAkeroydsDivas

Much love and happy reading,

G. A. Mazurke

xo

THE NEW YORK STARS

FORWARDS

42 Cole Korhonen LW
5 Ruben Kerrigan LW
26 Zeke McIsaac LW
28 Kyle Lewis RW
35 Liam Donnghal C (C)

DEFENSEMEN

15 Jude Gagné LD (A)
23 Jean-François Deschamps LD

GOALTENDERS

59 Ryan Greco
1 Roger Davies
31 Matt Ellison

Governor
Conor O'Donnelly

General Manager
Gracie Bukowski

Head Coach
Allan Bradley

Mia

The Charles

uncle
Chuck

great grandpa
Marty

found family
Dionne
Larry
Beanpole
Jarvis

The Bukowskis

parents
Hanna & Fryd

sister
Gracie

brothers
Trent
Cezary aka Kow
Noah

COLE

The Korhonens

peps
Clyde

mum
Lindsay

brothers
Colt
Cody
Callan

The billet bros

Liam
Gray
Matt
Oren

PLAYLIST

If you'd like to hear a curated soundtrack, with songs that are featured in the book, as well as songs that inspired it, then here's the link:

https://open.spotify.com/playlist/5X0tYTlOLXgoxuxmU5J8VO?si=7109cce6b43f498b

FIRST PERIOD

Glitterball - Sigma/Ella Henderson

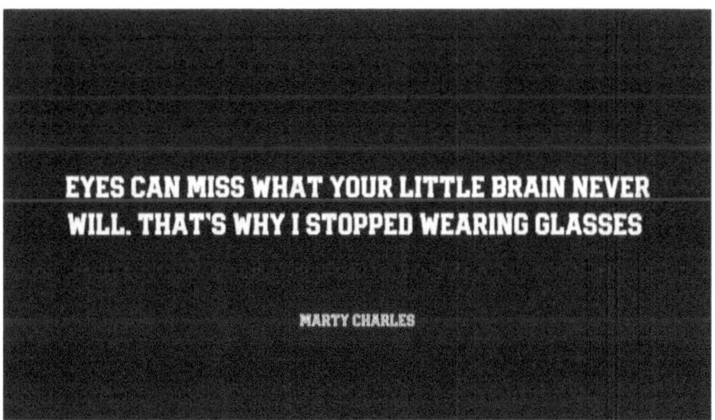

WHILE IT SUCKS that my team, the New Jersey Blue Demons, didn't make it into the playoffs, and despite the bad juju, I have to grin when I watch my billet bro, Liam 'Leprechaun' Donnghal, slide yet another puck into the back of the net for the New York Stars.

There's an advantage to my figure-skating coach being late—I got to read some Omegaverse why choose until the puck dropped, and then I started watching my bro in action. That means I can cheer to the empty rink when he scores without feeling like I'm betraying the Blue Demons.

Thankfully, my celebration is between me, the ice, and my Kindle app.

When a notification slides into my DMs informing me my coach has shown up at long last and has parked outside the rink, I switch from watching the game stream to my messages.

Sending her a thumbs-up, I move over to *Hooked-Up*, when I see a chick swiped right on me.

My nose crinkles as I study her profile.

I have nothing against hot blondes, but I prefer brunettes—they're the ones who know how to have more fun.

Checking out the next profile, I see a hottie from Midtown. One of her pictures shows her working behind a bar—her uniform has *Chuck's* embroidered on her tit—where another has her hugging a cat.

That's good. I like cats.

As I swipe right, a second later, a notification dings around the rink, echoing and making me jump.

Which is when I realize I'm not alone anymore because that notification wasn't mine.

I glance up, on the hunt for my figure-skating coach who's the only person allowed access during this private session, and my eyes widen as recognition hits.

The chick I swiped right on is the one skating toward me...

My grin makes an appearance as I straighten up and head onto the ice.

This whole session was born of watching Kyle Lewis, one of the first-string right wingers who plays for the Stars, spin pirouettes during his cellies. While other morons were giving him shit, until Liam called them out for it, I was watching his landing and takeoff.

Poetry. In. Motion.

Ballet isn't my thing, but figure skating *could* be.

Having seen my coach, hell, I'm more invested in my classes than ever because not only is she hotter than she looked on her profile, but that *ass* of hers?

Fuck. My. Life.

And all that brown hair—I should probably start worshipping her now and save us both some time.

Of course, I'm too busy checking her out to see the writing on the wall because Mia Charles, of *Hooked-Up* fame as well as a talented figure-skating coach who's supposed to be helping me with my edge work, skitters to a halt right in the center of the ice and bursts into tears before I even get the chance to ask, "How you doin'?"

CHAPTER 2
COLE

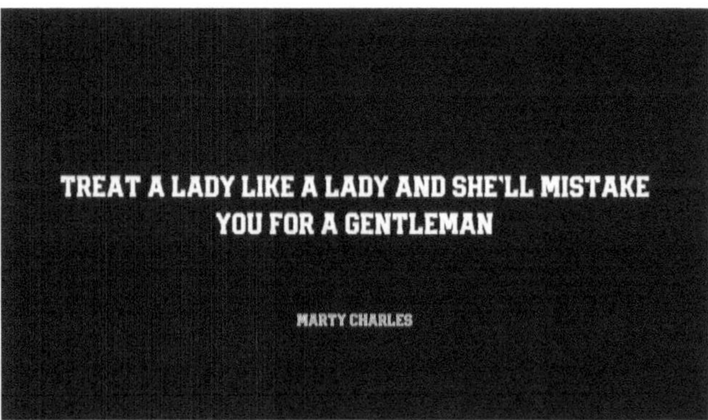

"YOU OKAY, MISS?"

Calling her 'miss' when I know my coach's name gives this encounter a faintly Victorian tang, but I do it anyway.

This is me unashamedly falling back on lessons my mum taught me. Ones that I've let fall to the wayside because hockey makes men entitled jerks—there.

I said it.

With my genes and career, I'm already on a losing streak.

Unfortunately for me, Mia doesn't recognize my Victorian-shaped sacrifice.

She keeps on weeping at center ice.

"Guess I know how Quasimodo feels," I mumble under my breath as I skate toward her.

Another guy might run for the hills, but my sister from another mister would have my balls if I didn't try to help her. Unlike my peers, I know to listen to the chicks in my vicinity. Not that Gracie is easy to ignore.

Mia doesn't stir at my approach, doesn't appear to even register my existence until I tap her on the shoulder in a *there, there* motion.

She jolts at the first tap, her head whipping back to look at me as if she didn't know I was standing in front of her.

This spontaneous outburst of emotion appears to have drained her.

Her eyes are rimmed red, massive, fat tears overwhelming the lashes and making 'em into little waterlogged half stars and... Fuck, she's beautiful.

On the one occasion I've seen Gracie cry, she went the whole hog. Snot everywhere. Tears rolling down her cheeks that wore grooves into her skin. Bright red in a whole cacophony of misery.

Honestly, she was crying like she does everything else—with serious gusto.

Mia, on the other hand, is delicate and fragile, and hell if I don't want to wrap her in my arms and hold on tight. While vowing to her that I'll not only make the world a better place, but I'll also ensure every impoverished nation has enough food to stop starvation as I singlehandedly figure out some refrigeration technique that'll get the glaciers to refreeze themselves.

That is how beautiful she is.

All glossy burnt caramel curls and piercing blue eyes that could cut through the average man like a knife.

"I'm so sorry," she whispers, trembling fingers swiping at her eyes. "This is embarrassing. I didn't mean to cry. I was panicking about being late... I promise this won't happen again."

Awkwardly, I shoot her a half-smile. *Awkwardly*, mostly, because I'm a complete ass for noticing how goddamn pretty she is when she's so distressed, but this is like a scene I've read in books.

The stars are aligning, and Mercury has to be blowing Venus—or do I mean Mars is jacking off Jupiter?

Whatever. Those light-blue eyes of hers are borderline freaky but I'm not afraid, especially as they accentuate the rich shade of her curls.

Her forehead is wide, culminating in a widow's peak. Her nose is dainty with a small, uptilted tip that leads to pouty lips, the corners of which are curved downward.

A part of me wants nothing more than to make them curve upward, but perhaps that's insensitive of me.

Then, I realize she's staring at me with bloodshot, watery eyes and I pick up on the fact she's expecting me to say something instead of gaping at her like a moron.

"You don't have to be sorry."

I try not to notice the tiny silver studs in her ears—cat silhouettes.

Even her goddamn ears are cute.

Jesus fuck.

Talk, Cole.

Act normal.

"Something's obviously going on and you can't help being upset."

"I'm really sorry I was late," she mutters, ignoring my statement that she doesn't have to apologize as she swipes at her cheeks again.

Her head bows, allowing me a glimpse of a tattoo she has behind her ear—the outline of a small cat, complete with whiskers and pointy ears. Where the tail should be, right at the end, there's a fletched arrow.

Odd.

"It's okay. I was reading," I admit.

"Y-You were?"

Accustomed to the disbelief, I grin. "*And* watching the playoffs at the same time."

"What playoffs?"

"*The* playoffs."

"Hockey ones?"

HOCKEY ONES?

Is she for real?

"Yes, hockey ones." I sound as if I'm being strangled. "It's an afternoon game."

"When I Googled you, you seemed to be a pretty big deal. How come you aren't in them?"

I scrunch my nose. "Are you prepared for my answer?"

She hitches a shoulder, but her bottom lip quivers so I know she's trying to distract herself.

She's come to the right place for a distraction.

"My coach refuses to listen to reason, the defense for the Blue Demons has more holes in it than a sieve, and the GM needs to get laid because if he cleared out his pipes, I'm sure his brain would reboot and he'd use the trade deadline to get decent players on our side while offloading the shitty ones. And if you ever tell anyone I said that, I'll deny it."

Her eyes widen but those quivering lips twitch into a small smile. "Is that a fancy way of saying that your team sucks?"

I try not to stare at her mouth because that would be weird. "*I'm* good at what I do. The rest, not so much. But that doesn't mean I don't want to improve. Which is why I'm here."

Cheeks pink, she nods. "Do you want to get started?"

"That wasn't a prompt," I dismiss even as I'm wondering why she's blushing. Clearly, she's trying to make my overactive imagination combust. "I was demonstrating that I'm not an arrogant asshole who can't accept there's always room for self-improvement."

"That's actually..." She shoves her hands in her pockets. "...refreshing."

"Consider me a cool glass of pop at a 1st July barbecue."

Her brow furrows. "1st July?"

"You Americans. I swear it's like you think you don't share a continent with anyone else—"

"Ohh, you're Canadian."

"How deep was your Google search?" I complain.

"Apparently not deep enough."

"I'm from Saskatchewan."

"Bless you."

"Har har."

This time, her smile is more genuine. "I've heard of it."

"Thank God. I was worried." I rub the back of my neck. "You sure you're doing okay? We can reschedule?"

The genuine smile disappears and is replaced with a forced one. "We're good to go."

"I can start next week if you've got—"

"My uncle died," she blurts out before I can finish the sentence. "It hit me that I won't be able to call him on the way home anymore."

"Aw, man. I'm sorry."

"Don't be."

"We should reschedule—"

"No! That won't be necessary. Thank you but I have to figure out how to pay for his funeral so I can't cancel the class because I need the money." Mortification has her cheeks blazing hotter than ever. "I'm so sorry that we ate into that time. We can stay longer—"

"There's no need." I raise a hand to further stall the torrent of words. "Okay, how about I still pay you for the session, but we head to the cafeteria and we can talk instead of practice?"

"Why would you do that?"

Because I want to get into your pants and I'm trying to impress you.

My brain sucks.

I'm such an asshole.

Recognizing it doesn't make it less true though...

"Because it'd be real shitty of me to force you into a coaching session when you're grieving."

There—I can sound like a decent human being if I try.

"I'll still be grieving next week. And the week after. No. I need to rip off this Band-Aid because..." A shaky sigh escapes her. "Never mind."

"When did he die?"

Her bottom lip is back to trembling but it's the devastation in her expression that hits me on the raw. "This morning."

I don't care that I'm doing a goldfish impression. "Are you being serious?"

"I need the money for more than his funeral," she confesses in a low, embarrassed whisper.

Immediately, guilt jabs at me and gets followed up with an uppercut of privilege.

Even without hockey, I'm a trust fund baby. The summer my grandma died, I took weeks off, never mind a few hours.

"I meant it when I said we can talk theory and about my expectations," I reassure her. "We never got the chance to discuss what my end goals are for the lessons and you shouldn't have to eat that cost. How do you feel about going for a coffee?"

"A-Are you sure?"

"Of course I am. If you want, we can even skate around the ice. I know that helps me clear my mind."

"Could we do that? Skate?"

I nudge her with my arm. "Of course."

"Thank you." There's a tremor to the words as, in a move that surprises me, she grabs a hold of my hand and drags me toward the boards.

At the gesture, I squeeze back then let go.

When, barely seconds later, my cell starts blowing up in my pocket, I huff. "Just give me a minute?"

She nods and doesn't even bother looking at me as I snatch my phone when all my chats explode.

I billeted with the Bukowskis from fifteen to eighteen alongside three others: Gray, Matt, and, of course, Liam.

I have a group chat with them. Then, we billet bros have another conversation that includes the three Bukowski sons: Kow, Trent, and Noah. *Then*, there's the family chat where the Bukowski folks and their daughter, Gracie, are included. *On top of those*, I have a thread with my siblings, multiple individual chats, as well as a team chat with the Blue Demons.

At that moment, every single conversation lights up with notifications and, Stanley Cup semifinals or not, I don't give a fuck.

Totally unlike me, I activate the 'Do Not Disturb' mode, tuck it back into my pocket, and give her my full focus.

"Everything okay?"

I hum my assent and change the subject: "So, what was your uncle's name?"

"Chuck, but we don't have to talk about him."

"Huh." *Chuck.* That reminds me of something on her profile… "Okay, so full disclosure, like fifty seconds before you came onto the ice, I swiped right on your profile on *Hooked-Up.*"

She brakes to a graceful halt. "Huh?"

"When your phone dinged as you came in, that was probably me. I don't say any of this to make you feel weird or obligated or anything," I rush to tell her. "Not that you'd need to feel… I'm saying that I saw your pictures. Your uniform had a 'Chuck's' patch on it. Is that a coincidence?"

Why do I know that name anyway?

Though she's busy blinking at me, it doesn't stop her from starting up again and circling the rink like the pro she is.

It's nice to be free and loose on the ice, and it's even nicer when I'm at her side because she skates like a fairy and I want to stroke her wings.

"You saw my profile on *Hooked-Up?*" she repeats.

"I did. And I'm infinitely curious. My sis would say I'm nosy but she's a harsh critic." I shrug at her soggy laugh, relieved to have lightened the mood some. "You're going to see the notification later so I didn't want to make this weird, you know? I hate miscommunication. It's my least favorite trope."

Her eyes widen. She brakes. Again. "You hate miscommunication? Least favorite trope? *What?*"

"I read a lot. Romance." I smirk at her as she restarts skating, backward this time so that we're face-to-face. Her stare is… bewildered. "Dudes don't know what they're missing out on. Chicks write banging hot sex." Then, I remember that her uncle died. "Sorry, we shouldn't be talking about this, but I like to maintain an open dialogue."

She clears her throat. "Apparently."

"I also thought I'd grown out of the habit of oversharing."

That does earn me a wry smile. "Okay, so, to answer your original question, yes, Chuck's bar was my uncle's." Her bottom lip gets sucked in and I see her nip it a touch. I'm suddenly jealous of her teeth. "It's mine now."

Still jealous. "Oh, he left it to you?"

"I've known it'd be mine for years. It's a family bar." She cuts me a look as her cheeks burn. "I know you're into hockey, but what do you know about baseball?"

I wriggle my head. "Fair amount. If I didn't get to be a hockey player, I'd have tried to make a career in baseball instead."

"You had the talent for it?"

"It's all in the hips." At my wink, she rolls her eyes. "My family were big Montreal fans before they moved to DC. My older brother has a pretty snazzy trading card collection too."

"You should have heard of Marty Charles, then."

"Marty Charles," I repeat, then, because of the context, my eyes bug. "*The* Marty Charles? CHUCK?"

Her smile is sheepish as my holler echoes in the barn. "My great-granddaddy as well as my uncle's namesake."

"No fucking way." Even if baseball wasn't my shit, I'd know that I was talking to the great-granddaughter of a legend here. "He and Yogi Berra are like *everything*. Didn't they both get ten World Series rings?"

"They did. Chuck used to say that Marty and he were best friends until Yogi caught up to him.

"I hate baseball so don't expect me to know his stats."

"Ah, that sucks."

"For who? My baseball-obsessed dad and uncle, you, or me?"

"All of the above." I grin at her. "So, I'm guessing the eponymous 'Chuck's' is a baseball-themed bar?"

"Uh-huh. No one knows that about the Marty Charles connection though. Not anymore."

"Why not?"

"Because my uncle's an idiot." Mia gulps. "*Was* an idiot."

"It's okay," I attempt to soothe.

"It's not. It won't be for a while." She sucks down some air like she's been holding her breath for ten minutes. "And that's fine. I got over losing my mom and my dad. I can deal with losing Chuck too." The words are hard, but how she clenches her eyes tells me she's two seconds away from sobbing again. Still, her grit shows through because she grinds out, "He wanted to do it on his own. Wanted to make Chuck's famous for its wings. He got it into his head in the 90s that that was the way forward. Instead, the bar's about five heartbeats from outright croaking."

"You can save it, though, right? Reconnect it with the legacy?" Then, a thought occurs to me. "Are you going to stop coaching?"

"Chuck's is a money pit," she counters with a swift head shake. "I'm going to have to burn the candle at both ends to keep it going, but that's fine."

She says that a lot but nothing she's saying is, in fact, *fine*.

"Anyway, enough about me. You were right earlier when you said we never got to talk about your goals for our training sessions."

My answer's immediate: "I want to do a spin without falling over."

"That's oddly specific. Surely you can do that anyway?"

"I want to improve my edge work *and* do fancy shit. I'm a powerful skater, but I need to carve out some finesse on the ice."

Mia snorts. "Just so you know... spins aren't fancy. Was that really your only goal for these classes?"

"I admit this is a whim."

"An expensive whim. My rates are high."

"They're market value. I checked." I'm not cheap but I was raised on a ranch. Wealthy or not, you nickel and dime like pros when you're a rancher because the profit margins are shitty if you're not smart about it. Every ranch is three crappy years from falling into the red. "There's a player who came onto my radar recently and I realized how tight his turns are. How he skates like… huh. *You*."

"Me?"

"Ya know, like a fairy."

"A fairy?" She chuckles. It might be watery, but it's better than her earlier tears. "I've been called worse things in my time."

"Like what?"

"Oh, a judge called me a skating elephant once."

"No fucking way. You're Tinkerbell on ice!"

She hitches a shoulder. "I sucked that day. My head wasn't in my routine. I stopped competing shortly after." Her tone's wistful. "Made it to the state championship and that's as far as I've gotten."

Considering she lost her uncle and hasn't had a major meltdown aside from that initial crying sesh, I think the distraction of chatting is working.

"Do you mind me asking why your head wasn't in the routine?"

She doesn't seem the type to not follow through with something because her life is falling down around her blades.

And yes, it's a snap judgment, but I believe that first impressions count.

Her gaze locks on mine. "Only if you're sure you want to know?"

CHAPTER 3
MIA

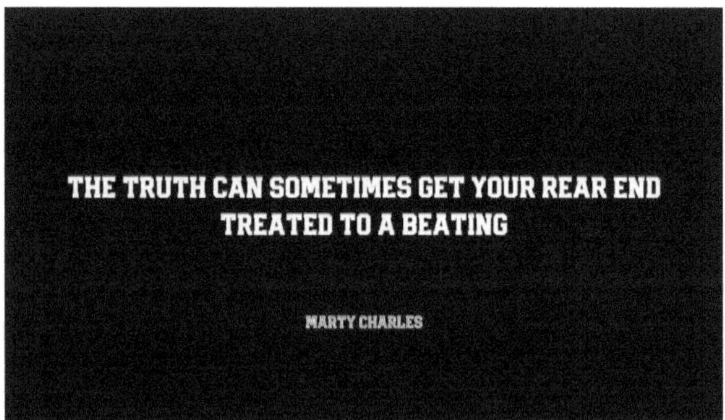

I KNOW my words were like a bad punchline. Why would he have asked if he didn't want to know? But there's a reason I always make sure —it's my version of a spoiler alert.

Cole, for whatever reason, appears to take me at my word.

He doesn't downplay my question, doesn't mock me, just frowns. "How bad?"

"Bad," is my gruff answer.

He tugs on the chain around his neck. "I'm a big boy. I can take it."

"My mom was murdered and my dad killed himself after he found out what happened to her."

It's a blunt answer, but the truth *is* blunt. There's no sugarcoating it.

Hell, it's not something I usually share with my 'students,' no matter their age, but nothing about this lesson is going according to plan and it actually feels good to get that off my chest.

What, with Uncle Chuck, the bar, the debts, the betrayal, it's been a shitty couple years in a shitty life.

My jaw works at the thought—*no fucking self-pity for you, Mia Charles. You're not allowed. Not after what you did to Gracie.*

"Your mom was murdered?" he blurts out, snow spraying as he skids to a halt.

"She's a New York City statistic," I concur bitterly.

"How old were you?"

"Nineteen, but I turned twenty shortly after."

More bitterness assails me as I recall what happened on that very day all those years ago…

"I wish you were joking."

"I do too."

"Jesus Christ." He scrubs a hand over his face. "So, you competed…?"

"I know it seems like a cold thing to do, but I needed to focus. I've always been able to compartmentalize and I figured competing would help. Ultimately, it didn't work."

"I get it. No one grieves the same and no one should ever shame another person for how they handle loss.

"When my grandma died, I decided I was going to take the summer off, but it made me wallow. Whereas when my gramps passed, I stuck with my schedule after I flew home for the funeral. It helped to get on with life. That's the only thing we can do sometimes."

"It is," I agree, my tone bleak. "Uncle Chuck and figure skating were what got me through. But I didn't have it in me to compete anymore."

"I'm sorry." A breath whistles from him. "On all fronts."

"You don't have to be. It was a long time ago." I elbow him in the side. "I should be the one who's sorry. I guess you didn't expect that answer, huh?"

"Definitely not." He shakes his head. "So, Chuck's your only family?"

"Yeah. I'm all alone now." My mouth quivers. "God, that hurts."

"It does." Surprising me, he snags a hold of my hand. "You don't know me, Mia, and maybe we'll never know each other more than what these lessons will permit, but you'll get through this.

"It'll suck. It'll hurt. Some days, you won't want to leave your bed, and others, you'll be hyper as you try to get through the hours without thinking of those you've lost, but you'll do it.

"And if figure skating is what'll help, both with your finances and mental health, then sign me up for an intensive training course."

The generous offer has me frowning. "You don't have to do that."

"Why shouldn't I? I need you to teach me how to be graceful on the ice and I've figured out what I want."

"Hit me with it."

"You heard of Torvill and Dean?"

My gaze turns distant as I search in my memory for the names. "They won the gold medal for Great Britain in the 80s?"

The reference is so specific that it makes me want to laugh. But then, there's something about Cole that's like that.

He *is* oddly specific.

It's in this shit about wanting to 'maintain an open dialogue.'

Maybe reading romance has trained him in how to be a decent human being?

"I remember them. Vaguely. They skated the *Boléro*, I think. Not that that narrows it down. Do you know how common—"

"Wait!" His eyes light up. "That's them!"

"My claim to fame is I'm a classical music buff," I joke. "Always used symphonies for my routines. I'm the woman you need on your trivia team."

"Good to know," he teases.

"Back when I was competing, I researched all previous Olympic wins, too, so you're lucky it registers on my radar, but what about them?" I inquire, shoving my sleeves up.

I can't help but notice that he stares at the cat tattoo on my forearm.

This sleeve depicts two of my cats, Curtis and Chloe, fleeing a tarot card when their tower falls apart after another member of my clowder dive-bombs it.

The whole background of the card appears to explode, leaving a part of it blank while the rest cascades over my forearm. 'The rest' includes furnishings and the culprit behind the attack—this one being bright white with a black nose—Cubert.

So named because of my uncle's obsession with the arcade game *Q*bert*.

Distracted as he scans my ink, he tells me, "I want to do that."

"Do what?" I ask, oddly aware of him thanks to his awareness of me.

Through my grief, it suddenly registers that he's a handsome man.

Mostly, his pictures on the Google search were of him helmeted up *or* with atrocious hair.

He must have had a cut recently because, um, yeah. I don't need to be thinking about his attractiveness.

Still, there's no denying he's all golden and smoldering—like a lazy panther who's pretending to be a pussycat.

There's a scar on his eyebrow that I know has to come from skating, but the rest of his face is literal perfection. Aquamarine eyes, a sharp blade of a nose, a wide mouth that looks eminently bitable, and an indent in his chin that should *not* keep drawing my eye.

"I want to replicate their routine," he exclaims, sweeping a lazy hand over his head, making his golden-brown hair stick up at all angles.

Not cute.

Not cute.

Not.

Cute.

So. Goddamn. Cute.

Still, his eager answer has my brows lifting. "You want to replicate their gold-medal-winning routine? In… You booked four weeks' worth of lessons, Cole."

"I did. But we can up the number of sessions per week. I'm free aside from collabs with my sponsors for the whole summer." He rubs his hands together. "Yeah, that's what I want to do."

Uneasily, I mutter, "Are you going to give me a one-star rating on Trustpilot if you don't finish the routine?"

He snorts. "No. Will you go on social media and talk about me to get followers?"

The words cut close to the bone. Really close. So close that it hurts.

Once upon a time, I'd have said I could never be such a scum-sucker. I'd have hit a mofo with one of the bats in Chuck's collection for so much as suggesting it.

But these past twelve months, my self-worth has taken a hammering.

I can no longer make that claim because I *have* done that—I've betrayed someone for clout like a grade-A asshole.

Rightfully so, she cut me out of her life. Which is ironic because if Gracie Bukowski were still friends with me, I wouldn't be so alone.

Karma—that's what this is.

And what's worse is that I know I deserve it.

"I would never betray your trust," I vow with a low whisper.

After everything that happened with Gracie, it was the height of bittersweet irony for a hockey player to hit me up for figure skating lessons.

While I might share a rink with some hockey players who rent out the ice for private training time, that's as close as I've come to breathing the same air as NHL players.

Until this past year.

Everything started to go wrong when Liam Donnghal—a dude I'd never heard of before that night—walked into my uncle's bar, took a seat in a booth, and Chuck saw him before Gracie cut out on her shift early to go home with the guy.

I didn't even know that Liam Donnghal was an NHL star. I thought he was a freak who came into a bar one boring midweek shift and ordered water.

That was the most memorable thing about him—his drink order.

I never realized that the moment he took a seat, some Pandora's box-level shit would gain ground.

Nothing's gone right ever since that night.

Entirely unaware of where my memories took me, Cole's smile practically beams from him. "We have a deal then."

I swallow. "It might not be as easy as you think to replicate the routine."

"I don't think it will be, but it's something to aim for."

"True. Do you mind me asking why you want to start with an Olympic gold medal-winning routine?"

Talk about aiming high.

"My mum's British and she traveled to Sarajevo when she was a teenager to attend the Winter Olympics where Torvill and Dean won.

"She loved it so much that she walked down the freakin' aisle to the *Boléro*."

"Yikes!"

"Uh-huh. Anyway, she still flies the Union Jack at the Olympics even though she agrees that Canada is the best country on Earth. I figure I'll get her to a rink if I tell her what I've been learning here."

"She doesn't come to watch you play?"

His smile tightens. For a millisecond. "Nah."

He wishes she did.

I clear my throat. "I used to know someone who was certain that Canada was God's country."

"Well, they sound like my kind of person."

"What about if you're playing?"

"At the Games? I trump the Brits then. Son's privilege." He holds up his hand. As I blink at it, he clucks his tongue. "You're supposed to high-five me."

"Oh. Sorry." I tap his hand, hard enough for him to whistle and wiggle his fingers with a grin. "I know what a high five is," I assure him, pink-cheeked. "I had a brain fart."

"I have that effect on women."

I mock-gag. "The retching effect?"

He smirks. "Do we have a plan?"

Sticking out my hand for him to shake, not high-five, and silently vowing that I'll hold my tongue for the rest of my life about training Cole Korhonen who wants to fly like a fairy on the ice, I assure him, "We have a plan."

Cole: I'm in love, bro

Gray: Shut up.

Cole: I am. Don't mock me!

Gray: I thought we got past this phase.

Cole: Which phase?

Gray: The juvenile one where you fall in love with anything with a big butt.

Cole: If that were the case, I'd have fallen in love with you a long time ago. Like, back when we first billeted with the Bukowskis lol.

Gray: *shudders*

Gray: Who are you in love with anyway?

Cole: She's my figure-skating coach.

Gray: Wait, didn't you meet her today?

Cole: Yes, Gray. Yes, I did. And WHAT a day. I swear angels sing when she talks. And her ass definitely deserves a poem dedicated to it.

Gray: *sighs*

Gray: You've been reading too much romance again.

Gray: Or did she blow you after your lesson? Is that what this is about?

Cole: No. Fuck, she's pretty when she cries.

Gray: WHAT?!

Gray: YOU MADE HER CRY?!

Cole: No! Of course, I didn't. You suck for thinking that.

Gray: What I know is that you've been with the Blue Demons for the past four seasons.

Gray: They recruit well-documented Neanderthals and romance books can only slow down the transmogrification so much.

Cole: Big word there, Gray.

Gray: *flips the bird*

Gray: I read too

Gray: Seriously, you need to suck up to the GM of the New York Stars so you can get your ass across the Hudson. Lucky for you, you should have an in soon lol.

Gray: They won. You see that?

Cole: By the skin of their teeth.

Gray: True.

Cole: Anyway, the Blue Demons aren't THAT bad.

Gray: Yeah, says you, the blossoming Neanderthal.

Gray: The one saving grace is that you still wear lime green and hot pink together and think it's a winning combination so they haven't tainted you completely.

Cole: Why did I even bother talking to you about this?

Gray: I don't know, Cole.

Gray: You clearly wanted to be insulted.

Gray: What is it about my face that makes people think they can tell me their secrets anyway?

Cole: This isn't a secret.

Cole: I'll shout it from the rooftops.

Cole: Also… color me intrigued. Which secrets? Whose secrets? What secrets?

Gray: Secret for a reason.

Gray: None of your beeswax.

Gray: So, the chick cried and you've fallen in love? We need to diversify your reading habits. When I said you read too much romance, you read too much fucking romance.

Cole: No such thing.

Cole: Everyone needs a HEA in their life.

Gray: Shoot me. Please.

Cole: Nah, who'd keep my 'secret' if I shot you? :P

Gray: So, you're gonna bang your coach. Nooooice.

Cole: Maybe.

Cole: Potentially.

Cole: If she said yes, I wouldn't say no.

Gray: Is this you being chivalrous?

Cole: *preens* I do rock.

Gray: Go away.

Cole: Where?

Cole: Oooh, I know. I'll check out her dating profile again.

Gray: You'll check out her what now?

Cole: Yeah, fun fact, I actually met her on Hooked-Up.

Gray: You're giving me a headache.

Cole: Sounds like someone needs to drink more water.

Gray: I don't need more water.

Cole: I think you're dehydrated.

Gray: Go. Away.

Cole: Only if you drink a glass of water.

Gray: *sends picture*

Cole: I said drink a glass of water, not flip me the bird IRL then send a picture of it to me.

Cole: Sheesh.

Gray: Lemme guess you want me to take a B12 supplement too.

Cole: *sniffs* You probably should

Gray: *sends picture*

Cole: Two birds in one conversation. Is that a record?

Gray: Never with you lol

Gray: You can't seriously think you're in love with this girl.

Cole: I'm only joking about that but I like her.
She's sweet.

Gray: You fuckers are turning me as gray as my
name.

CHAPTER 4
MIA

Fly Away From Here - Aerosmith

Chantal: So sorry about Chuck, Mia :(<3

DOES it sting that Chantal's the only one of my old friends to reply to the news that Chuck's passed?

Yes.

It stings *a lot*.

When I quit competitions, they began fading out of my life, but here's proof they erased themselves entirely—Chuck let us party at our apartment and gave us free beer though we were underage when we were on the circuit and needed a blowout.

Karma.

It keeps on kicking me in the metaphorical nuts.

I already didn't feel like going to work tonight, but it's not as if I have a choice.

Doesn't make it any better that the bar's as grody as ever when I make it back to Chuck's at nine.

Dionne and Jarvis are at the front of house as usual. We can't afford two bartenders but it gives me the freedom to coach. Beanpole and Larry, the short-order cooks, are in the kitchen, puttering away at our 'specialty' Buffalo wings which are the opposite of special.

Alongside the smattering of patrons who greet me with a warm welcome, I can't deny it's like coming home.

Especially when I see the grief on their faces.

Knowing that I'm not the only one in mourning comes as a massive relief. Chuck had such a huge presence that it's difficult to believe the universe could snuff that out, but it did.

It took him away, leaving me alone… Well, alone except for the regulars.

When Garry draws me in for a hug, I let him. Ordinarily, I'd be shoving him off me because he and I have never seen eye to eye, but this time, I sink into it. He tucks me in his embrace and I allow it. I even cry because I can feel his grief making my temple damp.

"I'm so sorry, Mia."

Someone claps me on the back—sounds like Walt—and I twist out of Garry's arms to answer him. "Thanks, Walt. Not for…" I swallow. "Thanks for being there."

"Of course."

The bar currently holds around two dozen souls, but there was a circle of guys that Chuck considered his buds—Garry, Walt, Robbie, and Biff. They were at the hospital with me when Chuck took his final breaths.

The memory has me wanting to down a few shots of vodka, anything to quench the chill in my soul that feels like it's taking over my whole being.

Chuck was... *Chuck.*

My uncle, sure, but my biggest cheerleader too. He had my back. Always. And I had his. No matter what.

I retreat from Walt's hug to dive into Robbie's then get a final one from Biff.

"You doing okay, honey?"

Dionne's relatively new so she didn't know my work-shy uncle that well, but she's the mothering kind. Her eyes are gentle with sympathy as she looks at me, seemingly aware that forming words is difficult.

"I-I want him back."

She pats my hand. "He's not suffering anymore."

My jaw works. "No, he's not."

"If you need anything from me, extra shifts, overtime, whatever, I'm here."

"I appreciate that," I tell her earnestly.

What I don't tell her is I can't afford extra shifts *or* overtime.

I'm not about to repay her kind offer with worries about job security though.

"And if you need to talk, my kids always say I've got the best ear in Queens."

I shoot her a timid smile in thanks then seek refuge behind the bar—I always tend and never serve—and take over for Dionne, who starts hitting up tables, asking if anyone needs a refill at the premature wake.

I don't charge the regulars even though the financial hit will have repercussions—Chuck would be very unhappy if there weren't a few rounds of drinks on him—but as some semblance of normalcy returns to the establishment, I let myself drown in the routine of a shift.

However, that normalcy makes it even weirder not to hear the pings and the dings from the small arcade Chuck had out back.

He used to be constantly playing those damn things when he should have been working. Instead, a game's on, and most of the patrons are watching it as they chow through hot wings and peanuts.

It's turning into any other night.

A night where Chuck's about to sneak outside with a cigar he's not supposed to smoke and which I always reprimand him for.

A night where patrons boo as a pitcher drops a ball. Where the grill sizzles out back and the scent of buffalo sauce and fried chicken skin is heavy in the air.

I suck in a cheek and gnaw on it, eyes darting around as my throat starts to feel like it's closing in.

Breathing is hard.

Sweat beads on my brow as the sudden flush of heat overwhelms my senses.

Suddenly, I know where I can't be—*here*.

Not now.

Whether or not I can afford this, my ever-tightening throat and increasingly narrowing vision make the decision for me.

With a quick sob, I snatch my purse from behind the counter and rasp at Jarvis, "I need a minute."

Before I can rush out, he mumbles, "You need to take some time off. Go home, Mia. We can handle things for a couple nights."

I don't have the luxury of taking a couple free nights, not anymore, but grief waits for no woman.

With a sniffled thanks, I make a swift departure, raising a hand in farewell when some of the guys call out as they notice me leaving.

Once the door shuts behind me, I race down the street.

Five minutes later, I arrive home.

Chuck's name might be on the rent-controlled apartment's lease but he barely lived here.

Most nights, he slept in his recliner in the back office at the bar, a beer resting on top of his belly, a baseball bat nearby in case anyone tried to break in.

I'm glad I didn't argue about his sleeping arrangements because while he'd amble his way here once a day for a shower and a change of clothes, that was pretty much it. Meaning I can breathe easier without the weight of *him* in my space, drowning me in memories.

What also helps is when Cupid and Cubert immediately yowl at me in welcome.

Cubie hisses when I try to pick him up, but Cupid lets me hide my face in her fluffy fur.

For what could be ten seconds or ten minutes, I stand at the entrance to my apartment, hugging her as tightly as she'll let me.

Like she knows I'm upset, she starts purring.

The low rumble has me releasing a heavy sigh as I stare into her bright green eyes. "He's gone, Cupid. He's not coming back."

She meows softly. I'd like to think it's *sadly*. She's probably just hungry.

Seeing as I ended up walking blindly around Central Park after Chuck passed until the reminder I'd set on my phone jogged my memory of the scheduled lesson with Cole, the stench from the hospital is still on my skin. My first port of call *was* going to be the shower, but my cats need feeding.

I slouch over to the kitchen, grimacing when I notice there are only enough packets of wet food for two more days.

"Guess that's me living on bread and jelly until my next coaching session," I mutter. "You're a foodie snob, aren't you, Cupid?" I laugh when she curls herself around my ankles, purring in agreement, totally fine with me going hungry so she can live her best bougie life.

Adding more dry food than they like to their bowls, I choke out another laugh when Cubie sticks his face in a second before I throw kibble in.

With a teary smile, I finish up, substituting old water for fresh, and once that's done, I head for the bathroom.

A shower doesn't wash away my grief, but it makes me feel like less of a zombie. Especially when I see Casper, another of my feline horde, hiding in the pile of towels.

Though I haven't eaten since breakfast, I don't bother with food and crash-land into bed, towel and wet hair and all.

For what feels like endless moments once Casper deigns to leave the clean laundry and to stroll over to the bed to cuddle with me, I stare at the ceiling and try not to cry. Then, a notification dings around my small bedroom.

I don't react because I don't care.

That's when the walls close in.

I swallow at the return of the pressure in my chest.

My mind races like it usually does, shitty thoughts dive-bombing me in the darkness until my lungs feel as if they're being squeezed in the hand of a giant.

Another ding sounds, then another. That's when I stop thinking about how hard my heart is pounding and I start caring when ding, after ding, after ding echoes around my room.

With a scowl and the onset panic attack forgotten, I clamber off the mattress and return to the bathroom where I scoop up my jeans and dig out my cell from my pocket.

There, I see the flood of notifications and my eyes widen when I realize Cole wasn't joking about him swiping right on me…

Attention well and truly snagged, I wander back to my bed, but I ignore his messages on the dating app and, instead, head to his profile.

How uncanny is it that we connected on *Hooked-Up*?

The clue might be in the title, and it might routinely be for one-night stands, but the site claims to work on compatibility too.

Are Cole and I compatible?

It seems unlikely, though the joker I met today can't be all fun and games—not when he's also a hockey star.

"'Likes pop music and horseback riding. Eating Hawaiian pizza and arguing with people about whether or not ham and pineapple are the only pizza toppings that count.'" I read the few lines off his profile to Casper, who grooms himself in response.

Because Cole's words are so *him*, I switch over to the messages and read what he's got to say there.

Cole: So, have you seen the notification yet?

Cole: It feels like the white elephant in the room.

Cole: Wait, no. That's mixing my metaphors and my aunt teaches English so she'd be ashamed of me.

Cole: I didn't want you to think I was being a creep or something earlier.

Cole: I'm not.

Cole: A creep, I mean.

Cole: Though, it's starting to look like that with
the number of unanswered messages...

Cole: Hint

Cole: Hint

Cole: Hint

Me: I didn't think you were being a creep.

That's what I settle on as a response, and before I can kick myself and decide to delete the message, he's seen it already.

Cole: That's always positive for our future
working relationship.

Cole: I totally expect you to transform me into
Christopher Dean.

Me: How much of an impact did those skaters
have on your mom if you remember Dean's first
name?

Cole: Google helped me. I watched the routine
again and came up with a bunch of trivia to
impress you.

Me: To impress me?

Me: Why would you want to do that?

Cole: Why wouldn't I? You need to be
impressed, Mia. You've yet to see how shitty my
edge work is.

Me: How bad can it be? You're a pro hockey
player, Cole.

Cole: It's bad. Horror-movie bad.

Me: Your skates are weapons of mass destruction?

Cole: I carve up the ice for sure. The Zamboni hates me. I cause it more work than two teams playing like brutes combined.

Cole: I think the technician is coming up with some form of vengeance against me, but that could be paranoia talking.

Me: That's some claim to fame.

The tension in my shoulders loosens up and I don't even realize it.

Cole: You really haven't seen me play?

Me: Hockey isn't my sport. TBH, nothing is. I hate sports.

Me: It might be for the best—I won't dread our first lesson.

Cole: Now I'm the one who's wounded. *sniffles* You're bad for my ego. Crying the first time you saw me, dreading the next lesson, not even knowing who I am...

Cole: Come on, you can be honest. How deep was the Google search?

Me: Rudimentary.

I'm not lying. I wanted to make sure the guy was who he claimed to be.

Cole: How rudimentary?

Cole: I guess we shouldn't be talking about this, huh? You're sad.

Cole: I didn't want you to feel lonely too.

Cole: There's nothing worse than being alone
when you've lost people who matter the most
to you.

His kindness comes as a surprise—chiefly because my 'rudimentary' search let me know that strange hair aside, the guy has seriously *bright* taste in clothes and a preference for going through hotties that *Page Six* can't keep up with.

Me: It's kind of you to think of me, Cole.

Me: I had a bit of a freak-out at the bar.

Cole: You went to the bar?!

Me: I have responsibilities.

Me: :/

Me: I guess I failed them.

Cole: Hardly. You're allowed to take some time
for yourself.

Me: We don't all have that luxury, Cole. I don't
mean to be a bitch about it, but my situation isn't
your situation.

Cole: You're right. And it's none of my business.

Cole: You wanna talk about the freak-out?

Blankly, I stare at the wall opposite when I realize that I do.

I want to tell this complete stranger something I would have struggled to share with a friend.

If I had any.

Me: Too many memories. They crowded me until
I felt like I was suffocating with the past.

Me: I'm going to have to suck it up though. I
need to be in there tomorrow for a delivery.

The notion has me scraping a hand over my face.

As many duties as I had at the bar, a number that increased substantially when Gracie quit after we treated her like shit, there are a dozen more about to be loaded onto my plate.

Chuck living at the bar made things easier for me in many ways.

In the past couple months, as things grew worse for him healthwise, he tried to prepare me, but I'm not ready for what's about to hit me.

> Me: Chuck taught me everything I needed to know but I didn't think he'd pass away as early as he did.

> Me: I was in denial about losing him.

Cole: He was sick?

> Me: Yes. For the last two years, but he only told me about the prognosis, like, nine months ago.

Cole: God.

> Me: Yeah. It felt so fast. One minute, he was Uncle Chuck, and the next he had a diagnosis and a pharmacy-worth of meds he had to take.

His sickness was one of the reasons he'd been so quick to double-cross Gracie—*money*.

His liver cirrhosis and the debts he'd incurred not only at the bar but for his medical bills were how he'd gotten me to betray Gracie live on air for the entire country to see that we were pieces of shit.

Fuck, I wish I could talk to her. Wish I could let her know that Chuck was gone.

Even after what he did to her, something I was complicit in, I know she loved him as much as he loved her. That was why she quit out of the blue without ever returning to the bar in the aftermath, getting some stiff to collect her dues—her hurt was substantial.

With that checkmate move, she made a liar out of us when we told the city that her hockey-star brothers were regulars in Chuck's, my not-so-smart uncle figuring he could strong-arm her into making that happen.

To be honest, I'm proud of her for quitting. She *should* have resigned. We betrayed her and we didn't deserve to have the chance to apologize.

But my guilt is a raw, festering wound and I'd give my left tit to talk to her. To say sorry and to mourn his passing with someone who *got* my uncle. Respected him. Didn't think he was an old, crazy coot.

Me: TBH, I knew he had a drinking problem but he was a functioning alcoholic so it became a part of his nature.

Me: Man, that's so fucked up.

Cole: His choices are not on YOU.

Cole: Are you going to get some rest? You should. It's been a hard day for you.

Though I've already processed his words, I stare at the ceiling again.
I stare and I stare.
And I stare.
And my heart pounds.
And my lungs squeeze.
And…

Me: Do you want to come over to my place?

I send it before I can panic.
I can't regret it. Won't.
The blue ticks are immediate.
There's no shame in finding solace in another person. If Chuck hadn't passed away today, I'm honest enough with myself to reason that I'd totally have contacted Cole to hook up tonight.

Especially after having met him at the rink.

Not only is he hot post-haircut, but he's cute—his personality. His quirks. Who wears purple cowboy boots with a lime-green Polo shirt? Cole Korhonen, that's who. But I like a man who owns the traits that set him apart from the rest. His very nature is extravagant and that's beyond appealing, so I can't complain about his unusual wardrobe choices when it all makes up the intriguing creature I'm inviting over to my place tonight.

Cole: To your apartment… Are you sure?

I'm sure that I don't want to be alone.

Me: Definitely

I switch to Google Maps and pull up my address.

Ordinarily, I wouldn't do this. I'd bring a guy back in an Uber to maintain some semblance of privacy, but Cole's in the NHL. I have to figure that privacy is more important to him than it is to me. Plus, he doesn't seem like the 'serial killer' type.

More… Tigger from *Winnie the Pooh*.

I said what I said.

Grabbing the link, I drop it in the app.

Me: Let me know if you're coming.

His response is reassuringly immediate:

Cole: Want me to bring food?

My stomach rumbles and my mind's eye veers to the empty fridge and less-than-full kitchen cabinets.

Suddenly, his coming over seems like a blessing in disguise. Which makes me feel guilty.

Jesus.

Knowing what he loves, I concede:

Me: Hawaiian pizza?

Cole: No other pizza exists.

Cole: Also, you checked out my profile, huh?

Me: I did. Before I answered you.

Cole: It's a great profile, isn't it?

Me: Your ego is massive.

Cole: Lots of me is, honey. LOTS of me is.

Cole: Okay, I'll bring food. And beer?

Me: I don't really drink

Cole: Pizza, then. See you in an hour or so.

Me: Traffic depending.

Cole: Sigh. Yeah.

I let him go then, content in knowing that he's on his way.

Now that I've let them loose, urges drift through my body.

Sex and I don't have the healthiest of relationships, but I'm not about to start questioning that when I need to forget. When I need to sleep.

I think about how big Cole is. As tall as I am, he's still got six inches on me—minimum. Then, there's that ass you could bounce a quarter on and thick thighs that make the seams of his pants strain. Those biceps of his are huge too. He's got veins that curl all over his forearms, and they stick out, which makes my tongue want to trace them. He's inked as well, and my fingers curl at the prospect of tracing the lines that an artist drew on him.

I know his hugs are going to be awe-inspiring.

I bet when he holds me, it'll be tight, so tight that it'll help me sleep. A living, breathing weighted comforter.

Tonight, that's exactly what I need—to forget, to be held, to lose myself in someone.

Even if that someone is a stranger.

Because that someone is a stranger.

CHAPTER 5
COLE

Born To Die - Lana Del Rey

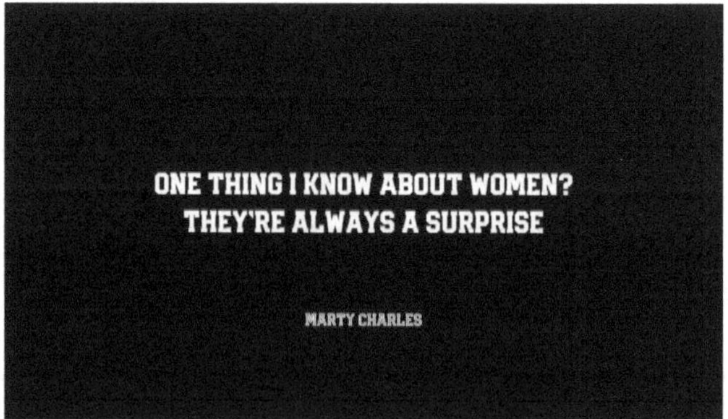

I NEVER LOOK a gift horse in the mouth, but I'm definitely surprised by Mia's offer.

Despite my billet bro's mockery, there truly is chivalry buried in my eagerness to spend time with her tonight.

I've been where she is and no one should ever be alone—I have three siblings and practically a baker's dozen of billet family in comparison to her zero. I'd never have coped if I had to get through my grief on my own, so why should she?

Traffic is on our side so it takes a little under eighty minutes for me to reach her street, and along the way, I phoned in an order at a nearby pizzeria so I collect that in ten.

Nearing midnight by this point, I arrive at her door with a bag full of different pops and a twenty-inch pie. As I knock, I half-wonder if I made up how hot she is, but nope. Even though she's clearly been crying again, she's so fucking pretty that it steals my breath.

Helps, I guess, that she's only wearing a towel.

And we have our green light.

Ugh. Gray's right. The Blue Demons *are* turning me into a prehistoric asshole.

I'm not beyond saving, though—I shove the pizza box at her first and foremost then order, "Food. *Eat.*"

Her puffy eyes focus on the box's fastener tab and she fumbles the catch as she steps away from the door to let me in. A small cat twirls around her feet, making the exercise twice as difficult.

"Who's this sweetheart?"

Her eyes gleam in the way that only a pet owner's can when someone else is talking about their fur kid. "Cupid." When she peers at the contents of the pizza box and finds a half-Hawaiian and half-cheese, her brow arches. "Thought the only true pizza in the world was Hawaiian..."

"I'm zealous in my defense of the Hawaiian pizza," is my solemn response, "but you didn't say you agreed with me, and tonight isn't the night for an argument on substandard pizza toppings. I thought this was a safe bet."

Her lips twitch. "For future reference, I'm a fungi gal."

My nose crinkles. "They grow on shit."

"What do? Mushrooms?" She waves a hand. "Good shit."

"Is there good shit?"

"If you like mushrooms, sure. Anyway, I don't think the ones that grow on cow poop are what they slap on a pizza, Cole." She dumps the box on the counter. I watch her snag a massive slice for herself, sigh, then take a bite. After a couple chews and a big swallow, she mumbles, "Thank you for this."

Her kitchen counter acts as a breakfast bar so I stack pop on it and haul my ass onto the stool beside hers. "You're welcome."

"I didn't think you'd message me."

I shrug. "I got home and I started thinking."

"Thinking is dangerous."

"It is," I agree as I pick up a slice.

"Don't you have to watch your carb intake?"

"You sound like one of my bros. You want the whole pizza, don't you? One glimpse of glistening golden chunks of pineapple and baked ruby squares on a slice of gooey heaven and you've become a turncoat."

She hides a smile. "Something like that."

I sniff. "I'm out of the playoffs—"

"You were robbed, I'm sure."

Nodding, I concur, "I was. But I wouldn't have won anyway. The Blue Demons aren't as good as the Stars. If they don't win the Stanley Cup, I'll swear off my weekly panacea."

"Your weekly what now?"

"Panacea."

"Panacea," she repeats. "Wait, you mean the pizza?"

"Oh, yeah. I'm being generous tonight. I'm sharing so I'm being screwed out of four slices of paradise. You've no idea how much of a sacrifice this is," I inform her sorrowfully. "But I'll take one for the team."

She outright chuckles. "It's the hockey player in you."

"Sure is." I wink at her then jolt when something fluffy scratches my calf.

Mia peeks at my feet the same time I do. "Meet Cubert."

My brows lift. "Cubert?"

"Cubert the Cuntie."

I snort. "The cuntie?!"

"What? He's an asshole."

"But he's so fluffy!"

"And his fluffiness means he lacks the motor skills required to be a complete and utter asshole?"

Cubert has a black nose while the rest of him is pure white fluff. Honestly, he looks like he's been sniffing around tar and got stained for the rest of his life…

The thought makes something click in my head—the tarot card tattoo on her forearm. The cat on it was white with a black nose. The same cat?

He meows at me, which has Mia shaking her head. "Don't feed him. He'll bite you."

"Sorry, dude," I inform him. "You've been branded a biter. No ham for you."

"He's worse than a biter, I can assure you. Don't even get me started on how he acts with the others," she grumbles, wincing when Cubert decides to play with the leg of the stool she's sitting on and scratches her with every pass.

"You said 'others?' How many do you have?"

"Five." She shrugs at my whistle. "They found me. What was I supposed to do? Get lost?"

Little hearts pop into being around my head at her admission. This is a cartoon-esque tumble into catching feelings.

It takes a special kind of person to bring in strays with all their illnesses, feralness, and foibles—I'd know, my mum used to do it all the time pre-divorce.

"So, five?"

"Yup. Casper the Charming, Chloe the Cheeky, Curtis the Cunning, Cupid the Cutie, and Cubert the Cuntie."

"You're weird." So weird.

I should buy her an engagement ring immediately weird.

"They live up to their reps," she dismisses unapologetically.

"It's uncanny that they all have names starting with 'C.'"

"Why?"

"Because my siblings do too."

"No way."

"Yeah," I say with a laugh. "Colt's the eldest, then there's Cody, followed by me, and then Callan."

"Your mom didn't mind?"

"It's a family tradition." She wouldn't have *dared* minding.

"Who's the charming one?"

"I'm wounded that you have to ask. I'm also the cheeky one. Cody's a cunning cunt, but he's a fighter pilot so I figure that's a part of his job description. Callan's pretty cute. But he's more curious. About everything."

"What about Colt?"

"He's an S-word."

"A what word?"

"Stoic. He always looks like he's in pain."

She pauses mid-swallow. "Sounds sad."

"Nah. He's happy. Sort of."

"If you say so."

I've no idea why I decide to share an old family truth with her, but I rumble, "We're ranchers. When I was fifteen and he was twenty-two, we had this big fire and we lost a lot of horses—he and I... *we* never got over it."

Her eyes grow round. "That's so sad."

I nod then pull up my hoodie, letting her see my stomach. Those round-as-a-penny eyes of hers widen even more.

"You tried to save the horses?" she rasps, taking note of my scars.

"We all did. Apart from Callan who was too young, none of us were spared from burns."

Her fingers trace the pockmarked and puckered skin. I don't normally like being touched there, as it's both sensitive and numb so it's uncomfortable, but I don't stop her. Not when there's sorrow in her eyes. Sorrow that's so tangible, I can almost touch it. Sorrow for *me*.

"How many horses?"

"Eight." Fuck, that still hurts to say out loud.

She releases a sharp gasp. "No!"

My pain feels like her pain and it makes it easier to share the fact that my grief is as raw as it was when I was a kid: "Lost my quarter horse, Betsy. I learned to ride on her. She was my BFF."

"Cole, I'm so sorry."

Her words are genuine and they choke me up, but it's the glossiness in her eyes that hits me harder. Those tears are why, gruffly, I change the subject. "I have more family than the 3Cs though."

"Jesus Christ, really?"

"Yeah, but they're bros by choice. Eight of 'em."

"Wow. How did you meet them?"

"You know what a billet family is?"

"Is that a military thing?"

"Well, 'billet' is, but not in this instance. When a kid in minor hockey gets selected, drafted, or traded to a team too far to commute from their hometown or, in the case of North American teens, country, they go and live with a family who's trusted by the organization. Like, I'm from Saskatoon, but I went to stay with a billet family in Winnipeg."

"That's pretty neat."

"It's how I came to live with the Bu—"

Cubert decides to live up to his name and attack my stool. I yelp when he manages to hook his claws into my favorite purple jeans and almost fall backward in response.

"Ah, shit," she whines, but her instincts are wired for this because she jumps off her stool and in seconds, the little bastard's in her arms.

He's also back to looking innocent as fuck.

I guess we have our confirmation that this is 'tarot-card, tower-terrorist' cat.

I crinkle my nose at him.

He hisses and spits at me.

"I'm so sorry, Cole. He didn't like you ignoring him," she mutters, dipping down to grab a hold of the beast when he attempts a second escape. Inadvertently, the move reveals another piece of ink on her upper thigh that's a crescent moon with a cat perched on it. "Say hello."

Warily, I wave at the cat. "Hey."

I receive another hiss for my pains as I twist to look at the cuffs of my jeans.

She clucks her tongue at the cat but walks over to the nearest window. He shows us his butt-star then leaps from the windowsill into the night once she wedges it open.

"Safety, at last," I joke.

"Told you he lived up to his name." She stares at my jeans. "Did he rip them? I hope he didn't. They're really nice."

I freeze.

Nice?

"You like them?" I sputter.

She hitches a shoulder. "They suit you."

They suit me?

Unaware that she's the only person who has ever said anything nice about my clothes, she takes a seat once she's washed her hands.

Unaware that she's sealed our freakin' fate.

Hooked.

That's me.

I'm so fucking screwed.

Because I need to change the subject before I start asking if she likes my bright Fanta-orange hoodie too, I point to the stack of pop cans I brought with me on the counter in front of her. "Pick your poison."

She eyes the smorgasbord of soda. "Couldn't decide what to buy?"

"Figured one of everything would suffice."

Mia reaches for the orange pop. "This is my jam."

After she pulls the tab and takes a sip, she sighs again. "Thank you, Cole. For… everything."

"My pleasure. I'll gladly be your pizza purveyor. We can even hang out after my sessions."

"Split a pizza?"

"Or we can each have one of our own." My brows bob. "Dirty talk, am I right?"

She whistles. "Sure is. Okay. Sounds like a plan."

Once I've demolished the slice in my hand, I go through the rest of my half like a lawnmower while gently prompting her with what I think she can handle.

I might not know her well, but I understand grief.

I know that it's a category one hurricane that can trigger an earthquake and a volcanic eruption in one fell swoop.

I know that it can shift into a torrential downpour one minute and the next, be nothing more than a bunch of gray clouds in a bright blue sky.

Grief is love that has nowhere else to go—that's floating around in a vacuum.

Humans don't like vacuums—be they the ethereal variety or the ones that suck up dust from a rug.

Before she starts on her third slice of pie, she asks, "Do you think badly of me for inviting you over?"

That gives me pause. "Should I? And why do you care anyway?"

Her gaze quickly drifts over to me before darting to the can of orange pop she's still holding in her other hand. "I don't normally invite my students here."

"I'm not an ordinary student though. I brought pizza. That's better than an apple."

Mia hides a grin. "Much better than an apple."

"Do you think badly of me for coming over?" I counter, watching as she relaxes at my question.

Only a jerk would judge her for not wanting to be alone on a night when she lost the last member of her family.

In silence, we continue eating until she peeps at me again as she takes the last bite of her third slice of pie.

"I don't want to remember. Not tonight," she says eventually.

There's no denying what she's talking about. Not that I want to hide from it.

I've had a slow streak for the past five or so months. It pains me to acknowledge that I'm getting to the point where puck bunnies aren't doing it for me anymore. Orgasms are great and all but…

This doesn't feel like one of my regular hookups.

"We don't have to do anything."

"That's not why I invited you over."

"No, you invited me for pizza."

This time, she huffs out a laugh. "I really didn't."

"Man, my profile reeled you in."

"Sure did." Dropping the can on the counter, she snickers then seems to come to a decision. The next thing I know, she's straightening up on the stool and locking eyes with me. "I'm going to bed now, Cole. Would you like to come with me?"

"Very much so," I rumble in return, the humor in my voice fading in the face of her direct request.

She doesn't wait for me as I get to my feet. Instead, she strides toward the bedroom, her intention clear—she wants to have sex. She wants to forget. And I'm the lucky asshole who was in the right place, at the right time.

As I follow her along the hall to the small bedroom, I watch her retreating spine as she steps into the bathroom.

This is a lot more clinical than I'm used to, a lot less grabby-handed, but I get it—I'm fulfilling a function tonight. One that might end with an orgasm or a bundle of sobbing woman in my arms. Either way, I'm okay with that for an ice-skating fairy who can appreciate my purple jeans, adopted five cats because they 'found' her, and knows Torvill and Dean off the top of her head.

Once I've stripped out of my tee, I drag off my jeans too, then in my boxer briefs, I clamber onto the bed.

With one hand behind my neck, I wait for her to come in, not bothering to turn on the light, quietly content to just lie here.

Though, I do think back to her dating profile.

I checked it out again before I messaged her earlier.

Hooked-Up has this BS personality compatibility test that you have to endure to get to the main site. I only went on the damn app because Gray recommended it—he's like me, sick of the puck bunnies.

That a computer algorithm thinks Mia and I are compatible isn't reassuring, but her profile *was*. It let me see that, beyond her grief, she has that same dry, quick sense of humor as I do, and having talked to her earlier today, I enjoyed how we bounced off one another despite the sad circumstances.

It's been a long time since I've had that kind of rapport with the opposite sex. Hell, if I've ever had it with anyone who isn't Gracie.

Though my lips purse at the thought, the opening of the bathroom door takes most of my attention. Especially when, the light as a backdrop, she walks out of there *sans* the towel she was wearing earlier.

She strides to my side of the bed then clambers on top of me much as I did her mattress.

Her silhouette alone was enough to give me a chubby, but I'm not going to rush this. Not after what she's been through today.

Instead, I let my hands find her shoulders and I gently rub them along her arms. I can feel the goosebumps pop up at my touch, and though, in the dark, she leans over me, her mouth seeking mine, I keep things slow.

I've had plenty of wham-bam-thank-you-ma'ams in my time. I know that's what she wants. But because I'm willing to be the dick that'll service her doesn't mean that I'm going to let her get away with expecting so little when there's potential here.

"Cole?" she whispers into the darkness.

I hum as she presses a kiss to the corner of my mouth. Her tits rub my chest as she wriggles against me.

"Are you wearing boxers?"

"Calvins."

"Why?"

"Why Calvins? Because I have a hockey butt, Mia. It'd be a crime not to showcase it."

There's a soft pause, then she chuckles. "I meant more, 'Why aren't you naked?' I wasn't dissing your taste in underwear."

Though I'm smiling, I cluck my tongue. "You need to be more specific."

"I'm learning that I need to up my game with you, for sure," she agrees, the tip of her nose gently rubbing over mine. "Are they purple?"

"Sure are."

She snorts but her voice is softer as she whispers, "Cole?"

"Yeah?"

"Thank you for being here."

I let my hands trickle over her arms again. "You're welcome. Getting to sleep with a beautiful woman is no hardship."

She stills. "Sleep with or fuck?"

"Either or," is my easy retort. "No pressure."

A breath soughs from her and with it, she seems to decompress. Her chest settles on mine and I wrap her up in my embrace. The skin-to-skin contact hits me in a way I didn't expect. There's low-level arousal, but this runs deeper.

It's as if we're connecting and she's not the only one who needed that.

"It's not even one AM."

"So?" I stroke her hair. It's like silk against my fingers. "You against cold pizza?"

"Cold pizza?"

"We can nap, wake up, share that last slice of cold pizza, which is better than hot, then go back to sleep if you want to."

"You're a heathen," she accuses, though she doesn't argue as I roll us onto our sides, keeping an arm hooked over her waist. "*Cold* pizza is so not better than hot."

"I think you'll find it is. All of the fat settles—"

"Congeals."

"—and the flavors develop. It's like how two-day-old lasagna is better than fresh-from-the-oven stuff."

"I want to argue with that but I can't."

"A woman who's prepared to admit she's wrong. I'm in love."

"I never said I was wrong about the pizza," she argues. "I'm not wrong. I'm right. The base gets solid if you let it go cold."

"It has a much better chew. And the pineapple is harder. You gotta work for the juice to burst on your tongue."

I don't know why but that has her clearing her throat. "You don't mind working hard for some squirting action, huh?"

She can't see it, but my eyes light up at her teasing. "Oh, you've no idea what I'll do for some squirting action."

"I've been on the competitive scene. I'm pretty sure I know the lengths the guys'll go to get some pussy. Whatever the sport, men never change."

I shrug. "We're depraved animals."

"At least you call it how you see it."

"That comes as a surprise after our multiple conversations?"

"Oh, yeah, so many. Three."

"Three's more than zero."

"Now I know you're clever."

"It's a gift. You really like classical music?"

"Good thing, too, seeing as I remember *Boléro* because of it."

"A match are we in heaven made."

She stills. "You like *Star Wars*?"

"Of course."

"*A New Hope* or *The Rise of Skywalker*?"

"Is that even a question? There was a while when Harrison Ford made me question my sexuality," I inform her seriously.

"I think he made a lot of guys question their sexuality and reaffirmed it for a lot of confused girls too," she teases, and I can't help but notice that she's a couple inches closer than she was before. "The last guy I dated refused to watch the old movies. Said he wouldn't sit through anything that wasn't 4K quality."

"He's clearly one of the Imperial forces."

"He gave off Stormtrooper vibes for sure."

"You were smart to dump him."

Mia laughs. "He dumped me."

"The man was obviously stupid."

"I like to think so. But in his defense, he was probably right. I couldn't give him the attention he deserved."

"'The attention he deserved?'" I repeat. "What was he? A newborn baby."

"I mean, he had that energy too."

"A squalling Stormtrooper—your taste is questionable."

"You're the one who's in bed with me."

I smirk. "Let's call it luck."

"It's a miracle that I can fit with your ego in it too."

"My ego is big for a reason."

"You live up to the fame?"

"The fame… Ah, you Googled me again, hmm?"

"I saw that you keep *Page Six* plenty busy."

"It's my duty." Though she snorts, I'm quick to answer, "Not my fault I haven't found the one yet."

"The one?"

"Oh, yeah, I'm looking." *And I might have found her.*

"For the one?"

"Yes. The one."

"Who's the one?"

"If I knew that," I say with a laugh. "I wouldn't be looking, would I?"

"Wait a minute. You mean like 'the one' the one?"

"Yes."

"I'm confused."

"Me too. You think I read romance for the hell of it?"

"But you're a fuckboi!"

"And? You don't know where you'll find that pot of gold if you don't go hunting for it."

"You're a romantic fuckboi. That should be an illegal combination."

"I can assure you it's deadly."

"Apparently. Still, you gained some experience… Are you a romantic fuckboi who's good in bed?"

"My reputation wasn't on Google?"

"It's yet to overtake your hockey stats. Unfortunately for your ego, most people seem to be more interested in that than your bed game."

I cluck my tongue. "For shame."

A chuckle escapes her. "I can't believe we're having this conversation."

I can.

Our rapport is chef's kiss good.

Not that I say that.

I trail a finger down the curve of her hip. "What'll it be? A ride on the *Cole Express* or sleep?"

"You a two-pump chump, Cole?"

It takes a minute for me to realize what she meant, but I snicker. "Two hundred pump."

She lets loose a choked laugh, but it morphs into a soft breath as she whispers, "Can we keep on talking?"

Tightening my hold on her, I smile into the darkness. "Uh-huh."

"Cole?"

"Yeah?"

"If we sleep, you can wake me up," she says in a rush.

"You need the rest," I start to argue.

"No. I mean, you can *wake me up*." For a moment, I don't say anything. But the lord loves a vacuum. "I'm on the shot."

"Good to know… You sure about this?"

"I'm sure.

"How sure?"

"Very."

A somnophiliac, hmm.

"You know you're supposed to be in a trusted relationship for this stuff, right?"

"I like what I like."

"If you wake up, you can wake me too."

"With your dick in my mouth?"

Cole Jr. twitches as she nuzzles into my side. "Yeah."

CHAPTER 6
MIA

WHEN MY EYES POP OPEN, it's four AM. The light from my clock is inordinately bright but that's not what woke me up.

A shudder rushes through me when I feel a thumb strumming my clit.

I've rarely shared this particular preference of mine with any of my partners in the past, but in this day and age, a guy who'll cross Manhattan for a hookup is a rarity. Getting him to come from New

Jersey, bring pizza, not expect sex, and talk about *Star Wars* and death before falling asleep? Unique.

I almost wish I were in the market of finding myself a man because this one might be a keeper.

I don't have time for my thoughts to run away from me—that thumb is doing wicked things to my clit and I immediately spread my legs in welcome.

"Fuck, that feels good." I whimper, enjoying how there's a tentative nature to his touch, like he's waiting for me to stop him. But all I can do is appreciate the mastery of his fingering skills.

Oooh, boy, he wasn't wrong about having game.

My heels dig into the mattress as I buck my hips into his hand, enjoying how he isn't rushing, taking the time to get me where I need to be.

His generosity doesn't come as much of a surprise when I think about how he's passed the night with me on his mind.

A finger slips around my slit, then he thrusts it into me. A quick dip is all I get before he retreats, and another is right where I need it. A third comes next, followed by a fourth.

The stretch is exquisite.

The burn is needed.

I cry out as he starts to finger fuck me while grinding the butt of his wrist against my clit.

As I come, with the shadowy tendrils of release bringing a relief in pressure with them, I sag into the mattress, only to find that, as I sink deeper into the softness beneath me, he's pulling me half onto his side.

When he draws my leg over his waist, I arch my back and grab his wrist. I can't stop myself from maneuvering his fingers so that I can suck one between my lips.

At his groan, I twirl my tongue around the length, tasting myself even as I'm focused on his pleasure.

"You don't have to," he assures me.

No, I don't.

I hum at the taste of him and me together and give his digit an extra suck.

Reaching between us with my other hand, I shape the bulge in his boxer briefs. Finding the fly, I let my fingertips rub circles on his dick before I pull him through it.

He's thick.

God, I love that.

Give me that over length any day of the week, though, admittedly, he's big in that regard too.

When I grip him, my fingers don't close around his girth, and I know that's why he shoved four of his own into me: because he's thicker than that.

Salivating at the thought, I kick my leg higher so I can straddle him.

"Fuck, Mia."

As my slick heat finds his cock, I sit up and rock my hips. Each thrust has my clit gliding over the fat vein pulsing down his shaft.

While sparks fly behind my eyes, his hands have found my tits. He pinches my nipples, making me hiss, but it feels good.

I *feel*.

That's enough sometimes.

When he palpates them, squeezing, jiggling them together even, I wince at the pressure but let my head fall back. Even go so far as to cover his hands with my own before I bend over him, allowing our mouths to meet.

My tongue flutters out to trace the generous lines of his lips. Though he grunts, he's swift to act as he snares me in a fast kiss, stealing my breath from me like a thief in the night.

That's when his hands break loose and shape my body, sliding along my curves, bringing the tiny hairs at my nape to life as he reminds me what it feels like to be touched.

Blanketing him, I let him fuck my mouth with his tongue.

It feels good. So good.

He's hard and wants me but he's also savoring me, and I need that—I need to be savored. I wasn't aware of that until he gave it to me.

When he twists us over so he's on top, his weight is welcome. It brings all my nerve endings to life, making me feel safe and sheltered.

He reaches between us, his cock finding my slit, and the tip starts to slot into me.

I try to relax as much as I can, but even I struggle with how fat his dick is.

My pussy flutters around him, a cascade of butterfly wings that squeeze and clench as he stops kissing me to grind out, "Fuck, Mia. Your pussy is killing me, baby. Bear down, yeah? Just a little more."

I try.

I really do.

There's nothing more that I want than for him to be inside me.

But it's a battle.

Then he's leaning up slightly, creating a pocket of space so that he can reach between us. His thumb finds my clit. He rubs it. Softer than before. More of a tease. Giving me what I want but not what I need.

I kick my legs up, rocking my pelvis back, which helps ease the pressure.

Finally, he's there.

Sinking into me.

Deeper.

Deeper.

Our groan is mutual as he claims every inch, impaling me on him until my poor pussy is choking on what he has to offer.

The sensation of being spread apart is overwhelming—*breathtaking*.

Then, I feel something—deep inside. My eyes pop open as I whimper. "Cole, do you have a piercing?"

His chuckle is low and long—a torment in and of itself as well as confirmation. Fuck. Why didn't I turn on the light to study it before I let him put it in me?

"You'll have to hunt the truth down for yourself later."

There's something going on.

I can feel it. It's stimulating something in me that's never been touched before, probably because of how wide he is.

Which is the moment my control shatters.

My hands grab the sheet, ripping and tugging as I whine, "More, Cole. More, please."

That's when he thrusts both his tongue and dick into me.

Simultaneously.

Until I can feel him fill me twice over.

The effect is instantaneous—it's like being zapped with a live wire.

It ricochets through my bones until every part of me experiences the delicious ache.

Then, I realize this can get so much better than it already was—he moves faster.

Faster.

Faster.

Honestly, if any other guy did this, I'd tell him to slow down, but the pressure is delicious.

My nails dig into his spine, dragging along the muscled length, scratching him until they find his ass and encourage him to pump that much harder.

But there's a ripple effect—my head is shifting ever nearer to the headboard.

Shoving my hands against it to ground myself, I brace as he rides me through an abrupt orgasm.

As I scream out my release, he pulls away, presses my legs together, then rests them against his chest and abs as he practically bounces into me.

I've never been fucked like this before, but it takes me higher until the darkness isn't in the room, it bleeds into my eyes and steals my vision.

I whine and mewl and whimper as I savor how thick he is.

God, he should be tearing me apart, but instead, my body is welcoming him like it was born to take his dick.

I want nothing more than for him to come inside me, but as I let loose a shriek when another orgasm hits, he's making a retreat, abandoning my pussy to clasp at nothing, leaving me feeling so empty that I sob in despair even as cum pelts my stomach.

The heat of it is intense, and I fight the urge to rub my clit with the mess he made, the lube exactly what I need to take me higher.

I don't have to though—he does it for me.

His thumb is there and three fingers are back inside me, pumping and thrusting until my spine bows with the intensity and my ruined orgasm is allowed to soar to unearthly heights.

As I sag into the mattress, I find he's still not done.

Suddenly, his mouth is where I need him. Tender and soft, his tongue slides through my folds, soothing my slit, antagonizing my sensitized clit, and the short, sharp shock of a final orgasm has me sobbing in relief and agony until he draws me back into his arms, tucks me between his legs, and cossets me with the hug that I've needed since yesterday morning—one that's all-encompassing, that smells of us, and that keeps me grounded to this shitty earth.

"Get some sleep," he orders, his fingers wet as he strokes them down my arm in an attempt to soothe me.

It works.

I fall asleep, unaware there's the softest curve to my lips as I settle in the safe cocoon of his embrace. An embrace that I never want to leave.

CHAPTER 7
COLE

Summer Breeze - The Isley Brothers

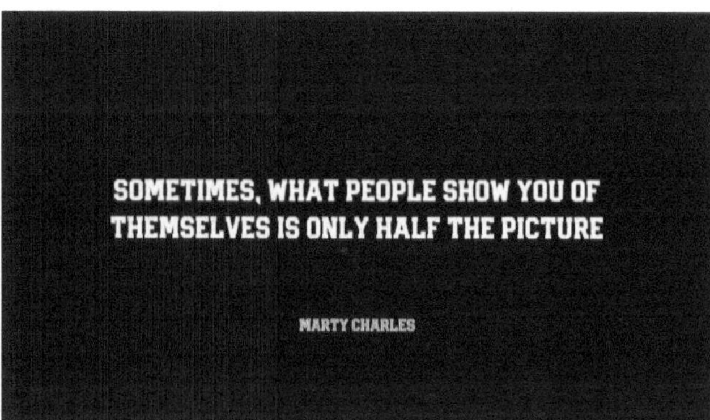

IT'S a happy man who leaves Mia's apartment.

I'm even fucking whistling.

I got a taste of her pussy in the early hours of dawn, woke up with her snuggling into me, shared a slice of cold pizza for breakfast, and am supposed to meet back up with her tonight—what more could I ask for?

Shelving the desire to remain between her thighs for the near future, I have plans for the day and need to get the ball rolling before I head to the stables in Brooklyn.

I discovered Camille O'Donnelly's project by chance last year and I spend as much time there as my schedule permits. Horses have always meant so much to me, but that they're therapy animals for underprivileged kids, too, speaks to my heart.

Still, I'm in the city and it's early, so I hit my billet bro, Liam, up—a man like me could always handle a second breakfast, and while he's a clean eater, I know since Gracie moved in, there'll be something naughty for me to chow on.

Me: Yo. You home?

Liam: Yup.

Liam: Why?

Me: Figured I'd come see you.

Liam: Why?

Me: Don't want me there? My heart is BLEEDING, Liam.

Liam: You're such a fucking drama queen.

Liam: I'm in. Will be until 1PM.

Me: Why so late? Don't you need to get to practice?

Liam: It's just light skating today.

Me: Did you win?

Liam: Like you don't know the score.

Me: I'll be there in thirty minutes.

Liam: K

As I grab a cab, I give his address to the driver, shut off my phone, and settle back in my seat until we make it to his place. A place that's become *their* place.

I'm almost annoyed at how he and Gracie kept their relationship under wraps and for so long, but hell, Gracie moved to NYC years ago and I didn't even know that until recently.

My sis is a professional at keeping secrets.

When one of my mum's favorite tunes plays on the radio, "Summer Breeze," I hum along, aware that I look like the cat who got allllllllllll the cream.

I slept great last night, only woke up the once when I realized Mia was crying.

Though she'd told me it was okay to wake her with sex, I'd still been hesitant to do so, then she was sobbing and I'd reacted blindly.

I have zero regrets, especially after what went down.

Man, her pussy was…

Well, there are no fucking words for how good it was.

Once I've paid the fare, I head toward the building and see that Quentin, Liam's doorman, is waiting for me with the door wide open.

"What a greeting," I chirp.

He beams at me. "Always a pleasure, Mr. Cole."

We bump fists before I wander over to the bank of elevators and start my way to Liam's apartment.

The door's also open when I get there, but he's not hovering so I know Quentin clued him into my arrival.

Liam became super freaky about security after his kidnapping—for obvious reasons. It's his agoraphobia that worries me more than anything though. He says he's not scared to go out because he can function, i.e. he can work and can travel for away games, but otherwise, he's always at home.

Always.

Sounds like agoraphobia to me but he denies it.

Slamming the door closed behind me, I call out, "If you two are kissing, you'd better stop. I don't want to see that shit."

"Fuck you, Cole," Gracie calls back.

I smirk at nothing as I wander into the kitchen where Gracie's surrounded by stationery.

Packs of it. And I'm talking *packs*. Stacks of books, pens galore, a gluttonous gourmand's array of highlighters.

I hook my arm around her neck and draw her in for a noogie. "You opening a stationery store and didn't tell me, Gracie?"

Liam eyes our byplay. "You have a death wish."

That's the only warning I get.

Suddenly, Gracie's fingers are literally in my nose and she's dragging my head back.

"UNCLE," I screech, but only because ya don't hit Gracie even if she's not afraid to punch first.

See, it's not the gentleman in me that knows that. It's the Blue Demons' Neanderthal who has the survival instincts.

Gracie will prank you.

She'll prank you *bad*.

Nothing is worth being the focus of her ire.

Gracie might be like a sister to me, but it's a fool who underestimates her.

Funny thing is, of course, that I figured she was like a sister to Liam too. Until she started wearing his number, 35, in a diamond-encrusted pendant. They're engaged, but she isn't wearing his ring yet.

She lets go of my nose the second I surrender and hops off her stool to go and wash her hands.

Rubbing my abused nostrils, I mumble, "You're more prickly than usual, furball."

"Gray calls me that. Don't switch out names."

Liam hides a smile. "She's angry."

"I'd never have guessed." I head over to the refrigerator and simultaneously give her a very wide berth. "What's up, G?"

"My cousin told her the contract's ready for her to sign. He's waiting until the playoffs are over to fire DeLaney and then it's going to happen."

I twist back to stare at them both. "Whoa, legit?"

Though I know that Conor O'Donnelly, the Stars' Governor, is

Liam's cousin as well as his boss, I also know that O'Donnelly offered Gracie the position of GM once she got her MBA and G's taking the job.

Sure, it's nepotism, but I've met DeLaney—he's an asscunt who'd give a twatwaffle hives.

"Legit," Liam crows, bumping fists with me when I hold mine out.

"That's awesome, Gracie, and so fucking deserved."

Her cheeks flush as she retreats to the counter, but that's all the answer she gives me.

My brows lift at the sight, and Liam makes a motion with his hand which I follow until we're stepping into the gym.

As he starts up his training session on the treadmill, I jump onto the elliptical beside him and ask, "Why isn't she doing a happy dance around the apartment? In fact, why's she pissed?"

"Firstly, have you met Gracie?"

My grin is smug. "You telling me she's never happy danced before?"

"Sure, but not for work reasons."

I snort. "Don't tell me. I don't need to know."

"I'd have to kill you if I told you."

Ugh, sex-related for sure.

"What's wrong with her?"

"She thinks she can't handle it, and that conversation with Conor made things very, very, very real."

"Gracie could manage three teams at once."

"Your confidence in me is admirable, Cole," Gracie inserts grimly. "*You* weren't supposed to say anything."

Liam peers at her over his shoulder, which is no small feat on a treadmill when you're running at level 9 as a warm-up. "He asked."

"You didn't have to answer. You'll jinx this, Liam—"

"This is bro talk," I dismiss. "What are you doing in here anyway, female? You should be choking on testosterone and heading for the door."

"If it were more *potent,* I would." She sniffs as I clutch at my heart. "I need to head to the store."

"Okay, *minou.* You taking your bodyguard?"

Gracie casts a look at me but sighs. "I will."

When she traipses out, I murmur, "You sure you still need a team of bodyguards?"

"She's going to be the GM of the Stars, Cole. Her worth tripled in the eyes of the world. You bet your ass she needs a security detail."

I hide a grin. "She was already a diamond in your eyes though, wasn't she?"

Liam's smile is dopey. "You know it."

For a couple minutes, both of us work out, seeing as Gracie answered for him—she's prickly about this all going south—then he breaks the silence with, "What are you doing here anyway? Not that I'm against a workout partner, but I figured it'd be too early for you as you're off for the summer."

"You had to mention that, didn't you?" I ignore his smirk to answer, "Hooked up with someone last night."

He nods. "That's what brought you to the city?"

"Uh-huh." I jump off the machine and head over to the small fridge in the corner. Snagging us both a bottle of electrolyte jizz, I toss one at him before I climb back aboard the elliptical. "It was weird."

"Weird good, weird freaky, or weird epic?"

I ponder the classification for far too long before presenting my conclusion: "Weird epic."

His brows lift. "Really?"

"Yup." I take a deep sip of the drink. "It was the craziest thing. I was waiting at the rink for my figure-skating coach to show up—"

"You finally decided to go through with lessons, then."

I nod. "Watching you and Lewis on the ice told me I needed to up my game."

"Yeah, we *are* the best."

"Only if you bring home the goods," I snipe. "Anyway, I was watching your game and then I got this notification on *Hooked-Up*. I check out my match's profile, it sucks, but after swiping left, I find this one who's hot as fuck so, of course, I swipe right, and as I do, a cell dings in the arena." At Liam's confused look, I clarify, "I swiped right on my figure-skating coach."

His confusion fades and is replaced with amusement. "Only you, Cole. *Tabarnak.* Luck of the gods."

"You know it."

"That's who you banged last night—your coach? That time with the masseuse really should have taught you not to piss where you eat."

I huff. "I'm a different man now."

"You're an older one."

"Precisely. Smarter. Quicker reflexes."

"Slower, more like," he mutters, but I ignore him.

"I see her, think about giving her some of the Korhonen charm—"

"You felt like terrifying her, then, huh? Or were you hoping to scare the shit out of her with that hoodie you're wearing?"

"Fuck off. She bursts into tears."

"I would as well if I weren't immune to your wardrobe choices."

I flip him the bird. "Turns out, her uncle died yesterday morning."

That has Liam hitting the STOP button. "Wait, so in a matter of minutes, you met your figure-skating coach—"

"For the first time," I insert.

"—on a dating profile, and as you swipe right, she comes into the building, and when she sees you, she starts crying, and somehow, you end up getting laid before the night's through even though her uncle died? Fuck, Cole. You're a classy piece of ass."

"Don't I know it." I dismiss his snort.

"I can see why you said it was weird."

"Weird *epic*," I remind him. "She's like Gracie. The banter is sexy as fuck." When his eyes narrow, I raise my hands. "Not that Gracie's banter is sexy. Mia's is. It's like that but without the fact she's my sis and I'd poke out my eyes before I thought about having feelings for Gracie."

"Nice save."

"I thought so too," I say wryly as I scratch my chin. "So, you heard of Marty Charles?"

Liam rolls his eyes. "Of course I have. Ten World Series and a massive gambling addiction that had him selling all but one of his rings for less than their worth."

"Huh, you know more than me then."

"Why does that come as a surprise?"

I punch him in the arm. "My coach… she's his great-granddaughter. Works at the family bar on the side, and it's like this legacy baseball dive or something. She didn't cancel the lesson because he left the business with a lot of debt."

Liam's eyes stop rolling long enough so that he can blink them at me.

"Anyway, you can't judge a person for how they act after they lose someone."

"No, but I wasn't judging them. Mostly, I was judging you," he mutters, but he's still frowning. "The bar…"

"What about it?"

"Was it called Chuck's?"

"You heard of it?"

Slowly, he nods. "Gracie used to work there. Remember?"

It's my turn to blink at him. "When?"

"Before I hired her."

I gape at him. "No way."

"Yes way." His tone is serious. "They're the ones who screwed her over. You remember she saved that kid from getting mowed down in the street?"

"I remember." My heart deflates like a compressed whoopee cushion. *That's where I knew the name from.* Fuck. "Her boss sold her out for some free publicity."

"The boss's *niece* did too. They were on the news. Don't you remember?"

Pissed, I snap, "I've slept since then." I slam a hand on the console and slow the elliptical down to a crawl. "I wouldn't have said she was the type."

"*Cibole*, Cole. You can't see her again."

I think about her smile. That beautiful face. How she rocked my fucking world. The way she made me laugh even when she was grieving…

Then, I think about Gracie.

Slowly, I nod. "Yeah, you're right. I can't."

"She hurt Gracie more than Chuck did. Mia's the one who claimed all the Bukowskis head in there to see her. Gracie said something about Mia being her 'work wife.' The betrayal cut hella deep.

"You need to cancel the lessons you have booked with her," Liam insists. "You can't support her."

That's when guilt hits me, but this time, it's double-edged.

Gracie might not be blood, but she's my sister by choice.

I'd do anything for her.

Anything.

Including cutting out on a course of lessons with a woman who's desperate for cash to keep her struggling business afloat.

Fuck, this guilt'll eat me alive.

"Chuck's the one who died," I rasp, a drowning man begging for a life raft.

But Liam just shrugs.

"The business is going under."

"You keep seeing her, it'll kill Gracie if she finds out. They betrayed her, Cole. What the fuck will that treacherous bitch do to you if she can do that to a close friend?"

The desire to smack Liam for calling Mia names is real.

I think about how she promised yesterday not to sell me out on social media. Did she appear genuine or fake? It seemed genuine to me.

Her grief was too.

Everything about yesterday was raw. You can't fake that but...

Scrubbing a hand over my face, I mutter, "I won't see her again."

"Cancel the lessons, Cole."

I scowl at him. "I will, Liam. Fuck."

"Do it now."

"You don't believe I will?" I challenge.

"I know what my brothers are like when there's a hot piece of ass at stake," he grates out. "I want to see you text her."

"Fuck you."

"Fuck you back. You didn't remember who she was so Gracie'll forgive you for touching forbidden fruit, but it'll kill her if you keep on seeing the bitch."

The urge to defend her resurges. As does the desire to break that pretty face of his for saying shit like that about Mia, but...

I remember how it was last year.

When Gracie started working for Liam.

How she'd been betrayed and how it hurt her.

Gracie, for all that she has the energy of a bull in a china shop, is very careful about letting people in. That someone else betrayed her to jump onto the Bukowski bandwagon for some free press led to her instantly cutting that poison from her life.

It was, in fact, how Liam took her on as his PA: because she'd quit immediately after her boss had gone to the media.

My hand feels like it's wading through maple syrup as I snag my cell phone from my back pocket.

I don't want to do this.

Even knowing what she did to Gracie, I don't want to cut ties with Mia.

But Liam's looming over me like the fucking Hulk, and Gracie... Gracie who cares so goddamn much about too much—how can I let her down when she's never let *me* down? When she'd cut off her right hand before she hurt me?

I head to our messaging thread.

> Me: Mia, I'm sorry to have to do this, but I'm
> going to need to cancel my lessons

Before I can hit send, my cell buzzes.

Spying Colt's name on the Caller ID, I frown and hit the connect button. "What do you want?" I snap at my eldest brother.

"You need to get back here, Cole. Pops had a heart attack."

CHAPTER 8
MIA

Dancing With A Stranger - Sam Smith ft Normani

Cole: Mia, I'm sorry to have to do this but I'm going to need to cancel my lessons. There's been an emergency back home. My pops had a heart attack.

I STARE AT THE MESSAGE, trying not to wonder if he's going cold turkey on me after last night.

Immediately, my brain goes to work, reminding me of how fat my ass is, of the fact I'm loud when I come, that I'm too clingy in bed—all reasons for a guy like Cole to back off, seemingly out of the blue because this sounds like the trashiest excuse in the world.

Rubbing at my eyes, I mutter, "You shouldn't have slept with him."

I needed that money.

But even worse, I liked him.

Really liked him.

Proof, yet again, that I have the shittiest taste in men. Shitty taste in everything.

God, I'm so fucking useless sometimes it makes me want to scream.

I spend the next twenty minutes second-guessing myself over whether I should reply or not, but in the end, I decide that just because he's rude, doesn't mean I have to be.

Even if I'm ninety-nine-point-nine percent sure he made this BS up.

> Me: I'm so sorry to hear that. I hope he recuperates. Let me know when you're back in the city and if you want to reschedule your lessons.

That's when the sweats start.

As does the desire to delete my message.

Instead, I suck in a breath because my chest feels tight and type:

> Me: All the best, Cole.

Awkward.

I hesitate again then, decide to go for broke:

> Me: Thank you for helping me to forget for a little while.

The check marks beside the messages turn blue, so I know he's seen my response.

But he doesn't reply.

That confirms it.

I grit my teeth at the brush off, but his radio silence does some good —it makes me angry. Enough that my anxiety fades and lets me approach this with a clear mind.

My first act: I immediately swipe on the text thread to delete the conversation.

I don't need that toxic shit in my life.

I should never have gotten involved with a student. That was on me, but I've learned my lesson, an expensive one at that.

With a quick look at my watch, I notice I have two hours before the delivery at the bar is due to show up. Down a student and without his tuition fee, I start my computer.

I wish I could say that I hate doing this—but it's easy money and it's… well, *easy* all around.

My relationship with sex has always been complicated, so when Gracie confessed to me once that she worked on a sex line to make ends meet during college, it was like a 'eureka' moment.

Despite being busy coaching through the day, I didn't make enough to cover all my bills, especially when I knew that I had to support the bar too.

Chuck's is always in the red.

I'm the one who's been covering our alcohol bill for the past two years when the distribution company stopped accepting credit and insisted upon cash on delivery.

Without me, the bar would have gone under three times as fast.

The internet lags as I log into my account so I quickly change the sheets and make the bed, trying not to think about what happened on it a few short hours ago.

That done, I close the curtains, turn on the backlights I set up for cam-girling, then drag off my clothes and switch out my bra and panties for a lacy ensemble that I consider my uniform.

I tug on a neon green wig and stick on some cat ears—my guys seem to love this and the Ahegao look.

When I'm changed, I click my status to 'online,' and I sit back until the clients roll in.

I don't have to wait long. I've been using this site for a while now and have a list of regulars.

Some are on the other side of the world so I could be busy at all times of the day.

The truth is I could quit coaching and offload the bar then use this for my primary source of income if I wanted to.

But those are the keywords here—'if I wanted to.'

I don't.

This is a means to an end.

A lucrative one.

When *ThomasEd104* hits me up, I invite him into a private room. Then, putting on my game face, I hit connect.

"Hey, Tommy," I greet.

His text thread takes over the screen so that I can see it from the bed if I need to.

> ThomasEd104: I missed you. Where've you been?

"A girl's got to live her life," is all I say as I start the usual with him—he's a tits man. Unfastening my bra, I shove my breasts together and croon, "You missed these titties?"

> ThomasEd104: You know I have. Fuck, they're so pretty.

As I smile at the camera, I don't think about the two hundred bucks I'll have at the end of the session and I focus only on the fact that I want to have an orgasm before this is over.

Maybe that'll ease the sting of that Dear John text message…

CHAPTER 9
COLE

Raging - Kygo feat Kodaline

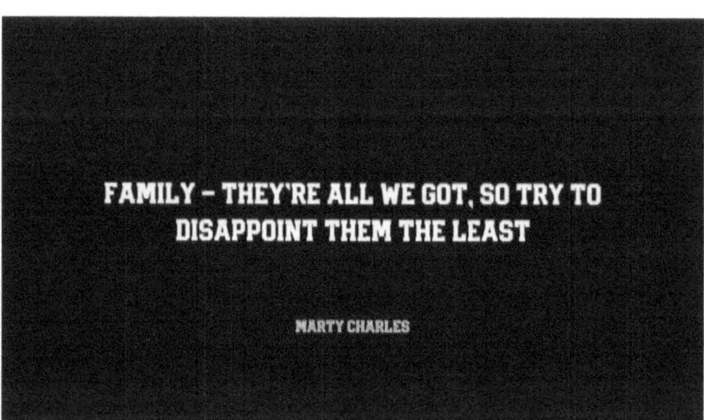

THE TRIP back to the family ranch is arduous *and* tedious.

It's one of the reasons I don't visit outside of holidays, and sometimes not even then.

Two connecting flights—ain't no one got time for that.

And seeing as Colt's refusing to get the damn helicopter fixed after Callan took it for a joyride—little prick—I've spent all day on planes, trains, and automobiles.

Moreover, the teeny town of Pigeon Creek isn't exactly a hotbed of activity worthy of me visiting often. However, I probably would head home more if we had an airstrip and I could hire a private jet.

#firstworldproblems

The longing for that airstrip consumes me as I merge onto the private road off the highway.

Driving toward the Seven Cs is, in itself, a pain in the ass, with so many bends and twists in the road that by the time you're done, you're ready for motion sickness meds.

When I finally make it to the gates, I find my way to the homestead where all the lights are blazing.

Because Callan is like Liam and gets off on security, I know the family will have taken note of my presence.

We might be at the back end of nowhere, but Callan's got us locked up tighter than Fort Knox.

When I get out of my rental, I straighten, crack my neck, then drag my luggage from the trunk in the bright spotlights from the house.

By the time my gear is on the graveled driveway, Colt and Callan are walking over to me. Callan isn't a toucher, but Colt's the big brother so he's the first to punch me in the shoulder.

"What took you so fucking long?"

"I told you that if you want me to visit more, then we need to get a private airstrip, seeing as you won't fix the damn helicopter."

"It's coming, it's coming," he mutters, but he casts Callan a glance.

Callan shrugs. "I don't have a problem with an airstrip."

"Since when? The last time I brought it up, you said you couldn't secure it."

"That was before," is my younger brother's simple retort.

"Before what? You broke our last ride and decided you want a new toy?" I demand, hooking my arm over his shoulder and drawing him in for a hug I know he doesn't want.

Tough shit.

It's been nine months since I last saw the little pest who crash-landed a million-dollar piece of equipment.

He might be seventeen, but he's fucking smart. Aside from when it comes to joyriding helicopters.

"Before I finished my security system," he corrects, his eyes big and shiny. "Every part of the ranch is wired, Cole. It's a work of art."

Snorting, I shake my head. "Your wife'll be made of wires and hard drives, won't she?"

"Never heard of the uncanny valley?"

"Nope. Is that around here too?" I counter as, with a crinkled nose, I stare at the house.

Six generations of Korhonens have lived and died here.

Mostly, I've never wanted to be the type of Korhonen who would too.

Give me the big city any day of the fucking week over my family's land.

Callan and Colt aren't like me though—they live and breathe the ranch. But they can, seeing as I don't want anything to do with it.

Cody's the same as I am. Spending one night here is too much.

"Nothing ever changes. You might stick up a couple new cameras and some motion sensors here and there, but it's always the same."

"I like it. It's nice."

I roll my eyes at Callan's simple answer.

Colt shrugs. "You never got the bug."

"Cole's always felt the pull of the city lights."

The softly spoken words come as a massive shock. Whipping away from my brothers, I see my mother standing on the front stoop of the massive log building that is the 'big house.'

"Mum?" I sputter. "What are you doing here?"

She holds out her arms for me so I lope forward. I don't wait for an answer, just let her embrace me.

"It's so good to see you!" I bite out, surprising myself with how much emotion there is in my voice. "It's been too damn long, Lindsay Matthews. You bad girl, you."

She smells like the perfume I bought her when I was fourteen—she's worn it ever since. "I missed you." Her laughter mingles with tears.

"Same." I hug her tighter, making her laugh as I lift her and twirl her in a circle. "God, it's been ages."

"I was in the facility for too long."

I don't give her crap for spending months at a time in some lab in an Amazonian rainforest, not when her work matters to her, but I enjoy the moment for what it is—a rarity.

"How long do we have you for?"

"I asked for a sabbatical," she stuns me by saying.

"A sabbatical? Why?"

"Because my boys need me. I might have wished that the heart attack took Clyde out, but I'm glad for your sakes that it didn't."

I swear she's so naive sometimes. How can she think we could ever forgive him for what he did to her? Deathbed, heart attack, or not.

"—you'll need me around if you don't kill him during his recuperation. He's a miserable patient."

Her statement has my lips curving.

Since their divorce, she stopped beating around the bush with him and ceased being afraid of the man who's made it his life's work to have the residents of Pigeon Creek quiver in their boots whenever he darkens the town's door. Never mind what he did to her.

I prefer to believe that I take after her because the prospect of being like him is discomfiting. Pops's never frightened me, though mostly I want to be on the other side of the continent from where he is.

How he treated Mum is one of the reasons I started reading romance. I wanted to immerse myself in something that was the opposite of what I saw every day—I needed the escape.

Until *she* escaped, that is, and got a divorce.

Then, I carried on reading because, hello? Romance novels are fucking awesome.

Slinging my arm around her shoulders, I complain to my brothers, "If you'd told me Mum was coming, I'd have gotten here sooner."

"Thought you didn't dick around getting here," Colt derides.

"I didn't, but I'd have found a way to travel through space and time," I snipe.

"We didn't realize she was coming until she showed up. You know how difficult it is to communicate with the facility sometimes. I thought we'd hear from her next week," is all Callan has to say on the matter.

It really is too—he doesn't hang around, just silently grabs my luggage, climbs the few steps on the front stoop, and walks into the house.

A smile dances on Mum's lips. "He's still the same as ever."

I nod but holler, "Love you, Geek!"

Colt slaps the back of my head. "Leave him alone."

"He loves me for it. I'm the only one who doesn't baby him."

Mum tuts. "Tough love. Is that what you call it?"

"He needs it," I insist.

And I'm not lying.

Callan's so beyond an introvert that he might as well be inside out.

I used to be the buffer between him and Pops, who doesn't understand why Callan isn't born from his image like Colt, Cody, and I were. If anything, he truly does take after Mum appearance-wise, and that's what Pops can't stand.

Mum's the one who got away.

At least, she's the one who divorced Pops despite him being the big-I-am. And that's something he's never gotten over.

Mum sighs. "Callan isn't going to be like any of you, Cole. You need to accept him for who he is."

"I do accept him. All of him. But if I don't get him to toughen up, then no one will, and I've been protecting him from Pops since the day he was born."

Having argued about this with me in the past, Colt grunts. "Until you left."

"I didn't *leave*." I had an opportunity.

Colt hoots. "Remind me to buy a dictionary for you this Christmas. Anyway, you ready to see His Majesty?"

"Ah, jeez. I thought he'd be in the hospital."

"We brought him home."

"Why? Is he dying?"

Mum clicks her tongue. "Don't sound so hopeful, son."

"I'm not hopeful. He's…" I don't even bother finishing that sentence, not with two of the five people who know him best in the world. Both of them nod at me in silent understanding. "Anyway, might as well drag the Band-Aid off." A thought occurs to me. "Did you go see him?"

"I'm not here for him. I'm here for my boys."

I smile at her. "Speaking on behalf of your boys, we appreciate it."

She squeezes my waist. "Go and do your duty, then come and sit with me. I'll order tea."

Because she's five-feet-nothing, I lean down and press a kiss to the top of her head. "It's great to see you, Mum."

Another squeeze. "Go on. Get."

Colt dips his chin at her like some kind of robot as he falls into step beside me.

I wasn't lying when I told Mia he's stoic.

"You okay?" I ask as he leads me into the house and takes me down what has always been my parents' wing.

Until Mum left, that is.

Most kids want their parents to stick together. They'll cry and sob. They'll even wail if the one parent they love is taken from them. But I know none of us ever did.

We were glad she got out of this hellhole.

We wanted her to be happy.

More than that, we needed her to be *alive*.

We stuck around, most of us biding our time until we were eighteen and able to make our own choices. Could, in fact, reclaim our lives.

Colt beat the shit out of Pops the second the minute hand ticked past midnight on his birthday.

Cody took off for the Air Force the millisecond he was of age.

I was already billeting with the Bukowskis so I was free to not return to this place.

I'm pretty sure Callan will stick around because he loves the comfort of the ranch and is obsessed with keeping it safe.

Once I know Mum's too far away to hear me speak… "Can't have been that bad an episode if he's back home already."

"Pops wouldn't let us in the room when the doctors gave their prognosis so I've no idea what's wrong with him. I'm pretty sure I was only summoned so I could arrange for a private air ambulance to bring him home."

"Wish I'd known. I could have hitched a ride."

"Stop downplaying this, Cole. Not everything has to be a damn joke."

I just purse my lips. "You think he was lying about having a heart attack?" I pause in the hall and grab ahold of his arm to drag him to a halt too. "*Was* he faking? No way he'd be home already if it was a cardiac episode."

"I don't want to think he faked it, but it's handy that he was in Prince Albert of all places when it happened.

"It took us three hours to get there, and by that time, he was already sitting up and looking okay to me.

"The doctors came in later, but he threw us out. Said he was a grown man who didn't need to be mollycoddled."

"Why did you tell me to come home if you thought this whole thing was bullshit?"

"Because it might not have been. Plus, he said he's changing his will, Cole. You have to be here for that."

"He can't touch our trust funds. Anyway, I don't want anything to do with the Seven Cs."

"I know you don't, but he's still in denial about it."

"You've earned it. It's yours."

Colt's smile is wry. "I never had a choice about whether I wanted it or not. But that's this place for you. It gets in the blood."

"Like malaria." When he rolls his eyes, I continue, "What about Callan?"

"He's my biggest concern," Colt admits.

"What do you mean?"

"I mean that he's claiming Callan's not his son."

"Not his son?!" I bark. "What the fuck? How can he not be?"

"Don't ask me. You know what he's like. That's why I thought it best for you to come home—I have a feeling that the changes to his will are about Callan. We need to deal with the repercussions of this together. I never expected Mum would be here though. I'm not sure if that helps or not."

"He's the cheater. Not her," is my fierce retort.

My elder brother claps me on the shoulder. "You're preaching to the choir, Cole. Whatever game he's playing, I need your help in protecting Callan. I won't have him cut out of his birthright."

"You *really* think that's what this is about?"

"I do."

"You could always give him his cut after the old bastard croaks it."

"Sure, I can. If push comes to shove, that's what I'll do. But if we're not careful, he could fuck with everything. Make it so that I can't. I know he's been talking with lawyers in Ottawa. Expensive ones. I have a bad feeling about this."

"You saw the bills?"

He nods. "It's been weird around here."

We start down the hallway again.

"What do you mean?"

"Water's low."

"Water's always low," I dismiss.

It's his turn to drag me to a halt. "Never been as low as this, Cole. It's looking bad. We have the money of ten kings, but we can't do dick if we don't have any water."

My brow puckers. "What's the solution?"

"I'm not sure."

"But you always know what to do." I can't help that my voice sounds panicked. Colt is our problem-solver.

Our fixer.

If he doesn't know what to do, then we're fucked.

He scrapes a hand over his jaw. "You seen Susanne McAllister recently?"

My brow furrows at the change of topic—the McAllisters are our family's arch-nemeses and have been for centuries. "No. Jersey's a big place, Colt. It's not as if we hang out with the same crowd. She's a lawyer, isn't she?"

There's a strange gleam in his eye as he corrects, "Paralegal."

"Is the old bitch still alive and kicking?"

"Yup. About as friendly as poison ivy."

That about sums up Juliette McAllister, the Bar 9 matriarch and Susanne's grandmother.

Still confused and somewhat annoyed, I challenge, "Why do you care about Susanne McAllister anyway? She's the one who set fire to our goddamn stables."

I haven't thought about the fire in years, but I've mentioned it twice now in as many days.

He rubs the back of his neck. "I told you she didn't do it."

"I know what I saw!"

"You were a kid. Hopped up on adrenaline and fear." He releases a long sigh. "Never mind, Cole. Let's get this over with."

CHAPTER 10
COLE

Fire - Fabrizio Paterlini

> **FATHERS ALWAYS MAKE MISTAKES.**
> **YOU GOTTA DECIDE WHETHER THEY'RE WORTHY OF**
> **YOUR FORGIVENESS**
>
> MARTY CHARLES

"YOU FINALLY MADE IT THEN."

"What a welcome home."

Clyde Korhonen grimaces at me. "I'm the one who's sick."

"You don't look sick. Only the good die young, Pops. You're fine for another eighty years at least."

A glint pops up in his eye. One of respect.

I hate that about him.

I hate that if I dole out as much shit as he tosses my way, the more he respects me.

That's not how it's supposed to be.

"You're here now. That's something at least. Saw you got kicked out of the playoffs. Told you playing for Jersey was a bad idea, but you never listen."

I ignore his taunt. "It can't have been too bad if you're home already."

"Is that a complaint?"

"No, I'm trying to figure out what's going on. I got a call from Colt so I rushed home and what do I find? You're not even hooked up to an IV."

"You sound like you're disappointed I'm not deathly ill, son."

I plunk my ass on the side of his bed. "No, I don't appreciate my emotions being toyed with."

Pops purses his lips. "I'm tired."

"Rest, then." I immediately get up. "I can come back later."

He snags my hand and drags me closer. "No. You don't get to go. You only just made it to the Seven Cs."

"I'm not leaving." I wouldn't go so soon, not after what Colt shared with me. And definitely not after learning Mum's here. "I can come and visit you later."

He narrows his eyes but, satisfied that I'm not lying, grumbles, "See that you do." He barks at Colt as if he's a fucking dog, "You. Stay."

When he doesn't argue, I head out, then a thought occurs to me. "Did you tell Cody to come home too?"

"Pops insisted on it."

Huh.

Maybe the family fixer is right—Pops has some shenanigans afoot.

Asshole.

Leaving them to it, I stride down the hall and find Mum hovering at the mouth of this wing.

"Thought I was supposed to come to your solarium?" I greet.

"My curiosity wouldn't let me wait."

"What are you curious about?"

"On how long it'd take for you to walk out."

My lips quirk into a grin though I complain, "You know me too well."

"You never could stand for his theatrics. You're the only one he seems to respect. Though I'm sure he's frightened of Cody now that he's in the Royal Canadian Air Force."

I wish I could argue, but I don't. "You doing okay, Mum?"

"I'm fine, son. Let's go for some tea. Mrs. Abelman's assured me she's set it up how we like it. I'm sure you need it after that long trip home."

"Definitely," I concede, though I hate tea and only drink it with her.

Sometimes, I forget how English she is. Then I have to drink her tea.

Mrs. Abelman's like a ghost with polite poltergeist tendencies. Shit happens around her that makes our lives easier, so she's not exactly anti-social, more all-knowing.

She's long since stopped being a housekeeper. After Mum had to leave, she became our surrogate mom.

Poltergeist Abelman's already acting up because there's a tray waiting for us in Mum's solarium. The water's boiling hot in the same silver pot that she's used since forever, and I watch her doctor the teacups in the only way that I can stomach it—three sugars with the smallest dash of milk.

When she passes me the cup, I study her, knowing that she's got a question for me, but unluckily for her, I have questions too.

"What are you doing here, Mum? It's not like you to leave Brazil if you can help it."

Her jaw works, though she's quick to control her facial expression. "To see my boys, of course."

"As great as it is to see you, you could have met us in Saskatoon. Why come here?"

She fiddles with the handle on her teacup. "Colton called me and told me what's going on with Callan."

"And? Is he not Pops's son?"

That has her hooting. "I only wish I'd been brave enough to find happiness with another man while I was existing under this godforsaken roof. No, unfortunately, Callan's his spawn as much as you are."

"Poor Callan," I mutter, but I'm not offended by her words.

No matter what the Canada Revenue Agency believes, Pops's main residence is hell—his kids are definitely spawn.

"So, you're here to defend him?"

"Partly. When Colton told me that he'd asked Cody to come home as well, at his father's request, I realized it'd be the first time in ages that I got to visit with all four of you at once. Plus, he's stuck in a bed so I'll never have to clap eyes on him. Win-win." She graces me with a concerned if perplexed look. "Why's he doing this, Cole?"

"He and Callan have never gotten along. Callan's too much of a thinker for him. It's like he's punishing the ones who are willing to stick around because he never gives Cody or me as much shit as he does Colt and Callan."

"He's a horrid man." Her hatred for Pops leaches into every word.

"He really is."

I want to ask her what the hell she was thinking when she married him, but I don't.

Victim shaming is *not* the way to go, even if, because of her choices, her kids became victims too.

Thank fuck for Colton is all I'll say. Without him, us younger kids would have had it a thousand times harder.

"I won't let him cut Callan out," she warns.

"You'd probably have to talk to him first." The prospect would make this trip home truly worth it.

She huffs. "You like hearing me yell at him."

"Hey, do you know how often I used to wish you'd stand up for yourself when he was screaming to the rooftops? It was only after you ran off that you started speaking up."

"He had me under his thumb. Not anymore. I already detest that I let him have full custody of you boys—"

"We never resented you for it," I quickly insert.

"I'm lucky that you don't because I resent it. What kind of mother leaves her children with a man like *that*?"

"I think you're being hard on yourself. It isn't as if he gave you a choice." What, with Pops having her declared as emotionally unstable, the judge handed us over without a second glance at the case files. "Plus, you know full well that Mrs. Abelman did most of the heavy lifting as an unwilling nanny."

"Who else could be as hard on me as I am?" she counters, lips pursed. Out of nowhere, she sighs. Relaxes. Smiles. "It's good to see you, Cole."

I shoot her a half-grin that morphs into a grimace as I drink my tea. "Good to see you too, Mum."

"Caught a couple of your matches this year."

"Games, Mom. *Games.* Not matches. This isn't England, and I don't play soccer."

"If only you did. I'd understand the rules." She sniffs. "How are the Bukowskis?"

She knows how close I am to Gracie's family and has always been grateful to them for bringing me in and treating me like one of their own. Not only that, but she was able to visit me more while I was living with them.

The only son she hasn't had much access to is Callan. She came to Winnipeg to be with me, and she's always traveled to wherever Cody has been stationed. Colt studied in Saskatoon and she spent months at a time there too.

Callan, who was locked here for endless periods of time, barely knows her outside of Skype calls.

If I feel bad for anyone, it's him.

"They're fine. Gracie's getting married."

"She is?" Her brows arch. "To whom?"

"Liam. He billeted with the Bukowskis too."

"What a good match. I remember he's very calming and Gracie is the exact opposite."

"Yeah, she's a little bit a lot." Though I grin, it starts to fade when I think about Mia.

My brow furrows.

I take a deep sip of tea.

And I don't even pull a face this time.

"What's wrong?"

"Nothing." I should be focused on the latest family drama and not a woman who betrayed my sis.

"Fibber."

Jesus, it's been a while since I heard that one.

"Tell me. Maybe I can help." Her eyes sparkle. "It wouldn't be women troubles, would it? Are you finally in a relationship?"

"You want to be a grandma," I complain.

"Is that a crime?" She stills a second. "You know I'd do everything I could to be a wonderful grandparent, don't you, son?"

"Of course."

"I wouldn't let your father stop me from seeing my grandchildren."

I settle a measured glance at her. "You think we'd let him?"

"No, you're right." She sags. In relief. *My old man is a piece of shit.* "You've always been on my side, haven't you, Cole?"

"Always." I snag her hand in mine and quickly squeeze it. "You're no longer under his thumb, Mum."

"I know." Her smile is tight. "So, come on then. What's wrong?"

It's not that I particularly want to talk about Mia, but I don't want to discuss Pops either.

Scraping a hand over my chin, I loop her in on what's been happening the past couple days. What I researched online during the flight too.

By the end of it, she looks as uneasy as I feel.

"Did Gracie know that the bar was struggling?"

"No, but she was an employee there. Why would the boss tell her how bad things were?"

"It's a shame he didn't because Gracie is the type to help if it's within her means."

That's so true that it makes this even more bittersweet.

"I really liked her."

"I can tell." She tips her head to the side. "But it can't be helped. You owe Gracie far more loyalty than you do a roll in the hay."

"I know."

While that isn't a lie, she's been on my mind throughout the trek home. Occupying more space than any one woman has in a long time. Not even a smutty audiobook distracted me.

"Hmm," is all Mum says because she knows me too well.

Peering into the dark sky beyond the many windows in this room, I get to my feet and stretch. "I'm going to catch some Zs."

"You sure you don't want anything to eat?"

"I grabbed something at a service station on the way in." Leaning over her, I kiss her cheek. "It's great to have you home, Mum."

"It's wonderful to be with my boys. Goodnight, son. See you in the morning."

I like that more than I want to admit.

I was one of the first to whoop with joy when she left him, and I wasn't lying about resenting him, not her, but that didn't stop me from missing her.

Mind oddly torn between Mum and Mia, I wander toward the wing where the sons have always historically slept.

Seven Cs was named after the seven boys from the original Korhonen who settled here.

Ever since, the unfortunate descendants were all doomed to be named with a 'C.' No one has ever been as prolific as the OG frisky Korhonen, though.

Thank God.

Back in the day, those seven sons worked the land, raised families in this house, and so it continued.

It sounds like my idea of hell, but hey, whatever floated my ancestors' boat.

It means, however, that the house is fucking enormous, but the unmarried sons always, *always* sleep in this wing.

Knowing that Callan will be in his room, before I head for mine, I go to his.

Not bothering to knock on the door, I walk in.

Then immediately regret it.

"Ah, Jesus H. Christ, Callan," I mumble, turning away from him when he nearly drops his laptop on the floor as he struggles to cover up.

"Have you never heard of knocking?"

"Oh, that feels so good, *CalKor*," someone moans, making my eyes widen as that's followed up with a *slap* sound.

Whipping back and around, I hear another deeper moan, and that's when my wide eyes bug even more.

Callan tries to slam his computer lid down but it's too late for that.

Mia's there.

On his screen.

Spanking herself?

What the hell is happening here?

"Don't look at her!" Callan spits as I drag the laptop from him and stare at Mia, who's fucking herself with a massive dildo in one hand and tapping her ass with the other.

I gawk at it, then her, then my baby goddamn brother.

"How the fuck did you get a credit card to pay for this?" I snarl because that's the only thing I can focus on.

I'm well aware that cam girls aren't cheap. Pops might have trusted Cody, Colt, and me with a credit card, but he's always been different with Callan.

I guess I know why now.

"Does it matter?"

He comes at me like he's Scrappy Doo while I hold the computer above my head and smack my hand to his forehead to keep him back as he tries to stop Mia from moaning.

God, the noises she makes…

It's weird that I have an erection at the same time as my baby brother.

"You stole the card from Pops?"

He immediately blanches. "You can't tell him."

There's genuine fear in his expression and it has my shoulders sagging. "Of course, I won't, but you have to pay back what you stole. You know better than to do something like this. How much have you spent?"

His white pallor burns hot pink as he mumbles something that sounds like, "Fourthouandfivecen."

"Four *thousand*?"

Callan glares at me. "That's nothing to you."

"Yeah, but I pay my fucking way and work hard for every dollar I earn. You're still in high school." His mouth puckers with a complete lack of regret. "You know I'm going to have to tell Colt about this."

His shoulders hunch. "Ah, no, Cole. Do you have to?"

"Yeah, because you'll do this again if I don't."

I'd never tell Pops. Ever. But, Mia aside, it'd be irresponsible to let him keep on doing this, right?

An X-rated loop starts playing in my head as I think of all the whacked-up shit I've done…

People in glass houses shouldn't throw stones.

But this is about Mia! Isn't it?

"I love her," he declares, breaking into my quandary and making things a hundred times worse. "I'm going to save her from doing this and make her a Korhonen so she never has to show her body to dirty old men again."

"You're not a dirty old man," I point out, but I'm not sure why that's the first thing I think of to say. Not when, to be honest, the idea of old perverts jacking off to her fucking a monster dildo riles me up the wrong way too.

"That doesn't matter. I. Love. Her. I won't let her go," he insists, his hands balling into fists at his sides.

"You're going to have to. I'll give you until tomorrow to tell Colton yourself, otherwise I'll do it. And I'm taking this with me."

"You're taking my computer?" he shrieks.

"Yeah, I am. If you've got a problem with that, you can always complain to Mum or Colt, huh?"

He glowers at me as I leave the room, the laptop in my hand.

I almost feel bad for doing this, but I don't have it in me to care.

Colt or Mum can be the parents in this situation. Mostly, I'm…

"Oh, fuck, this feels so good. It's so big. I know you'd be as big. I'm so wet. Can I touch my clit? Please, can I?"

Right there, in the middle of the hallway that'll take me to my bedroom, I stop and let my head fall back.

I heard those same noises last night.

I nearly busted my wad then and I'm close to doing the same thing now.

"Can I? Please?" she whines.

Sucking in a breath, I storm into my bedroom. Instead of cutting the video as I should have in my brother's room, I set it on the desk where I used to do my homework, and after I retreat to the door to lock it (I'll learn from Callan's lesson), I plunk my ass on the chair that creaked when I was one-eighty, never mind two-forty.

> Rog43: No. U can't toch your clit. Show us ur cunt.

The words immediately piss me the fuck off and make me want to slap Callan upside the head.

That's when I realize she's in a public forum—Callan didn't write that so he can live to see another day.

But this means…

Other guys are watching her.

Rage rattles through me until my attention shifts when she immediately pulls out the dildo and exposes her gaping slit.

"Fuck," I hiss.

She was hard for me to get into and her ease with that dildo tells me I'm bigger.

Nice pat on the back for Cole Jr.

She's so fucking wet that all I can think of is how I got to taste that. I got to eat her out to my heart's content.

"Why are you being so mean?" Mia mewls. "Let me come. Pleeeeease."

> Rog43: Shov 3 fingers into ur slit.

> HydraRoolz: Let us see how they shine in the light.

She obeys like a wet dream.

Her fingers make the deep dive as requested and then she's there, showing us the proof of how turned on she is.

Is it lube?

Or is it real?

I can't decide.

What I do know is that I don't like her showing these assholes that slick whether it's natural or lube.

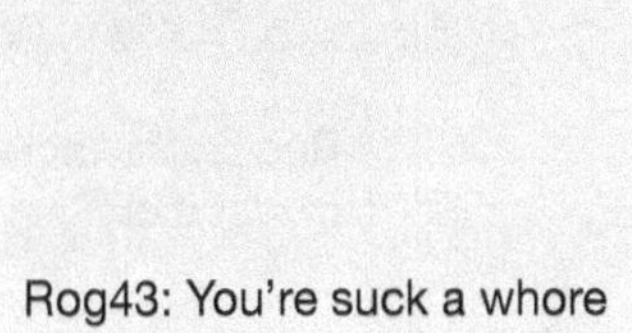

My mouth tightens.

Mia's too busy showing us how wet she is to see the insult but I fuck-ing do.

CalKor: Learn to spell, DUMBFUCK

HydraRoolz: Lick them clean.

Rog43: Who the fuck are you talking to?

CalKor: You, asscunt. There's no need to talk shit
to the lady

Rog43: What made u think this slat is a lady

CalKor: Asshole. You should apologize

She sticks her fingers in her mouth and slurps up her juices—noisier than necessary and ten times hotter.

It's confusing as hell, too, because as much as she's turning me on, my brain can't get over the fact these other pricks are watching what belongs to me.

She's mine.

I close my eyes at the thought.

Because…

She isn't.

Rog43: Man, ur such a dirty hore. Love those
noices

I grit my teeth.

> Rog43: Wish u were scking my coc

> Rog43: I'd choke u on it. Steal all the oxigun on my fat dick

The urge to throw the computer against the wall is real and raw. I'm so fucking close to doing that.

> Rog43: Bet u look so pretty wen ur not breathing

I slam my fist onto the desk.

> CalKor: You abusive piece of shit. Isn't there a moderator here? That was a fucking death threat!

> Rog43: STFU

A few clicks later, I hit 'report' on his username and I'm totally understanding why an impressionable kid like Callan wants to run away with Mia. Not because she's hot, but because he wants to save her from these fucking ASSHOLES.

Except, thankfully, *Rog43* gets kicked out of the chat.

Then I'm left with *HydraRoolz*.

> HydraRoolz: You're so beautiful, baby. I wanna see you come.

His praise rubs me the wrong way too.

Goddammit.

"Thank you, sweetie," Mia croons, making me crack my neck.

This is so fucking wrong. I hate that she's saying this shit to other guys.

Goddammit to hell.

That's when I see a couple more of her tats which were hidden to me in the darkness of the night.

There's one on her belly—another cat outline, but this time, the cat's standing on his back legs as it paws at a small, inked star.

Low on her other hip, she has a more playful one—two cats curved together, head to tail, one black and one white in a parody of the yin-yang symbol.

An obsession with cats shouldn't be a check in the positive column, especially after what she did to Gracie, but fuck if I don't love that about her.

HydraRoolz: Let me see your tits.

She shoves them together.

HydraRoolz: Titty fuck the dildo.

I scowl at his crass demands.

Sliding off the bed, she sets the monster cock on the table in front of the camera, letting the suction pads on the base do their job, then wraps her glorious tits around the toy.

HydraRoolz: Shit, I gtg. Stay beautiful xoxo

Suddenly, I'm all alone in the chat. For the moment, at least. And that changes everything.

As she starts to jack it off, she moans as if this is doing it for her.

I know it isn't.

At least, my brain does.

Little brain in Cole Jr. doesn't fucking care.

All I can think is how deep my regret is that I didn't do this last night.

That I didn't do *this* before I found out how she betrayed Gracie.

Not even thoughts of that are enough to get me to stop doing what I'm doing, though—I unfasten my zipper and release my cock from the prison of my fly.

"It's just you and me, *CalKor*. I know you love seeing me like this."

Shuddering, I rub pre-cum over the tip of my cock and start to roll it down my length.

A part of me hates that I'm doing this. Treating her like those other bastards. But fuck, I'm a weak, weak, *weak* man.

CalKor: I do

"I wish my tits were around your cock. Don't you, *CalKor*?" I wish she'd stop using his username. "You want me to be desperate to come? You want me to beg? I will," she whimpers, seeming to speed up as she jacks the fake dick off. "Please. I need to come. You've got me so hot. I'm so ready to explode. I wish you were here. I wish it were your cock I was jacking off—"

Like a fool, that does it for me.

The last time I was a two-pump chump, I was back in middle school. I'm almost ashamed of how quickly my cock spurts before I can stop myself. White ropes of thick cum quickly drench my fist, pooling in my Prince Albert piercing as I get off to her pleas.

I grit my teeth as I eke out every last ounce of pleasure and then, and only then, do I type:

CalKor: I'd love to see you on the bed. Watch you come. You earned that pleasure, baby. You worked so hard today.

The words fall off my fingers as I type one-handed.

She complies immediately, leaping onto the bed with a grace and speed that tell me it isn't the first time she's done this *and* that she genuinely does want to get off.

It makes it feel more authentic, despite nothing about this being authentic.

Including the bright purple wig she's wearing.

Rolling onto her knees, face to the mattress, ass in the air, she strokes her clit, moans getting louder and her wails forcing me to adjust the volume.

When she finds her release, my attention veers off course as someone knocks on my door and another guy jumps in the forum:

CaptainGeorgia11: Oh, man, what a way to start the chat!

Fuming, I press 'mute' because now that I'm the one caught with his pants down, I have no choice but to deal with whoever's on the other side of the door.

"Cole?"

Jesus.

"Give me a couple minutes, Colt. I'm using the shitter."

He grunts. "Come and see me when you're done."

Releasing a relieved breath, I watch as Mia sags into the bed I fucked her on yesterday and sigh at the sight.

She's so beautiful.

Why did she have to betray Gracie?

CalKor: I need to go.

I don't know how this works. I never had to resort to webcams when I was Callan's age—half the cheerleading squad was more than willing to take my V-card and teach me the ways of the pussy promise land—but my message must ding or something because she turns back to look at me.

Her pink ass, complete with handprints, is still pretty much all I can see.

I should have fucked that too.

"There are only so many hours in a night," I try to console myself.

It doesn't work.

I know I should log off.

This is weird.

More than that—it's creepy.

But I don't.

Instead, I perpetuate the crime and type:

CalKor: See you tomorrow. Be happy, beautiful

She smiles at that then curls onto her side and waves before saying, "How are you doing today, handsome? I missed you, *CaptainGeorgia11*."

That fucks with my mood as I figure out how to leave the virtual room we're in.

When I'm logged off, I get to my feet and head to the bathroom.

While I wash my hands, I stare at my reflection.

My cheeks are flushed in a post-orgasm glow and there's a hard glint in my eyes that says everything—there's no way that'll be the last time I see Mia Charles orgasm.

Once I've dried my hands, I return to the desk and stare at the interface of the site Callan uses, then I look at his tabs.

Spying that his email is open, I head to the user settings of the cam girl site and change the email address to mine, alter the password, then proceed to delete Pops's credit card info and replace it with my own.

Once that's done and Callan can't access the site anymore, I log out for good and then, to be on the safe side, clear the cookies and saved passwords.

He's a smartass, so he'll start up a new account, but for the moment, this is as much as I can do.

I hate to admit it, even to myself, but I need to stop him from having access to Mia.

If I could cut off those other jackasses' access, I would.

Knowing she's having to deal with that *Rog43* and his ilk on the regular isn't helping my blood pressure.

Fighting the desire to go pick a fight with Callan, I close the screen, snag it under my arm, and head for the door.

A few minutes later, I open Colt's.

"If I hadn't forgotten that you were raised in a barn, I'd have warned you that he's going through a phase," is his greeting, one that makes my hackles rise.

I stare at him, trying not to imagine how a fight between us would go. I'm strong but Colt's Colt. He knows all my moves. He taught me most of 'em.

Losing would piss me off even more.

Huffing, I join him at the window, where he's leaning with one arm on the sill, a glass of whiskey in his hand.

"Why you can't knock is beyond me."

I crack my knuckles as I try to work through my *futile* rage. "I forget."

She. Is. Not. Yours.

"Well, learn not to."

"You fuckers can lock the door."

"Or you could knock."

I sniff. "He went straight to you, huh?"

"Said you stole his laptop."

"He was watching a cam girl on it, Colt."

My cam girl, to be precise.

My older brother shrugs. "So?"

"So?! He's paying women to strip off and fuck themselves with monster dildos."

"You've probably got a chick in every state, but Callan, the kid behind a screen, is the one with the problem?"

"Two words, Colt. Monster. Dildos."

"I thought you'd be offering to pay." At my bewildered expression, Colt derides, "Weren't you screwing half the cheerleaders in your grade at his age?"

"That's different."

"How is it? Callan's awkward. He doesn't find it easy to talk to girls."

"He finds it easy to type to them," I grumble as I toss the computer on his bed. Watching it bounce, realization strikes. "Wait a minute, did you give him the card?" Maybe I misunderstood?

"No. I saw him take Pops's. I never said anything because Pops gave us cards at his age and it's not like he missed it. Callan's had it for nearly a year without the old bastard realizing it was lost."

There are so many levels of fucked up in that sentence that I mutter, "He claims he's in love with her. Wants to run away and stop her from having to sell her body to old perverts on the internet."

Colt finally turns to face me. "He said that?"

"He did. You think I'd make it up?" I roll my eyes and snag the whiskey tumbler from his grasp. We fight over it but he concedes and lets me take a sip.

"Little shit."

Colt's always been too old for his own good.

He acts like he's our dad and I can't fault him for it. He took the beatings so we wouldn't. He was the one who covered for us. He was the one we came to with problems…

"Is Callan doing okay?"

"He's fine. Happier since he started sorting out the security in this place. You know what he's like."

"Obsessive?"

Colt snorts as I hand him the glass.

"I talk to him at least four times a week."

"You're a good brother," Colt says with approval.

"I try."

And the little asshole tries to get with my girl!

Not that she is my girl.

"That's all we can do." He takes a deeper sip of whiskey. "I'll deal with him and this cam girl situation."

"It didn't occur to me that you wouldn't."

He grunts.

"Go easy on him, though. If he thinks he's in love, it'll be hard to stop him. I changed the password and email combo so he won't be able to access that account."

"He'll open up a new one."

"I know. But if you make sure he can't get his hands on a credit card, that'll stop this in its tracks."

"Until he's eighteen and he can do whatever the hell he wants." His lips curve when I grimace. "He's a sneaky little fucker."

"Gets it from watching Cody."

"True."

Studying him, I ask, "You doing all right, Colt?"

He looks… exhausted. Maybe even more than that.

"Been better, been worse."

I clap him on the shoulder again. "I get it."

And I do. Because that's confirmation there's definitely something going on with him. I also know he won't share it with me.

Not yet.

Maybe not ever.

"I'm here if you need me, big bro. You know that, right?"

When he tips the glass at me in silent assent, I turn to look out onto the Seven Cs' prairie with its rolling waves of endless darkness that no light pollution interferes with.

Though I hate coming back here and I can fight it as much as I want…

CHAPTER 11
MIA

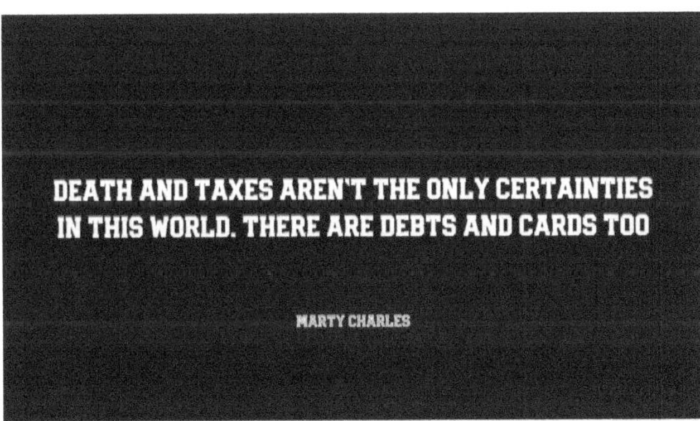

Formula - Labrinth

I CAN LITERALLY FEEL the blood draining from my face as I stare at the letter in front of me.

I always knew that Chuck played loose with the figures that he filed on his accounts, but not to this extent.

Back taxes owed: $198,056

A part of me feels like screaming, and another part wants to go home and cry myself to sleep.

The worst thing is that this is just one of the debts he's accrued over the years, with this 200k being a drop in the ocean. Even the bar is mortgaged to the hilt. Throw in his medical bills and the cost of a funeral these days, and I've come to learn that I'm well and truly screwed.

Two days ago, after Cole texted his Dear John letter, I headed into the office at the bar once my cam girl session was through. It was rough—really fucking rough—because this place is Chuck's. Every inch of it stinks of cigar smoke and the cologne he used to wear.

His battered recliner is angled away from the TV, much as if it's waiting for him to return from the bathroom. His cookie jar is stuffed full of the midnight snacks that he devoured while he watched baseball reruns to help him fall asleep.

If that isn't rough enough, taking a seat behind his desk makes me feel like an imposter.

I've staved off many a panic attack in this chair, but only because these accounts wait for no one.

Every morning has revealed more debts, making it necessary to go home, shower, and change so I can jack off in front of strangers on the internet in the hope that I can cover some bills with my body.

I'm going to have to cancel a couple of coaching sessions because the cam-girling pays more.

Feeling defeated and as if a stone has permanently settled in my stomach, I pull out the drawer that's filled with more of Chuck's denial.

It's as big as the river too.

He stuffed letters in there. Whether they were black or red, they made their way into this one fucking drawer.

But this is the worst of all. Especially as it's dated two months ago. Which means that huge debt has daily interest being added to it as we speak.

A part of me wants to cry, but another, bigger part of me is angry.

He dumped this on my shoulders, and somehow, I have to make this work. People are relying on me—not just my staff who need their salary but the customers too. This place is a safe haven for many.

Chuck, with his stupidity, put that at risk.

"Mia?"

I turn to the door as it opens. "Yeah, Dionne?"

"I think Cupid got out of the office again," she drawls, amusement lacing the words as she walks in with my cat in her arms. "I'm starting to see that she lives up to her name." She rubs her nose on her head. "Cupid the Cutie Cat."

Sighing at my rogue feline's antics, I ask, "Could you get her a dish of water, please?"

I decided to bring her with me because she's been sad. I get the feeling she misses Chuck popping in, and I figured the scent of this place might help. Instead, she's spent half the time getting into mischief.

"Of course. I'll make sure that she doesn't escape when I come in." Dionne studies me. "Do you need anything, Mia?"

Two hundred thousand dollars would be awesome.

Not that I say that.

Even if I really want to.

My smile is even weaker this time as I shake my head. She hums at me then fades away, leaving me to the pile of mail that feels like a scarlet letter.

When Cupid winds a path toward me, I let her jump onto my knee, finding comfort in her scent and in how she nuzzles my chin.

"What am I going to do, Cupid?" I ask, but she has no answer for me.

At least, not one that hasn't already occurred to me.

Staring blankly ahead, I sit there, absorbing the terrible truth that I might have to sell the bar.

That's the only light at the end of the tunnel.

The building is mine and the bank's, but without the building, there's no business.

Which means that what my great-granddaddy established is something I'll be the one to wreck.

Anger is what's getting me through this. I've always had anxiety issues, but I've mostly managed to keep a cage on them. Chuck's death unlocked that cage and let my fears out to party.

But I have to get through this so railing at my uncle's stupidity is helping. Selling isn't something I can abide—not yet. Not without trying to turn things around on my terms with no Chuck there to undermine my projects.

The door opens and Dionne steps in with a 'Chuck's' tumbler tucked under her arm while two dishes are in her hands. She places one beneath my nose and another in front of Cupid. She pours water from the tumbler into her dish and then hands it to me.

"You're not going to fix anything if you don't look after yourself, Mia," she chides when, grimacing, I thank her.

The tumbler's half-empty by the time I answer, "I'm not hungry."

"Sometimes, you just have to eat." She tips the dish toward me. "Everything okay?"

Awkwardly, I pick up the sandwich and take a small bite. It settles like ashes in my mouth but I chew on it and swallow because she's right —I've barely eaten since the pizza Cole brought to my apartment.

The 'no food thing' is part anxiety, part trying to save money and not eat into our meager profits.

"Not really, Dionne."

"Do I need to look for another job?"

The tentative question drowns me in guilt—she's a single mom, already working three jobs to make ends meet. I always accommodate her schedule as best I can.

That's partly why Jarvis is here.

Sure, I noticed him one day picking through our trash cans for food and that was my reason for hiring him, but he's turned out to be great behind the bar.

Having the pair on staff is expensive but it means I can coach. Or cam girl. Whichever the case may be.

Wishing I could tell her something different, I promise, "I'm trying to do everything I can to make sure that won't be necessary…"

Dionne perches her butt on the side of the desk and casts a shrewd glance at the piles of paper in front of me. "These letters aren't helping?"

Bowing my head in shame, I whisper, "No."

"It's not your fault, Mia."

"Of course it is."

"Chuck was the worst businessman I've ever known. I don't like to speak ill of the dead, but his tabs are longer than my eldest and we both know that he's nearly seven feet tall."

My nose crinkles. "I was helping run the place before he passed."

"More like you were covering the bills that he was running up." She tuts. "The last thing you need to be doing is taking the blame for any of this." She pats my shoulder again. "Could you let me know if I need to look for work? I'd appreciate a heads-up."

"You know I will."

"Can you still cover wages?"

I can if I work nonstop at the cam girl stuff.

I rub my tired eyes. "Just. But... I won't be able to be around the bar much."

"The coaching?" At my nod, she sighs. "It's a damn shame you're having to support this place with other work. You sure you shouldn't be selling it?"

"Selling what? No bar, no sales."

"How about the memorabilia on the walls for a start? That's gotta be worth something."

I shake my head. "It's all nostalgia. Chuck told me when I asked him to get it valued."

She purses her lips as she gets to her feet. "I know Beanpole was worried—"

"He doesn't have to be. I'll make this work."

His granddaughter's sick. How can I let him go when he's helping his son pay her hospital bills?

As for Larry, he's been with us since the Stone Age. He's practically a part of the furniture. I can't fire him either.

"You're a kind person, Mia." Dionne pats my shoulder. "I'll let everyone know that you'll be M.I.A for a while. We know what you're doing to keep this place running and we appreciate it. Now, eat that sandwich, honey."

With a soft smile, she fades from the room, leaving me with the mess of finances I've inherited.

Cupid noses at my sandwich so I pull off some pieces of meat to feed to her.

"It's not that I hate doing the cam girl stuff, Cupid," I mumble to my only confidante. "I just don't want to do it twenty hours a day."

Utterly unaware and uncaring, she meows at me.

"Yeah, I know you need cat food too," I say with a sigh as I tug off a few more bites for her then get to work on eating the rest myself.

The last thing I need is to faint on cam.

"Is cam-girling full-time a solution?" I ask Cupid. "It's a lot of pressure, a lot of work, but…" I nuzzle my nose against her head. "Three months. That's what I'll give myself. Enough to get a debt consolidation loan, see if I can ease the pressure, then earn enough to cover the day-to-day expenses and let some of my ideas kick into gear.

"Chuck got us into this mess so it's not like he had the right to shoot me down." My mouth tightens and for the first time in days, I start to feel like my old self. "If I'm going to save this place, then we need to think outside the box."

Cupid meows at me.

And call me crazy, but I take that as a 'yes.'

Nodding at her, I mutter, "Three months or I sell."

Another meow.

I blow out a breath. "Let's do this."

NEW YORK STARS ARE OUT

BY MACK FINNEGAN

The season's surprise underdogs, the New York Stars, were knocked out of the semifinals in a brutal game five that saw Chicago take one step closer to winning the Stanley Cup.

As has been the way this season, Coach Bradley's men forced overtime.

On this occasion, however, Lady Luck was not on the Stars' *or* 'the Leprechaun' Donnghal's side.

Though the captain and Kyle Lewis brought heat to Chicago's defense, the rest of the team fell short.

Last night's game was an all-round disappointment with lackluster performances by Raimond and Gagné in particular.

It's a devastating end for Stars' fans who were hoping the team would go all the way and live up to the promise they showed at the start of the season.

Chicago will face Calgary in four days.

CHAPTER 12
COLE

Streets – Joel Sunny

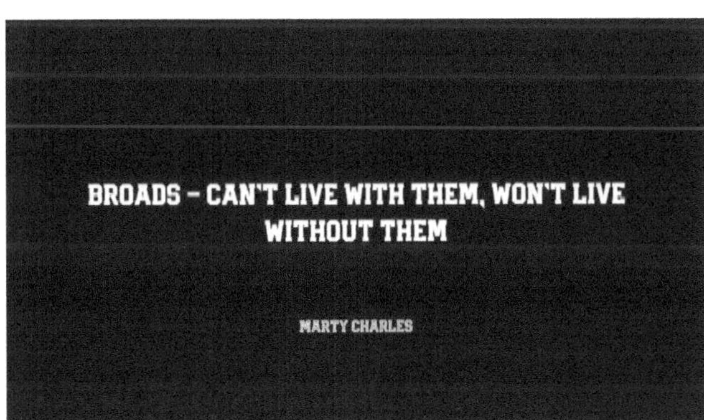

SHE'S NOT ONLINE when I first wake up.

Nor is she an hour later when the Bukowski chat is inundated with a barrage of messages in the wake of the Stars' loss.

Yeah, I've checked the website. Like, I've checked it a dozen times in the past few days.

This is a problem.

Fuck.

My.

Life.

"Why isn't Callan talking to you?"

Disturbed from my thoughts, I blink at Mum. "He is."

Her brow arches. "He walked into the kitchen, saw you, walked back out again. What did you do?"

Huh, I didn't notice that.

"We had a disagreement."

She purses her lips. "Are you planning on speaking with your father soon?"

"Unfortunately. Colt informed me that I've been summoned. Pops doesn't like that I've been avoiding him for three days."

"Will you tell me what his game is when you find out?"

I shrug. "Of course."

The prompt reminds me that I was heading to Pops's room before I got waylaid with thoughts of Mia.

Mrs. Abelman smacks my hand when I try to drink OJ from the carton. "I know I didn't see you do that, boy."

"I'll have you know I'm very much a man now, Mrs. Abelman," I drawl as I drag her in for a hug she doesn't want but accepts with an impatient sigh.

"Men don't drink from the carton," she tuts, making Mum snicker behind her china teacup.

"Oh, I see how it is. You two are gonna gang up on me, are you?"

"Damn straight," Mrs. Abelman assures me, though it doesn't escape my notice that the normally dour housekeeper-cum-surrogate-mom-to-us-all is unusually chipper.

Mum's influence, I guess.

Pouting at the pair of them, I pour half a bag of milk into a tumbler instead of OJ then start drinking it as I leave the kitchen with half an ear on their chatter.

I lose track of their conversation about Callan's celiac issues when I make it to the wing where Pops's rooms are situated.

He's sitting up and looks brighter when I walk in. That means he either feels better for real *or* he was wearing makeup the last time I saw him.

The thought of my misogynistic father wearing makeup is hilarious enough that I'm hiding a chuckle as I drink some more milk before I throw myself on the armchair beside his bed.

"What's so funny?" he grouses.

"Nothing."

"Cody got in last night."

"I didn't realize."

"He only came to see me," is Pops's smug retort.

I'm not sure why he thinks that's a burn but it clearly is to him.

That Colt didn't inform me or Mum, I have to reason he's not lying.

"Is he okay?"

"Of course he is. He's Cody. It's good to have my sons under my roof again. You don't come back home enough."

"I come back home plenty," I dismiss. "Now, why did you want to see me?"

He leans forward, wincing as he does so. "I need your help, Cole."

"You need *my* help?" I repeat. "With what?"

"Your mother's a liar."

Well, that's a way to get nothing out of me.

Eyes narrowed, I ask, "What makes you think that?"

"Callan ain't my boy."

"Of course he is."

"He isn't!"

"Why do you think he isn't?"

"He's a freak."

"He likes computers. That's not a crime. At least he isn't joyriding or getting into drugs."

"What, you mean if he did normal shit?" Pops shakes his head. "It's not right. Him cooped up in that room of his all the time. I'm telling you he ain't mine."

"So, you're going on the premise that you're not his biological father because he's an introvert?"

"Colt, Cody, and you aren't. You were normal."

I think about my penchant for Omegaverse why choose, big booties on women, and a new obsession for cam girls... "Normal's overrated."

"Why aren't you listening to me?"

"I am listening to you, Pops, but you're making no sense. Hell, would it make you feel better to know he's spent nearly four grand on cam girls in the past year and that's why he spends so much time in his bedroom?!"

Pops harrumphs. "You're lying."

"I'm not lying. Why would I fucking lie?"

"You can't sway me. I've been thinking about it since your slut of a mother had her so-called 'miracle baby.'"

I growl, "I've told you not to call her that."

He sniffs. "I got him tested."

Colt was right.

"For cooties?"

"No. To see if he's my son or not," he snaps.

"And the results were proof that you're wrong? As always?"

"I don't know." He snatches an envelope from amid the sheets and wafts it. "Got them here."

The door opens and in steps Cody. He looks, much as he always does, like he's got a stick up his ass.

Still, he's my brother and I haven't seen him in...

Fuck, years.

Getting to my feet, I grab a hold of his neck and draw him in for a hug. "Hey, asshole."

He smirks at me. "Hey, yourself. You doing all right?"

"Yeah." I cut him a look. "You heard this bullshit about Callan?"

"Let's get this over with."

I dart a look at the door and see Colt's arrived, though his phone is glued to one ear and his glower would make anyone not in this room wince at the sight. His presence and Callan's absence tell me Pops only wants his so-called biological sons around him as he opens the letter.

I'm used to the low-voltage anger I feel whenever I'm around Pops, but the desire to throttle him is increasing every minute I'm in his vicinity.

After Colt shuts the door, he strides over to the window and leans against it like he's got the weight of the world on his shoulders and only looking at our family land can ease his stress.

Cody remains standing at the foot of Pops's bed. I retreat to the armchair again, watching Colt finish up his conversation.

"I swear to fuck if you didn't check that fence—" Colt rubs his eyes but I know his growl has enough bite to get the other guy to respond: "Just goddamn do it."

Cody even straightens up at the tone—Colt really should have been the soldier in our family. He's got CO vibes for sure.

"Did your heels click?" I taunt Cody, who scowls at me.

"It was better back in the day when you could fire people without any warning," Pops mutters.

"Oh, yeah, no employee rights were the best days," I mock, crossing my legs at the ankle.

Pops ignores me. "The northeast quadrant again?"

Colt shoves his phone in his pocket. "Don't even pretend you know where that is."

I can totally believe that. Pops has never been one to get his hands dirty. He only inherited the ranch because his twin brother, older than him by five hours, died when he was forty-six—single and childless. Unlike Pops, Colt took after Uncle Clayton—they were both born for this shit.

Pops huffs as I snicker, but Cody snipes, "I told you last night that I don't appreciate being drawn back home on lies so get on with it—"

"I wasn't lying! I *am* sick. I could have died. That my sons are this upset about being dragged home tells me how much I'm appreciated."

My eyes ache with how hard I roll them. "Pops, you lied to us. This isn't your deathbed."

"I've got arrhythmia. I thought it was a heart attack. It's not. There— are you happy now?" He tears at the envelope and pulls open the letter, not that he glances at it. Instead, he wafts it again, declaring, "This'll tell me the truth. Your lying bitch of a mom was cheating on me. I know she was."

Though I frown at him, I watch as Cody snatches the letter from his grasp, and while Pops's flailing around for it, he opens it, scans it, and arches a brow at Pops before he tosses it on his lap.

"Callan's yours."

"It's a fucking lie," he snarls, snatching the letter and scanning the test results. "He's not my son. I'm telling you! Why will no one fucking listen to me?"

"Dammit to hell, Pops, you have the proof in front of you," Colt roars.

For the first time, there's dead silence in the bedroom.

Colt might not blow his gasket often, but when he does, it behooves you to listen.

"He's not mine," Pops insists like the spoiled brat he is.

"You took the DNA test, you sent it all in, and the results are back— he's your kid. And it's a disgrace that you thought otherwise." Colt pinches the bridge of his nose. "What were you hoping to achieve with this mess?"

Pops bows his head. "It doesn't matter now."

I shoot Cody a look but he only sighs.

"Sure it matters."

"Who did you think she cheated on you with?" I've no idea where the question comes from, but it suddenly feels like that'll get us to the source of this little issue we're having.

His jaw works. "Anthony McAllister."

His archnemesis.

Colt frowns. "She never had anything to do with the McAllisters. You'd have made her life hell if she so much as went near that place."

"She took his painting class in Pigeon Creek." He sneers. "There were plenty of opportunities."

"Did you catch them?"

"Almost did."

"I hope she did," I grate out though she told me herself that she didn't.

Cody nods. "At least she'd have known some fucking happiness while she was in this prison."

Pops gapes at us both like we mortally wounded him. "You're *my* sons. You're supposed to be on my side!"

"You made Mum's life a living hell," Cody drawls, peering at his nails. "If getting dicked down by McAllister gave her some peace then good for her. Whether she did or not, however, Callan is *your* son. Not McAllister's."

"What purpose did any of this serve—"

I don't even get the chance to finish that question because Colton is growling, "This is because he's turning eighteen soon, isn't it?"

Cody groans. "You're trying to screw him out of his trust fund?!"

"I don't believe you," I snap in outrage.

"I want that three hundred million to go to my *real* sons. *My* flesh and blood—"

"Callan is," I spit, "your flesh and fucking blood. Goddammit, man. What more proof do you want?"

Colton slides a hand over his head. "I want to say that I'm surprised but I'm not. You've always been a shortsighted idiot."

"I'm your father and I demand you speak to me with respect!" he blusters.

"You lost any right to being respected by your sons," I grind out. "I'm sick of this bullshit." And I storm off, leaving my older brothers to deal with him.

Which, of course, is when I get a text message.

> Gracie: When you get your ass back to the US, hit us up in Manhattan because I have some star-shaped pierogi with your name on them.

Confused as fuck, I stare at the message as I stride down the hall, trying to get far away from my asscunt of a father before he can spread his poison any farther.

> Me: I'm never going to say no to your pierogi, little bit, but what the fuck are you talking about?

> Gracie: Now that the Stars are out of the playoffs, my engagement as GM is official.

> Gracie: You're going to be a Star, dude. Don't make me regret making this trade...

NEW YORK STARS' GM IS OUT - GRACIE BUKOWSKI IS IN

BY MACK FINNEGAN

This morning, Justin DeLaney, GM of the New York Stars, quit in the face of a searing semifinals loss to Chicago. The team was quick to announce that new kid on the block, Gracie Bukowski, will take over as General Manager.

You might recognize the last name from her brothers, Kow, Trent, and Noah—all top-tier players in their own right—but Bukowski, an MBA graduate from NYU, doesn't exactly have the experience to back up the appointment.

Her first move as GM was to acquire Cole Korhonen from New Jersey in exchange for Lars Raimond and future considerations.

Korhonen, who billeted with the Bukowskis in Winnipeg at the tender age of 15, has mostly been wasted with the Blue Demons, though his place on their top offensive line had long been cemented.

It has been announced that he will be harboring number 42.

Ms. Bukowski's appointment is shattering glass ceilings in more ways than one. She becomes not only the first female GM but also the youngest.

Chatter of nepotism is already spreading. Ms. Bukowski, after all, is engaged to Liam Donnghal—the Stars' captain—and rumor has it that Donnghal and the new team owners are, in fact, related.

New York Stars' fans had this to say:

"Hockey's a man's sport. Not sure what the Stars are thinking, but it's madness bringing in Gracie Bukowski. Was sad they lost, though. Brilliant team this season. Real shame." William F., Buffalo, NY.

"Korhonen was wasted in New Jersey and that the new GM has all these contacts at her fingertips gives me hope for the future. Go STARS!" Juniper K, Staten Island, NY.

When a team promising so much falls short, oftentimes the one to pay the price is the coach. Amid these changes, one has to wonder about Allan Bradley's fate in the new-look Stars' future.

Cole: Glass. Ceiling. Shattered.

Cole: That should have been the headline

Gracie: Shuddup

Cole: Is it not the truth?

Liam: Sounds like the truth to me.

Gray: And me.

Trent: Me too.

Matt: Over here as well.

Noah: Yup. Way to bring it, Gracie. Woop!

Liam: Your mom and dad are still drunk from how much Champagne they drank last night lol.

Fryd: Can confirm. Head hurt

Noah: You could have warned us that she signed the contract! We could have been there.

Gracie: I didn't want anyone there. Not even them.

Liam: She thought Conor was going to pull the contract before she could sign it.

Gray: GRACIE! We did not raise you to be so dumb.

Gracie: Since when did you raise me?

Cole: We're a pack. We raise one another.

Liam: God help us.

Matt: That's why we're all fucking weird?

Noah: Sounds like it.

Trent: Speak for yourselves.

Cole: Haha

Cole: Still, this is awesome news. So fucking proud of you, little bit.

Gracie: <3 <3

THAT SAME DAY

Kow: How did I just find out that you were in Canada but didn't come to see me?

Cole: I went to Saskatoon, not the Peg.

Kow: And? No one comes to visit me.

Cole: That's because you're an asshole.

Cole: You almost die this year yet?

Kow: What's with the hate?

Cole: No hate. Facts.

Cole: But in this instance, it's not because you're an asshole. I had to get home fast.

Kow: Liam said something about your dad?

Cole: Yeah, he faked a heart attack. Can you believe that?

Kow: Woah. Crazy. Your old man is such a piece of work.

Cole: Tell me about it.

Kow: And nah. I haven't died yet.

Kow: Though there was that issue with a butt plug that wasn't a butt plug.

Cole: Do I want to know?

Kow: Some ER doctor got a good look in my ass, that's all I'm saying.

Cole: FML. You're asking to die.

Kow: Nah, you gotta live like today's your last.

Kow: Speaking of, you should have come down. We could have hung out. I wanted to show you this new strip joint. The chicks have booties that have your name written all over them.

Cole: I told you last time I was there, Kow, I don't like that shit anymore.

Kow: How can you stop liking strippers? It's ingrained in your DNA, dude.

Cole: Might be ingrained in yours, but it isn't in mine. I'm tired of that scene.

Kow: You're younger than me.

Cole: I can count.

Kow: Man, what the fuck is going on? First Liam, now you? Who've you fallen for?

Cole: I haven't fallen for anyone. I've come to realize that I'm sick of anonymous lays.

Kow: But they're the best. You gotta spread the love, dude.

Cole: You can spread the love for me.

Cole: I swear you got some kind of breeding kink or something so I'm doing you a favor.

Kow: BREEDING?! No fucking way.

Kow: No kids for me.

Cole: And the world rejoices. :P

Kow: You're pissy today.

Cole: Yeah, I guess I am. Sorry, Kow.

Kow: It's okay.

Kow: You're really down, huh?

Cole: Pops is a jerk. I wish he were like Fryd.

Kow: Dad ain't perfect.

Cole: No, but at least he cares.

Cole: My asshole father was trying to pull some long con with Callan.

Kow: Huh?

Kow: Callan's only a baby.

Cole: You don't want to know what the baby was doing a week ago.

Kow: Tell me more.

Cole: Little fucker only stole Pops's credit card and was using it to pay for cam girls.

Kow: Dude, I want to be him when I grow up.

Cole: Figured you'd approve lol.

Kow: Since when are you a prude?

Cole: I'm not a prude.

Kow: Sounds like it.

Kow: Thought you'd be the one sneaking him a card to pay for that.

Cole: Doesn't matter.

Kow: Sure it does. Not like you to be a freakin' hypocrite.

Kow: Why do you care?

Kow: No one's getting hurt and Callan's learning how pussies work.

Cole: I don't want to have this conversation with you lol.

Kow: Because you know I'm right.

Kow: Here if you need me, man. Can be there if the worst happens.

Cole: Yeah, I know. Thanks for that.

Cole: Since Liam pulled your head out of your ass, you've been better.

Kow: It's called personal growth.

Cole: That what it is? Figured you'd been taking more laxatives than usual.

Kow: HA HA HA

Kow: That news article… Gracie is doing us proud.

Cole: Yeah. I'm glad for her.

Kow: Me too. At least she'll be with Liam.

Cole: More like he'll be with her.

Kow: He needs her more than she needs him.

Cole: There's probably a lot of truth to that.

Kow: I'm capable of speaking the truth lol.

Cole: You congratulated her privately? I couldn't help but notice you were radio silent in the chat.

Kow: Nah. She doesn't need me ruining this moment.

Cole: Kow, listen to me, would you?

Cole: Congratulate.

Cole: Her.

Cole: NOW.

Kow: Why did you never tell me your agent was hot?

SECOND PERIOD

THREE MONTHS LATER

CHAPTER 13
COLE

SEPTEMBER

sirens - Maiah Manser

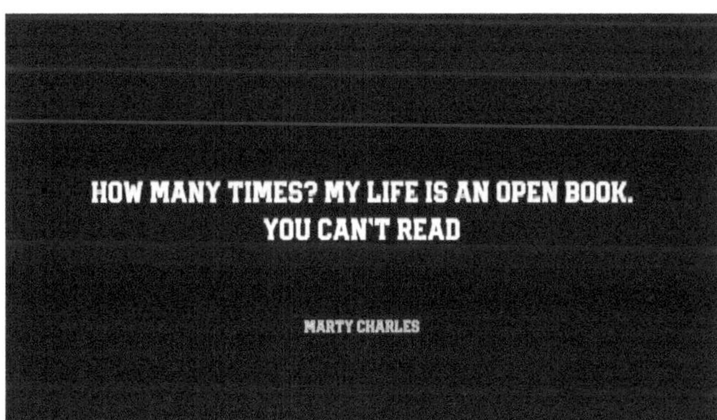

THERE'S no getting around it—Mia is my dirty little secret.

As she perches her ass on the side of the bed and expectantly tilts her head, however, there's nothing dirty or little about her.

And the last thing I fucking want is for her to be a secret.

These past couple months have been torture. What, with moving from Jersey to the city, then trying to coerce Callan out of his funk with me, and this whole looking but not touching thing with Mia—summer has both sucked and kicked ass.

I scrub my hand over my face at the shit that I want but that I can't have.

Me: You are so fucking beautiful.

She laughs, but her laughter is sultry. That's because it's early on in the session. "You say the sweetest things."

Me: Maybe, but I wasn't being sweet.

Her brow lifts.
Ever so faintly.
Her smile is less practiced and more genuine.
Progress.
Less cam girl, more Mia.
"What were you being?"

Me: Honest.

Me: Though you look like you've lost weight.

She snorts. "I'm still curvy."
She is but she's also a touch pale.
Concern has me frowning as I tap out:

Me: Have you eaten today?

"Yes."
Lie.
"How do you want me?" she croons.

Me: Did you watch that episode of The Windsors
I told you to find?

Her lips purse—gently. "I did."

Me: Told you it was funny. You didn't believe me
though, did you?

"How did you even know about that show?"

Me: I have eclectic tastes.

"Apparently," she says with a laugh. "I'm surprised they make shows like that in the UK."

Me: It's only satire. And sadly for the royal family,
the days of beheading dissenters are long
gone :P

Me: I'm glad it made you laugh.

She needs to laugh more.

Some days, that cloud of inherent sadness around her makes me want to—

Fuck.

The stalled thought has me pinching the bridge of my nose.

It isn't my place to make things better for her.

Even though I want to.

I'm not supposed to be talking to her.

Gracie's my sis. I've got her back—always—and what I'm doing with Mia makes me an asshole.

I can't help but want to do a whole lot more though.

She's... *Mia*.

An Achilles' heel-type problem that comes without the need for an orthopedic surgeon.

Except that doctor's appointment will come if Gracie finds out about this.

"I watched the whole season," she admits sheepishly. "I have the rest to watch later."

> Me: When you've finished that, I have a bunch of other random British shows to recommend seeing as you've torn through the Canadian satire I told you about.

Me becoming her 'watch next' feature only started when she confessed one day that it was her uncle's funeral and I wanted to make her laugh.

"Their sense of humor is different than ours, isn't it?" she muses, twirling a strand of bright purple hair around her finger.

God, I love that wig on her.

> Me: It's black humor. They're weird but I dig their comedy.

"Doesn't that mean you dig them?" she teases.

> Me: My mother is actually from the UK, so EWW.

"How can that be 'Eww?'"

> Me: It is.

"Your logic isn't logicking today."

> Me: Something I pride myself on.

Mia rolls her eyes. "Have you ever been to England?"

> Me: Sure. To see my mother's side of the family.

"Do you have a lot?"

> Me: Not really. A couple aunts. Some cousins.
> Me: Oh, and a great uncle.

"That sounds like a lot."

Me: Nah.

"It is to me." She smoothes her hands over her arms. "I wish I'd come from a big family. I'm an only child."

Me: I wish I were

"Liar."

Me: :P Siblings are pains in the ass.

"Somehow, I feel like you're more of a pain in their asses than the other way around."

Me: You wound me!

Her smile is the one I've come to crave seeing—genuine. "I'm sure."

Me: You do!

"Uh-huh."

Me: Anyway, you have a family of cats.

"That's true."
I've met a couple of them by this point—they tend to hijack her shows when she least expects it.
Honestly, it's pretty fucking hilarious when they do, even if they are cockblockers.
She kneels on the bed, her feet scooting under her butt. It's a move made for comfort, not to entice. "So, what made your mom move to North America?"

> Me: Couple reasons. My grandma never made it over here but she always dreamed of visiting... She fell for a soldier during the war.

> Me: So when my mother was younger and she was a veterinarian, she crossed the pond for work. That's how she met my father.

Man, it's hard being vague while also trying to share with her. She's so reticent that only a fair exchange of information gets her to open up to me.

"At work?"

Sort of.

> Me: Uh-huh.

"Is she still a vet?"

> Me: No, she moved fully into research. She spends most of her time in Brazil.

Her eyes widen. "Brazil?! Why there?"

> Me: Her research took her to the Amazon rainforest.

"Wow!"

> Me: We don't get to see her as often as we like.

"I'll bet. My folks... My dad co-owned, I mean, co-owns a diner. They..." She hesitates. "They work together."

So, that's what her parents did.

I don't mind the half-truth. I'm still a stranger on the internet, after all.

> Me: Cool. What's his specialty dish?

"She's the cook."

Me: Okay, so what's her specialty dish then?

When she stares at her knees and doesn't reply, I regret asking the question, especially knowing their fate, until, finally, she murmurs, "Apple crisp."

Her words are stilted, though, and her smile becomes forced as she spreads her legs slightly.

Conversation over.

I get the hint even if I wish I could bury my head in the sand instead.

Scraping a hand through my hair, I try to shift focus.

Because I wasn't lying about her being beautiful, my dick's never too slow to react to her, but there's the bitch of the situation—I could keep talking to her. For hours. And hours. Learning more about her. Fixating on making her smile. Wanting to know what's going through her head when her gaze turns distant.

She fascinates me.

And she shouldn't.

But she does.

"How the fuck do you get yourself into these situations, Cole Korhonen?" I mumble to myself as I focus on the new desk the furniture store installed yesterday in my office rather than how she drops one of her shoulders so her shirt strap tumbles onto her arm, revealing the upper slope of her breast.

Dick starting to twitch, I heave a sigh as I type:

Me: Let's get that pussy nice and wet for me...

CHAPTER 14
COLE

THE FOLLOWING MORNING

Star Shopping - Megami

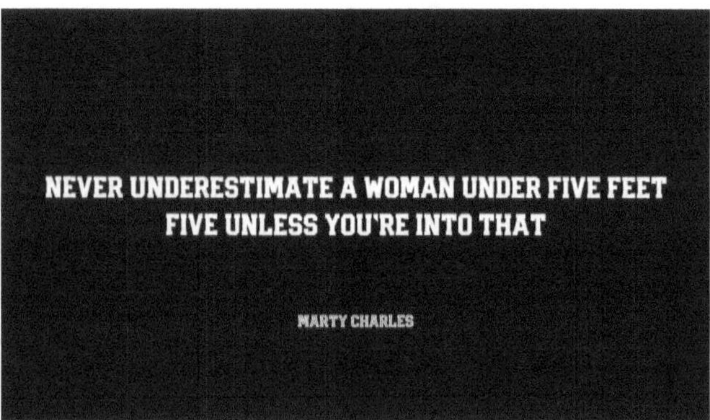

LIAM BUMPS FISTS with me as he draws me into the Stars' locker room for our first day of training camp.

You'd think that every locker room was the same as any other, but the investment Acuig, the owner of the New York Stars, put into the team is clear.

The Blue Demons weren't small fry by anyone's imagination, but this space is goddamn huge—twice the size of the one back in Jersey.

With a whistle, I sling an arm around his shoulder. "You ready to corral me, Leprechaun?"

He snorts and shoves me aside. "Not even going to try."

"Thought it was your job." I prod the 'C' patch on his pec. "Seeing as you're cap'n."

"Just call me Crunch." His nose crinkles. "I asked Gracie to demote me—"

"You did what?" I sputter. "You've been working hard for that patch as long as I have!"

"Want it? She might give it to you."

I glower at him. "What's going on with you?"

He hitches a shoulder. "Wanted it before. Shit's better but I'm not the same guy I used to be. Don't have the patience."

"No? You got the balls to fuck Gracie Bukowski, dude. I'm thinking you're not cutting yourself enough slack."

His smirk is smug. "She's a ball buster, isn't she?"

"Yeah, those are two words that fit her," I say dryly, but his pride shines off him like sunlight on a diamond and Gracie deserves that.

Hell, she deserves more.

A better bro than me, for sure.

Behind me, a barrage of players come wading into the locker room, bags slung over their shoulders, some barking at one another, others on the phone, a few shooting the shit.

Liam and I stride forward and find that we're cubby buddies.

"Awwww, do you think Gracie was worried I wouldn't make any friends?"

"Wouldn't surprise me. She's a real mother hen."

I dump my bag on my seat and grab the jersey that's waiting for me —42. Korhonen. It's a great feeling to be on board a promising organization with family.

"You know she's bringing all the billet boys here at one point or another."

"Likely," he agrees.

"Not her brothers though. You watch her make them work for it."

"Oh, yeah. You know how she rolls. She's forgiven them for giving her shit, but payback is a bitch with her."

My lips twist. "We gotta win the Cup for her this season. Let 'em regret fucking G over."

"With Raimond gone, we'll make that happen. Dude was bad for team cohesion. No wonder we didn't take it all the way during the playoffs."

"Thought you'd have worked some orgasm magic on Gracie to get her to dump Greco from the net too."

Liam squints at me. "You talk about Gracie's ass, tits, pussy, or orgasms, I'm going to fuck you up."

"Better than fucking me," I preach piously, hiding a smile when he rolls his eyes. I knock him with my elbow. "I'm glad you're together, bro. Don't mean I won't give you shit for it."

"Shit, I expect. But no references to anything that isn't PG."

"PG?" Kyle Lewis, a forward on the first string and my original inspiration for hiring Mia as a coach, pops up. "Lemme guess, he's giving you the lowdown on Gracie?"

"That's GM to you," Liam complains, punching Lewis in the bicep.

Jude Gagné, a defenseman, heaves a sigh. "You put a ring on the most terrifying woman in the league, Liam. You don't have to worry about anyone poaching her."

Liam jerks his thumb at Lewis. "You say that and dipshit here was drooling all over her—"

"Right, peewees, listen up!"

I roll my eyes at Coach Bradley's idea of an insult but turn to face him, smiling when I see Gracie standing at his side.

The new players cast bewildered looks at one another now that we have a chick in the locker room, but I'm not shocked—this is Gracie to a tee. Some even cover up like damsels in distress; others blatantly shove their bare asses in her direction.

I can almost see Liam taking notes on who he's going to punish once we're on the ice.

When he has our full attention, Bradley sneers, "This is Gracie Bukowski, our new GM—"

"I want to make it clear—" Gracie interrupts when Bradley's tone says he's not happy about her being his boss. Hell, the man looks like he's been chewing on habanero peppers. "—above the XX chromosome, bozos, the only letters that matter to you are G and M." Proving that she spied some of the peacock-preening going on, she continues, "Would I prefer not to see your asses? Sure. But I'm not afraid of your bubble butts and wieners so if you don't want me to comment on either, McIsaac, don't think about mooning me."

As a roar of laughter cascades through the locker room, McIsaac's cheeks pretty much glow as he gets cuffed around the head by his cubby buddy.

"For those of you who were here last season," Gracie continues, "I'm not like Justin DeLaney. For those of you who are new to the Stars, you're here because you don't suck but also because I made sure you were approached.

"I'm going to be hands-on, more than your coach would like, I'm sure, but we'll make it work because I'm not having any of this bullshit where we don't bring home the Holy Grail this season, do you hear me?"

Dead silence is her answer.

Even Liam's surprised by her introductory speech, which tells me she didn't run this by him.

Trust Gracie to take the bull by the balls and not be afraid of getting gored.

The silence perseveres until Gracie barks, "Do you hear me?"

A chorus of blurted "Yes, ma'ams!" greet her.

"Good. Chicago managed to steal the Cup right from under our noses, but that's it. The Stars are going to make history for more than being wise enough to have the first-ever female GM, and if we don't, you'll have me to answer to.

"Trust me, I live up to whatever you've heard about me.

"Before I go, I have an open-door policy. While Coach seems to think that isn't necessary, last season, it came to my attention that some players thought blackmail was funny—"

My brows lift. To Liam, I mouth, "Blackmail?"

He shrugs, but I notice the rest of the team, those from last season, are peering at one another blankly.

"—but I'm running a tight ship and I won't stand for any of that bullshit. Earn those bucks because, unlike DeLaney, I'm not afraid to drop deadweight before the trade deadline." She dips her chin and storms off without a backward glance.

Her statement has me grinning; a little pride mixes in with mirth at her take-no-prisoners' attitude, but my grin only widens when I notice that Liam can't decide on whether to check out her ass or to glower at the idiots who are busy gawking at her curves.

"Okay, peewees, now that the *woman* has left, let's focus on getting changed and heading onto the ice." Bradley stomps off, too, one of the assistant coaches hovering behind him as he makes a retreat.

"Was that with respect or disrespect?" I muse.

"He doesn't like her. Called her a nobody cunt from the Prairies last season."

"He did what?!"

His mouth is tight as he confirms, "Wanted to beat the crap out of him when she told me a couple nights ago, but she wasn't even mad. More amused—"

"Gracie found it funny?!"

"Said she wiped the floor with him." His lips twist. "You know how she is."

Oh, yeah, I do.

"Why didn't she get him fired?"

Liam pulls a face. "I think she's got payback in mind."

I whistle. "This season's gonna be…"

"An experience?" Lewis chimes in.

Gagné tacks on, "Fun as fuck?"

"Victorious!" Liam growls.

I grin. "All of the above."

WE'RE BARELY into the NHL preseason and already the drama and tension are through the roof!

And. I. Am. Here. For. It.

Last year, there were plenty of rumors about Lars Raimond floating around, rumors regarding Kyle Lewis's ex-girlfriend...

Unsurprisingly, the dislike between the Stars' players was evident, and despite Raimond's recent trade to the New Jersey Blue Demons, Lewis and he got into a massive fight in the nightclub, Russu, last night, a source told me.

Russu, a club I believe to be a front for the Sicilian Mafia, promptly had 'security' throw both players out where cops found them *still* fighting in the parking lot.

As soon as I discover the reason for the fight, you, my darling reader, will be the first to know.

CHAPTER 15
MIA

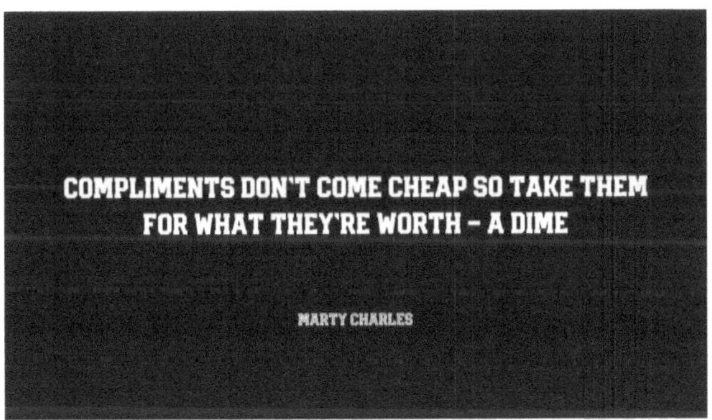

WHEN A KNOCK SOUNDS at Chuck's back door, I pull it open with a smile for Norm who grumbles, "You need to check the peephole, Mia. You ain't Chuck."

"I knew it was you," I reason.

He huffs. "What if it weren't? You're on your own here, chickie. Anything could happen if it wasn't me."

"When did you get so doom and gloom, Norm?"

The wizened delivery man scowls. "You telling me this world ain't getting shittier, Mia?"

"No—"

"You telling me that Chuck didn't think you were his princess? That he wouldn't want his old pal to watch out for you?"

I sigh. "No. I can't tell you that, Norm."

Is it bad that I wish Chuck had thought twice about leaving his 'princess' close to a million dollars in debt rather than leaving me with some dubious friends who keep an eye on me?

Oh, yeah—tallied up, I owe nearly seven figures to various financial institutions.

Thanks, Uncle C.

Norm dips his chin. "Exactly. So, you check the peephole, and while you're at it, get a door swing bar lock on these doors. No one would have broken into this place when Chuck was running the joint, but you're a different matter."

Norm continues his disgruntled diatribe as he offloads the day's order.

Until my uncle passed, I'd only met Norm a handful of times, but I've been coming face-to-face with him for months.

Months.

How has it been months since I last saw Chuck?

The thought has me biting my lip even as I hand over a wad of cash to pay Norm for the delivery.

On his way out, he grouses and grouches and I let him, until he stops to make sure that I lock the door behind him.

Smiling at the sweet touch, I head into the back office to collect yesterday's accounts and leave a note saying I'll be in around eight, as I've given Dionne the responsibility of opening the bar.

We had a great June and July, with a record turnover since I started serving more than goddamn hot wings and we had a couple videos take off on Instagram for this massive burger Larry and Beanpole created in the hopes that it'd be clicky on social media, but since the brief surge, it's quieted down—*too* down.

Once I'd undertaken a major accounting of all Chuck's woes, I managed to get one of those debt consolidation loans that they advertise on TV.

While the IRS is no longer breathing down my neck, that doesn't mean FedeLoans isn't.

September's payment is looming and I was two weeks late for August's.

My stress levels are through the fucking roof, but Chuck's is still going—that's all that matters.

If the fall season doesn't pick up, I know Chuck's will have to diversify into being a generic sports bar, not one that focuses on baseball.

I've also got some ideas for using a microbrewery that's super popular in Jersey—Satan's Sinners. IPAs are all the rage and because my uncle was old-school, IPA was a dirty word to him.

Still, it's adapt and evolve or die, and I didn't use the lot this bar sits on as collateral on an almost seven-figure loan to lose it to some predatory bank that literally only gave me the money because they're sure I'll default.

Dumping the books on the counter, I stand there a couple seconds, trying to come up with something weird that'll catch people's eye online.

I was sucking off a wolf dildo last night when I thought a burger made with donuts might take on a life of its own, but a brief Google search told me donut burgers have been done to death.

Still, I have to eat here because I can't afford personal groceries and I know the boys in the kitchen will make this for my dinner so I can sample it then.

I doodle a donut sliced in two and stack it with bacon, cheese, and a burger, then I proceed to cover it with more cheese—the melty kind. I stick a little toothpick with a US flag on top and draw some sprinkles.

Just the thought of the look on Larry's face as he decorates a burger with sprinkles is enough to make this attempt worthwhile.

Leaving that on the side as a guide, I lock up once I've collected my other stuff and walk home with the donut burger on my mind.

I'm thinking about it even as I feed the cats and pick up Cupid to coax her into eating a new, expensive-as-fuck pill she's on for the arthritis in her back leg.

I'm thinking about it as I shut myself in the bedroom, close the shades, switch on the rainbow strip lights, and get changed into my 'uniform.'

By the time I'm logging into my profile, I've come up with nothing fresh, then I see *CalKor* is online and I hide a grin.

He's become more regular than regular over the summer.

If I don't speak to him twice a day, that's unusual and, simply put, it's a relief because I only made August's payment, two weeks late or not, thanks to him.

Knowing what he likes, I quickly grab a pair of short shorts and the T-shirt I took off then drag them on.

"Hey, hey. How are you today?" I chirp once, pink-cheeked from dressing quickly, I've logged on and accepted him into my room.

CalKor: You look beautiful.

"Aww, thanks, Kor." For whatever reason, he hates it when I call him *CalKor*. Twisting around, I shove my ass in the camera and wiggle it. "I remembered."

CalKor: Good girl.

It's dumb to get turned on by one of my patrons, but hell if he doesn't know the shit that gets me hot and bothered.

A ding sounds on the screen.

I peer over my shoulder and see he's given me a fifty-dollar tip.

CalKor: A little 'thank you' for remembering.

"You didn't have to do that," I argue, stacking my hands on my hips. "You already pay enough as it is."

CalKor: You're not supposed to complain when it's a 'thank you.' We had a rule.

"Some rule," I grouse. "Obviously they're made to be broken with you."

CalKor: :P

CalKor: Sometimes. Apart from the ones that
stop me from showing you how much I
appreciate you.

He says things like that a lot.

Too often.

It makes me feel things I shouldn't for a dude who pays to watch me
jill off.

"You never answered my question."

CalKor: That's because I'm rude.

"Clearly. And you're not answering again…"

CalKor: I'm okay. Tired. Busy time at work.

"I feel that." I heave a sigh as I settle on the bed, scooting my feet
under my ass as I lean on one hand because I know full well that he
won't start anything without a conversation first.

That's sure been a learning curve seeing as most of my clients want
me to get my tits out…

CalKor: You need to rest more.

"I'll rest when I'm dead," I tell him with a wry grin.

CalKor: Not funny! I should have you spank
yourself for that.

I snort. "It's fine."

CalKor: Is it?

Taking a moment to give him a truthful answer, I slowly reply,

"Things have been better, but they've also been worse. I'm getting there and that's more than I figured I'd be doing at this point."

CalKor: That sounds positive in a negative way.

Chuckling, I nod. "I guess it does. But I'm fine."

He's pulled a lot of weight in making that so—I'd have been financially screwed without him. The only reason I can sleep at all is because of CalKor.

CalKor: I love to hear that.

"Do you want to talk about work?" I ask kindly. "Off-load?"

CalKor: Nah. It's all good. Just busy and I have a
lot to prove.

"Why?"

CalKor: I'm new to my job and my boss is an
asswipe. He didn't really want me on board but
HIS boss did so there are a lot of egos to satisfy.

I've never asked him what he does for a living, but I figure it's high-powered considering how much he pays me.

Because I'm curious where I shouldn't be, I change the subject. "Would you like me to help you destress?" I purr, leaning forward and shifting my arms so that my tits get squished between them.

CalKor: Fuck, beautiful. 'Course I would.

Though I grace him with a coy smile, I pull on the hem of my shirt then tug at it so my tits are practically popping out from the neckline.

Teasing him is always fun, but I have to make Kor work for being naughty—we agreed, *no tips*. The guy spends two hundred a session and he's upped that to twice a day.

It's both a blessing and a curse to know that I have four hundred dollars coming in from him alone, but I can't help feeling bad too.

That's a *lot* of money to spend on watching someone masturbate.
So he definitely doesn't have to tip me.

CalKor: You're such a tease.

I smile at the camera as I draw the shirt over my head.

CalKor: Fuck.

CalKor: How is it possible that you get more and
more gorgeous?

"Oh, hush," I chide, well aware I've gone red in the face from the compliment.

CalKor: Pinch those pretty nipples, honey.

Biting my lip, I do as he orders, pinching a little harder than I'm used to.
One thing I can say about my one-night stand with that Cole jerk was I realized I like the bite of pain from a hard pinch.

CalKor: You got the clothespins close by?

Like Kor read my mind, I reach under my bed for them.
Without prompt, I place one on my nipple, hissing at the brutal tension.
My eyes close, though, as I feel a tug deep in my core.

CalKor: Slide a finger through your folds. Let me
see if you're wet yet.

"I can tell you."

CalKor: You might lie. Tut. Tut.

I roll my eyes but drag down the zipper on my shorts and stick my hand under my panties. Carefully withdrawing them, I show him my fingers.

> CalKor: Let's get that pussy nice and juicy for me.
>
> CalKor: The second clothespin, please.

"So polite," I tease, knowing he prefers it when I talk to him.

That's the weird thing about *CalKor*—he likes me vocal. Not with the moaning, either. But actual conversation.

He was always online regularly but something happened over the summer. He went from being relatively quiet, shy almost, his only request that I bounce on a cock while I slap my ass, to upping things a notch with the clothespins, asking me to strip on cam during private, not public, shows, and preferring me to take bigger dildos.

Not that I'm complaining…

He also started to hate the Ahegao look. Though I don't seek tips from him, he gives me fewer if I cross my eyes and stick out my tongue when I come.

What can I say?

I listen to my clients' needs.

Grabbing the second clothespin, I pinch my nipple, settling the teeth onto the sensitive flesh.

As I let go, I groan through the pain.

My heaving breaths echo loudly in the room and my head bows as I take the strain and absorb it into me.

I don't have to look at the screen to know what he's asking me to do next.

I repeat my earlier move and this time, my fingers are slick.

> CalKor: Tell me how you taste.

"Like I need your cock in me."

> CalKor: Hmm. I love watching your pussy take a big, fat dildo.

CalKor: Turn around and take off your shorts.

I comply, bending over right in front of the camera to wiggle free of the clingy fabric.

When I'm only wearing panties, I straighten and go through the process twice, making sure that at the front, I snag them in my fist so that he can see the fabric pull taut over my butt and pussy.

CalKor: God, you are so fuckable.

I smile to myself when I read his reply before I take my underwear off too.

Once I'm naked, I turn back around and expect him to request the dildo he has in mind for today. But he doesn't.

CalKor: How much do you earn a day on here, honey?

"Why do you want to know?"
I'm not going to lie, that killed some of my buzz.

CalKor: I promise there's a reason.

CalKor: I won't tell anyone.

CalKor: I want to know.

"It depends on how often I'm on here. I take the higher 200 bucks' rate. I have other responsibilities though—" Like Jarvis, my spare bartender, being sick these past two weeks. It's either cover his shifts or hire someone else and stop paying his sick leave which I'm not going to do. "—so I can't be online as much as I could, say, back in July."

CalKor: A thousand?

"In June, it was nearer to fourteen hundred. But now it's about eight. Why are you asking?"

Of course, taxes take a third, and commission is high too. I only wish I came out with my full pay—I might have been able to manage without that legal loan shark.

> CalKor: How would you feel about stopping using this site?

"Why would I do that?"

> CalKor: Because I'll pay you two thousand dollars a day if you do this for me.

"Are you for real?"

> CalKor: Yeah
>
> CalKor: I bet the site takes a hefty commission on your earnings?

There's no denying they do. My best day *was* sixteen hundred in mid-June, but I came out with twelve hundred net. Phenomenal money for sure, but I need every cent I can get.

> CalKor: Do you have a Venmo account?

"Of course I do."

> CalKor: Give it to me.
>
> CalKor: I'll send a payment over so you know that you can trust me.
>
> CalKor: I'll pay in advance so if I don't follow through one week, you know that you can always come back to this site.

Bewildered, I sit there, staring at his text.

I have it set up so that I can't see myself because that knocks me out of the headspace I need to be in to do this. Still, I can imagine how I look

—*floored*.

"You're talking about paying me fourteen thousand a week, Kor. That's insane! How the hell would you afford that?"

> CalKor: I'm a trust fund baby, lol. At least this way, I'm giving it to someone I actually like.

That has my insides doing somersaults and it really shouldn't.

He's a client.

That's all.

I bite my lip. "How often would you need me to be online?"

> CalKor: Two hours a day. But it would be on my schedule, not yours.

"I have responsibilities at night. I can't work from eight until eleven."

> CalKor: That's fine. 8AM and 12:30AM work okay for me. If I need to reschedule, I'll inform you 24 hours in advance.

Those hours are workable.

God, I'm tempted.

"Would you want to do direct video?"

> CalKor: No. Same setup as this, on a different platform.

Fourteen thousand a week.

Commission free

Tax free.

Sweet Lord in a chariot eating cheesecake—a single week alone would cover my monthly debt repayment.

My jaw practically unhinges at the thought.

Even if he did this for a couple weeks, that would help me get ahead of myself, which has been my current problem.

FedeLoans refused to cover Chuck's medical bills, and the accrued debts are making me insolvent.

Nothing about my current lifestyle is sustainable long-term, but this will help me keep my head above water until I can roll out my plans for Chuck's.

Knowing that none of my private details are associated with my Venmo, I use the chat box, which I never do, and type out my username.

> Me: KillerCatQueen7

No less than fifteen seconds later, my phone dings.
Heart in my throat, I reach for it on my dresser.

> GretzkyWannabe42 has sent you a payment of $14,000

My legs wobble as I flop onto the bed.

A shuddery breath escapes me as tears prick my eyes, and even though he's watching, I don't care—I immediately forward that payment to FedeLoans.

The relief is so unreal that I sag on the bed.

For the moment, Chuck's is safe—I have another thirty days to prove myself.

Trembling hands cover my face before, remembering that he's there, I look up at the screen and whisper, "Thank you."

> CalKor: You're welcome.
>
> CalKor: My Skype has the same username as my Venmo.
>
> CalKor: Or if they need my email, add @gmail.com

Nodding, I switch over to Skype and immediately tap out his username.

The only problem is my name is all over my account.

"Just give me a couple minutes."

> CalKor: Of course. Are you having trouble
> finding me?

"The problem is on my end," I half-lie as I quickly change my username and alter my on-screen name and email to the one I use for cam-girling.

With that done, I log out and log back in, and once I'm certain that my identity is hidden, I find his username again and hit connect.

As the call goes through, he logs off on the other site so it audibly dings and then it's us.

It feels different on here.

Already.

It's not as if my regular site offers any protection, but the guy paid me a preemptive fourteen thousand dollars, for God's sake. That changes things.

> GretzkyWannabe42: I'll send that over every
> Sunday.
>
> GretzkyWannabe42: But I want you to stop using
> the other site.
>
> GretzkyWannabe42: Do you agree?

"I agree," I rasp, aware that I still sound shaky from shock.

> GretzkyWannabe42: If I go on there and see
> you've logged in, there'll be repercussions…

"What kind of repercussions?"

> GretzkyWannabe42: You'll have to wear a butt
> plug.

Neither of us is into that but I still pout at the screen. "Anal's no fun."

> GretzkyWannabe42: Exactly lol.
>
> GretzkyWannabe42: Are you okay?

My smile peeks out, a little stronger, a lot brighter. "I am. Thank you. You don't know how much you've helped me."

GretzkyWannabe42: I'm glad I could.

I clear my throat. "If you want to speak to me more than twice a day, w-we can."

GretzkyWannabe42: I'll bear that in mind.

"It's the least I can do."
I earned fourteen thousand dollars and didn't even lose twenty-eight hundred in commission, never mind that this is tax freakin' free…
How the fuck did I win the lottery?

GretzkyWannabe42: How are your nipples?

I blink at the question then sheepishly look down at my tits. If he didn't realize how overwhelmed I was, they give the game away—the clothespins are jiggling like crazy from my heavy breaths.
"They ache."

GretzkyWannabe42: Good.

I hum.

GretzkyWannabe42: Squeeze down on the clothespins.

I do as he orders until I hiss.

GretzkyWannabe42: Rub your clit.

I suck two fingers into my mouth and get them wet, then I slide them over my clit. The lingering tug from my earlier arousal is still there, despite him blowing my mind with his generous offer.

GretzkyWannabe42: Do you have a PO Box?

"I don't."

GretzkyWannabe42: I'd like to send you some
things. So, get one.

"Fine, but I won't use the gifts if I don't like what you send," I tell him as I rock my head forward, continuing to rub my clit as I spread my legs to give him a better view.

GretzkyWannabe42: Of course.

GretzkyWannabe42: Stick two fingers into your
cunt, honey.

GretzkyWannabe42: Spread that slit wide open
for me.

Shuddering, I grind the butt of my wrist against my clit. Sweet fuck, that pressure is phenomenal.

Honestly, with how often I orgasm, I should be walking around on cloud 9, especially with *CalKor* because he won't stop until I come at least once.

I've no idea how he knows if I fake it, but he always does.

Suddenly aware that I need to keep an eye on the chat box as it might not ping like on the other site, I read his text.

GretzkyWannabe42: That's it, baby.

GretzkyWannabe42: You spread that cunt.

GretzkyWannabe42: Fuck, it's beautiful.

GretzkyWannabe42: I wish I could taste it. God, I
bet you taste like fucking heaven.

GretzkyWannabe42: Pump those fingers into that
juicy pussy.

GretzkyWannabe42: Pump them and spread them.

With a mewl, I obey, spreading them as wide as I can.

GretzkyWannabe42: Wider.

I know I'm insane because I swear I can hear his voice growling the words in my ear.

I don't even want to question why he sounds like that jackass I was supposed to coach over the summer.

Whimpering, I do as he demands, but I switch hands so I can use my more nimble fingertips to rub my clit.

GretzkyWannabe42: Thrust your hips in the air.

Who am I to refuse?

I ride my fingers like I would a man's dick, and then he writes the magic words.

GretzkyWannabe42: Give it to me, honey.

GretzkyWannabe42: So loud that the neighbors hear.

A sharp scream escapes me as I let loose. Maybe there are some theatrics to the performance, but damn if it didn't hit the spot.

Amazing what fourteen thousand in the bank will do to lighten the load and have you fly that little bit higher, that little bit faster.

With a groan when I start to feel lightheaded, I slow things down, rubbing my clit in small circles while I stare at the camera.

Now, I know that it's my turn to take over.

"Did you like seeing me come, Kor? I hope I pleased you. Did you like how I screamed?"

GretzkyWannabe42: Next time, I want you to say my name for real.

Nodding, I rasp, "Of course, Kor. I will. And you can imagine it's me, moaning your name in your ear, and we can pretend that it's your cock that's in my pussy.

"Would you come inside me?" I continue, ignoring the tug in my core at the prospect. "Would you want to see your seed slipping out of me? Do you like the thought of that?"

GretzkyWannabe42: YES.

Aware I'm turning myself on, I smile at the screen as I move my fingers lower and circle my slit. "So white against all this hot pink."

GretzkyWannabe42: Fuck.

GretzkyWannabe42: YES.

GretzkyWannabe42: Take off one of the clothespins.

Biting the inside of my cheek, I release the pressure as quickly as I can. The sensation has my legs rocking against my stomach as I roll onto my side. The keening noise I release is loud, but it's nothing to the throbbing ache in my sex that might as well have its own chorus.

GretzkyWannabe42: Do you need to come again?

Nodding eagerly, I whisper, "I'll get one of the dildos?"

GretzkyWannabe42: The red one.

GretzkyWannabe42: It's my favorite.

Dipping over the side of the bed, I make a show of it by baring my ass and pussy to him then wiggling it from side to side as I snag the fake alien cock from my toy box.

Once it's in my hand, I turn to face the camera and immediately start rubbing it over my clit and slit.

When it's wet and lubed up, I place it against my entrance.

> GretzkyWannabe42: Yes, baby.

> GretzkyWannabe42: Let me see it fuck you.

On a shaky moan, I slip the tip into me. I bought this one after I slept with that Cole guy because they're about the same girth, though the dildo is a little smaller. There's no replicating that piercing, but ooh, boy, am I glad that this toy fits the bill otherwise.

> GretzkyWannabe42: I want you to let go.

> GretzkyWannabe42: Don't look at the text chat.

> GretzkyWannabe42: Focus on getting off again.

I whimper at the permission he gives me. Knowing that this decimates me, I lean against my pillows to prop me up.

With that done, I concentrate on me, my pussy, and I.

Inch by inch by inch, I take what the alien cock has to offer.

Every bit of give in my pussy is pulled taut because it's so fucking thick and I never realized how goddamn wonderful it is to feel like I'm being pushed to the edge.

My hips sink into the mass of pillows supporting me when I've taken as much as I can on my own. Then, I whimper as sweat beads on my temples from the satisfying fullness that makes me feel like I'm being torn apart.

I know that shouldn't feel good, but it does. It makes electrical tingles whirl up and down my spine.

It makes my pussy hypersensitive as every nerve ending is pulled taut to the max.

When I've taken as much as I can, I know from his angle it must look intense.

Good.

It is.

I keep my hips still as I pump the dildo in and out of me, fully aware that, by its very nature, it forces my clit to pop out of the hood.

With my other hand, I slick up my fingers with my juices and carefully, oh, so carefully, I tickle my clit.

Immediately, I release a keening whine.

"Fuck, that feels good. I'm so full. It's so thick. I could—" I break off to rock my head on the pillows. "I'm going to come. I'm going to come. I'm going to come! *Kor*!!"

His name is a litany I sing as I scream through my release.

It takes everything I have to give.

Everything.

And it feels so fucking good.

But what feels even better?

Still panting, still sweating, still fatigued from that surprisingly intense orgasm, I leave the fake cock in me and crawl to the foot of the bed and take a seat at the edge.

That's when I see something the other site didn't permit.

A picture.

Of a hand.

With cum on it.

Immediately, my pussy clamps down on the dildo inside me and I whisper, "Thank you, Kor."

GretzkyWannabe42: You're welcome, baby.

And that's how I found myself an online sugar daddy.

CHAPTER 16
COLE

42

Cruel Summer - Taylor Swift

I KNOW I'M CRAZY.

I know this is going to end terribly, but I'm not sure that I care.

Especially when the orgasms with her, using my own fist no less, are better than what I've experienced with other women since *before* I hooked up with Mia…

Yeah, she's the last woman I slept with.

I'm screwed.

Staring at the now-blank screen, I snag a tissue to wipe my hand then rock in my seat. I can't stop myself from grinning at the ceiling—I locked her down.

The satisfaction that rushes through me is as powerful as my orgasm.

So's my relief.

No other bastard is going to get to see her like that.

No fucker is going to be able to treat her like shit.

She's safe again.

Mine.

I can't help but tack the label onto her, even when she has no fucking idea who I am.

See? Crazy. But I admit it.

I've started to notice when she's stressed or upset, for God's sake.

Take today—that's why I mentioned the offer I cooked up in my head weeks ago. The shadows under her eyes were darker than usual, though she was still quick to smile.

I have the means to help her so why wouldn't I?

Before I can logic my way out of how messed up my feelings are for a woman I can't have, the alarm on my phone sounds and totally kills my buzz.

With a grunt, I snag it and switch it off then head for the bathroom to clean up.

I have an hour to get to the rink for practice. With the regular season about to commence, the intensity has upped a notch, and I can't deny that I'm loving it.

Having never played with Liam before, it's a fucking honor to be on the same line as him. Training camp is proving the Blue Demons were holding me back and that Liam, Kyle Lewis, and I have some true on-ice chemistry.

After a quick shower, I pull on some jeans, a hoodie, and my favorite lime-green cowboy boots—that's me ready to roll.

I live in Liam's building so I could commute with him to the arena, but I don't bother. Not when I have my own car and that car'll be taking me to Brooklyn later on in the day.

Slinging my ass in the back of my ride, I greet the driver, "Hey, Burrows."

"Good morning, Mr. Korhonen."

"Less of that, Burrows, my dude. You can call me Korhonen or Cole. Pick your poison."

We've had this same conversation every day since training camp started, and I reason it'll take a little while longer for him to realize that I don't need him to be formal.

I'm not Pops. *He* is Mr. Korhonen.

Mr. Jackass, too.

Now that I've hired the guy to be my driver full-time, it's even more important he stops with the 'mister' shit.

Liam gave me the idea when he told me the Stars hired drivers for the players as an inaugural season perk.

Why do I wanna drive through Manhattan?

Work smarter, not harder is my motto.

As expected, traffic is crazy on the ride over and I'm the last one in the locker room, which sucks because that means suicide drills for a 'warm-up' are in my immediate future as a punishment for tardiness.

Once I'm locked and loaded in my equipment, I head onto the ice and find that Lewis is on suicide drills duty with me.

"What are you in for?" I call out as I snow the boards in an abrupt stop.

"I got into a fight—"

Coach blows the whistle before he can finish and the torture commences.

By the end, we're both so exhausted that neither of us really give a fuck about why we're suffering; we just get on with it.

Because Coach is a grade-A dick, we're tossed into a scrimmage immediately afterward.

But even with two of his forwards fucked from the drills, we're game ready against the darks.

Still, it's a relief when he switches me out for Kerrigan and I plunk my ass on the bench and gratefully grab the bottle Liam tosses at me.

"Who did Lewis fight with?" I ask as I pour half the bottle down my throat.

It has to be bad because Coach hasn't let up on Lewis or benched him yet.

"Didn't you read the news?" Liam asks, his eyes on the game.

"No."

"Why not?"

"Because I choose to wake up and believe that the world is rosy and kind, Liam. What happened?"

My bro cuts me a look. "Remember Raimond?"

"How could I forget?"

Raimond played defense for the Stars before he became my ticket out of Jersey.

"Well, unfortunately for Lewis, they both decided to visit Russu last night."

"Russu? That nightclub over by the docks?"

"That's the one. Did you know my brother-in-law owns that place?"

"Does that mean you can score us free tickets?"

"Yeah, I'll ask him next time I see him because you can't afford your own," he mocks.

"Hey, I'll be doing the club a massive favor."

"How do you figure that?"

"Publicity?! Duh. Man, you really forgot how this shit works. I know it's different when you're stuck in your apartment all night—"

"Cut it out," he grouses.

I arch a brow at him. "Cut what out? Does Gracie stamp your hand before you go to bed? Maybe she should start integrating you into real life, huh? You have to miss nightclubs."

"Because there's so much to miss."

"You loved clubs before." *Before* his kidnapping. *Before* everything got so fucked up.

I asked Pops if he'd let me pay for the ransom—the bastard wouldn't sign a waiver with my trust fund for me. Even went so far as to put a block on transfers over five hundred thousand on the family accounts. Cody and Colt helped out and I threw it all into the ransom kitty but Liam was freed before we had enough to pay the kidnappers.

The whole extended family got a hard lesson about cash flow during that time.

Ever since, Mia aside, I've stopped spending like crazy because I've come to realize that I can't depend on my trust fund for the shit that matters.

"You said it yourself—that was before. I enjoy being at home."

Bradley calls, "Korhonen, get your ass on the ice."

Clapping Liam on the shoulder, missing him in a strange way despite him standing right next to me, I return to the scrimmage as Lewis flies over the boards. His face is redder than a fire engine and I can hear the clatter behind me as he half-collapses onto the bench.

But the second the puck drops, that's when my worries about Liam disappear and I focus on the game.

My love for it has never faded but it's intensifying now that I'm with the Stars, where Liam is my captain and Gracie is GM—I've found my home.

I have to keep at it to be worthy of this team.

I earned my rep for being a pest and I make it work with the Stars. Greco is cursing under his breath when I sneak a wrist shot from the slot after directing a pass from Gagné into the net.

Not three minutes later, McIsaac slaloms the puck to me from the boards and I slide it past Greco. He's not happy, so that means I've done my job right.

By the time the scrimmage is over, lights have won three-oh. Liam punches me in the gut to celebrate—it's a weird Bukowski celly—but I take it.

That's when Lewis backs into the boards with his hands raised as Liam focuses on him. He's laughing, though, as he cries, "I'm innocent I tell you."

Liam grins. "Shut the fuck up. We won. Gotta celebrate."

Lewis slugs him in the shoulder before Liam can get to him. "I'd be happier if that wasn't against our defense. You saw them—they were giving everything they got."

That has me humming in agreement.

Defense is a major problem for the Stars...

But mostly, I'm thinking it's Bradley because instead of releasing us, he shouts, "Last night, one of you assholes thought it was a good idea to get into a fight." Most of us try *not* to look at Lewis. "One of you does the crime, *all* of you are going to do the time, so let's get set up for bag skating."

"You have to be fucking kidding me," Gagné growls. "We didn't do anything wrong!"

"You fuckwit, Lewis," McIsaac snipes.

Even Liam's pissed. "You're picking up the fucking tab for the next month, dipshit." Which is saying something because Liam doesn't even go out with the team!

The promise of free drinks—we rich fucks love a freebie—has a cheer swarming around the crowd. Greco, who'll have it worst during bag skating thanks to all his equipment weighing a ton, even skates over to Lewis and mutters, "You beat the shit out of Raimond, dude. You don't have to buy me a drink."

That's when I get what Liam's doing.

From Bradley's dour expression, he was hoping to stir discord between the players.

Asshole.

Lewis swipes a hand over his bright red face—suicide drills, scrimmage, and now bag skating means the fucker's probably not walking without wincing for the next forty-eight hours. "I'm sorry, guys," he calls out to the team.

That earns him some grumbles, but most of us take up our positions on the ice when a dissatisfied Coach blows his whistle.

Twenty minutes later, Bradley dismisses us, but only when Lewis is puking from exertion.

The jerk-off still isn't done with his punishment—he keeps Lewis back for *another* scolding while the rest of us head to the locker room.

That's when Liam grates out, "You pick up on his game?"

"Couldn't miss it. Why does he want to fuck with team morale?"

Liam shrugs. "He's an asshole. Was all last season and he's looking set to suck this one too. Wait until Gracie finds out he brought back bag skating. She won't approve."

Stripping down at my cubby, I heave a tired chuckle. "Yeah, they're fucking exhausting."

"She's already not happy with him."

We head for the showers. "Why?"

"The plays Bradley came up with during the off-season. She thinks he's going to lead us down the same road he did before."

"Relying on shoot-outs to win?" I tack on over the running water as I set the shower to working.

"Yup. She encouraged him to trade a few defenders and that's working even though they're not as cohesive as she'd like, but the next step is the plays.

"Trying to fuck with the team spirit is going to put him even higher on her shit list, and frankly, I didn't know that was even possible until today."

"Why do I get the feeling she's going to be more involved than most GMs?"

Liam snorts. "It's almost like you know her."

Twenty minutes later, I'm in the whirlpool, trying to work out some of the kinks around my knee. I fucked it up a couple seasons ago and that combo of suicide drills and bag skating was a real bitch on it.

One massage later and fifty pages of my book devoured, I'm as good to go as I can be. Even better when, dressed and on my way out, Liam hurls a banana at me.

Snagging it in midair, I ask, "What's the game plan for today?"

"Don't know."

Together, we leave the locker room.

"Why don't you?"

"Because Gracie's interviewing new PAs for me and until that happens, I don't know what I'm doing."

"Interview them yourself, you big fucking baby."

"I did!" he defends. "But then she's vetting the rest. You know she's going to struggle putting up with someone else in our lives. I figured the least I could do was let her have the final say."

"You watch. You'll end up with some kind of Tolkien-esque troll."

Liam grins. "I don't mind. If she's jealous then it means I gotta up my game so she knows she doesn't have to worry about any bullshit like that."

I hook an arm around his neck. "You're soooooo thoughtful, Liam," I croon then smack a kiss on his cheek.

"Fuck off." He shoves me in the side even as he's swiping his cheek on his shoulder.

"Leave my fiancé alone."

Both our heads pop up at the reprimand as we spot Gracie walking down the tunnel that leads to the parking lot.

Liam shoots her a dopey smile. "Hey, *bébé.*"

"What did I tell you about using dirty words at work?" she grouses, even as she leans up on tiptoe and presses a soft but quick kiss on his lips.

"Since when was that a dirty word?" I argue, peeling the banana and taking a massive bite.

They look at me; Liam's expression is smug, but Gracie's is world-weary, like she's a parent with a bawling kid on a flight. "Piece it together, Cole. Jesus Christ."

"Ew," I whine, mock-gagging on the banana. "I'm too young to hear this shit."

"Then go outside, brat. I have to speak to Liam."

"Are you going to fuck in the tunnel?" I inquire with a fake leer.

Gracie frowns at me. "Do you think I'm shooting porn here, Cole? I got a Stanley Cup to win."

I raise my hands in defeat and toss the banana into the nearest trash can. "It's my role in life to give you shit. And, in my defense, I never mentioned you getting caught fucking in the hot tub last season—"

"Why did I trade for him again?" she asks Liam.

"Because he was wasting away with the Blue Demons."

Gracie winces. "Yeah, I forgot about that."

"It's wonderful to feel loved," I drawl, pressing a kiss to her cheek. "If you're going to ask Liam about Bradley, then I'll gladly snitch—the fucker's using bag skates as punishment." With a wink at Liam when Gracie turns bright red with fury, I murmur, "I'll see you guys tomorrow."

As I walk off, I find Burrows's one of the few cars remaining in the lot. When I jump in, he passes me a protein shake, and I accept it gratefully.

"To the stables, sir?"

"Korhonen, Burrows. Honestly, it makes me feel like you're talking to my father and no one needs that."

Burrows smiles a little. "Very well, Korhonen."

I grunt. "Yup. The stables."

A deep yawn escapes me as I rock my head back against the rest.

These earlier-than-usual starts and late nights are fucking with me. I'm already up before the sun, but this routine with Mia is killer. Still, it's worth it.

I grin at nothing when I think of what happened with her this morning until my cell buzzes.

Drawing it from my pocket, my brows lift when I see that she's sent me a message.

Oooh, I forgot we could do this now.

> **KillerCatQueen7:** I got a PO Box.

> **Me:** Someone's eager for gifts.

The thought has me smirking.

> **KillerCatQueen7:** I'm starting to think you're into FinDom.

> **Me:** Nah, I'm no paypig.

> **Me:** But I can buy you stuff I want to see you use, no?

That's when the guilt hits.

Gracie's flowery perfume is still fucking with my sinuses and here I am, trying to send her nemesis *gifts*!

The situation is so wrong, but it's like I can see that the only way is down and I'm still helpless to say no.

I know how sailors used to feel when they came across a siren.

Yet here I am, happily wading toward my Gracie-shaped and Mia-shaped demise because if anyone ever finds out about this, I'm fucked on so many levels, there'll be no saving me.

"At least I'll die with a smile on my face."

"Excuse me, Korhonen?"

I clear my throat. "Nothing, Burrows."

KillerCatQueen7: I'll take you at your word that you're not a paypig lol.

Me: You've been obsessed with pigs since I told you to watch Black Mirror.

KillerCatQueen7: Ugh, don't make me think about that damn show. It's too freaky.

Me: Reality often is :P

KillerCatQueen7: You're too cheerful about this shit.

Me: Hey, can I help it that I'm cheerful by nature?

KillerCatQueen7: Yes. You can. Especially when bestiality is involved.

Me: Well, I'm not a paypig or into pigs.

KillerCatQueen7: You've no idea what a reassurance that is.

KillerCatQueen7: *rolls eyes*

KillerCatQueen7: Bestiality aside, are you going to reveal some grody kink that I can't handle?

Me: Nah. Nothing grody.

KillerCatQueen7: That comes as a relief.

Me: I live to serve.

KillerCatQueen7: Are you a sub then?

I snort.

Me: Turn of phrase. Though I'd pay to see you in head-to-toe leather. Oh, man, we unlocked a new kink I didn't know I had!

KillerCatQueen7: We can live that fantasy out now, seeing as I got a PO Box for you.

She sends me a photo of her address.

Me: Thank you

Me: I'm honored

Me: To be able to buy stuff

Me: For you

Me: :P

KillerCatQueen7: The pleasure's all mine. Lol

KillerCatQueen7: Are you having a good day?

Me: It's okay. I'm tired.

KillerCatQueen7: I know how you feel.

Me: You eaten?

KillerCatQueen7: You're obsessed with my stomach.

Me: It's a sexy stomach. I love your tattoos. Did I ever tell you that?

KillerCatQueen7: Yes. After I told you why one of my inked cats wears a Phantom 'Erik' mask.

Me: That's not on your stomach though.

KillerCatQueen7: Nope. Ten points if you remember where…

Me: ONLY TEN?

Me: Criminal

Me: It's on your sit spot.

Me: Maybe you're the masochist in this relationship.

KillerCatQueen7: Very likely lol.

Me: How is the pussy patrol?

KillerCatQueen7: Driving me crazy. They won't eat the wet food I bought them.

Me: You have bougie cats.

KillerCatQueen7: I do. I almost have a heart attack every time I pick it up from the vet.

Me: Is that lunatic one still jumping out of the shadows to scare you?

KillerCatQueen7: Curtis? Yes. He's such an asshole.

When my cell buzzes and Gracie's name flashes on the Caller ID, the guilt that hits me is worse than being whipped by Mia in full Domme getup.

Me: See you at 12:30. I GTG

KillerCatQueen7: :)

Once I switch screens, I can't help but feel a little empty inside.
As much of an improvement as this is, the situation still sucks.
And it's only exacerbated when Gracie tells me to come up to their apartment later to collect the pierogi she made and put in the freezer for me last night.
Fuck.

KERRIGAN: WORTHY OF THE NEW YORK STARS?

BY MACK FINNEGAN

With Korhonen fitting in so perfectly in the New York Stars' first line, how long should Gracie Bukowski be patient with Ruben Kerrigan and his hefty salary?

After yet another disappointing performance where he barely held it together against Toronto, he has now been pushed to the 3rd line, a clear demotion for the player who used to raise hell with Lewis and Donnghal in their honeymoon season last year.

Crossing the Hudson has done magic for Cole Korhonen, tallying five points in three preseason games and bringing new energy to the Stars' offense.

Surely the Stars' GM is shopping around to clear up some cap room? Maybe a change of scenery is what Kerrigan needs to get inspired again.

The Stars could use help in defense and they also need a good backup to Greco with Davies being another headache for the rookie GM.

CHAPTER 17
COLE

Nothing Else Matters - Metallica

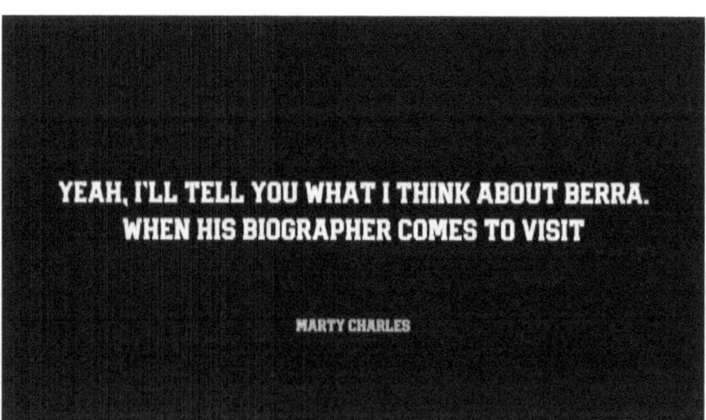

I ALMOST FLY into the kitchen when Liam punches me in the shoulder and Lewis decides to wade in by tripping me up.

"You're jealous that I got more *inches* than you," I crow at them, flipping them both the bird as I right myself.

Gagné chuckles. "You got more *something* than them. Not sure it's inches though."

I wink at him. "I'll have to flash you the next time we're in the showers and you can be the independent adjudicator."

He snorts then rubs his nose—not sure when the fucker broke it, but he's had a bandage on the bridge for the last day or so.

Grinning as they scoff all the way to their cubbies after I read the PSN article aloud on how fucking awesome I am, I head into the kitchen without their interference and blink when I see Kerrigan sitting to the side, his shoulders rounded and his back hunched.

In front of him, there's the same paper I was reading and a protein shake, but that doesn't hold my interest—it's how he's swiping at his eyes that does.

I don't know the man but I doubt PSN's cutting diatribe is why he's crying—we've all been annihilated in the press at some point, and I was only joking about being awesome.

Contentment from playing with my people has benefited me so far, but lucky runs don't last forever. You have to be an idiot to forget that.

I head to the fridge to snag some fruit and, with my back to him, ask, "Are you okay?"

"Yeah," is his gruff response.

"I'm sorry about that article."

"Finnegan knows how to hit a nerve," Kerrigan agrees before he chokes out a laugh. "Like I give a fuck if I'm traded or not."

There are hoots in the locker room as well as the 'slap' sound from a towel being snapped, but I ignore the chaos as I grab an orange and start peeling it. "You really don't care?"

Kerrigan's mouth is tight. "My life is caving in. What the hell does it matter if it's in New York or Tucson?"

"Fair point," I agree, brows low as I step over to him.

He's not sitting at one of the tables; if anything, he's off to the side, between two counters where two huge boxes of bananas are stacked in preparation for the mass consumption that'll go down over the next couple of hours.

Bananas are our god.

Not wanting to crowd him but not wanting to leave him either, I take a seat at the table, my back still to him, and ask, "Is there anything I can do to help?"

"Can you cure cancer?"

I freeze. "You're sick?"

"Donnghal didn't tell you?"

"That you're sick? No."

"Not me. I wish I were. Fuck. My w-wife." His guttural sob has me wincing. "She's dying."

My mouth works as I try to formulate a response, but what the hell can I say to that? "It's really terminal?"

"You think I'd lie about something like that?" he snarls, and I hear the boxes shift as they scrape against the floor.

That's the only warning I get before I'm dragged off my seat by the neck of my tee. He shakes me as he turns me around to face him, his fists balling in the fabric and pulling it tight. "Do you? You think I'd make something that fucking horrific up?"

I don't bother trying to shield myself. The grief in his expression, the yawning depths of his pain filling his eyes—if it makes him feel better to beat the shit out of me, then he can have at it.

"No. I don't."

In the doorway, I see someone hovering.

Liam.

I catch his eye with my own and faintly shake my head to the side. At my order, he doesn't move away, nor does he enter the room.

"She's fucking dying." His hands tighten around my neckline until it cuts into my throat. "And there's dick all I can do."

His pain has me placing my hands on Kerrigan's shoulders and gripping them tightly. "You sure this is where you need to be if you're going to lose her soon?"

Fat tears pour down his cheeks. "I get on her nerves. Hovering.

"What's the fucking point in having all this money if I can't fix her?"

He starts off hoarse, but the words are practically a scream by the time he's done.

"I know, man. I know. It fucking sucks." I squeeze his shoulders, offering what comfort I can. "But don't hover around her. Be there with her—"

He shoves away from me, letting go of his hold on my tee with a bewilderment that tells me he didn't realize he'd gotten in my face.

"What do you know about any of this?"

"My grandma died of cancer. And my granddad had to watch her fade."

His eyes clench. "She was old. My Lacey's *young*. We have a baby girl. She's not supposed to fucking leave me. I told her I could only have kids if she was with me. She fucking promised—"

"I'm sorry," I whisper.

"Your grandma got to live. She had a family. She saw you. My kid won't even see her mom at her first birthday." His shoulders heave. "What am I going to do? How am I supposed to do any of this without her?"

"I don't have any answers, but maybe you and she need to talk about that?"

His back's to me by this point, but I see him lift an arm and swipe at his face with it. "Talk about what?"

"About what she'd want you to do in her stead."

His shoulders hunch. "You mean, like, school for London?"

"I mean *everything*. Does she want to write a letter for London's birthday every year? Does Lacey want to make videos to pass on her guidance? Does she want to tell London how to deal with periods? I don't know, man, but you need to come up with a plan. It'll help you feel more in control."

"I think it's time you took some family and medical leave, Ruben." Liam finally wades into the conversation.

"What, so you can get rid of me and kill time until the trade deadline? Don't make out like you give a fuck."

"Of course I do," Liam snaps.

"You think I give a shit about hockey?"

"No, and I don't expect you to. Anyway, you know Gracie loves Lacey. I'm well aware of what she's going through. I wish there were something else I could do, but I think Cole's right, man. I think you need to be spending this time with her and not wasting it on slinging hockey pucks around a rink."

I arch a brow at such sacrilegious talk, but Liam changed after he was kidnapped. It isn't news to me that hockey stopped being his everything. I just didn't think he'd say *that* to Kerrigan.

The other man swipes a hand over his face, his thumbs digging deep into his eyes.

"You won't get this time back, Ker— Ruben," I correct, keeping my voice low too. "Liam's right—why waste it here? You know Gracie will hold a place for you. She's not like the other GMs."

I'm not sure why but that seems to get through to him.

"Hockey'll… I need hockey. For, you know, after."

"And you'll have it," Liam assures him.

Kerrigan sucks in a watery breath as he turns and stares at his captain. That's who he's seeing. Not the guy who's probably given him crap on the ice or the dude he doesn't particularly get along with.

In times of trouble, it's the 'C' patch we always look for.

"You mean it?"

"Gracie won't have a problem going to bat for you." His smile is sheepish. "She'll enjoy knocking some heads if that's what's needed."

"R-Right. Okay." He cuts a look at me. "Sorry about the…"

Tugging at the neckline of my tee, I shoot him a cheerful grin. "I'm used to it."

Liam snorts. "Yeah, he is."

As Kerrigan starts to walk out of the kitchen, I grab his arm and draw him in for a hug. He stiffens automatically, but in his ear, I rumble, "Enjoy this time with her. It's not as long as you should have had together, but that doesn't mean you can't make the most of what you *do* have. Be there. That's all she needs. You can't fix her. You have to accept it like she's having to."

He surprises me by relaxing then tightening his arms around me in a deeper hug.

Then, he stuns me more by sobbing his heart out in my embrace. My mouth works, reacting instinctively to the sound of his grief, but all I can do is hold on tight and be there for him.

Liam releases a deep exhalation at the sight but leans against the door, letting Kerrigan grieve while preventing other teammates from entering the kitchen.

I clap him on the back when he pulls away.

"Thanks, man." He slouches off, clearly embarrassed, head low.

I watch as Liam picks up the slack, talking about guiding him to Gracie's office.

I can't stop myself from reaching into my pocket for my phone as other guys wade in, throwing questioning looks my way.

I don't say dick to them though.

Ruben's pain shouldn't be a source of gossip.

Me: You there?

KillerCatQueen7: Hey! Yeah, I'm here. Everything all right? You need to reschedule?

Me: No, I wanted to check in.

KillerCatQueen7: Check in?

I grimace at the stupid urge that I followed through with.

KillerCatQueen7: You okay, Kor?

Me: I'm fine

KillerCatQueen7: Can I help?

Me: Not really. It's a co-worker of mine

Me: His wife has cancer.

KillerCatQueen7: :(I'm so sorry to hear that

Me: Yeah.

I wanted to touch base with you. Wanted to make sure YOU are all right.
I can't say that though. Not without sounding like a lunatic.

Me: I wanted to say hi.

Well, that just makes me sound like a fucking loser.

I slam my phone on the table and resume eating my orange. That's when she texts back:

KillerCatQueen7: Do you want to talk about it?

KillerCatQueen7: It helps sometimes.

Me: I don't even know the guy but his grief was so raw. It was like I could feel it somehow.

KillerCatQueen7: I understand. I was that way when my mom passed.

Ah, shit.

Me: I didn't mean to rake up the past for you. I'm sorry.

KillerCatQueen7: Don't be. I was a kid. I'm definitely not that anymore lol. I can handle talking about her.

KillerCatQueen7: My dad, less so. I still struggle with his loss.

Me: Do you mind me asking why?

KillerCatQueen7: My mom was hurt by some bad people and he couldn't handle her death. He ended up killing himself on my birthday.

I gape at the screen.

It's not like the news comes as a shock, not after she shared it with me that day at the rink, but that stuff about her dad taking his own life on her birthday was something she hadn't told me.

Me: Holy fuck.

KillerCatQueen7: :/

KillerCatQueen7: I'm less stuck on their passing and more triggered by the emotions around their deaths.

KillerCatQueen7: I didn't mean to make this about me, though.

Me: You're not.

Me: I'm interested.

KillerCatQueen7: Really?

Me: Yes. What do you mean you're triggered?

KillerCatQueen7: I'm sad about my mom. Like, it wasn't her time to go. It was stolen from her. I'm angry at the guy who took her life.

KillerCatQueen7: My dad loved my mom. He was besotted with her. They were a living, breathing rom-com movie, I swear.

KillerCatQueen7: I think, looking back, I always knew he'd never last long without her but I figured they'd be a lot older.

My mind drifts onto Kerrigan—how he feels about his wife. And I can't help but draw a parallel to Mia being like Kerrigan's kid, forever grieving something that was outside of her control.

With a heavy heart, I read her next message, surprised by how deep she's willing to go with a stranger on the net. But then again, it's always easier to open up to strangers, and she's come to trust me.

I might put my money where my mouth is, but she wouldn't have stopped doing the cam-girl stuff if a part of her didn't accept that, in this, she can trust me.

KillerCatQueen7: I'm angry at him for choosing that day. I know that sounds petty, but I already had the shitty memory to contend with, and now, my birthday's depressing. I stopped even thinking about it years ago.

Me: So, you're not resentful of him leaving you?

KillerCatQueen7: You never know what's going on in someone's head and I'm the last person to shame anyone, never mind my father, for that.

KillerCatQueen7: I struggle with anxiety myself. After they died, every morning, I had panic attacks, and when something bad is going on in my life, I still deal with them.

KillerCatQueen7: So, no, I don't blame him. I don't resent him for choosing to go that route. But I'm annoyed that he took that day from me.

KillerCatQueen7: Like I said... petty, huh?

Me: Not at all. But look at it this way. Would there ever have been a day that he COULD choose where it wouldn't wreck things?

KillerCatQueen7: Not really, I guess.

Me: I mean, if he did it the day after or before, it's still going to ruin the day in your eyes.

KillerCatQueen7: It's more that he didn't think about me at all. This is going deeper than I meant to but he was always the one who big-upped birthdays. Mom thought they were capitalistic nonsense that the greeting card industry reaped the benefits of.

Me: She's not wrong lol.

KillerCatQueen7: But my dad was all about birthdays. Every year before then, he'd fill the hallway outside my bedroom with balloons. So, when I woke up, I had to wade through them.

KillerCatQueen7: There was always cake and he ALWAYS pulled me out of school on that day.

Me: I understand.

KillerCatQueen7: Do you?

KillerCatQueen7: I guess I'm still being selfish.

Me: No. I don't think so. I get it. And I'm sorry.
He forgot you when he never had before.

KillerCatQueen7: You don't have to be sorry. It
was a long time ago.

Me: What happened to your mom?

KillerCatQueen7: She was mugged but she
wouldn't let go of her purse so the guy pistol-
whipped her. She went down and cracked her
head on the curb.

KillerCatQueen7: Just like that, I was an orphan
because Dad checked out.

KillerCatQueen7: I don't know what I'd have
done without my uncle.

My heart turns to ice at her text.

Earlier this year, Gracie was mugged.

Fuck, that that could have been her makes my skin crawl.

We could have lost her—just like that.

And hell, Liam's not as fragile as he used to be, but I know how much he loves her. What would *he* have done if we'd lost Gracie?

Feeling sick to my stomach, I hurl the half-eaten orange at the trash can.

As it's swallowed up by Oscar the Grouch, I turn my attention back to the text exchange and type out:

Me: I can't imagine how hard that must have
been for you.

Me: How old were you?

KillerCatQueen7: I was pretty young and hella
angry at the world for a long time afterward.

Me: My co-worker... they have a baby together.

KillerCatQueen7: Ah, Jesus. That's terrible.

Me: It really is.

Me: Thank you, queen.

KillerCatQueen7: Hehe. Queen. I like that.

KillerCatQueen7: Anyway, what are you thanking me for lol?

Me: You didn't have to share that with me.

Me: So you know, if you ever need me, I'm always at the end of a message.

KillerCatQueen7: That means a lot.

Me: Want me to tell you a deep, dark secret too?

KillerCatQueen7: It WOULD equal the balance.

KillerCatQueen7: But nah. It's fine.

KillerCatQueen7: You can owe me one next time.

Me: Deal.

KillerCatQueen7: I GTG—I'm at the vet's office picking up some cat food my damn cats won't eat. I'll see you later :)

Me: Can't wait. Have a good day, beautiful.

KillerCatQueen7: You too :*

I clamber to my feet. When I approach my locker, Gagné has one arm leaning against the wall and another is holding his phone.

The expression on his face...

I frown.

What's that about?

Wanting to jerk him out of it, I clap him on the back. "Everything okay?"

He jolts like I hit him then shakes his head. "Yeah, yeah, it's fine."

I watch as he dumps his cell in his cubby then starts to get ready.

Both of us look as if we're headed for the same place—the sack.

Though I doubt I'll sleep.

A blanket fort is what I need, and a book.

If ever there was a day where I needed to escape, it's today.

Colton: It's official—the asscunt has finally stopped milking this arrhythmia shit.

Cody: Man, he was still pulling that card?!

Colton: Oh, yeah, he's been spending most of his days in bed.

Colton: He finally got out when I told him I wasn't paying for him to flirt with his nurse.

Colton: We're lucky she hasn't tried to sue for harassment!

Cole: *shudders*

Cole: A leopard never changes its spots.

Cody: Comparing Pops to a leopard does leopards a disservice and they're practically extinct. Don't be snide, Cole.

Cole: Lol

Cole: Is Callan doing better, Colton?

Cody: Lemme guess, he's still hiding in his bedroom?

Colton: I'm starting to think he knows more about why Pops brought you guys home. Though it's funny watching him deal with Mum AND Mrs. Abelman.

Colton: Still, he'll get some space soon. Mum's leaving now that the jerk-off is showing his face around the rest of the house.

Cole: :/

Cole: Is he still pissed that I took his credit card away?

Colton: Why would he be? I gave him mine.

Cole: COLTON! Why did you do that?

Colton: Because he needs to buy shit. We had a vandal sneak onto the property last week. They tagged the barn. They didn't get the chance to do it again, though. Callan's cameras caught them right in the act. He deserves to be paid for his system.

Colton: Plus, I thought we'd gotten over this. You're not a fucking prude.

Cody: I feel like I'm missing half this conversation and I'm not sure I want to know either so…

Cody: Who was the tagger?

Colton: River McAllister.

Cody: Since when do they give us beef?

Colton: Things are weird up here. And I'm not talking about Pops.

Colton: We're having a really dry September.

Colton: Anyway, it's Callan's birthday next week.

Cole: Like we forgot *rolls eyes*

Cole: I'm coming up. He won't appreciate the fucking journey I have ahead of me, the ungrateful little asswipe.

Colton: I was thinking he'll be 18. We could add him to the chat?

Cody: Fine with me.

Cole: And me.

Colton: I thought I'd have a fight on my hands.

Cole: Why? It's about time we corrupted him and turned him into a son that Pops would be proud of.

Colton: Don't make me regret asking lol.

Cody: Pops wanted a boy reared in his own image…

Cole: He should be careful what he asks for.

Cody: Agreed ;)

THE FOLLOWING DAY

KillerCatQueen7: Is this for me to waft at the camera?

GretzkyWannabe42: You received it, then?

KillerCatQueen7: If you sent me a flogger, yes.

GretzkyWannabe42: Feel free to use it to swat flies, but I wouldn't mind seeing you turn your ass pink with it…

KillerCatQueen7: Hmm. Maybe.

GretzkyWannabe42: ;)

KillerCatQueen7: You're a strange man.

KillerCatQueen7: A flogger wasn't entirely unexpected but the rest?

GretzkyWannabe42: Do you like it?

KillerCatQueen7: Did you pick this stuff out for me?

GretzkyWannabe42: Sure did!

KillerCatQueen7: Seriously?! You went to Anthropologie and picked out a candle for me?

GretzkyWannabe42: I shouldn't have?

KillerCatQueen7: I expected sex stuff, lol, not a boo basket.

GretzkyWannabe42: Are you complaining?

KillerCatQueen7: No, it came as a surprise.

GretzkyWannabe42: A nice one?

KillerCatQueen7: A lovely one. Thank you.

KillerCatQueen7: Really.

KillerCatQueen7: I'm not sure what I did to deserve that, but I appreciate it very much. Especially the Netflix gift card. I had to pull my subscription.

GretzkyWannabe42: I thought you needed some pampering. :)

KillerCatQueen7: Stop. You'll make me cry.

GretzkyWannabe42: No tears! Unless they're happy ones.

KillerCatQueen7: You want to recommend weird shows to me.

GretzkyWannabe42: Guilty :P

KillerCatQueen7: I love the blanket you sent me. Even if it's still unseasonably hot where I am lol.

GretzkyWannabe42: My research indicated that a boo basket has basic requirements that I didn't dare deviate from.

KillerCatQueen7: *snorts* Well, I love it. And the Mai Tai mix... Did I tell you that was my favorite?

GretzkyWannabe42: You did.

KillerCatQueen7: A while back, wasn't it?

GretzkyWannabe42: Uh-huh.

GretzkyWannabe42: Anyway, I gtg.

KillerCatQueen7: I didn't know you were a hockey fan.

GretzkyWannabe42: My username didn't give it away, LMAO?

KillerCatQueen7: Oh, Gretzky is famous?

GretzkyWannabe42: *has a heart attack*

KillerCatQueen7: Oops.

GretzkyWannabe42: *swoons*

KillerCatQueen7: Can you swoon when you've had a heart attack?

GretzkyWannabe42: I can be shocked any way I want lol.

GretzkyWannabe42: Yes, I'm a hockey fan.

KillerCatQueen7: So, this jersey… that's a thing for you?

GretzkyWannabe42: Uh-huh. Can you wear it tonight for me? I wanna see you in it.

KillerCatQueen7: Korhonen… he's really one of your favorite players?

GretzkyWannabe42: He's a new pick for the Stars but I've always been a fan, yeah.

KillerCatQueen7: Right, okay. Fine.

GretzkyWannabe42: See you tonight. In the jersey.

KillerCatQueen7: Yep. Thank you again <3

CHAPTER 18
MIA

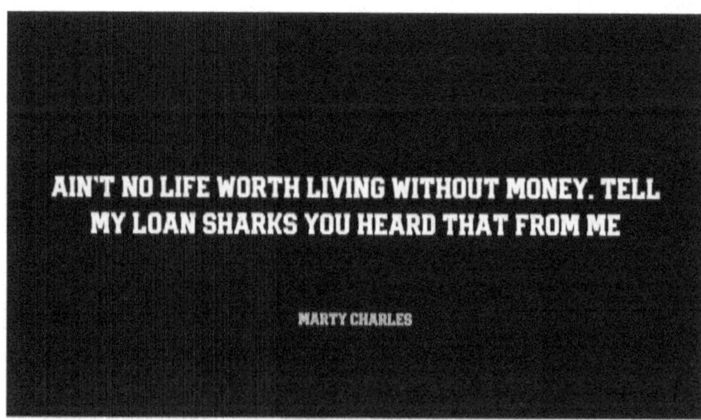

Strangers - Kenya Grace

MONEY MAKES things so much easier.

When people lie to themselves about it not making the world go around, it's all bullshit.

And, to be frank, I don't even have that much of it.

For five weeks, *CalKor/GretzkyWannabe42* has been paying me fourteen grand and every cent is going into my bank for future payments.

The payback model I have with FedeLoans doesn't allow for early buyouts so I'm saving it all up for a rainy day.

With several months to do *something* that'll revolutionize the bar and finally make it pay for itself, I'm feeling more hopeful than I have in a long while.

It's when I jump into the shower after my session with Kor, where I had to wear that motherfucker's jersey AGAIN, that I realize I've not had an early-morning panic attack in weeks.

An escape from the endless cycle of grief and worry and outright terror at losing everything that's been a part of my days since Chuck died is exactly what I needed and what Kor has provided.

See? Money is better than therapy.

Though, I'm half sure I need it every time I have to wash that goddamn jersey Kor sent me.

Fuck. My. Life.

Trust Korhonen to be my client's favorite hockey player. Trust my luck that he wants to see it almost every freakin' day.

With a groan, I hop out of the shower once I'm done and get ready. After, I retreat to Chuck's.

This week's payment, I've decided to take a risk with.

I don't see Kor pulling out of our agreement in the next seven days so I have fourteen grand to burn.

When I make it to the bar, Dionne's already opened up the place and coffee is in the middle of the table where the entire team is sitting, waiting for me.

"Sorry I'm late, guys," I apologize as I plunk my ass in the booth and retrieve a notepad from my bag.

"It's fine," Dionne says, but she shoots me a tight smile. "Only a couple minutes. What did you need to see us about?"

That's when I realize everyone's tense.

Even Beanpole, who I'm sure smokes weed in the back, looks stressed too.

I flip through my notepad and I shove it toward them. "I need your help."

Dionne frowns as she stares at the notepad. "These are…"

"Memorabilia?" Jarvis throws in.

Wanting to lighten the mood, I nod. "I've decided that being so focused on baseball is really bad for business. We need to diversify into all sports *or* switch out at the end of the season for something else."

Dionne blinks. "But Chuck's is a baseball bar."

"I know it is, but with the season winding down, what are we supposed to do?"

"What we always do—show all types of games."

"Yeah, but why would someone who's a football fan come here when they could go to a general sports bar *or* a football-themed one?"

Larry scratches his nose. "You think the baseball shit puts people off?"

"I think it doesn't help. And we have to try. This might not work but we don't know unless we give it a shot.

"So, my idea is to pick a sport and to get some memorabilia, cheap stuff to start with, and to pepper that throughout the bar—"

Picking at her nails, Dionne blurts, "So, you're not firing us?"

I gawk at her. "Is that why you guys were all tense? I'm so sorry. I thought you'd have seen that things were ticking along for the moment."

"We know you've been more cheerful this past month." Jarvis rubs the back of his neck. "Then you called us in and we didn't know why."

"It'd be easier for you to throw in the towel than carry on. We're not idiots, Mia. We know the bar's not covering itself."

"Chuck's has been here for nearly sixty years, guys. I won't be the Charles who quits on it. There *has* to be a way to make it pay in a city that's sports-mad. I refuse to give in."

Dionne pats my hand—my hand that I didn't even know I'd balled into a fist until she blankets it. "You can only do what you can do, honey."

"There's more fight in me yet." I make my nod decisive. "I want your input. What should our next step be?"

"I think we need to be careful not to offend our current clientele. They like it how it is. They came here in the first place because they're baseball fans," Larry points out.

"I agree. So, we do this slowly *or* we keep it all well-themed."

Dionne's nose crinkles at the bridge. "You think this place has a theme? To me, it looks as if it were last painted when the place was inaugurated."

I bite back a smile. "There's no denying that. So, that's our first move, then? Some paint?"

"I think so." Larry nods. "At least you won't have to bribe the health inspector the next time they come around like Chuck did."

"Are you kidding me?" I shriek, aghast.

"You didn't know?" Beanpole snorts. "Chuck always had to bribe them."

Tiredly, I rub my eyes. "I refuse to cheat." Inwardly, I curse Chuck before I continue, "Right, so a deep clean, some paint, and what type of memorabilia?"

"I think we should focus on two sports. I vote for hockey," Jarvis chimes in. "Since the Liberties became the Stars, it's getting more popular in the city."

Ugh.

"Isn't football more popular? You know Jason Griggs will be a pain if we settle on another sport."

"Hockey fans are loyal," Larry reasons, casting a look at Jarvis, who's nodding eagerly. "You get them in here, they're hooked for life."

I tap my nails on the table. "I *do* like the sound of that."

"You could split the place down the middle." Dionne points to the bar which, admittedly, is in the very center. It means that we have 360 degrees of seating. "You could have one half for baseball and one half for hockey."

"But that limits the seating."

Dionne frowns at Beanpole. "If that section is full, the other half can be the overflow." Then, she rolls her eyes. "It's not rocket science. I'm sure patrons wouldn't mind."

My lips curve at her tone—she tends to speak to everyone like they're one of her kids. "I love the sound of that.

"We may have to throw some of the stuff on the walls away because it might crumble to dust after it's disturbed for the first time in decades." I tap my nails on the table. "Half the room means we can make up for the lack better. But what about the hockey memorabilia? I don't have much money to burn on the theming. Even I know hockey equipment is expensive so, in turn, the memorabilia *has* to be costly."

"I can scope some out for you?" Jarvis queries. "I love hockey so it's no hardship for me to do that."

"If it's online, do the scoping during quiet periods at the bar. I don't want you working on your own time, okay?"

He beams a smile at me. "That's fine. I'll get started tonight."

"Perfect. I have some money set aside for it, but, like I said, not much. So if you can focus on smaller, cheaper pieces that'll fill up the space then we can try to save up for something worth having."

"Sounds great to me," Jarvis confirms.

"We could go with posters too," Beanpole adds. "Old ones and new. They're cheap. We should stick to the Stars—"

Words fading, he blushes bright red as Larry mumbles, "Way to go, Beanpole."

I grimace. "It's fine. It makes no sense not to be aligned with the city's team, even if the new GM is an old member of staff."

One I helped screw over.

Dionne and Jarvis peer around the table in confusion, which makes sense because she's the one who replaced Gracie, and he came after.

Not wanting to get into it and aware they'll gossip once I'm gone, I murmur, "'Stars' themed it is. As for the menu, I want to diversify some more. The monster burgers are selling, right?"

Beanpole gags. "They're fucking disgusting. Who wants sprinkles on their burger?"

"It's making a name for us," I argue, ignoring the old curmudgeon. "We need to keep that up. Maybe we could start dedicating burgers to teams or players?"

"The Gehrig Gherkinator," Jarvis throws out.

I snicker. "Yeah, shit like that."

Beanpole mock retches. "I can't believe people order that. I love pickles, man, but there's such a thing as too much."

"Stop bitching. People enjoy them. Right, let's brainstorm."

The meeting goes well despite running behind which means we open Chuck's late.

Even better, people are waiting to come in and drinks soon flow.

Everyone's excited and enthusiastic about not being fired, which gives the bar much-needed energy.

At eleven-thirty, I'm happy to leave with a game plan in mind.

Of course, that's when life has to fuck with me because when I get back to my apartment, Cupid doesn't greet me at the door.

I try not to freak out, but she *always* greets me. It's her thing. She's perennially pissed off that I stopped taking her with me after that one week of visits to Chuck's and she's determined to make it known that I'm an atrocious pet because, in her eyes, she's the owner.

Dropping my stuff on the floor, I race around the rooms for her favorite hiding spots but don't see her.

It's only when I remember her penchant for scuffling with Curtis over the spot where I stack the clean towels that I find her.

She's struggling to breathe, barely responsive, and at that moment, so am I.

KillerCatQueen7: I'm so sorry but I won't be able to make this session.

GretzkyWannabe42: Is everything okay?

KillerCatQueen7: I'll be online tomorrow. Thank you for your understanding.

All You Want - Dido

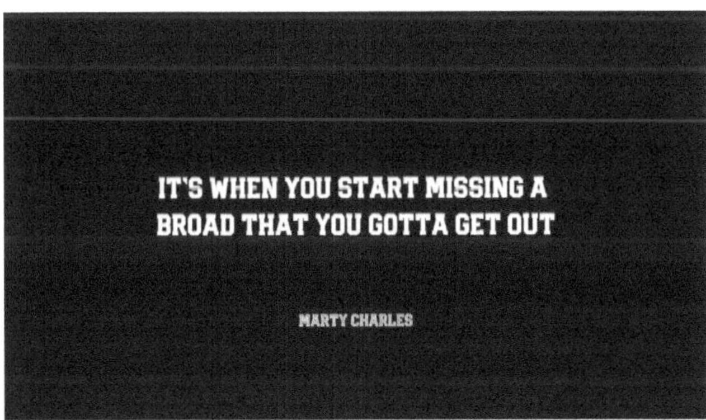

I MISSED HER LAST NIGHT.

How fucked up is that?

I'm awake at 5:45 and sitting in front of my computer, waiting for her light to turn from amber to green.

When she comes on, she looks raw.

Complete with wig and cat ears, she's wearing sleep shorts and an old tee. Not her usual uniform. But it's her eyes that clue me in more than anything—they're red and puffy like they were that day I first met her.

> Me: What's wrong?

My fingers race across the keyboard as I rush to get the message out.

Her bottom lip quivers. "My cat's sick. She had emergency surgery last night and they haven't updated me yet about her status this morning."

> Me: Fuck.

"Yeah." She shoots me a sad smile. "I'm really sorry that I missed last night's session."

> Me: You don't have to be sorry. I'm the one
> who's sorry that your cat's sick.

> Me: Which cat?

"Cupid."

> Me: You never did tell me why you called her
> that.

"Because it suits her. She's how I found two of my other cats." A soft sniffle escapes her. "She's my oldest."

> Me: How old is she?

Her bottom lip wobbles some more. "Seventeen."

> Me: Got plenty of matchmaking ahead of her
> then.

"Wishful thinking but I can live in hope."

I want to reach through the screen and draw her into a hug.

In fact, fuck that. I want to sit her on my knee, hug her close, make the damn vet fix her cat, and hold her until she knows her family is safe —because that's what her cats are to her.

Over the months of talking to her, little things have cropped up here and there and nothing about the woman I'm communicating with is anything like the clout-grabbing social media whores that I'm used to coming across in my world.

She doesn't have puck bunny vibes either.

She's shy. A geek. Those cat ears she wears? She has forty-three pairs of them. I asked because I saw her wear a new one every day for six weeks!

There's sticking to a character and then there's *that*.

Her favorite movie is *Phantom of the Opera*, and her fingers are rough and callused from hard work. The moment I moved to the city, I drove past the bar to see if it was for sale—it wasn't. Which means she's struggling through her grief and the money issues to keep the family legacy alive.

This woman, for whatever bewildering reason, betrayed Gracie.

The words 'betrayed Gracie' should be the only ones that matter to me about this whole situation, but they…

Damn, they're starting to mean less and less to me.

Not because I don't want to defend Gracie to the grave, but because something doesn't add up here.

I cut ties with her because Liam was right—I needed to.

Then I blew that, and months later, I'm so fucking certain there was a reason for what she did that we don't—

"Are you there still?"

I blink at her when I realize she's talking to me.

Me: Sorry, my phone rang.

"Is everything okay?"

Me: It's fine. Have you eaten this morning?

"We… We don't have to do this. You can pretend that I'm the same old KillerCatQueen7 and we can—"

Before she finishes that sentence, I type:

> Me: No.

> Me: Cupid matters to you.

"She really does." The words are a whimper and it breaks my fucking heart.

> Me: Tell me how you found her.

"You mean last night?"

> Me: No, I mean originally.

"How do you know I found her?"
Shit.

> Me: I mean, did you adopt her or buy her?

"Adopt don't shop."
Her outrage covers for me.
"And I found her at this bar where—" Mia clears her throat. "—I used to work. She was trash can diving. I lured her in with tinned salmon and ever since, she thinks she deserves that."

> Me: And she helped you find your other cats?
> How many do you have? You've never said.

She goes on to tell me about her other cats and how she found them. That's when I ask:

> Me: You have more tattoos than cats.

"You noticed them?"

Me: How couldn't I?

"Cupid wasn't my first cat. I lost some along the way." She lifts her shirt and shows me the one with the cat pawing a star in the sky. "Celeste. They don't stay with us long enough."

Me: I agree.

"Do you have pets?"

Me: No. I don't have a lifestyle that permits any.

"That's sad."

Me: I guess it is.

Me: I used to, though. When I was a kid.

"What kind of animal?"

Me: Horses.

"Ohh, really?"

Me: Yes. I've always loved them.

"Couldn't you have a horse? I mean, not to be funny, but you can afford to pay me fourteen grand a week so I'm going to assume you could afford to keep horses."
My lips twitch.

Me: I could. I never thought about it.

"Why not?"

Me: I don't know. I lost my heart horse and ever since, I guess I struggle with the idea of replacing her.

"You can never replace them, but our hearts are big and they find spots for themselves in there."

> Me: You think so?

"I know so. I never go looking for cats. They always find me.
"Anyway, you can pay me less next week for the missing—"

> Me: No.

"It's only fair!"
I shake my head at the screen, trying to reconcile Gracie's betrayer with this woman who's arguing over her payment.

> Me: No. I don't care if it's fair or not. You didn't skip out on a session because you wanted to go shopping, for God's sake. You had a family emergency!

> Me: Later, we can talk again if you want. You know, about the surgery?

She ducks her head. "I doubt I'll be lucid if anything…"
Her grief is suddenly my grief.
Just like it was with her when I told her about Betsy.

> Me: I'll be here if you need me.

> Me: Could you do me a favor?

"Of course."

> Me: Will you let me know what happens?

She shoots me the tiniest of smiles. "I will."

CHAPTER 20
COLE

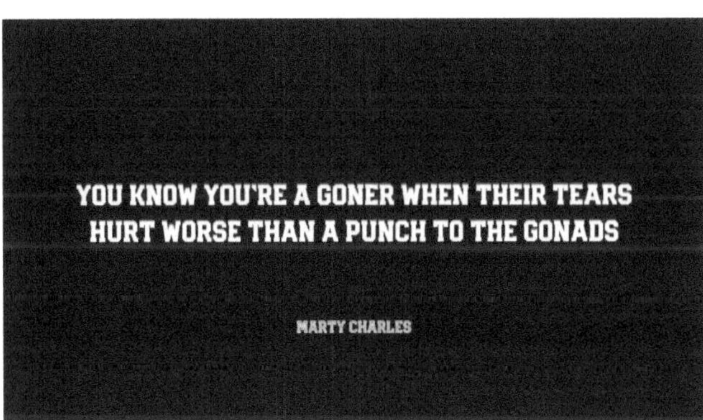

I CAN'T LET her deal with this on her own.

I'd be a bastard if I did.

That's why, even though I'm pretty sure that she's going to slam the phone down on me, I hit her number.

"Cole?" she inquires warily.

"I thought you might have blocked me."

"Why? We hooked up. That's what you do on *Hooked-Up*.

"Look, I don't have time for this. I need to get my head on straight."

"What do you mean? What's going on?"

"If you must know, my cat needed emergency surgery."

"Which one?"

"Cupid."

"She's the one who waited by the door, isn't she?"

She sniffs in my ear. "You think I'm impressed you remember that? Well, you'd be right."

I grin at nothing, relieved to hear some lightness in her voice. "I hope she's okay."

"Fuck. Me too. Why are you calling? Do you want to schedule some lessons?"

No, I saw you crying on cam and wanted to protect you from the world.

Somehow, I don't think she's ready for that answer.

Hell, I'm not ready for it either.

"I wasn't lying about going back home."

"Any bozo who makes up an excuse that involves their father and a heart attack needs smacking upside the head."

That doesn't mean she believes me...

"You haven't met my father, but ironically enough, *he* was lying."

She's silent for a second. "Wait, what?"

"He lied about having a heart attack to get my family to go home."

"Wow."

"I know, right? Who does that?"

"Your father apparently."

That has me grunting.

"Does he have Munchausen's or something?"

"Munk-what?"

"You know, where you fake illnesses to—" She pauses. "No, wait. That's when you make other people sick for attention. At least, I think that's right."

"I don't know if he's got that or a case of incurable massive egoitis, but whatever. He lied."

"You stayed home all summer?"

"Some," I hedge. "I came back because I got traded to the Stars."

"I saw. Do they suck too?"

I smirk. "Not now that I'm on board."

"I see the incurable case of massive egoitis is hereditary." I can hear the amusement in her voice though. That's a miracle in itself considering how she was on cam. She clears her throat. "So, *are* you ready for lessons? I can fit you in but the hours might be—"

"No. My schedule's crazy. I was wondering if you wanted to meet up."

A soft laugh escapes her. "My god, you weren't lying when you said you were cheeky."

"Fuck, you remember that?"

"It was a memorable conversation."

There's no way I can stop myself from preening at her admission.

"Then, what do you say?"

"Are you going to ghost me again if we meet up?"

"No."

"Would you have said that earlier this year?"

"Yes. But, in my defense, my circumstances changed."

She snorts. "I'm not sure if that's reassuring or not."

"It's reassuring. I'm not really a jerk."

"I did have higher hopes for a guy who allegedly devours romance novels."

"Are you trying to say that you don't think I have it in me to be a book boyfriend?" I gasp. "You're mean."

A snicker sounds in my ear. "You know I work at my uncle's..." She stills. Her voice gains ground. "I'm busy after five-thirty."

"We can have a day date then."

"You'd be fine with that?"

"Sure. It fits my schedule perfectly." I pause. "Will you let me know what happens with Cupid?"

"I will." Her gulp is audible. "Why do you make me forget things?"

"Like temporary amnesia?"

"No. You take my mind off stuff. It's annoying. A half hour ago, I was sobbing as I poured myself a coffee. Now, you've made me laugh twice."

"I'm going to take that as a compliment," I rumble.

"I'm not sure if it's that or a sign you should walk away. We did hook up and I was okay with you going radio silent then, but... I won't be so forgiving if you pull another stunt like you did last time."

"Meaning that you thought we connected too?"

"See, you told me you were a straight talker and that you wanted an open dialogue and then you ghosted me! Who's the one giving mixed signals here?"

"Me. I'm sorry about that. Honestly, my summer was a fucking mess."

"Mine wasn't much better."

"Coffee. Tomorrow. Two PM. What do you say?"

She sighs. "Okay."

"And you'll text me when you know how Cupid is doing?"

"I will."

"I'll send you the location to the coffee shop if you don't want me to come pick you up…"

"No. It's fine. You can."

"I'll be outside your apartment at one-forty-five."

"You remember where I live?"

"There isn't much about that night I don't remember."

She releases another sigh, but this one is softer than before as she confesses, "Me either."

LATER THAT DAY

KillerCatQueen7: She made it through the surgery like a champ!!

GretzkyWannabe42: What a relief!

KillerCatQueen7: It really is. I thought my heart was going to burst when I was in the vet's office waiting to hear an update.

GretzkyWannabe42: Do you mind me asking what was wrong with her?

KillerCatQueen7: She had something stuck in her gut. They had to take it out.

GretzkyWannabe42: Oh, damn!

KillerCatQueen7: Yeah. To be honest, they were more worried about the impact of the surgery on her when she's so old but they had to get it out.

GretzkyWannabe42: And did they?

KillerCatQueen7: They did.

KillerCatQueen7: Thank God.

KillerCatQueen7: And they cleaned her teeth when she was under too lol.

KillerCatQueen7: Anyway, we can talk later tonight?

GretzkyWannabe42: I'll be there.

THAT SAME DAY

Mia: Cupid made it through!

Cole: That's fantastic news!!!!!!!!!! I'm SO glad.

Mia: Me too! See you tomorrow <3

Cole: Can't wait.

Mia: Me neither.

CHAPTER 21
MIA

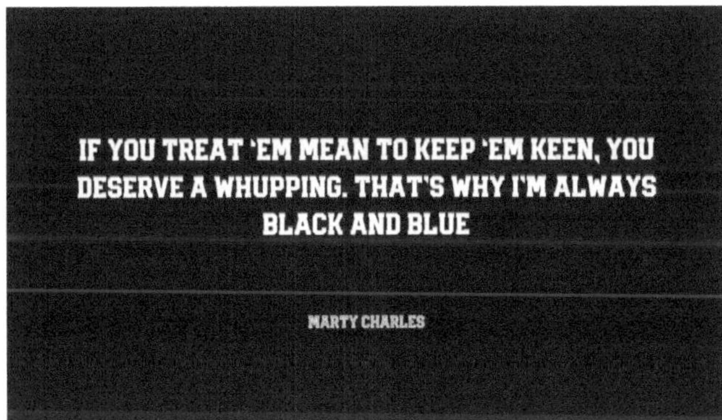

I'M SO dumb for agreeing to see Cole again, but I couldn't stop myself from saying yes when he called out of the blue yesterday. Nor can I stop myself from being excited as I get ready for our coffee date.

"I'm making it up," I tell Curtis, who hisses at me.

I hiss back.

Our interaction makes me miss Cupid even more than I already do, but the vet says she has to stay there for another day at least and I'm not going to push it.

While I need her home *yesterday*, I need her to be 100% more.

"My memory is faulty about how great the chemistry was between us," I continue like Curtis cares. "Or about how awesome his dick was. I mean, it had to be wishful thinking and, like, some kind of fugue state from grieving for Chuck."

Curtis stalks off, annoyed at being asked for dating advice, when Chloe meows in the other room. She's apparently far more interesting than I am.

"That's it. Stick with your own kind," I grouse at his butt-star. "I'm only the one who feeds you."

When I stare at my reflection, I tug on my jeans then decide that they're not informal enough and strip out of them. Snagging a mini skirt from the closet, I tug that one on, then I wonder if I should go for short shorts.

I may have had an orgasm this morning thanks to *Kor*, but the wolf dildo prepared me for Cole's dick and I wouldn't say no to some of that action.

Honestly, I've not had the time or desire to hook up with a guy this summer, but after I heard that Cupid was recuperating better than the vet expected, Cole's Coke-can cock (all the fabulous Cs) is the only thing I can think about.

Was it as thick as I remembered?

Did I make up how good it felt to be so stuffed full of him?

Did the piercing hit where no man has gone asunder?

I'm not against learning the answer to those questions in the near future. A reprieve from the stress of my life would go down better than an ice cream float.

And if a little part of me feels bad about *Kor*, I shrug it off. We're not dating. He pays to watch me masturbate. Nothing more, nothing less.

Brave words for someone who still feels guilty…

I stare at the mini skirt and drag on some Converse sneakers to see if that makes it low-key. Then, I grimace. It looks as if I'm trying too hard by dressing down. Ugh.

A glance at the clock tells me I have five minutes to make a decision, so like a crazy person, I strip and pull out a flirty little mini-dress that floats around my upper thighs.

It's lacy, boho-chic, and borderline transparent so he could get an eyeful if the light hits right.

The second it settles on me, I know it's the correct choice. I slide into some low-heeled suede booties, which add to my hippie vibe, and after another quick look in the mirror, I smile at myself, happy with my appearance because it'll tease him.

He totally deserves to be teased.

I drag a scarf from the closet too—a moss-green one—and then I snag my purse and sling that over my shoulder.

When I spy that I have less than two minutes until I need to be downstairs, I race into the kitchen and hurl cat treats into the middle of the living room to keep the pussy patrol away from the door.

"Mommy's outta here," I yell to no one before racing off.

Of course, Cubert decides to be a douche because he tries to head for the hall, but I snag him, dump him on a cat tower, and make for the front door in record time.

When I slam it closed, I hear a peeved hiss and a meow and know that he tried to beat me again—he likes to go to the stairs that lead to the roof.

"Little shit."

Still, I smile to myself.

After almost losing Cupid yesterday, even Cubert and Curtis' most annoying traits are sweet.

A snazzy town car is waiting outside my building when I make it downstairs. Immediately, I feel underdressed until the back door pops open and Cole climbs out.

Dressed in lurid green cowboy boots, he's paired them with black jeans and a rather snazzy black and silver shirt.

It's like Freddie Mercury decided to become a cowboy and it's oddly hot.

In greeting, I shoot him a shy smile.

Cole's not shy though.

He strides over to me, cups my chin, and presses a kiss to my lips.

I'm so startled that I let him do it, then I remember that the fucker ghosted me all summer so I whack him with my purse.

He doesn't jump back, just grins at me.

Whoa, boy, either I forgot how potent that grin is or I truly was in some fugue state that night.

"That was a celebratory kiss."

"A celebratory kiss?" I repeat.

"Cupid's okay!"

I blink at him, take in his excitement, and something deep inside me melts.

Oh, fuck, I'm fucking fucked.

He cares about my cats.

He remembered Cupid.

He knew she was the one that greeted him at the door.

The level of screwed I am is dangerous.

Because I'm a tad speechless, I mumble, "Yeah, she's doing better. I get to bring her home tomorrow, otherwise I'd be in bed sobbing."

"I need to send your vet a fruit basket in thanks then."

I hide a smile as he hooks his arm around my waist, like the last time we saw one another wasn't before midsummer, and he draws me over to his ride.

When he keeps the door open for me, I slip inside and move over so that he can slide in too.

I peep a glance at the driver in the rearview mirror and he dips his chin politely.

Cole slams the door and declares, "Burrows, this is Mia. Mia, this is Burrows. Get used to seeing one another."

My brows lift at his audacity, but, politely, I tell the driver, "Nice to meet you, Burrows," while I elbow Cole in the side.

I get the feeling I'll be doing that a lot today.

"Likewise, ma'am."

Cole groans as he rubs where my elbow collided with *thicc* muscle. "No, dude. I told you her name so you wouldn't call her that."

From the rearview mirror, I spy a gleam hovering in Burrows's eyes —one that tells me Cole's leg is currently being pulled and he doesn't know it.

"It's really okay to call me Mia," I chime in.

"There ya go," Cole mutters. "The 'ma'am' agrees."

I have two seconds to smirk at him before his arm is around my waist and he's dragging me into his side.

My brow furrows. "You've got some nerve."

He winks. "You love it."

I huff but repeat, "I think you've got some nerve."

"Why would you want to sit over on the other side of the car, all cold and alone, when you could snuggle with me?"

My lips twitch. "The other side of your car isn't in Outer Mongolia. And it's not even that cold." A sudden wash of heat blasts my ass which has me laughing. "I think Burrows's trying to blow your game."

"Burrows," Cole chides. "Did you put the seat warmer on?"

"Seeing as the back seat is currently in Outer Mongolia, I thought it was best, Korhonen."

I chuckle but I don't move away, which was totally proof he was playing a waiting game.

Cole smiles at me. "It's good to see you."

My own smile is shy. "It's good to see you too."

"So, this coffee shop we're going to…"

"What about it?"

"It's actually a bakery."

"All right. I'm not averse to baked goods."

He makes the sign of the cross on his chest, revealing a cacophony of ink on his forearm that looks like feathers. I've never wanted to lick a feather in my life until today. "Thank God for that," he drawls, freeing me from my wet dream. "Because I reserved the private room."

"The private room?"

"You know how restaurants have a chef's table?"

"Uh-huh."

"Well, this is like a viewing room of a bakery. This place went viral years back and ever since, the lines are insane."

"So, you thought we'd go into the kitchen and that would cut the line?"

"Exactly."

It sounds pricey…

Still, what a neat date.

Suddenly happy that I said yes, even without the prospect of carbs, I turn to him. "You put a lot of thought into this for an out-of-the-blue date."

"I pulled some strings."

"For me?"

He chucks me under the chin. "I let you down. You'd be a fool to waste time on me if I didn't do something special."

The flush of heat that rushes through me has nothing to do with the seat warmer and everything to do with being... *cherished*.

That's how, in that one statement, he makes me feel.

My mouth works as I try to figure out how to answer but he doesn't let me. He bows his head and presses his lips to mine.

It's a soft kiss. Tender. Much as his earlier one was.

"Are you okay, Mia?"

Nodding, I swallow. "Yeah, I am."

"Good." That's when he presses another kiss to my forehead this time, which has me wanting to melt *and* cry, which is too much for my body to handle, so I cuddle into him.

Let him hold me.

Let him make me feel cherished.

And hope against hope that tomorrow, this wasn't all a dream, that I'm not an idiot, *or* that I don't wake up for him to have ghosted me again.

CHAPTER 22
COLE

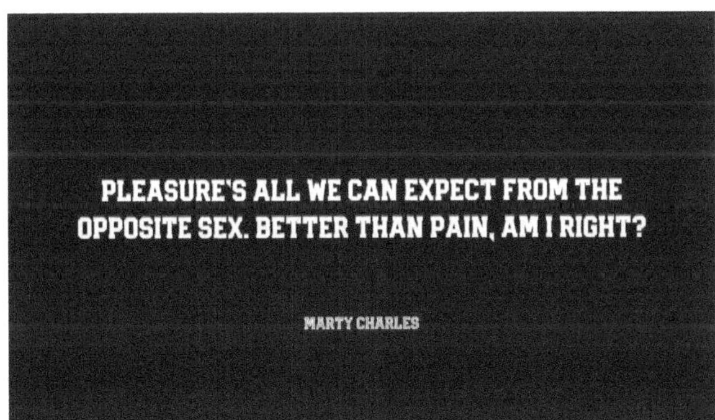

SHE'S WIDE-EYED when we make it into the bakery, and I get it.

The lines are fucking insane.

But that's what happens when a special brownie goes viral. Even if it has no weed in it.

"This place took off so many times online that it's famous overseas," I inform her as I guide her toward the back of the bakery.

As much as I deviate from my diet, I don't seek out carb heaven often so I only learned about it from Liam, who said his cousin's wife owns the bakery and is behind the recipe.

A few calls and I got my in.

And I know I suck for using Liam to get a date with Mia, but fuck, she deserves to be treated right. Especially after I pretty much pulled a *Coyote Ugly* on her.

Brushing off the thought, I peer around the establishment on the hunt for a single stand that Liam told me about. It isn't that hard to find—it's not dissimilar from a maître d's post.

We barely have to hover there before a door opens and a man steps out.

Unlike the other members of staff, who are wearing leather aprons and suede flat caps as a uniform, he has a dress shirt and pants on.

"Your invitation, sir?"

I open up the QR code that was in the booking reservation and show it to him.

He scans it with his cell then, beaming a smile, motions with his arm for us to follow him.

As we head down a small corridor, we're guided into a large room.

In the middle, there's a table big enough for six but it's set for the two of us.

There are tea and coffee pots, water jugs with fruit bobbing in them, as well as two more carafes of iced tea and coffee.

The server holds out Mia's seat for her as I take my own. "I'll return in a few moments, once you've had a chance to peruse the menu. Would you like anything to drink while you make your selections?"

I look at Mia, who shakes her head. "No, it's fine. We can serve ourselves from what we have here."

He smiles politely then fades into the background, leaving us alone.

Mia's eyes are wide as, once the door closes, a switch flips, making the wall in front of us entirely transparent.

"That's so cool." Getting to her feet and walking over to the wall, she waves, but no one waves back.

"You could have asked," I tease. "It's a two-way mirror."

"Neat."

What's neat is that dress.

It flirts with her upper thighs and in certain lights, you can see her tits.

Yeah, she's not wearing a bra.

Fuck.

After months of having access to parts of her she doesn't know I've had, I guess I'm being a little forward. She's still stuck on the day I ended it, whereas I'm in the here and now, but her behavior with me is telling— she was upset when I cut things off.

She wanted to see me again.

She chose a flirty outfit.

Green light.

And despite it all, I want to see her again, so I refuse to fuck this up.

I hold out a hand for her. "Come and decide what you're going to order."

She turns back at my prompt and her gaze locks on my hand. For a second, I wonder what she'll do—will she come to me or won't she?— then, she strides over and slips her fingers into mine.

Because I've been wanting to do this since yesterday morning, I tug her onto my lap. One arm bands around her waist to secure her in place; the other settles on her chin as I angle her head down to kiss her.

She sighs into the kiss so I take it as slow as I did earlier.

I've no need to rush.

We have all the time in the world…

Well, until midnight.

Still, I don't think about that.

I think about this—how good it feels to have her back in my arms. How great she smells. How the soft tickle of her hair on my skin is a wonderful caress…

Those things were absent from my life for four months.

It makes me take note of them more than ever.

I missed them.

Missed her.

Fuck, I'm so fucking fucked.

She presses her forehead to mine. "You said this place is famous for brownies?"

"It is. And bread, I think."

She hums then twists in my lap and grabs the menu. I read it over her shoulder and quickly settle on the sampler. She doesn't—she goes for an afternoon tea service. "Want to share it?"

I smile at her. "You've no idea how much I eat."

"You're a growing boy," she excuses before her brow slowly lifts. "Or at least, something is."

Her wriggle on my lap has me groaning. "It missed you."

A hoot escapes her. "Yeah, I'm sure." That's when I realize there isn't much I won't do to see that sparkle in her eye.

I am so in over my head here.

The server returns, but he doesn't seem all that surprised to find us with Mia on my knee. At least, he doesn't bat an eye, and that's all the confirmation I need to keep her there throughout the ordering process.

Once we've made our selections, barely five minutes pass before he arrives with the cake stand and all the accouterments of afternoon tea, followed by a large dish with various squares of brownies surrounding a grilled cheese sandwich on sourdough. It's a weird combo but with all that sugar, I know the grilled cheese is going to hit the spot.

"That's everything," I tell him once he's finished serving. "Thanks."

He smiles at me then motions to a button on the back wall. "If you need anything else, hit that and I'll be with you shortly. There are signs outside if you have to use the restroom."

"Thank you," Mia pipes up, but as the door closes behind him, she asks, "Do you think rich guys like you often bring chicks here?"

"I'm thinking that's the main purpose of this room, yeah," I state, amused by the question as I pick up a brownie and take a bite. "Holy fuck." I shove the square at her. "Try that."

She pops some into her mouth then releases the darkest, silkiest moan that makes my cock do the tango on its way to getting hard. "My god, what's in this? Crack?!"

I pull her deeper into my hold so she can feel my dick. "If you're going to moan like that every time you eat something, then I need you to feel the repercussions of your actions."

A soft smirk creases her jaw. "I've done nothing wrong."

"That moan was practically illegal," I grumble.

"I can't help that you're susceptible to sounds."

I stare at her tits. "And sights. Don't forget the sights." I lift my hand and gently hover it at the neckline of her dress. She watches me, her eyes locked on mine. "Can I?"

"You can," she rasps, then she shivers as I make a bridge between us.

Immediately, goose bumps pop up along her chest and her head arches back.

I've seen her come so many goddamn times, but I never had the chance to see *this*. The visceral reaction to *my* touch. I already know that it's more addictive than carbs, which is saying fucking something with the flavor of crack brownie still on my tongue.

I trail my fingers around the hippie neckline. "Do you forgive me?"

Her lips quirk up at the corners. "For what?"

"I deserve that," I tease. "You're gonna make me work for it, huh?"

"Technically, we hooked up. Bada bing, bada boom. Then, we didn't see each other again."

While she's right, I know she isn't.

We had a strong connection that night and only Liam derailed it.

Well, that's not entirely fair.

Her past actions derailed it—

Mia's sudden moan has my thoughts shattering to dust. Realizing I was still caressing her décolleté, I stare at her nipples which are budding through the thin fabric as she hisses, "God, that feels good."

"I'm nowhere even close to your nipples, honey."

Her smile is shaky. "I'm hypersensitive to touch."

Huh. "Could you get off like this? Is that something we need to experiment with?"

"If I tell you, you can't laugh."

That wasn't the answer I expected. "Hit me with it."

"I hate being touched."

My hand stills. "You do?"

"Yeah. I detest hugs. Hate shit like that. But during sex, I crave it. Weird, huh?"

Mid-thought, I reach for one of the sandwiches and rest it against her bottom lip.

I've noticed over the past couple of months that her curves have diminished some. Not gonna lie, I liked her juicy. Especially her ass.

She takes the bite and chews as I let my mind race.

"I guess with figure skating, it's pretty invasive."

Her shoulders sag at my retort—from relief.

It has me frowning until I realize she's relieved I don't think she's weird.

"Yeah. I grew desensitized to it in a way. You had to when someone's lifting you in the air by your ass cheeks. It got so bad that I switched from pairs to singles when I was eighteen."

"We need to start doing lessons," I insert, which has her grinning.

"You know what I mean."

"I do."

"It's one of the reasons I stopped when I reached the state championship. I didn't have it in me to take it further."

"You're too tough on yourself."

"I'm a realist. *But*, as desensitized as I was on the ice, I had to deal with the opposite problem off the ice."

I wonder if that's why it's easier for her to disconnect when she's on cam. She's accustomed to performing and to being intimately 'handled...'

That's something to ponder.

I didn't even fucking realize I was a voyeur until her—now, she gets me hard by taking off her damn short shorts online.

I guess I used to like watching strippers, enough for Kow to pick up on the preference, but I didn't have such a visceral reaction until her.

Doesn't make me Einstein that I figured out she's the common denominator.

Then, a thought occurs to me. "But you're sitting on my knee."

She hitches a shoulder. "I like sitting on your knee."

I shoot her a dopey grin. "Really?"

Her hip wiggles. "I get to feel you."

"Ah, fuck," I groan, as that friction, after using my fist for a literal eternity, is hella nice.

She twists on my lap until she's straddling me. It's such a smooth move that it reveals her dancing experience and it makes me wonder if she ever took a pole dancing class or something similar.

When she's facing me head-on, I settle my hands on the juncture where hip meets thigh and stare into her periwinkle blue eyes—yup, I looked up the color.

Then, she twists back and grabs half the grilled cheese sandwich, takes a bite, and, as she moans about how good it is, feeds me some as well.

The problem is, as delicious as the sandwich is, my dick is so fucking ready for action that I can *feel* that moan.

I admit it's more sensitive than a seismograph.

Her small smirk tells me she knows exactly what she's doing to me and is loving every second of it.

"You're cruel," I half-complain.

"Me? I'm feeding you some fabulous grilled cheese."

I huff, but my thumbs turn inward, rolling along the line of hip/thigh until they're adding pressure to her pubis. Her eyes flare as I dig in before tunneling ever deeper toward her crotch.

Her throat bobs. "Do you think this bakery knows people hook up in here?"

"For what they're charging, they should include a bed."

A soft bark of laughter escapes her. "You didn't have to spend a lot—"

I shake my head. "Hush."

She bites her lip though. "I'd have been happy with a Timmies."

"I wouldn't have been. You deserve better."

And yet again, she proves that she's not some clout-seeking missile who'll do anything to go viral when she turns shy on me.

What the fuck happened with Gracie, then?

"Anyway, I wasn't complaining about the price. Just saying… they'd be crazy if they didn't think people hooked up in here."

Her head tilts to the right where there's a whole staff of people working busily alongside us.

Her bottom lip pops in.

Her gaze tracks the staff.

And I know—I'm feeling it too—she's loving this.

I figured out that I was possessive over her when I decided to make that offer to hog all her time to get her off that damn site.

I don't want to share her.

But I like this.

I enjoy *this*.

And until her, I didn't even fucking know I was into it.

Watching her get herself off and talk dirty to me for two hours a day for months has hardwired my brain into believing that witnessing her orgasm is my God-given right. I don't want anyone else to see it too.

With her focus still on the staff, she takes a bite of my sandwich, then her eyes flare wider as I drag my hands down her thighs then back up again, taking the skirt of her dress with me.

That's when I see her pussy.

"Fuck!"

She doesn't turn to face me, but I can see her smile.

"You trying to kill me, Mia?"

No panties—shoot me now.

"Maybe torture you a little."

I can't help but laugh as I let my thumb trickle through her folds, watching her ass buck in response.

"God, that feels good." She turns to face me at last. "Fuck."

When I find her clit, Mia shivers then rocks forward until her forehead meets mine.

Reaching between us, she starts to unfasten my fly, and I don't argue, keeping on rubbing her clit as she delves beneath the zipper and pulls out my dick.

As we stare at one another, she starts to give me a handjob.

Just one stroke and my eyes narrow to slits, while hers flutter to half-mast.

Then, almost as one, we rock to the side so we're staring at the busy kitchen.

The feel of her forehead against me, her touch, her slickness, the tight grip of her fist, her weight on my lap—they're sensations I've missed and I appreciate them all the more for their absence.

Her tension is as hefty as my own when she starts to grind into my hand. She's already wet and, honestly, I know she'll soak through my goddamn pants, but that turns me on even more.

Though, I'm glad I wore my black jeans for once.

"I knew you had a piercing. How did that happen? I'm surprised it wasn't leaked to the press."

"A friend—" Liam. "— decided to hire a private piercer. Most of the..." I clear my throat. "A bunch of teammates—" The extended Bukowski clan. "— took advantage of the iron-clad NDA he had them sign."

"So, you all got matching cock piercings?!"

My thumb speeds up because the only reason she should hit that note is when I touch her. "Not all of us. Some got their nipples done."

I don't even wanna remember what Kow got done.

"Man, that's some slumber party."

I can't stop my cackle and it flows out of me when she shudders at my touch. "Couldn't let my friend get away with thinking he was the only one with a big dick—"

She moans. "You have to explain that logic to me. You fried my brain."

"Exactly how I like it," I croon. "You keep whispering sweet nothings like that to me, baby, and I'll reward you."

"That a promise?"

"Nuh-uh. It's a *vow*. You gonna come for me, beautiful?" I rumble, though our focus is definitely on the bakery.

She shivers. "Only if you come for me too."

My smirk is aimed at the staff up ahead. "You want that? If you do, I'm gonna come all over your slit."

The shiver becomes a shudder. "I'm still on birth control. But I'm clean."

"Me too," I rasp.

Turning to look at one another, we both whisper simultaneously:

"Haven't slept with anyone since you."

"I haven't been with a guy since you."

Heart pounding from her admission, I stop rubbing her clit and, instead, grab a hold of her wrist. My fingers dig inward until she's releasing her grip on me. Then, I snag her waist and drag her deeper onto my lap.

Though her forehead rocks on mine, she lets me maneuver her until she gets what I'm doing and is the one to place my dick between her thighs, parting her pussy lips to settle me against her slick folds.

"You're so fucking wet," I groan, voice thick.

"All for you," she whispers as she starts to ride me.

"Jesus Christ." My head tips backward. "You feel like heaven."

"Juicy and wet." She hums, hands settling on my shoulders, nails digging in and scoring my shirt. "Just for you."

Fuck, fuckity fuck, fuck.

"You're going to make me blow, baby." My laughter is husky but unashamed. "I can't even be embarrassed because your pussy is perfection."

Her smile is incandescent, and it's so much better because I can taste it when she props her arms on my shoulders then connects our mouths.

She thrusts her tongue between my lips but I'm ready for the battle—instantly, I tangle mine with hers and she's the next one to groan as I devour her.

I can feel her cunt—so soft and hot—all over my shaft. It's so much better than lube or my fist.

She.

Is.

Divine.

I wanna worship her until she knows how fucking perfect her pussy is for me.

Unable to stop myself from latching onto Mia like she's got one foot out of the door already, I use my hold on her hips to grind into her.

The pressure is so much better for us both because with every thrust of my tongue against hers, she whimpers and mewls—soft sounds that I've grown accustomed to but that are so much better when they're inches away from my ears and with a whisper of her breath brushing against the tender skin there.

For months, I've had to hold back the words, but I can't now. I pull away from her lips to tell her:

"I want you to come all over me, Mia. I want to be sticky with your cum. I want to walk out of here with your scent on my cock.

"I want to feel you get off on me. That's it, baby. Use my dick. Use it and get off on it. I want to see you explode—"

"Cole," she gasps.

"Yeah, that's it. Come on, sweetness. Let go. Give it all to me. I'm here. Ready to take it."

Her moan hitches, her body quakes, and then she shudders as she explodes.

Her keening wail sounds loud in the room, and from the corner of my eye, I see the nearest member of the bakery staff pause and turn toward the mirror, but I don't care.

They can hear her.

They can't look or touch.

She settles deeper onto me, hips squirming as she ekes out every last ounce of pleasure and her thrusts become shorter and sharper, meaning that every time she moves, the tip of my dick is cosseted by her hot slit.

Within seconds, I'm exploding too. My cum pours free, coating her cunt with *me*. My essence. My seed.

Suddenly, an image pops into my head.

Her waist thick and her belly round.

My baby in there.

My eyes clench closed because we can't have that.

Not yet.

Maybe not ever.

My heart stutters as she presses her lips to mine in a soft and lazy kiss, humming her satisfaction and murmuring, "Can you feel us? All sticky with each other?"

Jaw working, I rumble, "This is what heaven feels like."

She wriggles from side to side again, making my sensitive dick twitch until I hiss and put a stop to her ministrations.

With my eyes locked on hers, I cup her chin. "When you decide to let me back in that pussy, baby, I'm going to make you beg for my cum."

Her pupils turn into pinpricks. "I can't wait."

Mia: Cupid got the all-clear!

Cole: Woot! I know the place to celebrate too.

Mia: Where?

Cole: Katz's Deli.

Mia: You know it's not for 'cats,' don't you?

Cole: Duh.

Cole: But there'll be leftovers. Cats like meat, don't they?

Mia: Lol, of course. They're apex predators!

Cole: Then we'll have the pastrami on rye for her.

Mia: I'm sure she'll appreciate the sacrifice. Haha.

Mia: I'm so relieved.

Cole: I'll bet! Me too.

Mia: She's got to take her usual arthritis meds and an antibiotic. Thank God. And I have to keep an eye on things I leave around the house so this won't happen again.

Cole: <3

Cole: I'll see you later?

Mia: You sure will.

STAR'S ADMINISTRATION FALLING AT THE FIRST HURDLE?

BY MACK FINNEGAN

Rumors of tensions between Gracie Bukowski and Allan Bradley were confirmed today during a New York Stars' public practice when the head coach called a grueling session of bag skating.

The old-fashioned method has long since caused discord among devotees—some claiming it's great at managing the egos of multimillionaire players, others stating it's a legal form of 'corporal' punishment.

Upon discovering the team being put through some admittedly brutal paces, Ms. Bukowski blew up at the Stars' coach.

Twice, she called his name, and twice, he ignored her. When she whistled to gain his attention, the entire practice stopped, and Bradley continued to ignore her until she clambered onto the bench and outright roared his name—in full view of everyone in attendance, including the press corp.

Cornered, he had no choice but to storm over to her and, as he did, proceeded to call her an expletive that isn't fit for publication.

The feud between them came to a head when she ordered him to stop the session and he refused, spitting words at her as he physically crowded her. Only the fact that she was standing on the bench gave her a height advantage over the taller man. That was when she grabbed a hold of the pen he wears around his neck, dragged him to her, and, loud enough for everyone to hear, stated, "You either do as I say or you lose your job. Got it?"

It isn't the first time Bukowski's more modern mindset has come to blows with Bradley's older ways.

Earlier this week, Bradley was heard scoffing at Kerrigan's absence for family and medical leave. The reason for which is unknown to the public.

Then he defended his decision to have Greco, a top-tier goalie, splitting the starting role with Roger Davies 50/50. With a goal against average of 3.98 and save % of 0.799, Davies ranks 49 of 50 in the NHL goalies. Every Stars' loss this season has occurred with him in front of the net.

The old boys' club is evidently in play.

Sure to please Ms. Bukowski, Bradley's relationship with the Davies dates back a long time.

Mitch Davies, Roger's father, used to play for Toronto when Bradley coached there, and Roger has long since become Bradley's go-to goalie, especially during his time at the head of the Canadian Olympic team.

Bystanders are wondering how long a forward-thinking GM can work in tandem with an old-fashioned coach.

CHAPTER 23
MIA

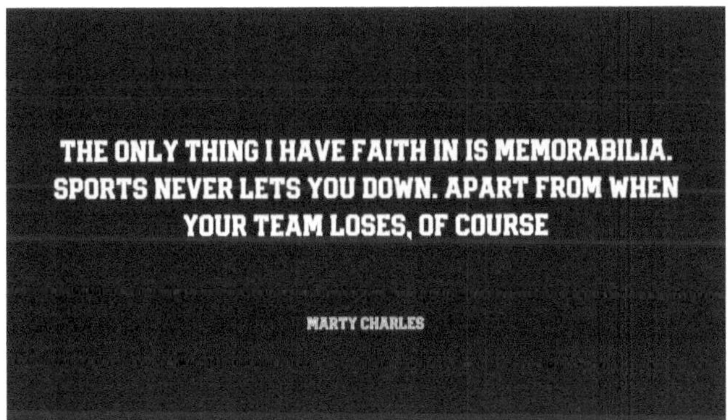

THE DAY DATE at the bakery was the first of many day dates with Cole.

There was a trip to the zoo and a visit to the National History Museum, then, my favorite, a trip to a spa.

Yeah, a spa.

Should have known with his choice of wardrobe that Cole'd be a metrosexual, but I'm here for it.

Honestly, there's nothing better than getting primped and preened while the guy you're dating is watching and taking part too.

Plus, it rocks because he doesn't have skanky feet and his skin is exfoliated and moisturized. Yet, he's also the most masculine man I've ever known, so sexy he blows my mind. The dichotomy is delicious.

Today's visit to the aquarium was surprisingly fun and it's put me in a great mood.

"Mia!" Jarvis calls as he dashes through Chuck's door with a massive paper bag in his hand.

"Time to stop daydreaming," I murmur to myself before beaming a smile at him.

Honestly, he's been so helpful—scoping out memorabilia from Facebook and thrift stores.

We don't have as much hockey merch as the baseball stuff which, to be fair, makes sense seeing as we've collected that stuff over decades and most of it is OG from my great-granddaddy's time, but we've put a good dent in one of the three walls that will make up that half of the bar.

"I'm going to show you something that I found and you're going to know that it's proof of my love for Chuck's."

Jason, one of the bar's more grabby-handed patrons, snags Jarvis by the arm and mockingly fights him for the package. "Your love of Mia, more like," he mocks. "Who can blame you, though?" He winks at me. "Mia is the prettiest thing in this dive!"

I roll my eyes at him. "Give him the package, Jason."

He pouts. "You're no fun."

The paper bag starts to tear as Jarvis snags at it, face bright red.

He's about half Jason's weight and I get the feeling some of the guys bully him. It's one of the reasons why I'm okay with him staying behind the bar because Dionne would break Jason's clavicle if he so much as sniffed in her direction.

Jarvis hasn't said anything to me, and those macho guys keep it quiet when I walk past so it's only suspicions until Jarvis confirms it, but it makes me like them less.

Ever since Gracie left last year, some of the patrons have been getting more rowdy and raucous and Chuck never did anything to stop them— only said that 'boys will be boys.'

I fucking hate that statement.

"Jason!" I snarl, my tone ten times more serious as the bag rips further.

Jason's already in my bad books because, one, he keeps on smoking despite repeated reprimands and, two, he won't shut up whining about the bar celebrating hockey during baseball's offseason.

He'd have preferred football, which is the reason his motor skills are below average—too many hits to the head during his time in the NCAA. Unfortunately for him, I don't mind if he never steps foot inside Chuck's again.

"What?!" Jason grouches at my rebuke.

"Let Jarvis have it back."

He pouts at me but drops his hold on the package, then he raises his hands in mock surrender when Jarvis isn't quick enough to stop it from connecting with the floor. "Yes, boss."

"If only I were your boss, Jason," I croon, leaning over the bar so I can poke him in the chest. *Hard.* "You'd be able to keep your hands to yourself."

He barks out a laugh as if that's the funniest thing he's heard in years, but I dismiss him and focus on Jarvis, who's still flustered.

"You okay?"

He shrugs, but his ears are hot pink. "I'm fine." He shoves the package at me. "I should charge a finder's fee for this."

Though I snort, I handle the bag with care as I, carefully, pull out a jersey.

My brow furrows at the name on the back, one that I've been seeing frequently—part of *CalKor's* other username.

"Gretzky?"

"He's only the best hockey player who ever breathed, Mia. And look, it has his signature on it."

I squint at the black speck on the back of the jersey. "Is that a signature?"

"It is. And I got it for twenty bucks. TWENTY FUCKING BUCKS, Mia! It's worth at least twenty-five hundred!"

My lips curve at his glee. "Good find, Jarvis!"

"Good find?!" He gasps. "My god, I should have kept it for myself. It's sacrilegious that you don't know who he is.

"You need to start learning more about the game, Mia. You can't run a hockey bar and not know Gretzky is a god."

"I'm slowly picking it up from the TV," I defend, but my smile deepens at his exasperated huff and, from the register, I hand him two hundred bucks. "This is me renting out the jersey from you, okay? You can take it back at any time, you hear me?"

Backing away from me, he holds out his hands so he can't take the cash. "You don't have to do that, Mia. I know things are tough and you need something like this on your hockey tribute walls."

"You *could* have kept this to yourself, but instead, it's going to make us look legit. Thank you for that. I couldn't have done it without you so this is only fair."

His chest puffs up at my gratitude and he beams a smile at me. "You're welcome, and thank you for this." He shoves the cash in his pocket. "I appreciate it."

"And I really appreciate you," I tell him earnestly. Clearing my throat, I ask, "You heard of Cole Korhonen?"

He rolls his eyes. "Honestly, Mia. You need to know the guys who play on our team."

My lips quirk. "He's good?"

"He's fucking awesome. And this season, he's playing on the first line with Donnghal and Lewis and they're deadly on the ice together." He smacks his lips. "We're going to *kill* it this year. We were robbed of the Stanley Cup in May—fucking Chicago—but this is our year. We're gonna win it. I can feel it."

I grin at his excitement. "I promise I'll listen to the TV more."

His nod turns brisk. "You'd better! Then I'll think the jersey is worthy of you."

Though I snort, I'm beyond grateful to him so I carefully fold it and tell him, "I need to get this framed. I'll take it to our usual place tomorrow."

"It needs to go front and center on the back wall next to the TV," Jarvis informs me. "Gretzky might have played for New York, not the Stars, back when we didn't suck, but it doesn't matter. He's beloved."

My eyes might glaze over. "Interesting." In my defense, there's a hell of a lot to learn!

"You need to be more believable. Hockey fans won't come here if they don't think you're jacking off to this stuff."

"Nice imagery."

"Beautiful imagery," Jason corrects, sneaking into the conversation. "The thought of you jacking off, Mia…" He cups himself.

I turn to him with a scowl. "You forget how handy I am with a baseball bat, Jason."

"You're making this hotter."

"Leave her alone, asshole," Beanpole barks from the kitchen door as he steps out with a monster burger order. "You know that shit don't fly here."

Flicking his zippo lighter, Jason sniffs. "This place ain't no fun no more."

"You know where the door is then," I tell him pleasantly.

I may work in the sex industry, but I swear to fuck, even the grossest of clients don't give me hives like Jason does.

With Gracie gone, and ever since Chuck died, he's getting worse too.

Glowering at me, Jason finishes his beer then storms off.

The atmosphere immediately lightens, and I turn to Jarvis. "Does he regularly give you shit?"

"Nothing I can't handle," is his response.

I hum. "You know I'd ban him if you said you *couldn't* handle him, right?"

"You'd do that… for me?"

"I'm not having you feeling like you aren't working in a safe space."

Beanpole snorts. "But it's okay for you to work in an unsafe environment, Mia? You think we don't know how he talks to you?"

"It's my bar. I gotta deal with this shit to pay the bills, but if he's cruel to my staff, that's another matter entirely."

"I promise I can handle him," is Jarvis's earnest answer. "But if that changes, I'll tell you."

"I'm not the only one who thinks he's getting worse, am I?"

Beanpole toys with a pen. "The guy's always been off his rocker. Too many hits to the head when he played college football. He's definitely worse."

Satisfied that he agrees with me, even if I'm unhappy to be correct, I turn my attention back to the TV and, now that Jason's gone, I switch it from college football and onto the NHL game.

Jarvis beams a satisfied grin, claps his hands together, and then immediately hisses. "That ref has it against us."

If I had a dollar every time I heard that…

"Ha! Too many men on the ice," he crows.

I'm treated to his running commentary during the period.

When I pull a beer and stand next to him, he points to the screen. "Look at Korhonen. See how big he is?"

Oh, yeah, I *see*.

I never thought hockey players were all that hot—I mean, have you seen their hair sometimes? But there's something about Cole. Even *with* helmet head.

Over the course of the night, my gaze tracks him, seeming to know when he jumps onto the ice, and I even do a happy dance when he scores two goals.

From his interactions with the team, I can tell he's liked. Not that I didn't already 'know' that. He's got a cheerful nature, but even I see how he's a team player.

If anyone gets in his teammates' faces, he's there, backing them up. He's the first to approach a goal-scorer and celebrate their win, (according to Jarvis) doesn't hog the puck, and isn't afraid to sacrifice his body on the ice.

I like that part the least.

Despite that, his inherent cheerfulness is contagious—I find I have a smile on my face for most of the shift.

That's what makes it suck harder when, quite by chance, I look up after I've served two guys a couple beers and I notice Gracie standing behind the team bench.

She's got her arms folded across her chest, eyes narrowed on the ice as she watches the men play.

"Shit's changing since she came on board," Jarvis informs me as he cleans the same spot on the bar that he's been scrubbing for five minutes —the patina's gonna wear if he doesn't move soon.

"Yeah?" I ask warily, though something in my heart soars at hearing how his tone turns respectful—Gracie deserves that. She's the best kind of people.

"She's making tidal waves. The first female GM in the NHL's going to bring us home the Holy Grail."

"Does the GM have that much input?"

"Well, she does stuff differently. GMs don't normally stand there, for example. She's got the coach by the balls and is trying to put pressure on him." Cackling, he motions at the screen. "Look how he glowers at her. There was a report of her yelling at him in front of the press. If he doesn't shape up, he knows he's out on his ass.

"Last season, we had a massive problem with our defense—"

"How do you know all this stuff, Jarvis? I wasn't even aware that you liked hockey, so why are you working in a baseball bar if this is your sport?"

"Because, one, I got bills to pay and, two, the hockey bars around here suck ass. Why do you think I suggested you turn this place into one? Plus, you're a great boss so you make up for the boring sport that is baseball."

"Say that any louder and you'll get punched by our regulars," I tease, amused when he peeks over his shoulder to make sure he's in the clear. "How come it's against the law for me to know nothing about hockey when we're a hockey bar but it's okay for you to diss the sport when you work in a baseball bar?"

"I conned Chuck into thinking I liked it. I know the rules. Can't help it in my family," he grouses. "But hockey's what makes my heart sing."

Though I shake my head, I smile at him. "So what was wrong with last season's defense?"

As I get a lecture on shoot-outs and overtime and all other kinds of crap I didn't think I'd need to know, my attention is split three ways— the bar, Gracie, and Cole.

That's when I see Cole bump fists with her. Tipping off his helmet, he drags her in for a hug before sitting on the bench.

The sight is like a punch to the solar plexus.
That's not a working relationship.
They *know* each other.
Well.
Shit.

CHAPTER 24
COLE

> TEAMMATES COME AND TEAMMATES GO. IT'S YOUR JOB TO STICK AROUND BUT ALWAYS GET THEIR AUTOGRAPHS. COULD BE WORTH A BENJAMIN FRANKLIN IN A FEW YEARS
>
> MARTY CHARLES

A MAN KNOWS he's in over his head when he turns down a party with his buddies and, instead, says 'yes' to his girl when she asks him to come over.

I accepted her invitation so fucking fast that it's a miracle I didn't break my thumb as I texted Mia my response.

"Who you turning us down for?"

I squint at Liam. "Don't bullshit me. You're not even going."

He smirks. "I don't have to. Gagné is."

"Yeah, I noticed you got him managing your captain duties off the ice."

"He likes it."

"I'm sure he does." I turn away from my phone and look at the defenseman. "He favoring his left side?"

"Got slashed during the game." Liam elbows me. "Come on. Why did you say no? You used to be a party animal."

"I still am," I argue.

"Bullshit. Kow already told me that you wouldn't go to a strip club when you saw him this summer. Then there was that date you asked me to set up for you at the bakery."

"A man's allowed to change."

"A man only changes if he gets with someone—"

"That's kinda sexist."

Liam hoots. "It is if it's not true. You forget how well I know you."

I grace him with another sniff. "Not as well as I know you. I'll go to the party if you do."

That's when his eyes narrow. "Maybe some other time."

My look is enigmatic. "Likewise."

"You got some kind of showdown going on here?" Lewis asks, wading into the conversation as he plunks his ass in his stall beside us to yank on some socks all while whistling the theme song to *The Good, the Bad and the Ugly*. "Do I need to be far away from the blast?"

"No blast," Liam excuses as he drags on some jeans. "Just a conversation. Between friends. Who know too much about each other."

My lips curve at the backhanded warning so I show him what I was doing in the whirlpool.

He rolls his eyes. "Only you, Cole."

Lewis peers around him. "What is it? Porn?"

"*Lady* porn," I preen. "But we shouldn't call it that. This is modern-day Austen, ya hear me?"

He doesn't.

"Lady what now?"

"Cole's a massive reader," Liam mutters, sounding put-upon.

"I'm a massive something," I retort as I drop my phone into my messenger bag and get dressed in earnest—I got places to be.

And finally, Mia might let me inside that sweet snatch of hers.

It's been ten days since our first date at the bakery, and every time, we sneakily get off which is hot as hell, but fuck if I don't want to slide into that gorgeous pussy.

What, with the dates and the cam-girl sessions, my dick hasn't been handled this much since I was Callan's age.

"What's lady porn though?" Lewis wags his eyebrows. "I think I need to get into this."

"There's a world of endless possibilities on Kindle, bro."

"You want me to *read*?" he blurts out.

"It's not a deadly sin, Kyle."

He studies me as if I'm a contagion, then, obviously uncomfortable which is hilarious, he shifts tacks.

"We rocked it out there," Lewis murmurs, his gaze unfocused as the press wades in. "They're late."

Liam hitches a shoulder. "Gracie probably waylaid them."

I snicker. "Looks like she's telling them off again."

"True. I know she's pissed at Mack Finnegan."

"Why?"

"For that piece about her showdown with Bradley."

"I bet you loved that article."

He winks at me. "I framed it. You know how hard it was for me not to get involved. But she's annoyed."

"Seeing her ream Bradley a new one made my year," Lewis agrees—Coach hasn't let up on him since that brouhaha in Russu.

"Made all our year," Liam mumbles to which Lewis snorts.

"Agreed." Lewis jumps to his feet and pulls on his pants, making sure to twist around when the press call out questions.

"Why are you flashing your butt at the press?" I inquire, well aware there are some hotties amid the crowd. "Or should that be to *whom* are you flashing said derrière?"

"Ah, fuck, Lewis. You don't shit where you eat," Gagné inserts, diving into the conversation headfirst. "You fuck one of them and screw 'em over, your name's gonna be mud."

"Who said I'll screw anyone over?" As he bends down, he winks at me.

I roll my eyes. "That adrenaline buzz you're seeking will bite you in the ass."

"Et tu, Brutus?!"

"Et who what now?" Gagné demands.

"BRUTE. Not Brutus. Jesus Christ," I grumble.

Lewis mutters, "Heretical douche canoes."

As I watch him wiggle his butt, I can't help but notice that one of the reporters is *definitely* checking him out.

Shaking my head, I focus on getting ready until I hear the others bitching about a fan.

"Why the fuck does she attend every game if she's going to cheer for the away team?"

"Who are you talking about, McIsaac?"

He snipes, "Some chick who never misses a game."

"But she always wears a jersey supporting the other side?"

"Yup."

My brows lift. "That's an expensive grudge."

"Tell me about it. She sits rink side too."

I rub my chin. "Wonder what she'll do when we host the All-Star Game in February?"

"Rotate through the jerseys every ad break?"

"That's some dedication to hatred. Wonder what that's all about."

"You and the entire team." Gagné's chuckle ends in a hiss as he leans over to drag on his pants. It's clear the woman's antics don't bother him, even if some of the guys genuinely are pissed.

"Should be illegal." McIsaac's words cut off when he draws on a sweater.

"How is it illegal to be a pest? Ain't that your job?" Lewis argues.

"On the ice," he defends.

Greco, on his way out of the shower room, lobs, "She's better at it than you—"

"Cole!"

Drawn from the bickering, I jerk my chin at Gracie and amble toward her because I'm good to go.

Little bit definitely micromanages—that's her all over though. Coach doesn't like it, mind you. He squints and scowls at her throughout the junket. Her hovering tactic might be unusual, but I kinda appreciate it.

Case in point…

"Finnegan with PSN News. Was it hard coming face-to-face with the Blue Demons again?"

"Not really. This is my new home, though I appreciate everything that Jersey gave me."

"Didn't seem like it when you slew-foot Hammonds."

"That's because I didn't. You think I'd have gotten away with that if I had?"

Pointedly, Gracie clears her throat, earning Finnegan's scowl.

"You've been acting very aggressively on the ice. Isn't this the second game you've spent time in the penalty box?"

"Didn't realize that was a crime."

"I'm not suggesting it is, but would you say there's a reason for it?"

"For playing a killer game on the ice?" Gracie turns the attention back to her. "What you call a slew-foot, Finnegan, I call a deke. I think you need to get your eyes checked."

Finnegan narrows said eyes at my GM while Coach huffs under his breath. "There's nothing wrong with my prescription."

"No? Then we're watching different games."

"The stats don't lie."

"Which stats are those? The ones that indicate we're in the middle of a winning streak?"

Finnegan grunts. "I never said you weren't. I was asking why Cole is playing more aggressively than usual."

"Who says he is?"

"I do."

When the pair of them lock horns, I hide a grin.

"Would you say you're playing aggressively?" Gracie asks, her gaze still fixed on Finnegan.

"Perhaps," I concede.

Gracie doesn't look at me. "Why is that?"

"Got a lot to prove."

"There? Satisfied with that answer?"

Finnegan is the opposite of satisfied. "I couldn't help but notice that you signed up with Mega X."

That has me blinking. "And?"

"Rumor has it they've got some special ingredient in there that—"

"Unless that special ingredient is testosterone, and seeing as Mega X is FDA-approved, Finnegan, I think we can leave this line of questioning and set it aside." Finnegan sniffs but Gracie isn't done. "If you've got some grudge against Mega X, take it up in your own time. Until then, if it's not about the game, don't bother asking."

"Any news on when Kerrigan will be back from FMLA leave and why he's been granted it?" Finnegan inquires instead.

Ten minutes later, thoroughly cosseted after G's mother-hen routine, I walk down the tunnel toward some of the fans who are waiting to spot their favorites as they leave the arena.

I'm trying not to feel guilty about the Mia/Gracie situation when a kid hands me a sucker.

Kneeling in front of him, I ask, "You sure you wanna give me that and don't want it for yourself? 'Cos that's really kind of you to share candy. Not sure I would have when I was your age."

He immediately turns bright pink and, though he glances at his mom, who's beaming at me, whispers, "It's sugar-free so it's not that great."

I bark out a laugh. "You trying to fob it off on me, huh?"

"Maybe," is his coy response.

Grinning, I get to my feet and retrieve a cap from my messenger bag I stuffed there for this purpose. "What's your name, kid?"

Shyly, he ducks his head. "Jack."

"You got a pen, Jack?"

His eyes are wide as he stares desperately up at his mom, who hands me a marker. I take it, sign the cap, then as I put it on his head, grinning when it sinks low and covers half his face, his mom asks, "We actually brought this along too if you wouldn't mind signing it...?"

The scarf's loaded with Blue Demons' signatures and it makes me whistle. "Isn't that cheating?"

"You've played for Jersey more than you have the Stars," the kid points out.

I snicker at his reasonable logic and sign the scarf. As I drape it over his shoulders, I murmur, "I'll take the sucker off your hands, kiddo."

"Thanks, Mr. Korhonen!"

Winking at him, I unwrap it and stick it in my mouth before I head on out.

My nose crinkles though—*what the fuck is this shit I'm eating?* Is this what they're feeding kids now? Sheesh.

Grumbling in remembrance of the good old candy days as I get in the car and give Burrows orders, I dump the sucker in the wrapper, grateful I didn't throw it away as I toss it in the cupholder, then snag my cell from my bag when it buzzes on my lap.

> Mia: You looked cute with that kid.

Me: You saw that? Stalking me, Mia? Good job. Keep it up.

> Mia: *snickers* One of my staff is a big fan and he's watching you on some livestream on TikTok lol.

> Mia: But I watched the game at the bar tonight. No wonder your head is massive.

I grin. Still...

Me: Chuck's is a baseball bar though. What are you doing watching hockey?

> Mia: We're diversifying.

Me: Diversifying into hockey?

> Mia: Baseball season's winding down. Revenues are dwindling so we gotta do something.

Me: Makes sense.

Me: You should have said. I could get you some jerseys for the wall. Get 'em signed for you.

Mia: I can't accept anything like that!

Me: Why can't you lol?

Mia: Wouldn't be fair.

Mia: Unless... I could reimburse you for them?

Me: Babe, I get free shit all the time.

Mia: It's not right. I won't take advantage of you like that.

What the fuck happened with Gracie, then?

I'm so tempted to goddamn ask, but I can't.

The question is starting to fucking choke me. As well as charming and cheeky, we can add curious-as-shit to the list of adjectives that describe me.

Me: Do you even like hockey?

Mia: One of my staff does.

Me: LOL. That's not an answer.

Mia: I thought you looked hot.

Me: /me is a hot hockey player

Mia: *snorts*

Me: Want me to dress up in my gear for you one night?

Mia: Not if you want in my pussy any time this year.

Me: *gasps*

Mia: You looked hot in it but you look hotter OUT of it so nah.

Me: I'm not offended anymore.

Mia: Good to know lol.

Me: Mind if I come see Chuck's?

Mia: It'll be closed

Me: That's fine. I'm curious.

Mia: If you want to. I'm still here closing up.

Me: See you soon?

Mia: K

"Change of plan, Burrows," I inform him. "Take us back to the arena."

His brow lifts in the rearview mirror but he does as I ask.

That's when I get a message from *KillerCatQueen7*.

KillerCatQueen7: I'm so sorry but I have to cancel. Everything's fine. Something's come up.

It's insane that I feel jealous of myself, right?

The lines between *CalKor* and I are blurring…

Things are more complicated than they need to be, but fuck if I didn't make my bed and now I'm having to lie in it.

CalKor: No worries so long as everything's all right. Speak to you tomorrow.

KillerCatQueen7: :*

The small crowd of fans has dispersed when I run down the tunnel. Only Gagné's still there along with a couple members of staff as I head for my cubby.

My brow lifts when I see him packing some ice against his side. "You okay, dude?"

He jolts then twists to face me. Immediately, he hisses at the abrupt movement. "Yeah, yeah, I'm fine."

"How hard was that hit?"

"Pretty hard."

"Could you have busted a rib?" I ask in concern.

He waves a hand. "It's all good."

That bruise on his side was the opposite of 'all good.'

"You got whacked with the puck?"

I didn't see that during the game—and his bruise seems hella localized. Like a puck caused it when it hit him rather than a fall.

He ducks his head. "No."

Confused, I stare at him for a couple seconds, then I remember why I came back and snag a bunch of shit from my cubby.

"What are you doing?"

"Stealing."

He chuckles as he gingerly wraps kinetic tape around his side. A side he shields. *Interesting.* "Why?"

"Because I got a friend who needs some of it."

"Want me to sign it?"

I grin at him. "Good man."

He digs out a marker from somewhere—unlike Gracie and apparently Gagné, I'm not a walking stationery shop—signs his jersey and helmet, then tosses it to me as I autograph a bunch of my gear too.

Noticing one of the housekeeping staff emptying the trash, I call, "Yo, dude, you got an empty bag?"

The guy blinks at me as if he's used to being nonexistent, which kinda makes me feel like crap, but he passes a roll of trash bags to me. "Here you go."

"Thanks," I tell him as I rip off four. "I've seen you around, man. What's your name?"

"Brody."

I bump his fist.

He shoots me a shy smile and returns to his business as I dump a bunch of stuff in each bag.

As Gagné grabs a hat from his cubby and tosses it to me, he flinches.

"You okay, bro?"

"Just didn't fall right." His shrug is dismissive as he departs. "I'll see you later."

Whistling, I leave the locker room with the bags in my hands ten minutes later and get caught by Gracie, who's done for the day too.

"You in the middle of a heist?"

I wouldn't ordinarily care, but seeing as this is for the bar that betrayed her... I wince. "Maybe."

She snorts but apparently gets distracted when she misreads my guilt, making me feel even worse. "You okay? Don't let that Finnegan POS get to you—"

"This isn't my first press rodeo, G." Together, we stride down the tunnel toward the parking lot. "Is Liam waiting for you?"

"Of course he is," she says with a laugh, then she twists back to point at something. Which is when I spy the two-man team following us. "You didn't hear them?"

"No."

"Where's your head at?" she asks, amused.

"Nowhere."

"Back in the locker room?"

"Nah, thinking about a couple plays that went wrong tonight." I flick a look at her and realize her eyes are a touch puffy. "You been crying, G?"

"You know, for a pain in my ass, you always notice shit."

"It's a gift." Though she chuckles, it's watery. I gently nudge her with my elbow. "Everything all right? Do I need to beat the crap outta Liam?"

Her lips kick up in a smile. "No. I was talking to Lacey Kerrigan earlier, that's all."

Oh.

"How is she?"

"Dying," is her flat response.

"That—" I blow out a breath. "—sucks."

"Yeah, life often does."

We walk outside and her bodyguards split off, moving around her as they check for...well, whatever Liam pays them to check for.

"I swear if he ever wonders whether I love him, I'll point to the gorillas and tell him I only put up with this bullshit because of him."

My lips curve. "Ain't love grand, G?"

She shoots me a goofy-for-Gracie smile. "Yeah, it is."

I wink at her as she splits off toward Liam's car. "See you tomorrow, little bit."

She waves as she jumps into the back seat. "You will."

As I head for my own vehicle, Burrows's waiting with the trunk open, clearly having seen what I'm carrying.

Five minutes later, we're on the road. Mum calls, keeping me company for a good chunk of the journey before she tells me she's off to bed.

Great timing seeing as we're almost at the bar.

I rub my hands together.

God, I can't wait to see my girl.

CHAPTER 25
MIA

WHEN A FANCY TOWN car parks outside the bar, I know it's Cole's ride without even seeing the make or model.

I go to the door and unlock it so I can let him in, but before he walks over to Chuck's, he stops at the trunk and pulls a bunch of bags out.

My eyes widen as I holler at him, "I told you not to!"

"What made you think I was a guy who did as he's told?" he hollers back.

My lips twitch when he walks toward me with four trash bags, but it's his outfit that has me smiling outright.

I'm pretty sure he gets dressed in the dark, but there's no denying I dig his vibe.

"Love the shirt," I inform him, watching as he preens.

"Knew you'd be awesome enough to like Taylor Swift, beautiful," he informs me as, ducking down, he presses a kiss to my forehead before shoving me into the bar.

He's still beaming from my compliment, which is hella cute.

Rustling sounds follow as he dumps his loot, then, having seen the place is closed with all the stools on the tables, turns to lock up behind him.

"What did you do?" I mutter as I stare at the bulging bags.

"I got you some shit."

"Literal shit?" I tease.

He winks at me. "For a non-hockey fan, it might very well be."

That has me snorting as I drop to my knees and pull out the goodies he's brought with him.

I gasp when I see how many jerseys he's purloined, and two of them are even signed! I squint at them. "Car Honk Ing?"

He grunts. "That's my best penmanship. Everyone's a critic."

Grinning at the jersey, I hug it to my chest. "I meant it when I said you didn't have to do this, but thank you."

Not so long ago, I hated this jersey.

Oh, how things change…

Still, it's a reminder his abrupt visit has brought to a head.

Not only is he in the dark about my connection to Gracie, he's unaware of my side gig.

Am I cheating on him right now?

These are the kinds of things they don't prepare you for in ethics class.

His smile is gentle. "You should have asked. This shit's expensive when you don't get it for free."

Chuckling at his logic, I drag out more and more stuff from the Mary Poppins' trash bags, seeing that the things with Gagné and Korhonen on are signed, but Lewis and Donnghal's aren't.

That has me biting my lip as I come to a swift decision.

"I need to tell you something."

He snags some of his loot and stacks it on the counter. "Oh?" Once he's done, he holds out a hand for me to take and helps me to my feet. Another kiss grazes my temple as he tucks me into him. "What's that?"

"I used to… Gracie Bukowski worked here once." I blurt the words, aware that my voice is hoarse.

Our eyes lock.

"I know."

I jerk back a little. "You know?"

"I do."

Then, I swallow. "You *really* know?"

But…

Why doesn't he hate me?

He sighs. "I wasn't lying about having to head home, nor was I lying about my father's heart problems, but what went down with you two was one of the reasons why I didn't get in touch over the summer."

Oh.

"Why the change of heart?"

His head tips to the side. "I'll answer that if you answer my question first…"

It doesn't take a mind reader to know what he's going to ask. And, to be frank, I've never not felt like a complete asshole for doing what we did to Gracie.

"Fine, but *are* you friends with her?"

"I am. Very close friends. I spent a couple years with her family. Remember I told you what a billet family is?"

"Yeah."

"So, what happened with Gracie?"

This makes no sense.

He's the one who contacted me out of the blue.

He's the one still holding me.

That he hasn't let go gives me the courage to whisper, "I'm going to preface my answer with a caveat."

"Fancy talk. I dig it."

Startled, I huff out a laugh. "Be serious."

His eyes twinkle, which makes this so much weirder.

Why isn't he angry with me?

Like he can hear that question, he drawls, "I spent all summer angry at you. If you want to know what changed, then you have to give me some logic."

I don't have to do dick.

With any other guy, *that* is what'd spill from my lips, but Cole's not really pushing me. The lack of pressure makes it easier to confess:

"The day before we went to the press, I had no idea what was going on with the bar."

"Your uncle was running an illegal bookie?"

"What?! No," I sputter.

"Did he hold cockfights out the back?"

"No!"

His nose crinkles. "What, then?"

"My god, your imagination is wild."

"Plenty about me is, babe. So, what was going on in this baseballer's idea of a den of inequity?"

"You read too much romance," I complain.

He winks at me. "There's no such thing."

"He showed me a couple of debts."

"Huh. Boring."

Annoyed, I glower at him. "Boring for someone rich!"

"True. Sorry. You can't deny that mine were more interesting."

"You should write a book."

"Maybe I will when I'm old and gray."

"*Anyway*, he showed me—"

"Wait. You said 'a couple of debts.' As in, he didn't show you all of them?"

"No." My laughter is bitter this time. "He left those for when he died." I can't stop myself from tipping my head forward and resting it on his chest. "Those two were terrifying enough. He owed forty-two grand to the people who deliver our beer every day."

He whistles. "That's why you sold her out?"

I recoil but face the bullet. "Yes. I-I knew things were bad because I'd started using my own cash to pay for each delivery."

"That's fucked up. Especially as it wasn't your business then."

"It was though. It's a family business."

He grunts, so I know he disagrees.

"It's not like I needed the cash," I argue. "Uncle Chuck handled my rent for me."

That has him humming. "If you say so, babe."

"I *do*. But that week, they informed us that it wasn't enough to pay for the deliveries. They wanted some of the debt to be covered too."

"Makes sense. They're not a bank."

"No, and I got it. That's why…" I swallow. "I hate that I did what I did."

"Still did it though."

I bite my lip at his flat response. "Yeah."

"Would you do it again if you had a do-over?"

Here's my chance to make everything right, but I don't sell either of us short by taking the easy way out.

"T-This bar was Chuck's everything. I noticed him watching Gracie leave, didn't think anything of it because he was getting himself a beer, but I-I saw his expression as he stared at the guy she was with.

"When I tell you that I know nothing about hockey, I mean it. Seriously, I don't really know who Gretzy is and I got his signed jersey—"

Cole jerks, making me jump, then screeches, *"IT'S GRETZKY, MIA! Jesus H. Christ! Greh-tzz-kee."*

My nose crinkles but I repeat the surname until he's satisfied—so, nine times.

Because that's such a Cole move in the middle of a massive confession, I have to huff out another chuckle.

To be honest, I'm surprised he hasn't asked to see the jersey.

"I went into the back office later that night, and he's staring at this pile of bills on his desk.

"I was bringing him a sandwich and I asked him if everything was okay, and he picked up the bills and handed them to me.

"I still remember that feeling of my heart sinking. Like, I knew that things were bad, but I didn't realize we were on the brink of losing everything. And my god, that was the tip of the iceberg." I lock eyes with him. "The bar's seven hundred and fifty thousand dollars in debt, Cole."

His brows lift. "You're shitting me?!"

"No. I wish I were. I thought that forty-two Gs was horrific. His face when I saw those bills..." I shake my head. "He was bright red and breathing heavy. I thought he was going to have a heart attack. But he was facing facts—no booze, no bar. And no bar equaled no Chuck.

"I didn't realize until later that no other distribution company would touch him because he already owed a handful of others a bunch too."

He winces. "I'm sorry you were in that position."

"God, so am I. But it doesn't make it right. Doesn't make things better with Gracie. The bitch of it is—"

"She'd have helped you if she knew."

I close my eyes. "I can see that now, but I was panicking. It was the craziest thing. This bar's worthless aside from the ground it stands on. I don't know why it's got such a pull on us—"

"That's what a legacy does. It gets its hooks into you, digs 'em in deep, and won't let go until you'll do the whackiest shit to keep it going."

My eyes pop open. "Sounds like the voice of someone who's been there, done that."

He hitches a shoulder. "I told you my family owns a ranch back home. My brother's... well, he's like you—would pull crazy stunts to save it."

Though his tone lacks judgment, I bow my head in shame. "I understand if you don't want to see me again."

"That's the thing, Mia. I can't stop seeing you. I tried over the summer." He rubs the back of his neck. "And failed because here I am, standing in front of you, with a bunch of stolen shit from my team because I want to help you."

"Even though I hurt Gracie?"

"Even though you hurt Gracie."

Desperately, I try not to allow the hope unfurling deep inside me to inflate. He could still pop it like a water balloon. "Why?"

He stares at me for so long that I'm not sure if he's going to answer, then he rumbles, "Confession time."

That has me frowning. "What do you have to confess?"

His grin is more of a grimace. "Plenty."

CHAPTER 26
COLE

Love Me Again - John Newman

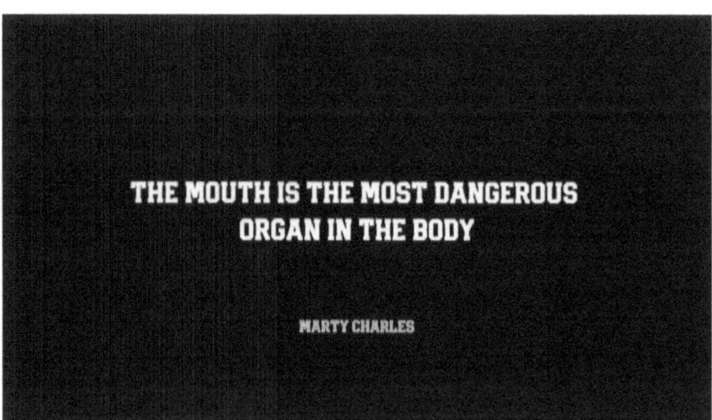

I KNOW that I can keep my mouth shut.

I don't have to say dick.

But like I told her, there's no such thing as reading too many romance novels and of the tens of thousands I've devoured over the years, shit like this is what breaks people up.

It always comes out.

Usually at the worst moment.

That's why I do it.

That's why I tear off the Band-Aid though I could totally have seduced her tonight.

"I'm GretzkyWannabe42."

She blinks at me.

Then blinks again.

"Also *CalKor*, but that's my brother's fault."

Another blink.

"I went home, walked in on my brother jacking off as he watched you—"

Finally, we have some movement—she gasps.

"—and when I recognized you, I kind of lost my shit."

She pulls away from me, but I consider it a positive that she doesn't slap me.

Instead, on wobbly legs, she retreats to the bar where she pours herself a massive glass of whiskey.

There are so many fingers in that glass, it might as well be a hand.

Whistling, I also head to the bar, surprised when she shoves the glass at me and pours herself one too.

"You've..." The croaky words freeze before she can get them out. Then, with her hand still trembling, she lifts the glass to her mouth and takes a deep sip.

I'm almost impressed when she doesn't cough.

She guzzles it down, turning bright red as she does. Then, she gulps some more, and I lean over the counter to snag the rest from her before she can polish it off.

"I get that this is a conversation worthy of a bender, but let's not end it in the hospital, eh?"

She scoffs. "I grew up in this place, Cole."

"Does that mean your liver's immune to alcohol?"

That has her grimacing.

"Going to assume that your uncle wasn't the best case of having a healthy relationship with booze..."

That earns me a wince.

She gives up the tug of war with her drink then rests her hand on the counter. Her fingers starfish as she bows her head then mumbles, "That's why *CalKor* went through the personality shift."

She noticed that?

"Yeah, I guess so."

Her throat bobs. "You paid me a small fortune this summer."

I hum. "Worth it."

That has her gaze hunting mine down. "How was it? You paid tens of thousands of dollars—" She croaks out the words. "—to watch me bounce on a dildo."

"I can afford it." My jaw works though. "I hated that you were doing that. My brother told me how he was in love with you and that he wanted to run away with you to save you from having to do the cam-girling." I bite off a dour laugh. "I thought he was insane until I found myself offering you fourteen grand a week to be my private cam girl." I purse my lips. "I have no regrets."

"Jerk."

I sniff. "How can I regret it? I've clearly been propping this place *and you* up. If anything, I regret that you know now because we'll have to stop with that stuff or you'll think I'm treating you like a hooker when I'm not.

"All I want is to support you. It killed something in me to see you so worn down even if you tried to hide it.

"I don't want my legacy whereas you want yours, but I get how it is."

She gnaws on her bottom lip. "You think that I *want* this place? What alternative do I have?"

"Coaching, of course. I think that you can't let it go," I muse. "I also understand how that feels.

"I spent my childhood watching my mum get beaten by my father, watched her turn into a shadow as he yelled at her, and then I witnessed her breaking free of her chrysalis and getting the hell away from him. All on that land." I take a deep sip of my drink. "You ever heard the sound of horses dying by being burned alive in a stable fire, Mia?"

Her gasp is horrified. "No!"

I close my eyes. "I can still hear them some nights." When I open them next, I know I'm crying. She has tears in hers too. "They were fucking terrified and there was nothing I could do.

"Pops ended up tying me to this railing at the front of our house with rope. My adrenaline was so jacked that I pulled down the porch to get free but it was..." My head shakes of its own volition. "I fucking hate that place. I hate it with every goddamn part of me, and yet..." I sigh. "It's still home. I only go back there for *that* and my brothers."

"That's fucked up."

"I agree." I take another deep sip of whiskey. "Don't think I misunderstand your devotion to this place. You're lucky, in fact. Because I *do* get it. I get it too well.

"But that's why I'm telling you this now. You can be mad at me and feel as if I lied to you, and then we can get over this because we *will* get over this hump.

"Just like I've gotta tell a woman who's practically my sister that I'm falling for the woman who betrayed her." I tip up my chin and lock my eyes on hers. "Some stories start hella complicated—"

"This isn't a book." For the first time, she sounds angry.

"Maybe it isn't. But that doesn't mean we can't have an HEA."

"An HE-what?"

I grunt. "I need to get you reading my shit, Mia. You need to know this stuff. I mean, we're not third-act breakupping this. No fucking way."

"What does that even mean?" She rubs at her temple. "I'm..."

"Don't pretend that you're annoyed with me."

Her temper flickers to life right in front of me. This is the only kind of fire I don't hate. "Don't you dare tell me how I should feel."

I hide a smile. "We can keep up the cam-girl stuff."

"You're digging your own grave here. The second we were dating, you should have shut the whole thing down!"

"I kinda liked talking to you twice a day. Mostly, I felt shitty for lying to you about who I was and for hiding this stuff from Gracie, but at least I can jack off in peace tomorrow—" *Plus,* how else could I keep paying her?

"We're not doing that again," she shrieks.

"Shame. I really will miss it."

Her glower would terrify any normal man. But I've spent too much of my life with Gracie Bukowski. Not that I tell Mia that. That'd be encouraging her to up her glower game and no man'd be that much of a fool.

"I think I need some space."

Though I want to argue with her, I don't. She probably does need space.

I ponder what a hero in one of my books would do. Some would turn into a caveman and haul her over their shoulder and kiss her until she forgot her own name. But then, there are some who'd give her space.

I know she deserves it—I heaped a whole lot of crazy at her feet.

Because I don't know what my next move should be, I just stare at her.

She stares at me too.

Apparently, that works because she stomps her foot. "Stop looking at me like that."

I shrug. "How am I looking at you?"

"Like you fucking love me," she screams, then she covers her face. "How the fuck can you love me? You barely know me. Oh, my god, this is insane. This is… You're batshit. Absolutely batshit."

"Maybe I'm fucking nuts for you."

"Why aren't you… I don't get it. We… You…"

"I had time to get to know you, Mia. Time that you didn't have in return. I know that's unfair and I don't expect you to love me back yet—"

"So generous," she growls, more of that temper sparking in her eyes.

"You're right. That's me in a nutshell," I agree, mostly to rile her but also because I kind of am. "Do you know what Gracie means to me?"

"Stop bringing her up. What I did to her and what you did isn't some kind of karmic response—one doesn't cancel out the other."

"I did nothing wrong. You said it yourself—we hooked up. That's it. When I saw how upset you were and you told me about Cupid, I had no choice but to call you."

"It's creepy," she complains, but she flushes at my admission.

"Perhaps. Only if you're ashamed of what you do. Which I don't think you should be—"

"I'm not." Her hands ball into fists at her sides. "I make a lot of money and I kept people in jobs because of it."

There's my girl.

I hide another smile behind my glass, but she sees it anyway.

Her eyes narrow. "Cole."

"Mia."

"You've been hit in the head too many times by a puck."

I beam a grin at her. "It's good that you know that but I have it on better authority that women like crazy guys."

Her scowl is so pronounced, I snort at it. Her words are beyond satisfying though. *Jealousy—I'm in paradise.* "Which women?"

"You should see the book groups I'm in. Feral." I sigh in happiness. "My true people."

"What are you talking about?"

"Book groups. Facebook. The Smuthood. Get with the program, babe."

"The Smuthood?"

"Oh, yeah. Thirsty ladies are my jam."

She rubs her temple. "The lime-green jeans should have warned me."

"Hey, you said you liked those."

"Oddly enough, I do." Mia rubs her temple some more. "I..." She almost chokes. "...*like* you too. Even if you did pay me a small fortune to watch me jill off with various dildos."

"You did a great job. Only right that you get paid the big bucks." I smirk at her. "At least this time, you'll be ready to take every inch of my dick."

"Is that a challenge?"

"More a statement of intent."

She taps her nails on the bar. "I should throw you out."

"Where'd be the fun in that?"

Her exhalation is so heavy, it might as well trigger a hurricane. "You're lucky you're pretty."

"My face has always been a blessing."

She pinches the bridge of her nose then counts to three.

Softly, I murmur, "You know I'm teasing."

"I do. But this is still crazy. *You* are still crazy. And I'm even crazier because I don't want to throw you out.

"I was scared you'd storm off when I told you about Gracie, and yet here you are, drinking my best single malt and telling me that I look good stuffed full with a dildo."

"I don't think those were my actual words." At her returning scowl, I raise my hands. "It's one of those things, baby. You take the rough with the smooth."

She rolls her eyes then rubs her cheek. "Your brother's in love with me?"

"Oh, yeah. Wants to be your Daddy Warbucks, but I wasn't going to let him get away with that. Recognized you the first time you moaned."

"Is that supposed to be a compliment?"

"It means your moans are very memorable."

"Jesus Christ." She shakes her head as she rounds the bar again, swiping past me.

At first, I think she's going to the door—that's her trajectory. But it isn't. Instead, she bends over, gracing me with a glorious view of her ass, and picks up the gear I brought with me and shoves it in a bag. Ignoring me entirely, she drags it to the rather empty side of the bar.

Reading her intent and knowing her silent acceptance of my gift is a silent acceptance of me, I traipse after her and collect the stuff that's still on the floor.

When I plunk it down, we stare at the loot.

"Do you do everything in excess?"

"Everything," I promise.

"God help me."

Though I chuckle, I murmur, "You should let us carry on—"

"—with the cam-girling? No way."

"Think about it." When she shakes her head, I grunt. "Just think about it for *me*. And if not that, then let's start up the classes again."

She bites her bottom lip but nods.

I'll take that win.

Deciding a change of subject is necessary, I grab a jersey and shove it at her. "You should wear this."

"It's signed."

"You already have—"

That's when she lets loose an explosive shriek. "Oh, my god! I could kill you for sending that damn jersey to me when I wanted nothing more than to throttle you for ghosting me!" She whacks me on the arm. "You suck!"

I wink. "I can lick far better than I suck. Let me prove it to you later."

"You'll be lucky if anything gets licked or sucked for the next century!"

"You're a hard taskmaster," I chide.

"You know it."

Though she sniffs, she doesn't toss the jersey down.

I hide my smirk—I'm not an idiot—then plead, "You know what would make my year?"

Her glance is suspicious to say the least. "What?"

"If you wore it on game nights. You can be my good luck talisman."

Her brow furrows. "Why would I be that?"

"Because I said so." I bat my lashes at her. "Plus, the thought of you wearing my name gives me an erection, therefore it's a win-win."

"Huh. So, what you're saying is it's not about being a good luck talisman and about everyone in my bar knowing that I'm yours?"

"Exactly," is my smug retort.

"I should wear Gagné's to put you in your place."

Well aware she's teasing, I pout. "Not nice."

That earns me another eye roll, then she surprises me by dragging it on and doing a turn.

"Fuck." My voice is beyond guttural. "You look so hot."

"You're easy."

"For you. I figured that out months ago," I dismiss.

"I don't get it. I-I'm not that special."

"I need to prove to you that you are then."

"Is that really your job?"

"It is if I make it so."

She harrumphs but positions the gear I brought with me onto the shelves, muttering again, "I should toss you out of the bar for your nerve."

"I warned you months ago that I was cheeky," I inform her piously. "You can't blame me—"

"Sure I can." She clucks her tongue. "I'll wear it on game nights but you have to make it worth my while afterward."

"That is a deal my entire body can stand behind."

Her harrumph morphs into a laugh when she notices I signed one of the tumblers. "Look, it even has remnants of the authentic Cole Korhonen protein shake in it."

"The black mold will be priceless in ten years."

"If you say so." She smirks as she props it on a shelf.

"Did I tell you that I love how tall you are?"

"Used to be a curse on the ice. Had to get hella tall partners. They're a rare commodity."

"You really do need to teach me how to figure skate."

She gives me the side eye. "My rates aren't fourteen grand a week."

"They can be." I wiggle my eyebrows. "I need special aftercare."

At first, I think she'll be angry at my teasing, but she blows out her cheeks. "You think you're charming, don't you?"

"We both know I am."

That earns me another harrumph. "Can you put this helmet up there, please? I'm not tall enough to reach that shelf."

"If you wanted to check out my ass, you should have simply said so."

She slaps said ass. "Get moving."

Expression deadpan, I do as she requests. Mia even steps back and points out where she'd like certain pieces to go and I maneuver them where she wants. I don't even grumble when she has me turn them this way and that.

When she's done, she chuckles. "You filled up my shelves. Thank you."

There's something about how she says 'thank you.'

I could get addicted to it.

It's not throwaway. It's genuine. In fact, it's so genuine that the words take on a life of their own.

"It's my pleasure."

"You really didn't have to."

"And that's why I had to."

Stepping back to stare at our work, I accept that she's not lying—the walls are fucking *full*.

"You're weird," she comments, and I know why.

"We established that already. I didn't even realize I'd stolen so much. No wonder Gracie asked me if I'd pulled a heist."

That has her tensing. "I saw you hug her tonight."

"I told you—she's like my sister. Anyway, she's with Liam."

"I know. I didn't mean I was jealous." That earns me my fourth harrumph of the night. "I mean… I saw her and you and I knew I had to tell you."

"You didn't invite me over to fuck my brains out?"

"I didn't invite you over…" She rubs her brow. "I guess something is easier now."

"What?"

"I felt bad about two-timing you guys. Mr. *CalKor*."

"I get it."

Her brow furrows. "This whole night has gone completely differently than how I imagined it would."

"Are you pleased about that?"

She swallows. "I'm not ashamed of how I've earned money, Cole."

"I don't think you should be either. You were rolling in the dough. Hell, I'm jealous."

That lightens up her solemn expression but not for long. It shifts until… "You didn't… tell anyone, did you?"

I squint at her. "Are you for real?"

"I know how guys can—"

Turning to face her, I cup her chin. "Baby, I wanted you to go private so that no one else could look at you like that. You think I'd tell my team?"

Her bottom lip gets sucked in between her teeth. "Does Gracie know?"

"Of course she doesn't. No one knows about you apart from two of my bros, and they don't know that you do cam-girling. One knows your name and Liam's the one who told me I had to break things off with you for Gracie's sake."

Her eyes flutter to a close. "You need to tell her, Cole. I can't betray her again."

I pull a face. "I know I need to tell her and I will. I couldn't before. You were a one-night stand. What could I say to her? What'd be the point of hurting her? But then, I got to know you—"

"We've barely talked," she chokes out.

Barely? Ha.

"You told me more than you know."

"Like what?"

How do I piece together my impression of her?

"You're generous too. You're not cheap or money-grabbing. I've never had someone sulk at me for tipping them before, never mind this supposed demoness who double-crossed my sister for clout." She flinches, but I ignore her to continue, "You're genuinely kind.

"I remember I told you about that time I hurt my wrist, and you were prodding me to go and get it checked out. We discussed grief and family and things that made us laugh on TV. And you remembered me. I didn't expect that."

Her cheeks flush. "I liked you."

"But we barely talked," I mock.

She shoves my shoulder. "I know what you mean. But it's still only an impression."

"An impression these past ten days continue to confirm." I hitch a shoulder. "I can wait. We can see this through. Maybe give it three months or so until we know we're serious—"

"You think we'll be serious after twelve weeks of dating?"

"I'm serious about you now."

"Who talks like you?!" she shrieks. "You're supposed to be freaking out and avoiding this kind of conversation."

I sniff. "How many times? I'm a *romantic*."

"You read the books for the dirty sex. Admit it!"

"I do not," I grumble. "That's an added bonus, and don't shame me for reading what I do! You need to read it too. You'd fit right in with one of the characters, trust me."

She squints. "How?"

"You like being fucked while you sleep. That's a whole separate group on Facebook. Never mind the monster cock stuff. Plus, the cosplay and that praise kink thing you've got going on. Then there's the exhibitionism, and you've made me realize I have kinks I didn't even know about—"

"Which ones?"

"Well, voyeurism for starters. Man, watching you strip out of your shorts gives me a chubby."

"Your dick lives up to that. The alien cock is my biggest dildo and you're still bigger."

"You're stroking my ego."

Her lips roll inward.

I smirk at her. "See? Your kinks and my kinks are like a match made in heaven. Okay, fuck a few months. Give me eight weeks to prove to you that we work, Mia, and then I'll tell Gracie."

She huffs. "This has disaster waiting to happen written all over it."

Like I'm approaching a pissed-off momma bear, I tentatively cup her cheek. As my thumb swipes over her jawline, I wink. "There's beauty in chaos, gorgeous."

THIRD PERIOD

WEEK ONE

CHAPTER 27
MIA

WHILE HE LETS me maneuver him around at the side of the rink, he complains, "I thought we'd be doing this on the ice!"

I grunt at him as I curve his arm around me, showing him how to hold me. "You're the one who chose the *Boléro*."

"I'm regretting that."

"If you expect me to let you lift me, we have to prepare you for that here."

"I'll pick something easier."

"Whatever routine we decide on, you'd have to practice off-ice. It makes no sense to risk it on a slippery surface."

"Can I at least lift you up by the ass?"

Twisting back to look at him, I grin. "You're begging to get slapped, aren't you?"

He pouts.

Shouldn't be cute, but wouldn't you know… it is.

I shake my head at him as I motion how I want him to do a spin.

His nose crinkles but he does as I ask, holding his leg out to match my angle and slowly moving around in a circle mid-hop.

We've been practicing this every class, but he has balance issues so I always start and end a session with him this way.

When he falls again, I tilt my head at him. "Aren't you grateful for padded yoga mats?"

His chest puffs up. "I know how to fall on the ice."

"Yeah, but best if it's cushioned at first."

He flops onto his back. "This is harder than it looks."

The muscles he has to use are both the same and somehow not.

Despite that, I didn't think he'd struggle as much as he does. Still, that's how this all started—he came to me for lessons for a reason.

Drifting to the floor beside him, I murmur, "I wish you'd get better too, you know?"

"Charming!"

I elbow him. "I miss the ice. I couldn't go all summer."

He turns his head to the side. "We could do a couple laps now."

"No. Because you're a huge child who'll end up trying to do a spin on there because logic reasons that if you can't do a spin with a flat foot, you'll be able to do it on a blade.

"I refuse to be the one who takes out *the* Cole Korhonen."

"It's annoying how well you know me."

I smirk. "You're easy to read."

"Speaking of…" He leans over to grab his bag. I roll my eyes when I see the new branding. Spotting my eye-roll, he pats it. "Snazzy, huh?"

"What was Mega X thinking?" I mumble. "It looks like you've got blood spatter on the bag."

He studies the canvas. "It does now that you mention it."

"Anyway, if they wanted to get you something personalized, why didn't they borrow from your personal color scheme?"

That has him blinking at me. "I have one?"

"Yeah." His confusion has me blinking back at him. "You always wear something purple or lime green. Always. They're your favorites."

"Huh. Just thought I liked 'em."

"That's the definition of 'favorite,' isn't it?"

"True. Smartass."

I grin.

Then, when he gets a book out of his duffel bag, I groan. "No, Cole! No fair."

"Yes fair. I'm going to read that encyclopedia snor-annica you gave me—"

"It's Isaac Asimov!"

"This is my version."

I stare at it. "This is...strange." It's not like any paperback I've ever seen.

Is it leather?!

He shrugs. "It's been bound."

"Bound?"

"I made it. Specially."

I gape at the book. "For me?" I look at the embossed front. The leather. The braiding on the spine. The gold scrollwork. "*You* did this?"

His lips twist into a sheepish grin. "I was taught how to do some leatherwork when I was a kid. Plus, I know you love *Star Wars*, and while you seem to have a personal grudge against romance, we both agree Reylo should be a thing."

I refuse to cry. "You bound a fan fiction for me?"

"Hey, there's a whole universe of smut out there, so I gotta start you off slow."

I stare at the book a tad dubiously. "Is the world building good?"

He kisses his fingers. "Would I give it to you if it weren't?"

"True."

"I mean, you're not as kind as I am because I think you gave me a dud. I can read a whole book a day, Mia, and I've barely cracked the spine on that Smirnoff book."

"Asimov!"

He sniffs, but there's a pleased smile on his face as he watches me riffle through the pages.

"I can't believe you did this."

"I can't either. Trust me, it was fucking hard."

I snicker but it's soon replaced with a shocked gasp when I see some illustrations. Naughty ones.

His grin widens. "Hot, right? Trust me, the writing's hotter. I didn't draw them but I had them commissioned for you."

I clap the book to my chest. "You gave me porn!"

Cole knows I'm teasing, but he still looks smug as he settles back on the mat and hooks his hands behind his neck. "I only give out the good shit."

I hide a smile as I lie flat at his side, holding the book above me.

A moment later, I slip past page one to two.

His head falls on my shoulder and I can tell he's reading with me.

My throat feels… clogged.

I know that makes me sound like I have nasal drip, but it's more emotional than that.

This feels good.

Better than good.

I blow out a breath and continue reading, hyperaware of his skin against mine…

An hour later, we haven't moved apart from him switching over to holding the book when I got pins and needles in my arms.

That's when he yawns. "We're really not going on the ice today?"

His yawn triggers one of my own as I straighten up and half-crawl across the mat toward my purse that's shielding something I know he'll loathe.

"No freakin' way!" He crosses his pointer fingers like I'm a vampire he's trying to avoid the second he claps eyes on them.

"You need the toe picks."

"I need my *real* skates."

"No, you need figure skating skates."

"I don't use them during games," he exclaims.

"These aren't to be used during games. Just for our practice. If you want on the ice with me then this is your only path to achieving that." I proffer them at him, hiding a smile when, pouting, he trudges over to me to take them.

He looks at them like they're shit in his hand and, grumbling, huffing, and muttering too, puts them on.

His eyes widen when one's fastened up tight. "These are so fucking heavy."

"Stop whining."

I plunk my ass on a nearby bench and strap myself into matching skates.

He wiggles his foot. "My ankle feels tight."

"Supported."

"My toes are pinching."

"Cry me a river."

He pouts again as he waddles forward. "How do you move in these?"

"With ease," I counter as, a couple paces later, I slide onto the ice.

The chill of the air, how it feels on my skin, the smell… it's home to me.

As I turn into a fast spin, I settle so that I can watch him wobble toward me.

"This is impossible."

"Nothing's impossible."

"This is. Why do people wear these? Hockey skates are so much better."

"Big baby."

He harrumphs but when I skate toward him and gently guide him, he improves quickly. He meant it when he told me he had to learn finesse—Jesus Christ.

By the end of our short twenty minutes on the ice, he's puffing away like he ran a marathon. But he managed a couple 'mini' spins with only one fall midway through.

"You're going to need a massage on your thighs," I inform him as I remove my skates. "You'll have used different muscles with these."

He pulls a face. "I haven't fallen like a noob in years."

I know he's genuinely hurting because he doesn't ask me to 'rub him off' later.

Doesn't make me cut him any slack, though.

"Lies. I've seen you during a game."

"There's a difference between being fed the stick and being forcibly tripped and skating in a straight line."

My lips curve. "Are you going to be this much of a brat throughout every class?"

His only answer is a grunt.

I'll take that as a yes, then.

Once he's on *terra firma*, he's back to the regular Cole I know and… *like*.

"We should grab coffee. I need to be at the rink in an hour for the game."

Nodding, oddly relaxed and happy from being in his company even if part of that included him whining like a toddler, I gather my things and dump them in my bag as he does the same.

Admittedly, I don't dump the book.

I place that carefully in my hoodie, well aware that the cafeteria here is heated below temperatures befitting the gateway to hell so it'll be more useful as padding for my gift.

From the pleased glint in his eye, he notices my careful handling of the book.

As we drift upstairs, he snags a hold of my hand.

It's only a light knotting of our fingers but I like that too.

So I squeeze back.

Then, we make it to the cafeteria and he orders my usual—he remembers from our day dates—and he also requests my favorite sandwich—egg salad with pickles.

When we take a seat, he watches me guzzle half a bottle of water before I unfasten the wrapper.

"What?"

He shrugs. "Nothing."

I roll my eyes at him—I do that a lot—then eat before I bombard him with questions about the book.

"I'm not going to tell you how it ends." He gasps, his tone horrified. "That would spoil it!"

"But I'm asking for spoilers!"

"I don't care. I don't do spoilers and neither should you." He shoves the sandwich at me, making me realize that I left half. "You want that?"

I nod.

"Then eat it before I do."

"You could buy your own," I grumble, holding the sandwich in my hands like it's lost treasure.

"Where'd be the fun in that?"

He grins at me as I take a big bite then tries to steal my coffee. It'd be rude not to lick the opening.

Of course, it has the opposite effect—his eyes darken.

"You think some spit is gonna stop me? Shared more than that with you, baby."

"Stop stealing my food!" I snipe, peering around the cafeteria to make sure no one is listening in.

He smiles once he notices what I'm doing then settles back in his seat. "You thought about my offer?"

"And we were having such a wonderful conversation too!"

Cole sighs, but his expression is sheepish as he scratches his jaw. "When we start dating publicly—"

"If," I correct.

"*When* we start dating, it'll be a PR nightmare if someone catches you on that site, baby."

His tone is soothing, but it still agitates me.

"I have to work."

"I know you do, and I support that wholeheartedly."

"I won't let you pay my bills! It was different before. I was earning market value for my services and as much as I love talking to you twice a day, I'm not going to charge you for it."

"But I'll—"

"No! It cheapens what we have and that's the last thing I want. You can't just cover my bills. My debts are too big. It wouldn't be fair on you. And, no, I'm not charging fourteen grand for figure-skating lessons either."

He scrubs his hand over his head. "I'm not sure what to do, Mia."

"I have enough to cover me for a couple months. I don't have to do anything yet," is my calm retort.

"Yeah, I guess."

I know he's not happy about it, and I get it.

I grab his hand. "This is my problem. Not yours."

"If we're dating, which we are…" His words are pointed. "It's *our* problem."

"Maybe in seven weeks it is, but for now, it's not."

Even then, I can't just take money from him.

"The idea of you being on that site—" He digs his fingers into his eyes but he doesn't finish the sentence.

I'm not happy about the idea of cam-girling when we're dating either. I'm out of options though. Unless the bar suddenly takes off or an influencer visits…

Crazier things have happened, right?

It's foolish to put this conversation off but I want to bury my head in the sand for a little while longer.

He squeezes my fingers. "Did anyone ever tell you that you're stubborn?"

My smile is sad. "Why do you think Gracie and I got along so well?"

LATER THAT NIGHT

Mia: *sends image*

Cole: Oh. My. God.

Cole: You can't be sending me porn before a game, babe.

Cole: I know I gave you the good shit, but I didn't expect you to reciprocate.

Mia: *snickers* It's me. In your jersey.

Cole: I repeat. P.O.R.N.

Mia: Shut up lol.

Cole: No shutting up.

Cole: How can I shut up? I get to see you in that AND touch you now. Do you know how fucking torturous it was watching you on cam with my jersey on?!

Mia: Poor baby.

Cole: Yes. Very poor baby. I SuFFeREd, Mia.

Mia: You suffered, or was it your dick?

Cole: My dick belongs to me.

Cole: So, both of us.

Mia: I know it's big but it's not its own entity.

Cole: Says you.

Cole: That's it. This is a thing. You're going to become a part of my pregame rituals for real.

Mia: Your pregame what?

Cole: Hockey players are superstitious.

Mia: You're not superstitious.

Cole: I am in my own way. I always tie the laces
on my left skate first, have to listen to at least
one Taylor Swift song, and if I don't eat a banana
then the world WILL come to an end.

Mia: You're so melodramatic.

Cole: It hurts that you didn't know that already.

Mia: *plays world's tiniest violin*

Cole: You will, though, right?

Mia: Find the smallest violin in the universe?

Mia: Sure.

Cole: NO. Send me porn before every game.

Mia: *snorts*

Mia: Sure

Cole: You made me a happy man

Mia: You're too easy sometimes lol

Mia: xo

Cole: You have to include that as well.

Mia: Include what? Aren't you busy listening to
Taylor Swift and tying your laces a certain way?

Cole: Send me an 'xo.'

Cole: Them's the rules.

Cole: No porn without an 'xo.'

Mia: *sighs*

Mia: xo

Cole: :D

42

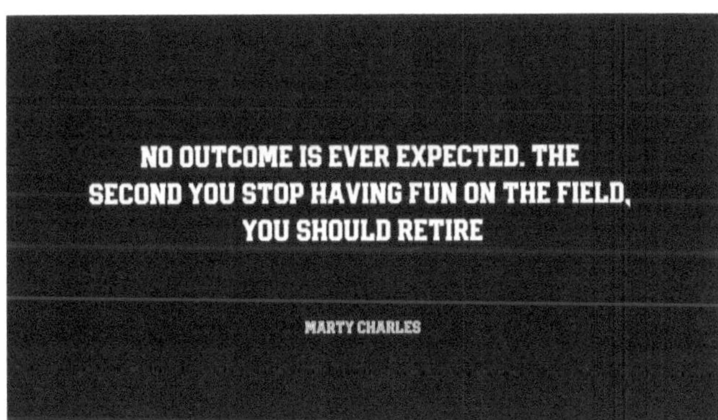

"WHY ARE YOU IGNORING ME?"

The holler comes over the crowd, making my head whip around to find the source.

My brows lower when, rink side, I spy my agent, Hailey Pirenzi, with her arms folded and a dour glower aimed my way, *and* wouldn't you know it? That chick who always wears the other team's jersey is sitting beside her.

McIsaac is right about her being a pest.

Aware my focus has shifted off the game, I try to snatch it back, but that split second of inattention has one of the jerks from Tampa Bay, Berg the Big Bastard, slamming me into the boards.

Lewis slides past, feeding the asshole his stick.

And, of course, the ref is going to call *that* and not the boarding that happened seconds before.

Kyle gets sent to the sin bin, leaving it up to Liam and me to kill this penalty while trying to even the score.

With us trailing by one, I refuse to let this game head to overtime.

Tampa Bay wins the face-off, but it's like Liam and I are playing with the same brain. He swerves around one of the forwards, getting in his face, as I sweep to the side and sneak the puck out from under his nose, tipping it through their goalie's legs.

The crowd roars as it hits the back of the net and a barrage of Stars' players jump on me—these are the best kinds of hugs.

But a sharp whistle sounds, cutting our celebrations short.

We look for the source and see it's Gracie. She's practically vibrating in the mouth of the tunnel—Coach had a massive hissy fit the last time she was behind the bench.

Noticing she has our attention, she sticks her fingers in front of her eyes and points it to Liam.

I've no idea what any of that means, but he apparently does and nods in understanding.

Everyone's confused but with Gracie as the big boss, it's becoming par for the course.

I can tell some of the defense are annoyed at her interference when Liam calls for a time-out.

As we huddle together, Gagné demands, "What the hell's the GM doing?"

"What Bradley's too chicken shit to," Liam derides. "Okay, we need to rile them up and Cole's the way to do that."

I don't bother arguing with him—he's right. "Berg's got a massive problem with me since I told him that he needed to stop checking out my ass."

McIsaac blinks. "You told him that?"

Liam snickers. "That's why he hates you?"

"One of the many reasons why."

"Be the pest that you are," Liam prods. "Distract him."

Contemplatively, I chew on my guard. "However I want?"

"Aside from mooning him, yeah," he warns, earning a bunch of chuckles from the rest of the team. When my eyes grow round with the promise, he quickly tacks on, "And anything that'll get your big ass hauled into the box."

Pouting, I mumble, "Honored my big ass is."

"Kick it with the Yoda shit. Look, Berg's the only one on their offense who's worth anything. We fuck with his head, we can maybe gain some ground and keep those two points for ourselves."

That's when he breaks out a quick play that's not in the playbook we study like it's a Bible.

He finishes by rallying, "Let's take care of business, guys."

My brow puckers at how well he laid down the law but the others look uneasy.

"Hey, he's our captain," I holler, elbowing Deschamps a couple times until he glowers at me. "In Liam we trust, right?"

Apparently, I said that louder than I thought because the front rows start chanting it.

Liam shakes his head as the chants turn into an outright roar but he ignores it to call, "We got this. RIGHT?"

As he receives a bunch of wary nods, we break out. A few look at Bradley, who's bright pink with rage at having 'time out' called without his approval, but somehow, that seems to seal his fate.

We glance at each other, smirk, and tip our chins in accordance.

That's when I line up at center ice, ready to win the draw.

Berg skates in front of me, looking as if he's got shit under his nose. I grin and pucker my lips then smack 'em together. The asshole reacts like I stuck my tongue down his throat—he wishes.

I waggle said tongue before the whistle blows, my mouthguard back in place, but Berg's too busy being offended to win the face-off, so as the puck drops, it'd be rude not to take possession. I pass it back to Deschamps who spots Liam at the Tampa Bay blue line.

True to the moniker of the early days of his career, he flies like Peter Pan toward the goal. Highly aware that the clock is ticking and that we are in the last minute of play with a man down, I rush the net to crowd their goalie as Liam ordered.

Through some inspired stick work, Liam takes aim at the top left corner of the goal. One wrist shot later, the puck beats the buzzer and gives us the win.

"What was that?" I roar in Liam's ear.

He pulls that DeNiro move that Gracie made earlier but his grin is wider than the Cheshire Cat's. "She said to do what Bradley can't. I listened."

"What can't he do?"

He winks as he slaps me on the shoulder. "Coach."

With a 3-2 win, two points for us and zero for Tampa Bay… *in Liam we fucking trust.*

And twenty minutes later, when I lock the door to the locker room so none of the coaching staff can get in, a roar of cheers explodes as we cele-brate the win that one of our own drafted.

If Bradley threatens us with more bag skating in the morning from the other side of the door, that's not enough to dampen our mood.

The only reason we open up?

Because Gracie asks.

Nicely.

If tonight's stunts didn't severely damage Bradley's ego, then my name's not Cole Korhonen.

CHAPTER 29
COLE

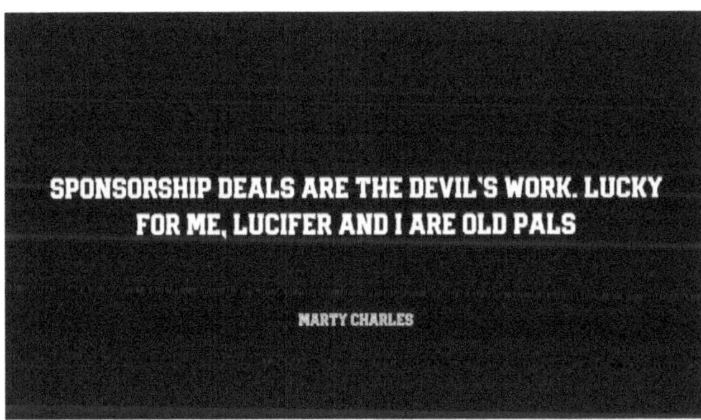

"THAT WAS SO IRRESPONSIBLE," I mutter when Hailey Pirenzi accosts me in the tunnel outside the locker room. "I was concentrating."

"Irresponsible is locking your coach out of the dressing room. Anyway, you've been ignoring my calls."

"For a reason."

She dismisses that with a frown as she scans me up and down. "What's with this ensemble, Cole? How many times do I have to send you clothes from Nordstrom for you to wear the damn things?"

"I never like what you send me," I reason as I stare at my jeans, shirt, and oversized sweater. "What's wrong with my outfit anyway?"

"It's pink and purple. Those brands I send over would like to use you in their campaigns."

"Yes, and I don't agree with their ethos. Fast fashion is destroying the earth," is my pious reply.

"Bullshit. If I threw some bright blue pants in there, you'd be A-OK with whatever I sent. I'm telling you since you started playing with the Stars, your dance card floweth over.

"Why aren't you answering your agent's calls, Cole? I'm starting to get offended."

I stride a few steps ahead of her toward the exit, where I sign a couple of the waiting fans' memorabilia. Only when we're outside do I answer, "Because I've been busy."

"That's no excuse."

"Sure it is. I've decided not to worry about sponsorships this season."

Her brows lift. "Why would you make a foolish decision like that? You're at the peak of your career."

"I'm not arguing that, but I've already had my morals called into question by having Mega X as a damn sponsor, Hailey. Don't you think we should cool it or, you know, you could vet the sponsors better?"

"That's bullshit about the added 'benefits' to their shakes," she dismisses, jumping into my car before I can tell her to get lost.

"Whatever, I had to face that in front of the press so…"

"I heard Gracie Bukowski handled that rather well."

"She's willing to get mauled to protect her players."

"Unusual."

"That's Gracie. First female GM and all—she's bound to do things differently."

"I said unusual, not different. Don't underestimate her. Tigers can turn on their own."

The words, unfortunately, cut close to the bone.

But not for the reason she might imagine.

"Of course, you're in the safe zone seeing as you were a Bukowski billet boy."

I sneer at her. "Thank fuck for small mercies, eh?"

"Speaking of Canada—"

"When were we speaking of Canada?"

"You said 'eh.'"

"Sue me."

"I will if you don't live up to the promise of your contract. Why would I keep you as a client if you're not willing to take on any sponsorships?"

"Is your commission suffering?" I mock.

"You're my top player, Cole! I won't let you waste the opportunities that are being thrown at you."

"Then find brands that align with my ethos."

"Since when do you have an ethos? What is it anyway? That purple and green are a great color combo?"

"They are."

"Only if you're colorblind or the original Joker." She pinches the bridge of her nose. "Tell me what your ethos is/are and I can tailor the offers to your requirements."

Ah, shit.

She called my bluff.

Mostly, I want to be left alone to play hockey and date/fuck Mia…

Still, Hailey's looking at me expectantly so I mutter, "Something green."

"Clothes?"

"No! Something that saves the earth."

"You play a high fossil fuel-consuming sport and come from a family of ranchers—your carbon footprint is the size of the Amazon that you're stomping on—"

"All the more reason to do something that counts."

That's when I realize Burrows's pulling into the underground parking in my building.

Fuck.

Five minutes later, Hailey's still grousing at me as I make it to my front door where Liam and Gracie are waiting.

Gracie scowls at Hailey. "What the fuck are you doing here, Pirenzi?"

Hailey merely smiles at her. "Gracie, what an honor that you know my name."

"All I know is that you got my player clipped today. What the fuck was that about?"

Hailey folds her arms across her chest. "I had to speak to him."

"Do it on his own time."

"What do you think I'm doing?" Hailey retorts.

Finger prostrate, Gracie narrows her eyes and wags it—Liam and I automatically shuffle to the left. "You should get lost."

Hailey sniffs. "Maybe you can talk some sense into him. He's refusing sponsorships."

"That's his prerogative."

"No, that's monetary suicide. He's got eight years at the most to make enough money to live off for the rest of his life—"

"You do know who his father is?"

Hailey scowls, knowing she's lost her argument. She slaps the button to the elevator and, to me, snarls, "Send me more of this mission statement of yours and I'll find you the fucking brands. Don't bitch at me if they can't afford to pay exorbitant fees for a suddenly eco-conscious hockey player."

With that, she steps into the elevator and, a mocking smile locked in place, flaps her fingers at Gracie.

As the doors close, I wouldn't be surprised if that turned into her flipping us the bird.

Liam's brows skyrocket. "You're not taking sponsorships?"

Awkward.

"I'm busy," I excuse as I unlock the door.

"Doing what? Playing with yourself?" Gracie responds.

When I think about how I spent most of the summer, I snicker. "Something like that, G, yeah."

She rolls her eyes and heads into the kitchen. Before I can ask why they're here and not in their own pad, I realize she's holding—

"HOLY FUCK, ARE THOSE PIEROGI?"

"They are," she drawls.

Liam slaps me on the shoulder. "Well done tonight, bro."

"You scored most of the goals," I dismiss, focus locked on the carb-heaven in Gracie's arms.

No one makes 'em like Gracie or Hanna, her mom.

"Yeah, but you were your usual annoying self and it worked like a charm." He smacks his fingers to his lips. "When you waggled your tongue at him, I thought Berg was going to cry."

"It wasn't even my best work," I jeer. "How did you know I'd piss him off?"

"I've watched you play for years," Gracie reasons with a laugh. "I've never known anyone to get into more shit than you."

"Hey!"

"What? It's the truth. You're lucky you're damn good at what you do, otherwise you'd be off the roster with that pesky attitude of yours. How you've only broken your nose twice is a miracle."

"You make me sound like Shaggy!"

"From *Scooby Doo*?"

"From where else?"

"God, you'd try the patience of a saint."

"Maybe that's who you should be a spokesperson for," Liam jokes. "Hanna-Barbera."

I shove him and, like magic, he ends up with his head under my arm as I scrub the top of it with my knuckles.

"Boys!" Gracie barks.

Of course, we ignore her.

She isn't GM here.

Liam manages to sweep my feet out from under me, and as I plunk on my ass, he winks as he hauls me back into a standing position.

"That's all that experience you have under your belt," I mock as I rub my hip.

"Watch yourself, Cole, seeing as I'm older than both of you."

I point my fingers at my eyes then at her. "I see you, Gracie."

She smirks. "It worked, didn't it?"

"Since when are you running plays?"

"Wasn't really a play. Just something Liam and I talked about last night. He said that if you were on your way to overtime, he should position you at center because you'd be a pest and it'd make for easy possession. The focus would shift to you and he could swoop in and score. I told him he was right about you being annoying and to run with it if I gave him the bat signal."

I have to shake my head at her. "Bradley looked real happy about it."

"Oh, I'm sure he'll complain in the morning." She prays to the sky. "I'm so tired of his bullshit. I had him revisit all his plays because it's happening a-fucking-gain. Shoot-outs! I refuse to lose the Cup this season because he's stuck in the last century."

"I thought you'd have fired him already."

She purses her lips. "We're not even two months into the season."

"You're quick to react."

"If we fire him, we'll have to pay out of his contract."

"So? Not like the team can't afford it."

"Of course we can. I don't think he *should* get paid out."

Liam snickers as he steps around the counter to hook his arm over her shoulders. "So, you're being petty, *minou*?"

"Just for the moment. Until he pisses me off." Her eyes darken. "He's on borrowed time though."

"We'll bring it home for you, *bébé*. With or without him."

"You better." She nuzzles her head against his chest in a gesture that makes my heart ache with how raw and real it is. "I intend to break those glass ceilings Cole won't stop talking about."

Because I know she means it, I murmur, "We will, G."

She looks at me. "I *know* you will."

I shiver. "That sounded like a threat, little bit."

"I *am* your pierogi dealer."

Her doubling down on the threat has me staring at her with big, wide puppy-dog eyes. Still, I have to point out, "Not much of a pierogi dealer when this is only the second time you made them for me since I became a Star."

When she throws a frozen one at me, I catch it and wink at her.

Korhonen: I wondered when you fuckers were going to let me into this chat

Korhonen: I'm officially labeling this 'Stars. Huddle. In. Text' BTW.

Lewis: We didn't know you were worthy of being included in the conversation

Lewis: But you just confirmed it lol

Donnghal: More like you forgot to add him

Gagné: After I prompted you TEN times, Lewis

Gagné: AFTER it took you almost the whole of last season to make it

Donnghal: Maybe we need a new keeper of the text chat lol

Lewis: Hey!

Greco: What the fuck was that last night?

Donnghal: Which part?

Greco: The part where you and the GM had some kind of silent conversation and suddenly, you're running HER plays?

Donnghal: You got a problem with winning, douche? Anyway, it was something I came up with recently.

Greco: I wanna know what the fuck's going on.

Lewis: We won. Does it matter?

Greco: Of course it matters. How the hell are we supposed to keep on winning if we're not running the playbook?

McIsaac: I don't see why it matters.

Greco: Because you're all being shortsighted.

Greco: Look, I hate Bradley as much as you dipshits do.

Greco: If mutiny is the aim of the game, then I'm down for that, but we need to be on the same page.

Korhonen: IS mutiny the aim of the game, Liam?

Donnghal: You said it yourself—Bradley isn't liked.

Korhonen: His plays ARE ancient.

Gagné: Plus, he's a bigot.

Korhonen: What did he say?

Gagné: He doesn't like that you wear hot pink.

Korhonen: That ASSHOLE. My hot pink pants rock.

Donnghal: A sentence I never thought I'd read lol.

Korhonen: It's official. I'm on board.

Greco: All it took was him dissing your pants?

Korhonen: My pants are special to me.

Greco: Jesus H. Christ.

McIsaac: You noticed we're doing more and more bag skates?

Lewis: Yeah. But I'm faster than I was so as much as I hate that, it's working.

Donnghal: You think Gracie wouldn't have given him hell if it wasn't old school? Punishing us like that is antiquated. So are the rest of his moves. He has no control over us and this is how he's trying to dominate us.

Greco: So, we all know you're related to the owners… Why don't you get them to toss him out?

Greco: Oh, and Davies, if Bradley hears anything about this conversation, I'll make you one with the posts. I.e. they'll become part of your body. You hear me?

Donnghal: Yeah, what happens in the chat, stays in the chat.

Davies: Of course!

Donnghal: Who'd we get to replace him?

Korhonen: Is that crickets I hear?

Donnghal: Gracie's looking for a replacement, but she'd actually like us to win the Cup so we're stuck with him until she finds the right guy.

Korhonen: Doesn't mean we can't make his life hell until she figures shit out.

Lewis: I'm all for that.

Lewis: Pussy power!

Donnghal: How many times have I told you not to mention her pussy, Lewis? You got a death wish, I swear.

Korhonen: He can dream, Liam. Let's face it,
Gracie'd chew him up and spit him out.

Lewis: What a way to go though.

Korhonen: Okay, I'll hold him down, Liam, and let
you have at him.

WEEK TWO

CHAPTER 30
COLE

Blank Space - Taylor Swift

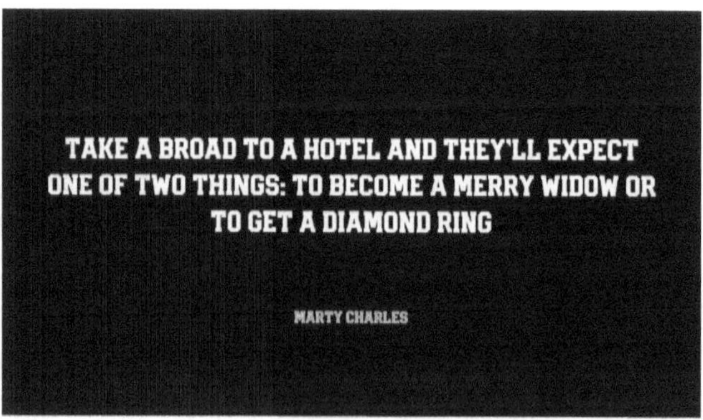

"GOTTA GO, CALLAN," I inform my baby bro when I see Mia's limo drive onto the hotel forecourt. "Lemme know how the history project goes."

His huff is all the farewell I get, but Mia more than makes up for it.

"You are crazy and I'm here for it!" Mia crows as she steps out of the car, arms wide in a silent invitation for me to wrap her up in a massive hug.

I grin at her. "Baby, you can't tell me that you've never left the tristate area before and not expect me to make that right."

She beams a grin back at me as she twists in my hold to stare around the hotel entrance. "I can't believe I'm in Nashville. I work out to country music all the time."

My brows lift. "You?"

"Yeah. My dad loved it. He used to make Mom dance around the kitchen to some of the greats almost every night. I think, eventually, he made her a fan too, but she'd never have admitted it."

Normally, when she brings up her parents, she gets sad. But not with this memory.

She smiles, so wide and free that it feels like I've been blasted with sunlight after a long, cold winter on the ranch.

Huh.

Maybe home wouldn't suck so hard if she was there…

"How did I not know you were into country music?"

She hitches a shoulder. "It's a part of my mystery."

"Oh, that's what it is, huh?" I tease, but I draw her in for a hug. "It's so fucking good to have you here."

Technically, it's only possible because Liam is having to sit this game out thanks to stomach flu.

When I heard that Gracie also had to stay put in the city, I knew I could bring her here.

"We don't have much time before the game," I warn her.

"That's fine. It'll be neat to watch you play. I can see for myself if you've gotten better on the ice."

"Everyone's a critic," I complain. "And I didn't bring you out here as my coach!"

Her lips twitch. "No, you brought me out here for my company."

"That too." I curve my arm around her waist and decide to be fancy and twirl her into me. Though she laughs, she moves with me, swirling into my hold like she does during our practice. "Come and see our room. You won't want to leave it."

"Oh, I bet. Don't you bunk together when you're on the road?"

"Nah, not anymore. Anyway, you think I'd let you share with one of my teammates?" I hoot. "They'd be all over you like white on rice!"

A sparkle hits her eyes, one that doubles down as I take her into the hotel lobby.

She misses nothing—her gaze darting here, there, and everywhere with an excitement that I know I never had because this has always been my life.

Even without hockey, we traveled first class. Whether it was to five-star hotels or the luxury apartments that Pops owns all over the continent.

But Mia, I know, grew up poor. She oohs and ahhs at the most random shit, and her excitement is not only palpable but contagious. Enough that someone like me, who's hardened to this stuff, is feeling giddy too.

When we make it to the suite and a butler opens the door for us, I swear to fuck that she's about to start crying.

"This is for us?" she breathes.

I nod. "All for us."

For you, baby.

Her throat bobs as she stares at the massive crystal chandelier, then she darts into the bedroom where she releases a shriek of joy as she uncovers the massive tub in the center of the bathroom.

Then, she's by the wall of windows which have her peering onto the city.

Next, she ducks into the living room only for her to coo over the small kitchen that's stocked high with Champagne and all kinds of goodies and is gasping about that.

The butler's as stoic as ever but I'm chuckling at her antics, pleased that I could give this to her. Even more pleased as I watch her go that her butt is back to wiggling—I've cottoned onto her and know how to work my wiles on her appetite.

"That's all. Thank you," I inform the butler.

"I can return later to unpack Mrs. Korhonen's luggage."

Ah, damn.

That's so hot.

So fucking hot.

Logically, I know it's too soon but…

Mrs. Korhonen.

I wish.

I smile at him. "I don't think she'll have brought much for an overnight stay."

And she wouldn't be in it for long if I had my say, that's for sure.

Thankfully, he disappears, leaving me with my butterfly of a girl-friend who's still cooing in the living room whenever she flips on the switch for the big crystal chandelier.

When she sees me leaning against the doorjamb, watching her, she immediately flushes.

But I tut. "None of that."

"Sorry. I know I'm being gauche."

I watch as she maneuvers between items of furniture to get to me. "You're not gauche. I'm happy you're happy."

As my arms slide around her waist, she sighs as her hands settle on my chest. "You didn't have to do this."

I press a kiss to her forehead, enjoying how she nuzzles into me.

The gentle affection is something I've been missing without even knowing I did. That she doesn't like being touched makes it even more special.

Makes *me* feel even more special.

"Stop saying that I didn't have to do this. If I didn't want to, I wouldn't have. Simple."

"But it's true."

"If you keep on telling me that 'I don't have to do this,' I'm going to be worse than ever."

"Worse, how?"

"I'm not sure yet, but leave it with me and I'll figure it out."

She snorts. "Only with you does that sound like a threat."

I preen. "It's good that you know how this'll work."

Her lips curve as she stands on tiptoe to press a kiss to my lips. "I heard your little chitchat with the butler."

"Huh?" *Innocence is my middle name.*

"The 'Mrs. Korhonen' part."

I arch a brow at her in a silent demand to continue.

"You didn't correct him."

Just call me cherub.

"You, in fact, looked pleased that he called me that."

Ah, hell. I wasn't made to be an angel.

Allowing my hands to slide down to her ass, I draw her into me so that she can feel my erection. "That's how pleased I am."

She swallows, but it's how her pupils turn to pinpricks that has me hiding a smug smile.

"It's too soon for any of this kind of talk."

"Nah."

Her head rocks forward. "It is. But I feel it too, Cole. This is nuts."

"Deez nuts."

She rears back to scowl at me. "Be serious! I'm having a meltdown here. I'm standing in a gazillion-dollars-a-night suite with a man who makes me think about stuff I stopped believing in when my mom and dad died, and it's both terrifying and—"

That's when *she* scares the shit out of *me*.

Mia starts gulping down air like it's being rationed and her hand cups her throat. For a second, I watch her, certain that she's pulling my leg or something, but then she fights free of my embrace, flops at the waist, and starts gasping.

"What the hell?" I bend over so that I can see her face. "Do you have asthma?!"

Her cheeks are bright pink but her eyes are terrified.

Then, I remember that text chat we had weeks ago, back when I was *Kor* to her.

She said she dealt with panic attacks.

Unsure if I should be offended that the idea of being with me triggers one, I focus on getting her into a sitting position.

I hustle her around, something she permits because she's used to it after our daily sessions at the rink, and I get her to settle in the corner.

It might be the worst thing to do for someone who can't breathe, but it makes sense to me and she doesn't argue.

Then, encouraging her to raise her knees, I roll her forward so that she can dangle her head between them.

Slowly, I stroke my hand along her back. "Just breathe, baby. Breathe."

Gradually, she does, and the panic lessens. Sniffling, she turns into my side. "I'm so embarrassed."

"I think I should be the embarrassed one." I keep my tone gentle and maintain the slow passage of my hand down her spine. "The idea of being with me triggered that!"

"I can't be like my dad and you fit too well."

It's more of a wail than I like.

I sigh. "I mean, it's hard being perfect—"

"Cole!" When she slaps me on the chest, I grin at her. "Be serious."

"I am serious," I argue. "You don't know how tough it is going through life being this awesome, but you're lucky you get to sit on the sidelines and be a witness to it."

"Man, you're really selling the idea of a relationship," she complains, but her lips are curving into a smile.

I chuck her under the chin. "There's what I like to see," I rasp, smoothing my thumb along the curve of her bottom lip. "Does it terrify you so much? Us being together?"

"It terrifies me how much I like you."

"Why would that terrify you?"

"Because what if I *am* like my dad? What if—"

My brows lift as her words wane but I ask, "What if you're not?" She processes that in silence, though I softly tease, "I'm not averse to waking up to balloons filling the hallway when it's my birthday though."

She peeps up at me. "I loved it when I was a kid."

"I'm not a kid and I'm pretty damn sure I'd love it too."

Her bottom lip gets sucked in between her teeth to nibble on. "Stop being perfect."

"Again with the impossible missions, Mia. Who do you think I am? Hercules?"

"Let me guess, you were reading a book about that last night?"

"Yup. But his twelve trials were dates. It turned into an orgy. The minotaur's dick would have scared even you."

Though she laughs, she cuddles into me, tucking her knees against her chest then leaning them on me too. "I'm sorry for ruining this—"

"For ruining what?" I'm not about to let her keep on thinking that. "You haven't ruined anything."

"It's been a while since I had an episode," she admits. "It happened a fair bit after Chuck died, but I developed a plan of action and once the will was executed, it helped me cope."

"So, what triggered that?"

"You're starting to become someone I don't want to lose, Cole. But I have things that I need to do that don't align with your life. I'm not sure how to make it work."

Her tone might be weak, but the words hit me as if they're bullets. "We *make* it work," I rasp, my voice guttural. Loaded with my sudden desperation that this might not last.

Suddenly, I get why she lost her ability to breathe.

The prospect of her not being in my life…

I swallow down the sudden blast of terror. "No matter what, I'll always be here. I'm not going anywhere. Didn't this summer prove that?"

"It proved you're a creeper."

My heartbeat settles down at her teasing.

This is us.

This works.

We can make it last.

I know we can.

Lewis: Yo, saw that hot chick you were with…
Name?

Korhonen: Fuck you.

Donnghal: Hot chick?

Lewis: Yeah, thought I'd keep you in the loop
that your bro's pipes are being cleaned tonight.

Donnghal: Why would I need to know that?

McIsaac: We're all having to hear it in the locker
room. Why shouldn't you be involved because
you have the shits?

Donnghal: Christ, don't remind me.

Donnghal: PLEASE.

Lewis: Name!!

Korhonen: Why would I give you her name?

Lewis: You're only worried because I'm hotter
than you.

Korhonen: HA

Gagné: You're a big fat chirper, Lewis.

Lewis: NAME?!

Korhonen: Wun NiteStand

Lewis: BOOO

Donnghal: *snorts*

Greco: She really is banging.

McIsaac: Yeah, banging Korhonen :P

Korhonen: Since when was everyone interested in what goes down in my bedroom? Is it because I'M so hot that you're all jealous and wish you were her?

Gagné: Bahahahahaha. He's got you there, Lewis.

Lewis: I don't swing that way… could manage a threesome though.

Lewis: If your dick is as big as your ego lol.

Donnghal: Ah, shit, you made that ten times worse, Cole. Hahaha.

Korhonen: *sniffs* Don't you have a ton of pasta and ranch dressing to eat, Lewis?

TWENTY MINUTES LATER

Mia: I wasn't sure if you still wanted this tonight but…

Mia sends image

Mia: xo

Cole: *gulps*

Cole: You took that ahead of time, didn't you?

Mia: Maybe. It seemed important to you.

Cole: Thank YOU

Mia: Now, enjoy your Taylor Swift soundtrack

Cole: ^^

Cole: I should never have told you about that

CHAPTER 31
MIA

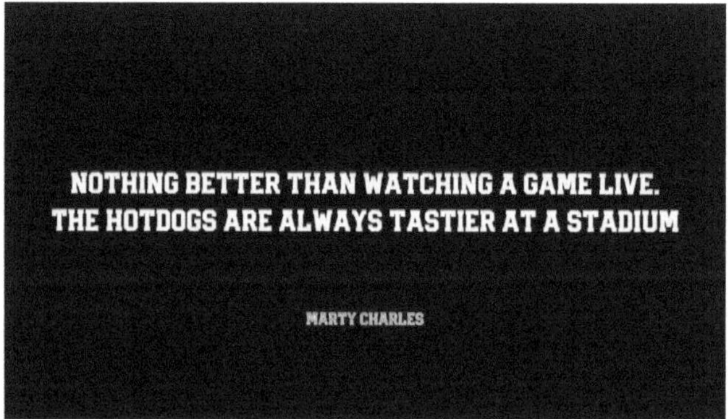

THE LIVE GAME is so much better than watching it on the TV.

For obvious reasons, reasons I agree with, Cole got me a seat in the nosebleed section.

He groused about it as he gave me the ticket, muttering that there was still a chance Gracie and Liam could see me on TV, and his grumbles grew even louder when I refused to wear his jersey in enemy territory.

I might need to squint at the ice and rely on the Jumbotron to keep updated, but the energy is vibrant. And, mostly, I'm just grateful.

Grateful that he wanted me here.

Grateful that he's willing to take a risk on me being spotted by people we're trying not to hurt.

Grateful that he cares.

Grateful that he brought me.

Grateful.

It peppers every interaction, every play, every moment, enriching the experience.

Despite Jarvis's lessons, I haven't learned much about the sport, but sometimes, you have to cut it down to the bare bones—there's a puck that both sides are trying to get into the other team's goal.

Two-hundred-pound guys armed with sticks will brutalize their way across the ice.

And, to make it more difficult, there are offside rules to comply with.

My favorite part is how they throw down helmets and gloves to start fighting—who does that?!

Hockey players, that's who.

My eyes are locked on Cole throughout the game. Even when he's on the bench, studying the iPad for plays, I'm assuming, I flicker my focus between him and the action.

An anticipatory buzz whistles through the arena, drawing my thoughts from him and onto the ice.

The game makes me think back to when I was a kid. All wide-eyed as I stared at the big beyond that's the world, trying to make sense of it, attempting to find some semblance of understanding of what's going down.

I grew up in stadiums like these; they're practically my second home, but it's different tonight. The *emotions* are different. People are excited and I'm literally breathing that in.

My focus darts around like a butterfly on crack because there's too much to take in so I'm taking in nothing at all, but I know I like this.

I like being a part of it.

The crowd suddenly goes wild.

My gaze narrows in on the action on the ice where I can see that Cole is being besieged by players in blue and white, all of them either clapping him on the back or punching him in the shoulder.

I have no idea what happened until there's a replay on the Jumbotron and I pump the air in celebration and grin wildly as I watch him being lauded by his teammates.

Unfortunately, that's when a Bobcats player skates past—someone shouts something and, from the epicenter of joy, a fistfight breaks out.

Linesmen try to drag the mob apart, but to little avail. That's when one of the Stars falls to his knees.

Which is when the 'fun' starts to derail.

Shocked, I gasp then squint as I try to make out who it is, but they're not getting up. And Cole's there, holding the others back as they almost trip over the fallen player in their haste to get a punch in.

Finally, the ref gets things under control and a paramedic runs onto the ice to tend to whatever the hell went down while I blinked.

Seriously, that's how fast it was.

Shortly after, the audience learns it's Gagné who was knocked down. Gagné who's unconscious. Gagné who hasn't woken up yet.

The glee from before has been replaced with outright fear as it's clear Cole's teammate isn't responding to what the EMTs are doing. A few minutes later, he's being carried off on a stretcher with an oxygen mask covering his mouth.

All around me, the crowd starts clapping, and on the ice, the players tap their sticks.

It's one of the most moving things I've ever seen in my life and my eyes prickle with tears at the sight.

I know, whatever's going on, I won't understand until the game is over, but Cole, more than anyone, is distracted. Somehow, he scores again, but the celebrations aren't as effusive as before.

Everyone, it seems, is thinking about Gagné.

Me included.

CHAPTER 32
MIA

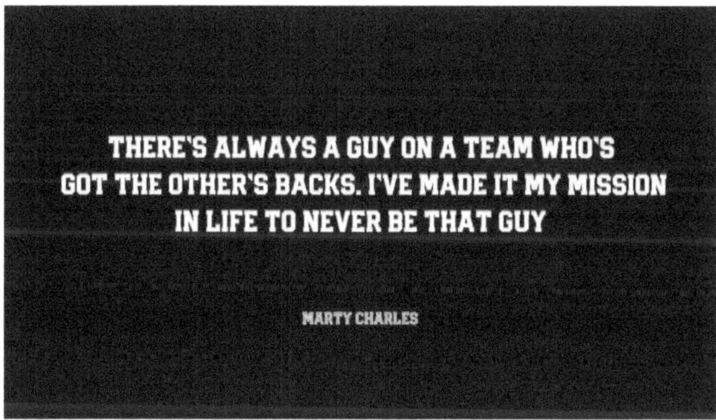

BY THE TIME we're back in our suite, my heart still hasn't stopped racing.

The whole game was a nightmare.

Gagné was taken to a hospital, Greco somehow broke his nose despite wearing his cage-helmet-thing, Lewis sprained a finger, and there were *four*, count 'em, *FOUR* fistfights on top of multiple busted noses. Never mind McIsaac, who got hit with a puck in the mouth and still came back to continue the game.

It'd be exhilarating if Cole weren't on the outskirts of every single one of those fistfights.

After Gagné, my glee shifted into fear as the realization struck—this sport is dangerous.

I mean, I knew that. Logically, I did. But seeing it with my own two eyes? Having skin in the game because Cole's out there dropping his gloves?

It's a miracle I didn't have another panic attack in the nosebleed section.

They won, but what consolation is that to my heart?

Their victory won't stop me from going into cardiac arrest.

Not that he knows.

He's been talking about points and where they're positioned in the standings and how Greco has a great GAA—whatever that is—since he got off the team bus.

I know why though—every two minutes, he's checking his phone for updates on Gagné but there's no news yet.

"We're going to do it, Mia. That Holy Grail is gonna be mine. I mean ours." He pumps his fist as he moves over to the small kitchenette. "Just wait until you see the ring. I need to add another to my collection—"

Toeing out of my sneakers, I turn to him, watching as he moves around the suite, utterly unaware that I'm feeling a little green around the edges.

Still, this conversation is almost… normal.

It makes me feel like this is actually happening.

Today has had a dreamlike quality to it, from the business class lounge to the seats in the air. Then, there was the car that picked me up and this suite, followed by the chance of watching him play in person.

With the panic attack and the game, this, *us*, feels real.

"I still can't believe how Gagné went down with the smallest hit. That hothead Bobcat punches like he's got a fist made of glass—" I don't want to think about how he knows that. "—so there's no way he got hit that hard. It's impossible."

"Is that supposed to reassure me?"

"Yeah, of course." He chugs down some water. "We had to get that fucker back for the hit. You saw that, right? Gagné goes down and that asshole wants to keep things going."

"It's pretty dangerous out there, isn't it?"

"Nah."

"There were *four* fistfights!"

He makes some 'pow pow' noises as he punches the air. "Got 'em good."

I swallow. "You got punched."

"Only because that asshole tried to—" My tone must register because he pauses. "Mia, you're used to bar brawls!"

"Not when the guys are walking on blades!"

He pshaws, then he sees my expression. "Are you okay, babe? You look… on edge."

I gape at him. "On edge?! Bet your damn ass I'm on edge. There were *four* fistfights, Cole! There were so many broken bones on the ice, the local ER is going to be crammed with hockey players! Gagné's in surgery!"

"It's only a punctured lung." When my already gaping mouth gapes wider, he clarifies, "You don't die from punctured lungs. Not when you're surrounded by EMTs and get airlifted to the nearest hospital. He won't die."

"He *won't die?*" I shriek at his weak reassurance. "He's playing sports! He *shouldn't* die."

He grimaces. "You've watched games before."

"Yeah, but live, it's different."

"It's better." His wink has me rubbing my temple.

He enjoys this. Not my horror. But this nightmare game that's both terrifying and exhilarating at the same time. Even beneath the concern for his teammate, the love is there.

"I didn't think it was so… so… *so…*"

"Hands-on. Fucking awesome, isn't it?"

"You could get hurt."

"Nah."

"Yes!"

"I mean, it doesn't happen a lot."

I narrow my eyes at him. "Why do I think you're lying?"

He rubs his chin and checks his goddamn phone. "It's not not a lie."

He's such a liar. I can smell his anxiety from here.

"It's not not not a truth."

Glee trickles into his gaze. "You're worried."

"Duh!" My hands go flying. "Four fistfights, Cole. A surgery. Broken bones! What's going to happen tomorrow?"

"We win again." He snorts at my huff but he snags a hold of my arm and draws me in for a hug. "I like that you care," he whispers, nuzzling his nose against mine.

I huff. Again.

"You're not used to dating people, are you?"

My brows lift at that out-of-the-blue question. "Not particularly. I'm better at hookups."

"That makes sense."

"It does?"

"You're more fidgety than a newborn filly."

He tugs me deeper into his embrace.

"That's what you're comparing me to?"

"Call it how I see it. I'm glad you were here tonight, Mia. Thank you for coming."

"Aside from… *everything*, I'm glad I came too."

He shoots me a goofy grin—I love how quickly his moods shift. "Aside from… you know… you enjoyed the game?"

"Aside from *everything*, I did. It's better live. More *real*."

"Of course it is! It'd have been ten thousand times better behind our bench."

"Yeah, I got some looks when you scored that final goal."

Cole chuckles. "You were the only one who was cheering for us in your section, huh?"

"For sure—"

His phone buzzes. His 'I'm so cool' mask drops as he fumbles it when he rushes to read the message.

His relieved sigh has me asking, "Gagné?"

"Out of surgery." Holding me tighter, he declares, "The next time you come to a game, you'll wear my jersey."

I can *feel* his relief. God, he cares so much. How could I not have all these crazy feelings for a guy like him? "I fail to hear the request there."

"That's because it isn't a request." His grin turns smug. "And after, I'm going to fuck you in it."

Amused by his dual nature, I trail my fingers over his jaw. "What if you lose?"

"You're going to fuck me and make me feel better about myself."

"Like you have confidence issues."

He graces me with another wink. "I'll have them for you."

"Gee, thanks."

Before I can continue, his mouth settles on mine.

I suck in a shocked breath, not expecting him to end our conversation that way. Though, from his boner digging into my stomach, I was short-sighted not to realize this was his intention. And hey, as a distraction, it's working.

With his tongue dominating mine, he picks me up and settles my legs on either side of his hips. The new position has my crotch rubbing against his dick and I let out a soft moan at the delicious friction.

He grabs a hold of my ass. The pinch of his fingers feels unexpectedly delicious, especially as he uses his grip to grind me onto him.

My arms settle on his shoulders and I clasp him to me as I fight fire with fire and begin the battle for dominance—it might have started in my mouth, but I won't settle until it's my tongue in *his*. But, the sneaky bastard knows my game.

Soft grunts escape him as I fuck his tongue while he walks us forward. I assume he's taking me to bed, but then he drops down in a somewhat controlled manner—though I still shriek—and he plunks my butt on a less-than-cushioned surface.

Popping one eye open, I see that he's placed me on the coffee table.

"Really?!" I watch him as he untangles his limbs from mine and gets to work on unfastening my jeans.

As he pulls down the zipper, he hisses when he sees the soft fluff of my pubes. "No panties?" he whines.

I smile at him.

"Why didn't you tell me?"

"Because I wanted you to win."

He snorts but slides his fingers through the neat curls before dragging my jeans off. "Jersey next time. And a skirt. That black one. The denim one."

"You like that, huh?"

"Yup. Can almost see your asscheeks. But definitely wear panties."

"Maybe I won't," I tease, watching his pupils contract. "Ooh, you like the idea of that. Someone in the stands seeing what belongs to you."

"Yes. *Mine.*"

My smile is cocky. "You could even fill me with your cum before the game."

He groans.

"You said all athletes have pregame routines. We could include that in your new one."

His eyes close. "You're killing me."

"I don't think so." Lowering the zipper on his jeans, I release his waiting cock into my fist and stroke him, rolling my thumb over his piercing with every pass. "And when you're away, I can leave you a little reminder of what's waiting for you when you get back."

As I clench down on his dick, hard enough to hurt, he grits out, "We'll video call?"

"Oh, no. I think we should record something special for you to watch before a game."

His eyes widen. "Are you being serious?" I know he likes that, not because his cock bobs in my hand, but because he pushes forward and practically climbs onto the coffee table to cover me.

"Deadly serious," I agree with a soft croon.

"Don't tease me, Mia. I'm on the fucking edge here."

"But it's so much fun."

His jaw turns to obsidian. "I want you more than I've ever wanted any other woman."

I blink at that declaration and it's stunningly easy to whisper, "And I want you more than I've ever wanted another man."

I seldom date, but my whole adult life, I've used apps like *Hooked-Up* to take the edge off. My 'urges' combined with Gracie's confirmation that there was great money to be had while working on sex lines was what spurred me on to register with the site.

But I'd gone one step further.

Though Cole has discovered kinks through me, I've always known I love being on display.

That *look but can't touch* thing gets my juices flowing.

"Have you made a sex tape with anyone else?"

I shake my head, wondering if he knows how special that makes him. But I'd love for him to think about the next time he can touch me. *Only him.* So this'll be fun.

He has to prod though. I *am* talking to Cole, after all. "Because you trust me?"

I nod.

"You trust me more than any man you've dated?"

"I don't date."

"You're dating me."

I hum.

"There's a compliment in there, right?"

I smile.

"Thank fuck I'm not alone with this. I swear to God, Mia, you drive me crazy. At least we're in this together."

I make a knot of our fingers. "I don't know how to be 'together' with someone. But I'd like to learn to be together with you."

His eyes narrow as he lowers his mouth to mine again. When his dick brushes my slit, both of us jolt, but then I moan as he starts to ride me. With every thrust, his cock slides through my folds, getting wet with me. Wet with what he brought out in me.

Then, he taps me on the nose with a reprimand of, "You won't distract me, witch."

My lips quirk but I let him do as he wants because I don't feel the need to take control—over months of us talking, I've learned that there's no fun in this for Cole if I don't get off too.

Multiple times.

The thought almost has me purring, but I prop my head up in anticipation. I'm so ready for him to fuck me that I might combust on the spot.

He doesn't disappoint.

One second, he's staring at my pussy, and the next, he's feasting on it.

I spread my legs wider to give him access to all of me, then I lean down and clutch at his head to make sure that he doesn't stop.

That he never stops.

I know he must taste his pre-cum but that doesn't faze him. He eats me out like he's been fasting for months, munching on me as if I'm his favorite snack. Maybe, given time, I could be…

As his tongue torments my clit with ceaseless pressure, his gaze locks on mine.

My eyes widen at the intensity in his, and I know there's no way this is ending without my orgasm.

His tongue shifts lower so his nose burrows into the upper half of my cunt. I'm not even surprised when it gets to work too, nudging the small nub as he thrusts into me, tasting me, sampling me…

I screech when he bites one of my pussy lips, the sudden shower of pain making the exquisite pleasure he's gifting me with all the more powerful.

That's when his teeth bite harder than before.

He follows that up by suckling my clit long and hard so that the pleasure and the pain combine, whittling down to my very core until it's practically a bomb blast that detonates inside me.

I didn't expect to come with the force of a battering ram, but I know that's what's happening because the glass of the coffee table is rattling against the frame.

A keening wail escapes me as he doesn't let up, not stopping until I'm sobbing from the continued brute force attack on my clit.

That's when, desperate, I scream his name and beg, "Cole, please, fill me. PLEASE. Fuck, I need your cock. Fill me. I need it. Tear me apart until I'm full of you—"

He snarls, gracing me with a final bite—on my clit this time. As I shriek in pain, his dick is there. Suddenly sliding into me. And I'm…

Confusion has my brow puckering, but it doesn't pucker for long.

Fuck, he's so wide.

I both forgot and remembered how goddamn big he is. Not sure how that's possible but there ya go.

My eyes clench closed as I struggle to take him all thanks to my pussy being tight from the repeated bolts of pleasure he gifted me.

He pushes forward.

Endlessly.

Until the folds of my sex tug apart from how wide he is and my bare clit is exposed to his pubis.

But it all felt easier than that first time.

Slippery.

Slick.

I stare down and realize he upended a whole bottle of lube between us because sweet fuck—

"Cole!" I cry, hands curving around his arms before I drag my nails along his biceps.

Where did he even get that bottle from?!

"You want my cum, baby? Tell me what you want," he demands, making my already sensitive clit throb.

"Give it to me. Give it all to me."

His fists fall to either side of my shoulders and he uses that as leverage to pump into me.

The thrusts are hard, but they're short. He's as deep in me as he can be, but it's the width that is agonizingly good.

I always knew I preferred girth to length, but this is so painfully good, I'm pretty sure I'm going to black out.

And how drenched we are means the friction has shifted until there's no discomfort, just pure pleasure.

God, the mess is going to be unreal afterward—I'm sorry for the maids who'll have to deal with it.

As I writhe on the coffee table, he continues plowing into me. I'm almost deaf to the noises I'm making because the one thing that's grounding me is the one thing that's making me fly free.

His teeth find my ear. Nipping the sensitive lobe, he forces a shudder out of me. "Beg me for it, Mia. Beg me for my cum."

I feel like I've been swallowing down nitrous oxide for the past twenty minutes—I'm giddy and light and happy—so it's no punishment to whimper, "I need you, Cole. I need you to fuck your seed into me. I want to be full of you. I want you to rub it on my clit. Please, please, please. Give it to me. Everything. I want everything…"

With a hissed *fucccck*, he blasts me with his release, pumping it into me for endless, torturous moments. I feel the edge of the peak he's had me hovering at, and I let myself tumble over the side into the waiting chasm.

It goes on forever but it could be seconds or an eternity.

I've never felt so connected to someone as I do with him. Never experienced such an intense welter of pain that's almost primal as it morphs into the most bittersweet of pleasures.

It rings in my ears, makes dark spots glimmer in my eyes, and sends a quake through my nerve endings that floors me.

When, eventually, I come to, I feel his weight on me because his head is resting atop my tits and it's hard to breathe.

I don't complain though.

I stroke my hands through his hair, feeling deliciously sore and beautifully sated, and let us both relax.

When he kisses my breast, that's when I realize, at some point, he tore open my shirt. But it was worth it to feel that soft caress.

After anointing both breasts with a kiss, he straightens, and that's when I see the state of him.

At some point, he also lost his sweater and his chest and arms are a mass of scratches. Because my nails are short, they're more like red ravines that I dug into him as he tormented me with pleasure. The softly puckered scar tissue on his abs wasn't spared either—Jesus, he turns me into an animal!

When he stares at himself then focuses back on me, I can read his smugness.

"I think someone lives up to their rep," is what he tells me.

My brow furrows in confusion, and when I rasp, "What do you mean?" I realize how loud I was screaming because my throat hurts.

He winks at me. "*KillerCatQueen7* has claws."

As I blush, he hauls me around until he lifts me into his arms and takes me to the bathroom.

I watch him putter after he places me on the counter. I let him run the bath, knowing we'll both end up in there once it's full.

As he moves, I study him.

He's a work of art, a conundrum, and my idea of dessert all rolled into one.

I'm not sure if I deserve to be this lucky, but I'll take it for as long as he lets me have him.

I'm not sure forever exists for people like me, but he makes me wish it did.

CHAPTER 33
COLE

LATER THAT WEEK

> **TEAMMATES WILL DRIVE YOU CRAZY.
> BUT THERE'S ALWAYS A CHANCE YOU CAN KNOCK
> 'EM OUT DURING PRACTICE**
>
> **MARTY CHARLES**

"WHAT'S THIS ABOUT?" Liam strides into my apartment once I open the door, not happy about the summons. "I see you assholes enough without eating into my free time too."

"Greco called the meeting." I shrug but pass him a kombucha because I know he prefers that to beer nowadays.

"And you let him host it at your place?"

"Knew it was the only way you'd come."

His harrumph tells me I'm correct.

What a surprise. Not.

"You're the last to arrive and you had the shortest journey," I taunt, earning myself the bird he flips at me before storming down the hall toward the furor that comes from hosting the whole team.

My apartment might be big, but it's bursting at the seams with so many of us hanging out here.

When Liam strides into the living room, however, he barks, "What the fuck is this about?"

"Killjoy," I mumble as I sidle in too.

Ignoring me, he folds his arms across his chest. "Some of us have better things to do than *this* so, Greco, get on with it. What's wrong?"

Though I shake my head, I don't say anything.

Liam's the most atypical captain going. I know he depends on Gagné for the 'caretaking' side of managing a bunch of egos, but the dude has yet to learn that you catch more bees with honey.

Plus, with Gagné still in the hospital, their power duo isn't worth shit.

"Is it true about Matthew Ellison being injured?"

The question takes everyone aback—Liam included. "What does that have to do with you? I figured this would be about Gagné."

"We all know how he's doing—he'll be back on the ice in a month or two," Greco retorts. "Answer the damn question. Is Ellison injured?"

"He hasn't told me if he is or not." Liam glances at me. "Has he told you anything about an injury?"

I scratch my chin. "No, but Matt's been pretty quiet now that I think about it."

Liam frowns. "Yeah. He has."

"That's unusual?" Greco prods.

Matt's relatively zen for a Bukowski billet brother, but that doesn't mean dick—zen for a Bukowski billet brother is like a regular person being hopped up on Adderall.

"I guess." Liam frowns. "I watched his game last night."

"He got switched out after the first period," I insert. "Maybe he *is* injured."

Liam unscrews the cap of his kombucha. "Why are you asking, Greco?"

"I heard a rumor that I need confirmed." He takes a sip of beer. "The Bulldogs want him gone."

Liam's brows lift. "Doubtful."

Greco hitches a shoulder. "You know Mack Finnegan? The PSN News' reporter?"

"That's your source?" I inquire.

"Sure is. Never let me down in the past… but if it's true, which I think it is, he'd be a cheap buy for the team."

"He's not a BOGO cut of meat from the grocery store."

"Aren't we all?" Lewis grumbles.

"Depressing but true," McIsaac confirms with a grunt.

Liam sips his kombucha. "You want me to tell Gracie about Matt, is that what this is about, Greco?"

"I figured it'd be smart to snap him up. I know the last time he was in New York, he sucked, but he was on fire last season. Dealing with an injury would be worth it to get him on the roster seeing as you're fucking useless, Davies."

My mouth gapes. "That's harsh, man."

"Fuck you, Greco," Davies barks.

"I can't trust you for shit when I'm not on the ice." Greco scowls at the dude who *should* be his backup goalie but isn't. "You let that puck in tonight when a kid in bantams could have stopped it. You're too busy thinking about who you're banging and that hair of yours to worry about your job."

"Who the fuck do you think you are?"

"You do worry about your hair a lot," McIsaac mumbles.

"I have sponsorship deals!"

"Don't we all, but we don't let them get in the way of our real job," Greco counters.

"You let pucks in too, Greco," Davies accuses.

"Not as many as you. We need someone who recognizes that his job is to keep the puck out of the net, not in it."

"You're an asshole."

"The truth hurts and the truth is you don't even belong in the ECHL. You're either sucking Bradley's dick *or* blackmailing him—"

Liam cracks his knuckles. "This conversation is devolving."

I get it—it's been a long fucking day.

"I can't believe this," Davies sputters, glancing around the room and finding that no one is on his side. "This is so out of order, it's unreal."

He has a point but…

"We've got one of the best teams on the ice and we're barely scraping through our wins.

"We need to up our shit because otherwise, we'll end up losing. *Again.* I didn't move across the goddamn country to lose," Greco continues, utterly remorseless as he lays into Davies.

His declaration, however, has most of the guys fidgeting like kids after one of the team dosed our gear with itching powder.

None of us want to lose. None of us came here to lose. And there's no denying—we tend to lose when Davies is in goal.

"You're going to let him talk to me like this, Donnghal?" Davies jerks to his feet in outrage.

Liam hitches a shoulder. "The stats don't lie, man."

"Some fucking captain you are."

"Maybe it's time you learned a few things in the minors," I insert. "No shame in needing some extra training where the pressure isn't as intense."

"I helped win the gold medal for Canada," Davies roars. "And you want me to play in the minors?" Looking around the team and yet again finding no allies, he shoots a glower at Liam then, like an idiot, throws a punch.

Before he can reach Liam, I field his flying fist and drag his arm behind his back. "You wanna rethink that?" I snap. "Cool your jets, dude!"

"This is bullshit. You're trying to clear house so you can get the whole Bukowski 'team' together. You think I haven't seen the papers? They're all begging for that to happen since the GM got appointed—"

"I'm not an ex-Bukowski billet kid," Greco denies. "Grow a pair and accept that you suck."

"Fuck you."

"Play better and I wouldn't want to get rid of you—"

Before he can finish the sentence, Davies storms out of the room, hurling his beer bottle at the wall.

Annoyed at the damage, especially when one of my pictures falls to the floor and smashes, I shout, "You asshole," but he's already slamming the front door.

Lewis scratches his nose. "That could have gone better."

Liam, ignoring him, studies Greco. "You didn't have to bring that up this way."

"Fucker needs to know he's useless. His ego is bigger than his brain and I'm tired of dealing with him. You'll speak with Ellison?"

Slowly, Liam nods.

"If he *is* injured," I point out, "it's not like Davies can go anywhere yet, which means we made the locker room situation hella awkward."

Greco shrugs. "Probably, but it's worth it. At least he knows his shit doesn't stink of roses to anyone whose last name isn't Bradley." He gets to his feet. "Keep us updated, okay?"

When Liam nods, everyone takes that as their cue to head out too.

I'm not the most gracious of hosts, but I know to wait for them to leave by the door which means I'm well aware that Liam stayed behind.

Finding him in the living room, collecting the glass from the broken bottle, I tell him, "You didn't have to clean that, man."

"I should have handled that better."

He didn't handle it at all, but I don't need to kick him when he's down.

"The C doesn't sit easily on you," I say simply. "Greco could have gone about this better. He's the one to blame."

Liam grunts but thanks me when I pass him a wastepaper basket. "Do you think Matt *is* injured?"

"Only one way to find out."

"Agreed."

Snatching his phone, he sends a message that has my cell buzzing to life.

Opening the conversation, I read:

Liam: Dude

Matt: Sup?

Liam: You got an injury that you're keeping under your vest?

Matt: No.

Cole: Then why did you get switched out last night after the first period? You're better than Reeves. He let in three goals after that switch.

Matt: Coach knows best.

Cole: Don't tell Gracie that lol.

Matt: Fuck off.

Liam: Nowhere I want to fuck off to.

Matt: How about outer Antarctica?

Liam: God, I wouldn't wish that on my worst enemy.

Cole: Is Liam really that?! :O

Cole: If so, you need to send me there too. I'll keep him company. We know he gets lonely on his own.

Matt: Screw you.

Cole: Nah, I don't swing that way, though it's interesting the reaction I've been getting from other guys since I pulled off wearing those hot pink pants *waggles eyebrows*

Matt: Cole, I don't have the patience tonight for your bullshit

Liam: One of our guys happened to hear a rumor that the Bulldogs are floating you…

Matt: They are

Liam: Why?

Matt: My meniscus is about to give out

We break off to share a worried look.

Liam: Why didn't you tell us that?

Matt: Because it's none of your business.

Cole: Of course it fucking is. Are you resting it?

Matt: I'm trying. It's not easy. Coach isn't letting up on me

Cole: Why the hell not?

Matt: Got a grudge against me.

Liam: What did you do?

Matt: Fucked his daughter so they're dumping me before the trade deadline. Now, he's making sure I remember him.

Liam rubs tiredly at his eyes. "What a dumbass."
"We all pulled similar stunts at twenty-four, Liam," I excuse.

Liam: Jesus H. Christ. You guys are a piece of work.

Cole: Not sure that means he deserves to be played within an inch of his meniscus snapping, Liam.

Liam: Never said it did, but how do you guys get yourself into these situations?

Matt: Luck of the draw?

Cole: I was gonna say bad luck lol

Liam: Your meniscus is in really bad shape?

Matt: I can feel it's on its way out. :/

Liam: How about Gracie gets you onto the
Stars?

Matt: I'd take you over the salary cap

Liam: Not if you're put on the LTIR

Matt: You want me to play second fiddle to
Greco?

Liam: You won the Cup yet?

I snort. "Burn."

"Little punk deserved it."

Liam: You know we're gonna get the Holy Grail

Matt: No guarantee that you will...

Liam: No guarantee that YOU will if your
meniscus's fucked

Cole: Don't be a dipshit, Matt. You know you
want to come

Matt: Says who?

Liam: Gracie'll look after you

Liam: She'll make sure you get the right
treatment and she'll keep the coach off
your back

Matt: You think she would?

Cole: Dude, it's Gracie!

Cole: Of course she would.

Matt: I'm not averse to the idea

Cole: Look at you using fancy words.

Matt: Jerk-off

Cole: :P It's like you know me or something

Liam: Shall I bring this up with Gracie, then? I didn't want to say anything without talking to you first because you're right, we're at the upper limits of our salary cap

Cole: It's weird how much of the backend of the business you know

Liam: Perks of being with the GM. Means I get to see a lot of behind-the-scenes' shit

Cole: Shit that you're not usually interested in…

Liam: Nah, I'm interested in the Stars.

Cole: Why?

Matt: Duh. Because Gracie's managing it. Don't you know that you're supposed to take an interest in your partner's work, Cole?

Matt: Maybe this explains why you're still single

Liam: I thought it was the hot pink pants lol

Matt: Those too

Cole: My hot pink pants are perfect

Matt: Say that ten times without stuttering

Cole: Like you've had any major relationships anyway, pretty boy

Matt: Was that supposed to be an insult?

Matt: I've had more than you

Cole: Says the man being tortured by his coach for fucking someone he shouldn't have touched

Matt: Have you seen Bianco's daughter?

Liam: Who is it?

Matt: Penelope Bianco

Cole: Wasn't she in Sports Illustrated last
month?

Matt: She was

Cole: Was she worth the torture?

Matt: A gentleman never tells...

Matt: But yeah

Cole: Bahahahahaha

WEEK THREE

CHAPTER 34
COLE

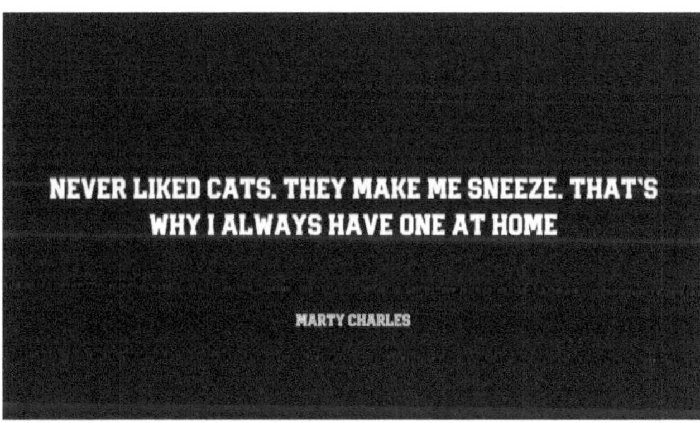

"I CAN'T BELIEVE you're still making me wear those skates," I grumble as we jog down the river walkway after an early morning session on the ice.

Though my thighs genuinely ache, I cut her a look to measure her reaction.

"You haven't managed to commit to a camel, upright, or sit spin in figure-skating skates yet, so why would I let you switch?"

I release a relieved breath.

The figure-skating skates are fucking hard to work in, don't get me wrong, but I'm not as bad as she thinks I am.

Hey, this is the only way she'll take any money from me—I can be creative when I need to be.

The trick is not being so bad my act is unbelievable.

Honestly, sucking takes skill.

"You said you'd get me doing that by week two," I half-taunt.

"I underestimated your balance issues."

I sniff. "Issue. Singular."

"Issues. Plural."

"*One* issue."

"Nope," she mutters.

I grunt at her as I speed up, which is a dick move, but I know she'll match my pace.

She does but she's starting to pant.

I quickly draw back so I get to see her ass jiggle, but mostly so she won't expire from the run.

"You're a pervert," she calls out as if she read my mind.

"Who's the pervert? The one who puts the ass in front of an innocent bystander or the one who merely looks at a beautiful sight in front of his very eyes?"

Her head whips to the side so I can see her grin.

I'm not sure I'll ever get tired of that. Especially when I helped bring it to life.

Mia, by nature, is quiet and solemn.

Apart from when I'm around.

"You know, you never did give me the full scoop about your pregame routine."

The change of subject almost has me decelerating.

"Cheater."

Tilting her face toward the low morning sun, she smirks. "I'm interested. I know about the bananas, lacing your skates, Mia P.O.R.N, and Taylor Swift. What else? Lemme guess… there has to be some smut involved."

I sniff.

"And oranges."

"How did you know that?"

She slows down to match my pace. A pace I only set so that I can watch her fine ass in yoga pants. "Whenever you're at my apartment, you always ask me to peel an orange for you."

"Sherlock Holmes, that's your real name, huh?" I tease, but I snag her hand to kiss her knuckles.

"You got that right. So?" she demands, entirely aware of my nefarious intent.

She's as bad—I've seen her drooling over my pecs when we shower together after our runs. I've never been self-conscious about the scars on my abdomen, but if I were, her appreciative eyes would have cured me of it.

"I read the last twenty-five pages of a book I love. But that's after. Not pre. In the whirlpool."

"And the oranges?"

"Two before I have a banana."

"Boring."

"Lewis eats cooked dry pasta with ranch."

"Ew. Yours is relatively normal, then."

"Don't sound so disappointed."

"You do everything with flare," she jokes. "I thought your pregame ritual would be appropriately dramatic too."

I chuckle because she's not wrong. "What about you? You must have had your own rituals?"

"Twenty minutes of yoga to calm my breathing, a shot of espresso that I had to sneak past my coach, and a vitamin B tablet."

My brows lift. "Why vitamin B?"

"I had a cold once and my mom force-fed it to me. I felt like I was dying but I won—"

Her voice wanes off so I gently murmur, "And so the tradition commenced."

Mentions of her parents still come few and far between so I let her shift focus onto the path ahead without prompting her to talk, knowing she will when she's ready.

Be that in ten minutes or ten years, I'll be here, ready to listen.

Both of us maneuver around a kid on a tricycle who's racing alongside his mom on the path as we merge toward the business district for a coffee shop we found last week.

Without saying a word, both of us speed up.

It's become this stupid competition—who'll touch the door handle of the coffee shop first.

While Mia races toward it, she's two feet from touching the door when she brakes to a sudden halt.

It's so sudden, in fact, that it's borderline comical.

Her head whips around again to face me but now, she's scowling. "Not funny, Cole!"

Confused, I stop running and quickly shift my gaze higher. "What are you talking about?"

"Meowing like that."

"I didn't meow," I deny, utterly bewildered by her annoyance.

I mean, generally, I'm annoying but I don't think I did anything *this* time…

She stacks her hands on her hips. "Sure you did. You were trying to cheat."

Because that's ridiculous, I huff out a laugh and mimic her stance. "I don't need to cheat."

"You haven't won the race once."

"So? I'm getting faster." Her ass is my version of hanging a carrot in front of a donkey. Except it's worth losing to watch her run.

"You meowed."

"I swear I didn't."

She scowls at me, then her head jerks around. "There! That was that noise again."

"I didn't hear it."

"Are you deaf or something?" she grumbles, but she stalks toward the corner of the coffee shop building.

Call me a jerk, but I make sure to tap the door handle before I take off after her.

At first, I don't see her.

Then, I realize she's kneeling on the ground amid the shadows.

"Oh, Cole," she cries.

"What is it?"

Rushing over to her side, that's when I hear it too—the lowest, quietest, weakest meow.

And I barely hear *that* over Mia's sudden sobs.

"There were three," she moans, her tone miserable. "Only one made it."

Looming over her, I see the tiny bodies that are forever still and I clasp her shoulder, fingers digging in.

This world is so fucking brutal.

"Is that one even…?" I start to ask, well aware that my voice is thick with emotion, but the little thing is barely moving.

Animals are my kryptonite. I know they're hers too, but unlike me, the coward, who runs from them because I can't handle losing another, she welcomes them into her heart.

"Just."

I dig into my pocket with my spare hand and find my cell. A quick search has me saying, "There's a vet around the corner."

"Some bastard dumped them here. Look, they're in a carrier bag."

"I hate people."

"Me too."

I drag off my jacket and hand it to her. Carefully, she tucks the weak kitten into its warm folds and holds it to her chest.

"What do we do with the others?"

"The vet will…"

When her words wane, I nod. Hating the necessity but unwilling to leave them to rot like so much trash, I pick up the bag and carefully carry it across the lot.

In silence, we wend a path through the myriad streets to the nearest vet.

It's with relief that we make it there and the kitten is still meowing weakly—louder, though, as if it's clearly pissed off about its current state.

Who the hell could blame it?

I open the door for her and we head straight to the front desk.

The second the receptionist locks eyes on me, I know that she recognizes me, and in this instance, I'm not afraid to take advantage of my fame.

"My partner found a kitten in the trash. It's an emergency—it was with two others and they…didn't make it."

When I pass her the bag, the woman's eyes soften but she nods her understanding, and then rushes toward the back of the clinic.

"We'll fix this," I promise Mia.

She stares at me with tear-drenched eyes and nods. "I know."

I grab her shoulder and haul her into me, both of us studying the tiny face peering blindly in our direction.

"I have no idea how you heard it. Thank God you did."

She shivers and tucks herself deeper into my side.

A few minutes later, the vet bustles out and takes charge.

Mia stands there, hovering in place, uncertain what to do now that the vet has the kitten, but I cup her elbow and direct her toward the unisex bathroom.

It might seem weird, but I draw her in and wash her hands as she lets me tend to her as if she's frozen too.

Then, I rinse off my own and get ours dried.

When we're done, I guide her back to the waiting room and plunk her on my lap.

Immediately, she buries her face in my throat. "I hate people," she repeats my earlier mantra.

"Me too."

We sit there for close to an hour. My phone buzzes with calls but I dismiss them, willing to take the penalty for missing practice, and together, we wait.

Eventually, the vet returns. Her expression is calm so I gently rub Mia's arm. "The vet's back, baby."

Head whipping around, she faces the other woman. "Is it alive?"

"*She* is. You got her here in the nick of time."

Mia releases a soft sob. "Thank God! Can we see her?"

The vet nods. "Follow me."

She drags me along with our joined hands. I almost smile because there was nowhere else I was heading other than with her, and together, we step into the vet's office.

The kitten is in a tiny bed, surrounded by blankets, and only her eyes and ears are visible.

When she sees us, she noses out of the blankets and stands on weak legs.

As we approach, however, it isn't Mia the little beasty wobbles toward.

It's me.

Surprised, I freeze as her small nose nuzzles my finger.

Then, I realize why—the scent of my jacket.

Mia's smile is watery. "I think she knows who she wants."

I choke out a laugh.

I don't have the kind of life that'll fit having a pet, but in that moment, with her smiling at me and the kitten warming my hand, I know I own a cat.

Or a cat owns me.

Mia clings to my arm. "I think she'll make a perfect Betsy."

The name hits me like a Bobby Hull slapshot to the head.

Not only because she's right but… she remembered.

"I'm not crying," I mutter. "You are."

I told you so… BLOG

RUMOR HAS it that a certain Canadian hockey player was seen in a veterinarian's office with a lady…

Not news in itself, but Cole Korhonen appeared to have brought a stray cat with him.

While the kitten was tended to, my source tells me that Korhonen and his 'lady love' sat snuggled together as they waited for an update.

Korhonen, notoriously single, as well as an active user of *Hooked-Up*, *(See blogpost, Hooked-Up—a dating app or Russian spyware? Hint Hint, it's more than dating)* looked very cozy…

As for recent Stars' chatter, there's Ruben and Lacey Kerrigan's absence from the majority of this season's games.

You'll hear it here first if any whispers make it out of the Stars' locker room…

Cole: Hey, Gagné, you doing okay? I wanted to check in. See how you're healing up

Jude: Yeah, I'm fine. I'm ready to play but the doctors don't agree lol.

Cole: Fucking doctors. What do they know?

Jude: Right?

Cole: Your wife must have been upset?

Jude: Mercy wasn't happy about it… no. Frightened her :/

Cole: Ugh, shit.

Jude: Yeah. Things aren't too good between us, tbh

Cole: That sucks to hear.

Cole: If there's anything I can do, just let me know?

Jude: Will do, but I doubt it unless you can get me off the LTIR sooner rather than later lol

Cole: I know I'm awesome, but I can't dole out miracles yet

Jude: Shame, haha

Jude: TTYL

Cole: TTYIAB (Watch out for a delivery from me. Everyone needs cookies when they're on the LTIR. It should be an NHL bylaw)

Jude: Cheers, man

WEEK FOUR

CHAPTER 35
MIA

Work Song - Hozier

YOU'D NEVER IMAGINE that something as tiny as Betsy could be so much trouble/work, but she packs a helluva massive punch to both mine and Cole's schedules.

Because he has no idea how to look after cats, never mind kittens in need of bottle-feeding, my apartment has become ground zero for the chaos.

I'd complain but Betsy is cute as fuck, and Cupid, who's recuperated from her surgery but has been down ever since Chuck's passing, is enjoying having the kitten around—especially when I'm out at night.

She'd always complain when I got back, pissed at me for leaving her in a lurch, but not with Betsy around.

Plus, there's the added benefit of watching a massive hockey player bottle-feeding a kitten.

Be still my ovaries.

We spent Thanksgiving together. The day after, he had to head to Dallas and they just flew into Boston for tonight's game. It's the first time since we got Betsy that he's left her and I'm not sure who he's missing more—me or the cat.

Standing behind the bar, I grin at the thought as I watch him slide onto the ice.

Jarvis nudges me in the side. "I got eighty on them to win."

"Why eighty?" I ask, wincing when I see Cole get slashed with a stick, straight to the back of the calf.

Even Jarvis grimaces. "Why not eighty?"

Distracted as Cole goes down, I question, "I meant why not a hundred? It's an oddly specific number."

My eyes lock on a strange interaction between Cole and the goalie who helps him to his feet. Liam Donnghal takes over, helping Cole get back to the bench, but he also interacts with the opposing team's goalie— they bump fists.

"That's Matt Ellison," Jarvis explains when he sees my confusion.

I grab my phone and shoot off:

Me: That looked nasty. You okay, babe?

"Matt who?"

"Do you know what a billet family is?"

"Yeah."

His brow furrows. "How do you know that? It's not exactly common knowledge."

"I read," is my mild retort/lie.

Gleefully, he asks, "You've been reading the sections of the paper I've been leaving you?"

He's sweet enough that I dip down and press a kiss to his cheek. "You've been very patient with me."

"Wooot, Jarvis looks like he's about to get some action," Jason, the asshole, hoots. "About damn time you put out for someone, Mia. Was starting to think you were into pussy, not dick."

I narrow my eyes at him. "What are you even doing in here, Jason? It's game night for a sport you hate!"

Lighting a cigarette, he sniffs at me. "Since when is it a crime—"

"That cigarette is a crime. Put it out. *Now.*"

He glowers at me but he accurately judges my annoyance levels because he grunts and plops it into a used bottle on his table.

"If you're going to disturb the game for everyone," I continue, "you can leave."

He jumps to his feet, hands slamming on the table, making the bottles rattle at the force. "I used to be welcome here no matter what game was playing."

"That Chuck let you back in after the stunts you pulled with the servers is yet another sign of his poor judgment and critical thinking skills."

"What?" Jason snaps, mostly because he's too dumb to understand what I said.

"The lady said that Chuck was a fool for letting you get away with the crap you have," Jarvis mutters.

Jason barks out a laugh. "You're one to talk. I've seen you sniffing around her. Why the fuck do you think she'd be into a weed like you when she could have me?"

Bewildered, I look between them both. "This is insane. Jason, I don't want you. Jarvis..." I pause to collect my words as I have no desire to hurt his feelings. "I'm dating someone. You know that, right?"

His cheeks flush with heat. "Of course I do."

I get the feeling he didn't. And his disappointment is as clear as day. *Shit.*

When I glare at Jason, his smug smile has me grinding my teeth together.

I'm not in a position where I can afford to turn business away, but that he was trying to hurt Jarvis, *in front of my goddamn eyes,* robs me of my reservations.

"Jason, you're not welcome at Chuck's anymore."

He gawks at me, mouth open wide enough to catch flies. "You can't be serious, Mia!"

"Sure I can. You've disrespected my staff for long enough. I won't allow it anymore."

"You frigid bitch!"

"I'm not sure what my sexual activities have to do with you being barred, but I don't give a damn about what you think or say or do. Get the hell out—"

"I don't know why I stick around this shithole anyway," he snarls before storming off.

When he moves over to his friends, I watch him duck between them, angrily jerking his thumb toward the door, but then his expression flat-lines as neither man gets up. They let him leave on his own.

As he does, he picks up the A-frame sign outside and slams it at the door.

Jolting in shock, I recognize how lucky I am his aim is shit because it collided with the sidewalk first and smashed there. Not the glass window in my door that I can't afford to replace.

There's an odd welter of silence after that ringing noise before, out of the blue, everyone joins in a round of applause at his expulsion.

It's definitely unexpected and, flustered, I twist around to find even the new patrons are getting in on the action. Never mind Chuck's old buddies.

"About damn time," Biff grumbles, one eye on his peanuts, another on the game—don't even ask me how that's medically possible but it is.

"Chuck was a fool for letting him stick around," Walt agrees.

"I'm glad you think I did the right thing." Turning to look at Jarvis, I see his shoulders are hunched and the despondency in his expression has me thinking Jason *was* onto something… Lightly, feeling horrible as I wonder if I led him on, I ask, "You were saying about a billet family?"

Without looking at me, he mumbles, "Cole stayed with the Bukowskis when he played in Winnipeg as a teen. But he wasn't the only one. Matt Ellison was another of those kids."

"How many were there?"

"Three Bukowski boys. As for the billet boys, four."

"Jesus Christ. Mama Bukowski must have had her hands full."

He bites off a laugh. "You could say that. When most of them came out in the first round of their draft, the papers started asking if they should be bottling the water at the Bukowski house—"

"It's good to be in the first round of the draft?"

"Yeah. It means every team wanted them."

"Huh."

"Korhonen and Ellison were two of them. It's unusual as fuck for a goalie to be a first-round draft pick, practically unheard of, but he's not only got magic hands, he's the eye of every storm—so calm all the damn time. I hate Boston and even I'm big enough to admit that he's fantastic."

So, Cole grew up not only with Gracie and her brothers, but with a bunch of other boys too...

Fascinating.

When I throw into the mix the fact that Cole also has three male siblings, I have to wonder how he got into romance novels after being surrounded by testosterone overload his whole life.

My cell buzzes as if the man of the hour knew I was thinking about him.

Cole: Thanks for stalking me, beautiful. TTYL.

A nonanswer if ever I heard it.

Jarvis shakes his head as he shoves his phone at me. "Look at this guy."

My brows lift when I spot Cole on TikTok with a bunch of players—they're clearly walking into the stadium so it's from before the game.

Which, of course, is when I remember it's been so crazy that I forgot to send him his damn pregame porn.

"I wish I had his self-confidence."

Chuckling despite my guilt, I say, "I do too."

Hot pink jeans—not many would have the guts to wear them but Cole does.

My mouth curves at the sight of a supposedly feminine color that Cole does weird shit to.

His dick is *there*.

Seriously, you can't hide something that big. And his muscular thighs distort the dyed denim. Yet, combined with a black Oxford and a dark gray sports coat, I can't say that it works but he's sexy AF.

My gaze locks on his ass when he twists around as one of his teammates yells something.

Damn, my man is smokin'.

When did he become my man?

And my brain decides to remind me of the fact that I told Jarvis and pretty much the whole bar that I was dating someone…

With my head abuzz, I bite my lip, but he keeps me going as I finish up the shift.

When I answer my cell at half-past eleven on the walk home, waving bye at Dionne as she continues onto the bus stop at the end of the street, I grin at nothing, well aware that it's him.

"You looked gorgeous tonight."

He did.

He might also look like he got changed in two different locker rooms, but he was fine as fuck.

Cole hums. "You're good for my ego."

"Like it was in any way, shape, or form damaged." I pin my cell to my ear as I unlock the door to my building and walk up the stairs.

"You're rough on it," he denies, but his tone is laced with satisfaction.

"I'm sorry about forgetting to send you the picture. The calf injury… that's not my fault, right?"

"Ah, baby, you even thinking that is cute as fuck to me. But no, of course, it's not. Still, don't forget again to be on the safe side, huh?"

That has me smiling as I ask, "How is it?"

"Not good, but I've dealt with worse." From his tone alone, I know he doesn't want to talk about it. "I finished that godawful book today."

"We agreed that we wouldn't diss each other's choices," I chide.

"Why would you want to read about massive ants taking over the universe?"

"That's not the point," I mumble. "Anyway, don't lie to me. I know that sci-fi romance is a thing."

"Yeah, but it's with hot aliens who have massive cocks. Plural."

My brows lift. "Plural?"

"Oh," he croons. "I'm so ready to corrupt you. There's a whole world of smut out there waiting for you, babe."

"One book at a time."

"Don't tell me that scene with the fisting didn't get you hot," he argues. "You like being stuffed full of my dick too much not to enjoy the imagery."

"While I enjoyed the imagery, Cole Korhonen, have you *looked* at your hands? You would tear my pussy apart. It wouldn't be a pussy anymore."

"They're not that big!"

"You have hands the size of trash can lids."

"I do not."

"You fucking do. Who's the one who gets your fingers shoved up her cooch every couple days? Me. That's who."

A snicker sounds in my ear. It's so juvenile that it's oddly charming. "True. I concede to your experience."

"Thank you," is my prim response as I reach my apartment.

When I unlock the door, it's not so much of a surprise that Cupid isn't waiting for me. I don't freak out anymore, mostly because I know she's with Betsy.

And sure enough, Cupid's got a hold of her scruff as she finally walks toward me with a determination that tells me I'm late with the food.

I hold up my hands. "I'm coming, I'm coming—"

"You are? Oooh, is this when we do cam sex face-to-face?"

I roll my eyes. "I was talking to the cat!"

"That a euphemism for pussy? I don't think it's gonna stick, babe."

"Cole!"

He laughs some more and it gets louder once I put him on speaker.

Of course, that's when I take a picture of Cupid with Betsy in her mouth because that's cute as hell.

"Awwwwwwwww," is his response as he receives the photo. "I mean, it's not your pussy, which I'd prefer a picture of, but I'm glad they're getting along."

"You'll see it shortly."

There's silence on the other end of the line. "I will?"

"I saw the pregame shots. You turned around to flash your ass on the screen to get me hot and bothered, didn't you?" I tease as I switch the voice call over to video.

That's when I see his face is as hot pink as his pants were earlier.

He grins sheepishly at me. "I wish I were as devious as you think I am, babe, but nah. Liam called my name."

"What did he say?"

"That I looked like a Ken doll on the bottom and Batman on top."

"A dastardly combination."

"You know it." His tone turns sulky. "He said my butt was getting bigger too."

"I like it. It's a bubble butt."

"You're not making me feel better here."

"Why? Because you're the only one in this relationship who can appreciate when the other's butt jiggles?"

He seems to ponder that for a second, then he grants me a decisive nod. "You're right. I'll stop being sexist."

Snickering, I pour kibble into bowls, distribute meds to both the oldest and the youngest cats under my roof, then put out a couple pouches of wet food on a plate. In the nick of time, I snag Betsy from Cupid before she drops the kitten into the dish of wet food.

With her in one hand, I press her to the camera. "Say hello."

"Hey, Betsy. Looking cute with the little mohawk."

"Don't get any ideas," I tease, smoothing my finger over the ruffled fur that's mussed from the grip Cupid had on her. "I like something to hold on to."

He grunts, but that's when he lowers the camera and I see he's in bed, naked, with a boner on full display.

I mock-gasp and gently hover my hand over Betsy's eyes. "Behave yourself in front of the children, Cole!"

Though he laughs, his eyes have gone to half-mast, and dayum if that doesn't get me moving on the double.

"I saw you were limping down the tunnel."

"That whack to the calf fucked me up. It'll be fine. It's more tedious than painful."

"Pain is never tedious. It's *pain*."

Harrumphing when he shrugs, I get Betsy sorted with a bottle. When she doesn't want more than half, I'm grateful because it means I can head to my bedroom and leave her in Cupid's care.

Who knew I had a cat nanny all lined up?

"Be good," I shout to the pussy patrol in my living room, ignoring Curtis the Butthead's displeased meow.

"I'm always good, babe. You wound me."

I stick my face in the camera. "Not you."

"Does this mean I get your full attention?"

"Do you want it?"

"Hell, yeah, if it means you're getting naked too. Oh, I'll be back tomorrow at nine."

I hum my understanding as I set up my cell in a stand and position myself in front of it so he can watch me strip off.

"You going straight to your apartment?"

He clears his throat. "Nah. Yours. Plus, my calf needs the..." Eyes glazing over at my striptease, he rasps, "Um, rest."

"Ohh, so I get to spend the morning with you?"

"If you want to," he mumbles, his gaze locked on my tits which bounce in my bra before I snap the fastener at the back. "Damn, I need to titty fuck those."

"Thought you were supposed to be charming, Cole."

"You know me—I live and breathe charm." He groans. "Do a twirl. Let me see your ass." Another pained moan escapes him. "What are you trying to do to me, woman?"

I make sure to twerk a little because he's got a weird fixation on my butt bouncing which is when he growls.

"I need to slam into that."

My back still to the camera, I bend over, resting my hand on the foot of the bed and spreading my legs so he can see my pussy.

"Ah, God damn," he grates out.

A second later, I hear the telltale sound of him jacking off.

He's either coated in lube or his dick is leaking pre-cum because he sounds wet and the prospect has my head rolling forward to look at the very small viewfinder I've given myself between my thighs.

When I notice that he's tilted the camera down so I can see more of him, I realize how much better this is than talking to him as *Kor*.

Which is an entirely bizarre thought to have because I never once wanted to see any of my other patrons.

Of course, those patrons likely weren't hockey stars with the bodies to match...

Sue me for being superficial.

"I wish that dick of yours was sliding into me," I mewl, letting my fingers find my slit. "Can you see how wet I am for you?"

"I wish that pussy were here," he grumbles. "And your tits... I want to drown in them."

"They're not that big," I croak out with a laugh.

"They're perfect. The perfect size for grabbing, for holding onto, and using as a pillow."

My lips twitch even as I roll my fingertips over my clit. "You want me to get one of the dildos?"

"Ah, fuck. I really do, but also, I really don't. This is the first time we've done this..." He clears his throat. "I'd like it to be me and you."

And he's back to being charming and sweet.

With a deep sigh, I twist on the bed and sit on the side. Curling my toes around the edge of the mattress, I use that to spread my thighs as wide as I can.

He licks his lips as I rasp, "I'd shove your face into my cunt faster than you could say my name."

"I'd eat you out until you were begging me to stop."

"I'll never say stop."

"Liar."

"Shame you're not here to prove that."

His eyes narrow in a silent warning, but I distract him by rolling my head back and crying out as tingles of pleasure radiate from my core.

It's not 'Cole eating me out like I'm water and he's a man dying of thirst' pleasure, but it's better than nothing.

I thrust a finger in and pout at him. "It's not thick enough."

"I'll be there soon," he promises, his voice a low, dark rumble. "And I'm going to split you apart with my dick."

My body responds viscerally—my hips rock backward. I hump the freakin' air, wanting to get off.

As I move, he starts to grind out, "That's it, baby. I'll be home soon. I'll make you feel good. You just gotta lie there and take my dick. Can you do that for me?"

I let loose a sob, not in release, in wonder at what his words tell me. *Home.*

Then, he continues, "I'm gonna stuff you full of my cock and when I come, I'm going to hold you down, keep my seed locked in you, and when I'm hard again, I'm going to fuck you. You'll be so drenched in me that you won't know where I begin and you end—"

"Cole!" I cry out as I hit my peak.

It's nothing like when he's in charge of my body, but it's enough to have me pulling taut against the bed, hovering in place as I hold the position to maximize those sensations rushing through me.

When I sag against the comforter, I watch as cum rushes from his dick, pelting his stomach with the mess he makes.

My jaw works as I watch him, slowly circling my clit to keep those sparks floating through my veins until, gradually, he lets his dick flop against his abs.

One arm slides under his head, propping it up, and the other lazily strokes his shaft much as I'm teasing myself.

"You're beautiful," he assures me.

I shoot him a surprised but happy smile. "Thank you."

"You don't have to thank me for the truth."

Sagging on one arm, I stare at him. "You're beautiful too."

"Nah. I'm all scarred and shit."

He isn't seeking compliments, nor does he sound like his esteem has taken a hit, but it's the first time he's ever been in any way vulnerable about his appearance.

"Those scars were founded in strength. *Courage.* They show me the type of man you are."

"What type of man is that?"

Mine.

God, the word sits on my tongue for the longest time.

"The best type," is what I settle on.

It falls flat though.

At least, to my ears it does.

He mock-sniffles. "Spoken like my favorite romance heroine." But he blows me a kiss in true Cole fashion—exuberantly—telling me he's not making fun.

Chuckling, I shake my head at his antics as I snag my phone and throw myself back into bed.

That might have been a long-distance quickie, but it zapped my energy levels.

"What I want to know is when you stopped reading anything that wasn't romance?"

"When my parents' divorce came through. He used to beat her. I liked to escape into the happily ever after and then, once she was safe, I didn't want to read anything that didn't have an HEA." As usual, he floors me, but he doesn't give me time to respond, just asks, "Have you eaten? Romance heroines are supposed to eat."

Spying his gimlet stare, I roll my eyes. "I'm too tired for food."

"I never have that problem."

"Hey?"

He arches a brow.

"Iknowthisisdumbbutdoyouwanttogotosleepwiththecamerasonsowe-canpretendtobenexttoeachother?"

"Did you speed up, or was it me?"

"You don't have a concussion. At least, I don't think that you do." It's my turn to give him the stink eye. "I'll whup that tush of yours if you have a concussion and didn't tell me."

"Kinky. But I don't think I'm into that." He hums. "Who am I kidding? I'll try anything with you."

My chest feels super tight at the declaration. I'm lucky I can breathe, what with his earlier admission about why he only reads romance. Apart from the books I suggest for him…

When he sees I've gone quiet, he winks, sucks in a deep breath, and says, "Yeswecansleepwiththecamerason." He pauses. "That reminds me of that *Dr. Who* episode—"

That's when I flop back into my pillows. "Of course, you're a Whovian."

He flashes a look at me, reads my expression, and murmurs, "I got more perfect, didn't I?"

I scowl at him. "Your head's going to get too big."

"We can watch it when I'm back."

"Who's your favorite doctor?"

"Matt Smith."

"Matt Smith."

We say it at the same time.

We share a smile.

"Wanna know why my number is 42?"

I pause. "Maybe."

He studies his nails. "Six words."

"Cole Is A Very Bigheaded Studmuffin?"

His grin is like quicksilver—despite having gotten off, if he were here, I'd have jumped back in the saddle and ridden him like a cowgirl. *The Hitchhiker's—*" His grin widens as I clap a hand to my heart. And together, we finish, "*Guide to the Galaxy.*"

"You might have odd taste in books, but your viewing habits are *this* fabulous," I inform him as I grace him with a chef's kiss.

His wink is pure cockiness, but he's earned it by being too perfect for my own good. "Er, excuse me. I *read* that. Well, I listened to it. Colt used to read it to me before bed."

Chuckling, I shake my head as we part ways.

Upon my return from the bathroom, I mess with the pillows until I have a perch for the cell and I watch him lumber and hop as he returns from the restroom and falls onto his bed. A couple moments later, he does the same with his pillows and then, on his side, he stares at me.

"Few months ago, I'd have gone partying with the guys."

"You still can. But you'd have to hop everywhere."

"Nah, you're more fun."

"I'm about to go to sleep."

"Still more fun."

My chuckle fades as I slip into slumber after the horrendously busy day I've had, but my smile lingers when, on the cusp of drifting off entirely, I'm sure he whispers, "Even if you only want to read sci-fi."

CHAPTER 36
COLE

> INJURIES? MOST OF THESE GUYS NOWADAYS
> TAKE A FALL LIKE THEY TAKE AN ASPIRIN.
> IN MY DAY, WE PLAYED WITH BUSTED BONES
> AND WE GOT PAID LESS. BET YOUR ASS I WISH
> I WERE OUT IN THE FIELD TODAY
>
> **MARTY CHARLES**

WHEN I HOBBLE up a couple stairs, the crutch the doc is making me use has me grumbling as I try to juggle all my cargo.

Finally accepting that it's impossible, I descend with a pained hiss so I can put the pan on the floor. Then, I snag my cell and call her.

"You here? Why didn't you use the key I gave you?"

"Because I have too much crap and I can't manage it with my crutch."

"You have a crutch?!" she shrieks, but before I can answer, she disconnects the call.

Next thing I hear is a slamming door and pounding feet as she races down the stairs toward the building's entrance.

"There's no fire," I call out.

"You should have told me. I could have gone to your apartment!"

My nose crinkles. "I like your place better."

"I could have brought Betsy with me!"

"Could you have packed up the apartment as well?"

When she skids to a halt at the top landing and can frown at me, she asks, "You *really* like my apartment?"

"You have that window seat I love, plus it smells nice."

"The smell is in a bottle and you could have a window seat too." She takes it slower now that she can see I'm okay, just leaning heavily on a stick. "What's the damage?"

"A week off to let it heal properly."

"A *whole* week?"

My eyebrows waggle.

"But, wait, isn't Gagné still benched?"

"Different positions. I thought you were learning about hockey?"

If a sniff can be nasty, then hers is.

Smirking, I explain, "Gagné's different. He's on the Long-Term Injured Reserve, not *benched*. That means he'll be out for ten games or more."

Nodding her understanding, she stares at the bags I brought with me. "What do you have here?"

"I got two of my billet bros to sign some gear for you."

"Don't they think it's odd that you ask them for this stuff?"

"The perks of being *odd* is that nothing I do ever fazes them. Anyway, Matt gave me some padding as well. It got sliced up in the game. You can always throw it out, but he did sign it." I point at the tray. "This, Noah assures me, is good shit."

"Noah?"

"Gracie's baby brother."

Her chin tips in understanding. "What is it?"

"Something called hummingbird cake. I had it a bunch when I was in Dallas; it's good but this place he gets it from is ten-out-of-ten so he brought me some to try. Because I'm a fantastic boyfriend, I decided to wait to sample it with you."

I use that label intentionally—just to see her response.

She doesn't flinch or anything. Not that I figured she would react with horror to the label—she got that out of her system in Nashville—but her smile comes as a surprise.

A nice one.

She tears the seal and pulls back the silver foil to stare at the gooey frosting on top. "This looks good."

I hum. "He bought me this to try after telling me that Texas sheet cake was better than Deep N' Delicious, but I told him that he's Satan reincarnate. This was his penance."

"You said a whole bunch there that I don't understand."

"When we visit Canada, you can try it then."

She blinks. "When?"

I clear my throat. "If?"

"Nice save. Cake for breakfast?"

"You didn't eat dinner." I let her change the subject.

"And?"

"We should have an omelet. I can order in?"

"I'd prefer cake."

"Me too. I'm supposed to be the corruptive influence."

"Speaking of which, when your alarm went off, it woke me—"

"Ah shit, I thought I hung up in time."

"It's fine. But I started reading."

Knowing what's on her Kindle because I put it there, I lean forward. "Can you still tell me that vampires aren't hot?"

"You can't make me say it."

"That's all the answer I need, sugar."

Mia starts to shove me, but before her hand can touch me, she freezes in place and stares at my crutch. "How bad is it?"

"I told you. Not that bad."

She glances at the stairs she descended. "Can you manage?"

"Yup."

"Should you?"

I grimace. "Probably not."

"Wanna get Burrows to pick us up?"

"No. Once I'm in there, I won't move."

"That sounds practical. *Not*." She hesitates. "Is this because you share a building with Gracie?"

I'm not having her feel like I'm ashamed of her. "No. She's at work. I live in one of the biggest skyscrapers in the city, Mia." Quentin *could* mention her to Gracie and Liam, but I don't care.

Okay, I do.

I want to tell them.

I'm already sick of hiding her.

She's the lo—

"Let me get my stuff and I'll come with you to your place, then."

I harrumph when she ignores my, "We don't have to—" and stomps up the stairs with my trash bags of hockey gear anyway.

Appreciating the view of her ass and enjoying her assertiveness, which doesn't always shine through if she's concerned about Gracie, I call my driver once she's out of sight.

Burrows assures me he'll be here in fifteen—gotta love Manhattan traffic when he literally left five minutes ago—and I stand in the hall like a hazard waiting to happen.

Luckily for me, Mia's there soon after. I can hear her lugging something because it bounces off each step. When I see her, I chuckle because she's got a cabin bag in one hand, a cat carry case in the other, then on her back, there's a rucksack.

"Are we climbing Everest and I didn't get the invite?"

"You have a baby. You can't travel light."

"How is baby Betsy?" I ask, peering into the shadowy carry case on the hunt for her tiny face.

I can't see into the murkiness but I hear a soft, disgruntled meow—apparently, she prefers other methods of transportation.

Like my shirt and Mia's tits.

My girl's got her priorities straight.

"Doing well," she assures me. "You need to feed her when we reach your condo."

Nodding my understanding, I hobble toward the door and open it then use my crutch to drag over the bag so it holds it open.

With me out of the way, Mia can make it to the bottom of the steps.

When she moves toward the door, she pauses to press a light kiss to my lips. "Good morning. Love the pants."

I preen at that, especially when she shimmies against me before heading outside.

Once she carefully lowers the carrier, she returns to my side for the cake.

It takes another journey to the curbside for her to get us ready for Burrows's arrival.

My driver jumps out and, leaving me to feel useless, coordinates with Mia so that we've got everything.

When I plunk my ass on the back seat, I take a relieved breath to be off my feet before she joins me.

I'd have hobbled up the stairs, but I can't deny I'm glad I don't have to.

Elevators FTW.

Mia places the kitten between us. "Betsy's taking the milk well."

"Good. We need to return to the vet soon, don't we?"

"Yeah."

"I'll book the appointment today."

Her brows lift. "*You* will?"

"Sure." I tilt my head to the side. "Any reason why I shouldn't?"

She laughs. "No. Most of the cats were Chuck's too. Cupid even lived at the bar with him for a while, but he always left that stuff for me to handle."

Chuck sounded like a real jerk.

Not that I say that out loud.

Mum didn't raise no fool.

"I'm a big boy and Betsy's technically my responsibility because I'm the chosen one."

"'Technically,' she's ours."

"She likes my smell better though."

"You smell good, but she still comes to me for food, plus Cupid's like her cat mom."

"Are we really arguing about cat custody?"

"Bet your ass we are." She winks at me. "How's the calf?"

"Shit." I wiggle my leg slightly when it starts to ache from how I'm sitting in the car. "Thanks for offering to come over. I know that was awkward."

"As if that matters. You should have said something. I could have met you there."

I shoot her a smile. "I like being at your place."

No lie.

"Only you'd prefer a grungy dump like mine in comparison to yours."

"Yours is lived in."

"Oh, is that what it is?" Another chuckle escapes her as she unzips Betsy's carrier and draws her out.

When she rests her on my chest, I cup under her fluffy butt and murmur, "You like Daddy best, don't you, Pumpkin?"

"She's either Betsy or Pumpkin. You can't have both."

"How about Betsy the Pumpkin?" I mock.

"No, that's not the rule. Betsy the Beautiful, I'll accept."

"How did that start?"

"Alliteration rocks."

My lips curve. "You're as crazy as I am."

She mimics my trademark wink. "What took you so long to figure it out?"

"How's the bar doing?"

The change of topic has her grimacing. "We're going to paint it. Hopefully, that'll help with our rep. I wanted to do it sooner but I couldn't afford to shut the place down. I accepted there'll never be a good time so I'm tearing off the Band-Aid.

"Apparently, Uncle Chuck used to bribe the health inspector and ever since I've learned that, it's been skeeving me out. I doubled down on our cleaning schedule and I put the job at the top of the 'imperative' list."

"Understandable."

Chuck's such a douche.

As I gather more and more intel about this guy, I can totally see how he sold out Gracie. But it's a complete contrast to what I'm experiencing with Mia—she's got a beautiful soul. Generous and kind. Her uncle, on the other hand, not so much.

"We're starting to make videos for social media too. Slowly trickling out information about my great-grandfather, focusing on some of the memorabilia. We'll see if that'll boost our sales."

"Marty Charles could be a massive draw. Do you want help with a publicist?"

"You're too kind, Cole. Thank you, but we'll figure it out." She gives me a kiss though, so I know she's not mad at me for interfering.

It kills me that I can't star in a couple vids for her.

The constraints of our situation are really starting to piss me off.

"How's the turnover?"

She frowns at me. "Why are you asking?"

"Because we're about to hit December and I stopped…" I clear my throat, not willing to finish that sentence when Burrows's in the car. "*You know.* And I'm not going to be able to figure skate for a while." I'm skating more than I ever have with these daily classes on top of practice. "I need to rest up. How are your savings looking?"

"Turnover's improving." Her gaze is soft as it settles on me. "Thank you for caring."

"Of course I do," I grouse, but I snag her hand in mine, raise her fingers to my lips, and press a kiss there. "I don't want you working yourself to the bone."

"That's what you gotta do to survive in this city."

My nose crinkles.

It wouldn't if you'd let me keep on paying you…

Not that I say those words aloud.

I do value my balls.

See above: *Mum didn't raise no fool.*

My classes don't even cover a quarter of what I originally paid her, so when the money from her time as my private cam girl runs out, I'm going to have to do something.

I may still be sticking to our original agreement and I haven't told Gracie yet, but it's only a matter of weeks until I do.

And for the first time in months, though Gracie will have stuck a death threat on me for betraying her, I'll be able to breathe easy *and* plan accordingly.

WEEK FIVE

CHAPTER 37
MIA

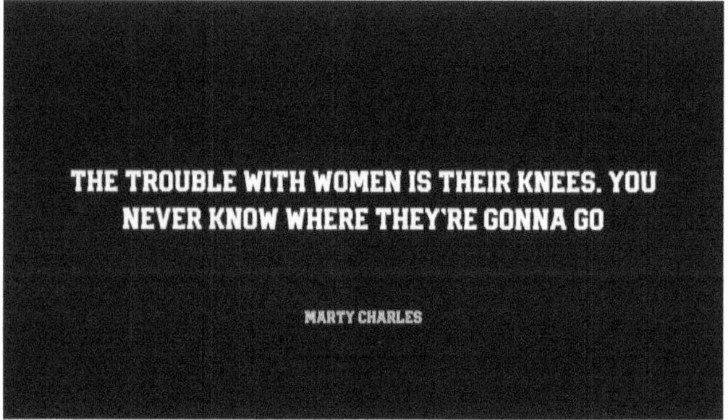

"WHAT ARE YOU DOING HERE, JASON?" I demand as I walk into the bar later than usual thanks to an overrunning kissing session with Cole at his apartment.

Jason beams a smile at me. "I figured you were messing, Mia."

"Why would you 'figure' that?" is my cool retort.

He flushes and, around him, the barflies he hangs with duck their heads as they focus on the screen in front of them. "I've been drinking here for years!"

"And? You've been mistreating staff for all that time too. Chuck let you pull those stunts but I'm not Chuck. I gave you plenty of warnings—"

"What warnings?" he bites off.

"If you chose not to heed them," I continue like he didn't speak. "… then that's on you. Not me."

His nostrils flare. "You can't do this to me!"

"Sure I can. It's my name on the license. I can do whatever I damn well please."

He jerks to his feet so fast that his stool tips onto the tiles with a slam. "You won't get away with this."

"You come in again," I snap, "and I'll call the cops."

When he smashes his bottle of beer on the floor, I don't even bother wincing. Dionne and Jarvis do, but I'm used to worse.

He storms over to me, gets in my face, and snarls, "You think I'm going to let some frigid cunt talk to me the way you do?"

I stare at him, and because he's taller than me, I rock my head back. I'm not scared though. I was raised in this damn bar—I've faced worse than this dick.

Because his focus is on my face, I hit out and slam him in the junk. As he releases a howl, I hiss, "If you threaten me again, I'll call the cops. If you step foot on these premises again, I'll call the cops. If you come anywhere near me or my staff, I'll call the cops. Are you getting the picture, Jason?"

With a wispy groan, he rocks onto his knees then sidles onto the floor as he cups himself.

Sniffing, I step over him and stride toward the counter. "Eyes on the game, folks."

Heads whip around to the screen, but Dionne warbles in my ear, "W-Was that wise?"

That the bastard made my intrepid server stutter like that? Oh, yeah, Jason definitely deserved a knee to the balls.

"He needed to learn his lesson. If he comes in again," I warn, "you call the cops."

"Will they do anything?"

"Maybe not, but he's a bully and we have to face off against those types of jerks." I tip my chin at the game on TV. "If I've learned anything from hockey, it's that."

Jarvis shoots me a weak grin at my play on words, but I can tell he's nervous.

No one so much as offers Jason a hand up, and a couple minutes later, he staggers out.

When he turns back to look at me as the door closes, I flip him the bird.

This time, he leaves my A-frame sign alone.

I doubt it's the last we'll hear of him, but it feels damn good to assert my authority.

Chuck's, after all, is mine.

And if I want to throw out handsy motherfuckers who can't take 'no' for an answer, that's my prerogative.

Do *not* ask me why, but it's that moment when I remember Cole and his jersey thing.

Fuck, this is such a nuisance.

But it doesn't stop me from running into the back office, earning myself worried looks from my staff, dragging on his jersey, and taking a snapshot for him.

Mia: xo

Mia sends image

Cole: Fuck.

Cole: I'm not playing, but keep up the good work, babe.

Cole: Thank you xo

Combined with my Wonder Woman act out front and his 'xo,' I can't deny that I'm walking on air when I return to the bar. Jason's going to be a problem, but I find I don't care. Maybe I'll have to walk home with Dionne for a little while, just to be on the safe side, but it doesn't kill my mood.

How that man makes me feel should be illegal, and I can't be anything other than relieved it's not.

Hanna: What are you boys doing?

Kow: In general or specifically?

Hanna: That you have to ask is terrifying in itself.

Gracie: I thought they were mostly behaving?

Hanna: Two of them are injured, and Liam's only just over his stomach flu!

Hanna: And why are none of you wearing neck guards?!

Liam: We kinda play a rough sport, Hanna, lol. It comes with the territory. Not that stomach flu has anything to do with hockey o.O

Hanna: I heard about that boy puncturing his lung

Liam: Gagné isn't a boy

Gracie: No, he's definitely not, and I need him off the LTIR stat. He's recuperating but I need him out of convalescence and on the ice, dammit.

Kow: Look at you bringing out all the big words.

Gracie: Here's one: DICTIONARY

Gracie: Some even come with pictures, Kow, so you can figure out what a word means.

Kow: Actually, I was gonna say that you're talking like a GM.

Gracie: Huh?

Liam: What?

Cole: Really?!

Matt: o.O

Gray: :O

Kow: For fuck's sake, I can be nice.

Trent: What do you want?

Cole: There's always a catch with you, bro

Kow: Man, you're going to give me a complex

Fryd: You big boy now. No time for complex

Kow: You can have a complex at any age, Dad

Fryd: You too old

Kow: I'm not!

Liam: Do you want to see my shrink, lol?

Liam: He's starting to specialize in hockey players

Noah: Huh?

Liam: NVM

Gracie: I'm sorry that I jumped down your throat

Kow: It's okay. I'm starting to see that I've been more of a dick than I thought

Liam: Meaning you meant to be a dick, just not as big of one as you were?

Kow: Something like that

Cole: *snorts*

Gray: Hanna's right though.

Hanna: I like to think I am sometimes. But about what in particular?

Gray: We're all dropping like flies.

Cole: Hardly. I got whacked in the calf, dude.

Gray: I hurt my wrist.

Fryd: Come in threes

Hanna: Well, we've had three with Liam's stomach flu so that's done then.

Hanna: All of you, I want to make sure you're getting plenty of rest in between practices and games. Only Noah and Matt are young enough to bounce back

Gray: The rest of us are decrepit

Cole: TBH I feel that lol

Cole: But it's good to know that I'm ready for the retirement home at 25, Hanna. You know how to make me feel good about myself

Hanna: I care, that's all

Gracie: I'm looking after your boys, Mom, don't worry. Matt's coming to NYC soon

Hanna: He is?!

Kow: @Matt, YOU ARE?

Noah: Dude, not cool. Why the fuck didn't you tell me?

Matt: Because I didn't know what was going to happen.

Gracie: Your lack of faith in me is appalling.

Matt: Contract renegotiations aren't always a matter of A, B, C.

Noah: Why do you need to renegotiate?

Gracie: He has to fit under my salary cap. We might be shipping Davies to the minors but I still have numbers to juggle.

Matt: Worth taking the hit to my wallet to play with Liam and Cole, but I don't know if Boston will go for it.

Gracie: I'm offended you don't believe in my powers of persuasion.

Gracie: You'll soon be whining about the cost of living in New York, fret not.

Matt: Yay. *rolls eyes*

Liam: And the traffic

Cole: Fuck, that really is the worst.

Hanna: Cole! Language!

Fryd: Boy!

Cole: Sorry but it's worth the expletive

Gracie: At least Matt will be able to rest that damn meniscus. That's my biggest concern.

Hanna: You're injured as well, Matt?! But that's FOUR!

Matt: Liam's stomach flu wasn't a third, Hanna

Fryd: They strong boys, Hanna. Not worry. They be fine

Kow: Mom, you just figuring out we get hurt every game?

Fryd: Cezary!

Fryd: No make Mom cry

Hanna: When do you move to New York City, Matt? I'll make sure Fryd, Ollie, and I are down there. We can help you like we did with Cole.

Matt: Ah, Hanna, thanks :) I'll let you know

Gracie: He'll forget so I'll tell you first, Mom

Hanna: Good girl

Trent: That'll be three Bukowski billet boys playing for the Stars lol.

Gray: I hope I'm next. You need a full set, furball

Gracie: I'm working on it

Hanna: What about your brothers?

Gracie: Ha. I'm not working with them

Kow: *pouts*

Trent: Not sure I want to work with you either lol

Noah: Same

Liam: You wait until we bring home the Cup ;-)

Gracie: :D

Kow: Winnipeg is a serious contender this season

Liam: In your dreams

Kow: Trust me, I dream about it plenty

Cole: Nothing's stopping us this year, Kow. We got plans.

Noah: What kind of plans?

Cole: That'd be telling…

Liam: Yeah, hate to say it, Noah, but you're kind of the enemy ;-)

Hanna: Now, now, boys. None of that. We're all family here.

Gracie: Of course we are, Mom.

Gracie: It's on the ice we're not.

Ten minutes later

Hanna: Don't think I forgot about the neck guards.

Gracie: Leave it with me, Mom.

Hanna: Good girl.

CHAPTER 38
MIA

Peaches - Justin Bieber feat Daniel Caesar, Giveon

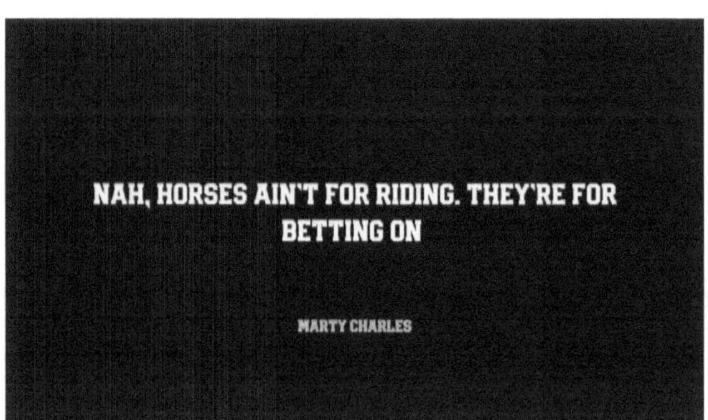

"YOU SURE WE should be doing this?" I grumble as I step back from the horse in front of me when it whinnies.

"There's no need to be scared, Mia," Camille O'Donnelly, the owner of the stables, assures me. "They're very gentle creatures."

Gentle, my ass.

One nearly stepped on my borrowed boot and I don't feel like having a broken toe any time soon.

Still, Cole's in his element, which is weird but sweet. As are his cowboy boots. I didn't know you could tan leather neon pink and green, but Cole apparently worked out where to get them from.

I'm not sure if he's vain or has self-esteem issues, but getting out of those monstrosities will likely heal both.

As Camille gently tightens the tack, she promises me, "Gloria's a very kind soul."

It takes one to know one.

I've barely chatted with this Camille lady but she's already been so sweet to me. I guess she could sense my nerves from the get-go.

Unlike Cole, who, the moment he hobbled out of the car and stepped into the stables, was accosted by no less than three horses who tried to get in his face.

I understood why a couple minutes later—my dude has more sugar in his pockets than a candy factory.

He's still being followed around by a tiny one like he's the pony Willy Wonka.

Camille snags my hand and squeezes it. "You'll be fine on her, I promise."

I eye Gloria dubiously. In return, she studies me as if she and Camille are not on the same page.

"If you say so."

"I put the youngest kids on her," is Camille's third reassurance.

I'd never even heard of this charity project until Cole brought me here today because he claimed he was getting stir crazy in his apartment.

He's the biggest baby when it comes to being injured, and the proof of that is in how quickly I agreed to this disaster-waiting-to-happen because horses and me have never gotten along.

I'd have agreed to go cliff diving if it had shut his whining up though —sheesh.

Camille helps me onto Gloria and gently leads me into the main part of the stables, where Cole is waiting.

He beams a grin my way even though I know my posture is all

wrong and says in his best Western drawl, "Don't you look as purdy as a Georgia peach, Mz. Charles. You'd sure win a Ms. Cowgirl pageant if I were one of the judges."

"Is that supposed to be a compliment?"

Even Camille's laughter is sweet—it's more of a tinkle than a chuckle. "I think in Cole's warped mind it is."

He scowls. "Warped?! Camille!"

She winks at me so I smile/grimace back, more focused on not falling off Gloria than Cole's attempt at easing my anxiety.

Seeming to sense it didn't work, Camille shoots me a worried glance. "Are you going to be all right? I can come with you. Guide you out there."

"Nope," Cole answers on my behalf. "I'm going to take it real slow and show her how I was taught."

"She has more of a drop-down than you did when you were four, Cole," Camille argues, stacking her hands on her hips.

"Gloria's quiet as a mouse. She won't toss Mia. You think I'd put her in danger? She's precious cargo, Camille. I got plans for that butt and it doesn't involve bruising it."

Laughter bursts from me but Camille tuts. "Honestly."

"Hey! No need to be a prude. I've seen what you and that husband of yours get up to when you think no one's around."

Her eyes flare wide. "Shut up."

Cole's smile is smug. "Don't worry. I turned around and headed back here like a good boy."

She flushes. "I didn't—"

Cole winks but I grumble, "Leave her alone, Cole. Like you're innocent."

"I never said I was. I live for filthy sex."

Camille shoots me a dry smile. "My husband's the same. We should join forces."

"And what? Out-filthy them?" I smirk as Cole pouts and declares:

"Impossible!"

"He thinks he's a romance book hero."

Camille blinks at me. "He does?"

"Yeah, he's delusional."

"Hey!"

Snorting, Camille gently taps Gloria's butt. "The things you learn." She leans closer to me. "We should exchange numbers. I need to leverage some of his secrets to keep him in his place."

My lips twitch. "Gladly."

Cole sighs. "Is this how you thank your most beloved donor? The one who spends weekends in the summer helping out with your programs?!"

Okay, so my heart might flutter at his words.

Doesn't stop me from giving Camille my number though. My old skating buddies have been quieter than church mice since Chuck's passing so the potential for a new friend is a pleasant one.

"I'm never going to live that down," he complains five minutes later when we amble out of the stables.

"You love not living stuff down," I retort easily. Then, I query, "Which part?"

"The book boyfriend stuff."

I dismiss that and peer at Gloria's hooves. "It's a long fall up."

He pauses. "That's a strange way of describing it."

I think back to what I said and pull a face. "Yeah, I meant the ground is somehow both farther and closer than I'd like." I tug on the reins. "Do we have to do this?"

"Yes. It doesn't hurt my calf." He bats his lashes at me. "You wanted me to exercise, didn't you?"

I huff. "You didn't need me here though."

"Where'd be the fun in that?"

"I'd have more fun talking to Camille." I click my tongue like he does to get Gloria to shuffle forward.

Of course, she doesn't.

I kinda bounce on the saddle to make her move, but no dice.

"She's offended."

"Shut up."

He shrugs. "She is."

"She doesn't know what I said."

"Sure she does." He pats his ride's neck—Thunder. "They're intelligent."

Could he look more gorgeous? It's obvious he was pretty much born in the saddle, but I didn't know I could be turned on and terrified at the same time.

New level unlocked—check.

He glances at me in concern. "Mia?"

I clear my throat. "I'm sorry, Gloria."

She actually freakin' neighs.

Cole motions with his hand for me to continue. "It'll need more than that."

Knowing I'm crazy for indulging him, I still mutter, "I like Camille, Gloria. That's all. It's nice to be around another woman who doesn't think Cole walks on water."

Gloria neighs and steps forward.

I shoot him a smug smile as he cries, "Not nice, Gloria!"

"Nah, Gloria knows your sass too well. She's used to Thunder preening and hogging all the limelight when *she's* the one who's purdy as a Georgia peach."

That earns me another neigh.

Apparently, Gloria approves of my sweet-talking because, finally, we start moving forward.

"I know you wouldn't tell Camille my secrets."

His cockiness has me rolling my eyes, even though, deep down, I'm relieved he believes that. Especially after what happened with Gracie.

"Keep getting kissed in coffee shops by random strangers and I might unzip my lips."

Cole decides to bring his death forward a few decades early: "That really riled you up, huh?"

I arch a brow at him as I think about our interlude at a coffee shop. "You wouldn't be jealous if someone tried to kiss me over a caffe latte?"

"You know I don't ask for it."

"And I don't have to like it."

"Jealousy." He holds out his hand to high-five me. Begrudgingly, I tap his. "I can deal with that. Week five, baby. Only three to go."

I hide a smile. "You trying to frighten me off?"

"Does it frighten you?"

"I have nothing to lose and everything to gain," I point out as we pad toward a cluster of trees. "I don't want *you* to lose Gracie."

"I think… I have to worry more about her payback."

"Payback?"

"Oh, yeah. She's a real bitch when she gets the bit between her teeth. Like Gloria, eh?" he chirps as he leans over and tries to rub Gloria's nose, but she lifts her head to avoid his touch.

"That's it, girl. You show him he's not a hockey god out here." That has him snickering. "What kind of payback?"

"She's an evil genius, a prankster."

I think about the woman I worked with for years… "Gracie?"

"Yup."

"*Gracie* pranks people?"

"Well, she pranks her family," he reasons. "Liam used to be called 'Peter Pan' in the early days because he flew around the ice. Then, one day, her brother gets it in his head to fuck her best friend. I still don't know how she did it, but she put something in the whirlpool that turned them green."

My brows lift. "She dyed them green?"

"Yup. It was an important game too."

"But what did Liam do?"

"Got caught up in Kow's bullshit as usual."

"So he was an innocent bystander?"

"Yup. She's not afraid of collateral damage."

"So, what happened?"

"They came onto the ice looking like the Phillie Phanatic's twin brothers, and Kow got into a massive fight with the other team. He was kicked off and Liam morphed from Peter Pan to the Leprechaun because he scored his first-ever pro hat trick… while bright green."

I whistle. "She's hardcore."

"Oh, yeah, she definitely is." He winces. "I got mine coming to me. But I'll take it like a man."

"My hero," I breathe, though a second later, my lips roll inward at his doomed tone.

Maybe I wasn't wrong about his premature demise.

He visibly braces himself. "It's all good. Worth it to have you."

I tug so hard on Gloria's reins that she stomps her feet in outrage. Cole turns back to find me staring at him. "Say that again."

His smile is gentle. "Her payback, whatever it may be, will be worth it if I can have you and not hide you."

My throat feels full with the sudden storm of tears that's gathered there. "Truly?"

He grabs my hand and squeezes my fingers. "I knew that week one, Mia."

"How did you know? We barely—"

"Sometimes, you know." He taps his nose.

"Is this because of your romance novel research?"

He bows his head like the pious man he isn't. "I'm erudite by nature." Then, he spoils it. "And I know some real kinky shit because of those books. You're a lucky lady."

My mouth works as I try to figure out how to respond to that, but in the end, only the truth will suffice: "I know I am."

My serious tone has him clicking his heels and bringing Thunder to a standstill. Gloria, because she's a traitor, does the same thing.

Gloria doesn't seem too happy, though, when he brings his stallion close, but she settles down when Thunder starts nuzzling her nose.

Funny how that same trick works on me.

Cole leans into me, rubbing his nose along mine before bringing our mouths together.

It's the sweetest, softest, gentlest kiss we've ever shared.

Lacking in heat but so full of warmth that it'd make my toes curl if my lower body wasn't frozen in place thanks to the horse between my thighs.

Still, I sigh into that kiss. Breathe into it and into him.

His lips part and I thrust my tongue against his, stroking but not inciting. Connecting. Letting him feel what he makes *me* feel.

Showing, not telling.

Because if ever a man deserved that, it's him.

CHAPTER 39
MIA

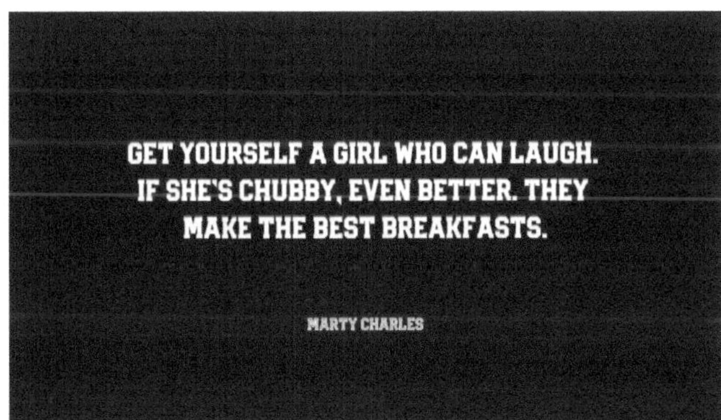

"WHAT ARE YOU DOING?" I ask around a laugh when he stands in front of the bed and starts dancing. My grin hurts it's so wide, but he begins—there's no other word for it—boogying.

With his hips swaying, he takes off his jersey and flings it at me. "Put it on, baby."

"I thought we were reading." I do as he requests, though, because I know seeing me in it drives him nuts.

Well, nuttier than usual.

"We were. Then I read a hot sex scene *and* I saw that reel you did on your great-grandfather had hit two hundred thousand views."

Chuckling, I murmur, "What'll I get if it hits a million?"

"Just you wait and see."

I arch a brow at him as he puts his hands on his belt and whips it out from the loops. "Were you a stripper in a past life?"

"You know it."

While he shimmies his impressive pecs, I sit on my heels, mimicking the move to fuck with his routine.

"No fair," he complains before he turns around and starts doing a semi-peek-a-boo with his jeans that involves half-mooning me.

I attempt to pinch that bubble butt but he dances out of reach. "No touching the talent."

That has me crowing as I cascade into giggles. "You're insane!" Still, I fling myself backward to enjoy the full show.

It doesn't escape my notice that I did this a bunch of times for him, and here he is, readdressing the balance.

God, I lo—

No.

I don't.

It's too soon for that.

But fuck if my feelings for him aren't getting bigger than his massive cock.

"Show me the goods!"

He winks at me over his shoulder before he wiggles out of his jeans and toes them off, revealing a welter of ink I've explored with my tongue. He whips the denims into his grasp at the last minute then uses it like a feather boa around his neck.

With his dick flapping in the breeze, I murmur, "Get that over here."

He treats me to a helicopter move, dick whirring in a full circle, then, while I'm distracted, pulls a cell phone from out of nowhere.

"Do I want to know where you put that?"

"Set it on record."

Ahhh.

That is what this is about.

His tone has shifted though…

Fuck, he's adorable.

"Nervous?"

"I mean, I don't want to get performance anxiety."

I see his dick is down for this even if his head isn't, so I grin at him. "You're the one who instigated this."

"You suggested it first."

"I'm not against it, but if you're nervous…"

"I'm not nervous."

"You look nervous."

"I'm not!"

I raise my hands in surrender but I stare at his dick. My brows surge. "It got soft."

"I have to concentrate."

"You never have to work at that. I literally blow in your direction and you're hard."

"Sounds like you take my erections for granted," he mutters as he stares at the cell in my hand as if he didn't give it to me.

"You don't have to do this."

"I want to."

Aware of the massive trust exercise this is, I strip out of his jersey and my oversized tee then crawl forward, watching his dick twitch but not pop to full mast.

Snatching the stand on my dresser, I set it up as he asks, "Is it rolling?"

"Yes, but we can switch it off."

Cole stares at me, then the phone, then back at me.

He goes through a couple rounds of that, and as I'm starting to wonder if it's *me* he doesn't trust because of the past, he surges forward, hands scooping me up like I'm pocket-sized as he tumbles us both onto the mattress.

Okay, then.

His Adam's apple bobs but he mumbles to himself, "This is like any other night. Mia's hot as fuck, Cole Jr. You need to focus on that."

"Cole Jr.?" I sputter out a laugh.

"What else would I call it?"

"Should I call my pussy Mia Jr.?"

He glares at me, but it's more absentminded than annoyed. "If you choose to, I'll call it that too."

Hiding a smile, I wink at the camera. He notices and immediately stiffens—everywhere, that is, apart from Cole Jr.

Taking matters into my own hands with a smile, I crawl farther down the bed, watching his attention switch to my tits, which sway with the motion as I settle between his knees.

"This is for the times you're away, baby," I croon. "Something for you to remember me by."

He gulps, gaze darting between the camera and my tits. "How did you get used to doing this?"

I hitch a shoulder. "Been on cameras my whole life in one form or another."

"So have I," he argues.

"Yeah, but you're dolled up to the nines in padding. I went out on the ice wearing spandex and had a guy with his hand up my skirt for lifts." I smile at his glower, and recognizing that I've taken his mind off the camera, I put his dick between my breasts and stroke him. "You wanna do that the next time we're at the rink?"

"You haven't let me lift you on the ice yet."

I suck the tip of his dick between my lips for a quick tease. "That was because I didn't realize you were faking it."

His eyes widen before they instantly narrow. "Huh?"

I knew it.

"I saw you on that horse. Your balance is perfect. I've also been watching you on the damn ice. Now, I have to figure out why you're procrastinating… though I'd hazard a guess and say that it's so you have to pay for more lessons with me."

His lips pucker. "Nah. I'm shit."

"Yeah, *okay*. I should have realized sooner but I believed you when you said you had finesse issues." He stares at me, wide-eyed. "Don't look at me like that. I run a hockey bar. Games are on all the time now."

He pulls a face. "Fuck."

"For some unknown reason, I find you at the center of my attention a lot."

"Screwed over by my own sexiness. Damn."

Barking out a laugh, I stroke his dick with my tits again, watching him tense, then murmur, "Don't worry, baby. I won't punish Cole Jr."

"You won't?"

I lower my head to nip his piercing between my teeth and tug. He yelps but I let go almost immediately and plop his cock against his abs.

Settling on my knees, I plunk myself higher on his belly so that when I rock against him, he gets some good friction.

That piercing glinting at me is a distraction—I swear he did it so you forget how wide he is.

Braver women than me have probably run screaming for the hills at the prospect of taking all that girth.

"What do you want to jack off to, hmm?"

Gaze locked on my pussy, he rumbles, "I want to watch you sit on my face."

His admission relaxes him some, but his body is still locked up tighter than a prisoner in a supermax jail cell. Which, considering how he started this, is really something.

"That we can definitely do," I purr.

He wriggles his shoulders then starts to slide down the bed so his head is flat on the mattress. When he grabs a hold of my ass, he lifts me, bodily, so that I'm straddling his face.

How he handles me tells me he'd maneuver me perfectly on the ice, and after a career of subpar partners, that's more of a turn-on than I realized.

"I want you to face the camera so that I can see your expression on the video," he instructs, helping me shift on my knees until I'm looking straight at his phone.

In all honesty, this is my comfort zone.

I've done it so many times that it's actually nice knowing I won't have to take care of my own pleasure for once.

"Fuck, you smell good."

A choked laugh escapes me that is immediately bitten off when his hot breath brushes over my sex. Then, his tongue flutters out and my head rocks backward slightly before I remember that this is about him watching *me*.

I like the idea of being the star of his personal porn stash.

Shuddering, I lean forward to press my hands to his chest as I grind into his mouth.

"That's it, baby. Take what you need."

My brow furrows at his muffled words, words that are only muffled because my pussy is taking up the entire real estate of his gorgeous face.

When he starts to suck on my clit, I have no compunction against humping him because that feels phenomenal.

As I roll my hips, I see his dick twitching on his abs and lean over to jack him off.

"Oh, fuck," he mumbles into my slit.

Like his words were a forewarning, pre-cum spills from the tip, easing the passage of my hand along his length.

It will never cease to amaze me how damn thick he is. My fingers barely meet as they curve around him, but my handjob has the added benefit of making his tongue hit turbo speed—clearly, he's concerned about coming too fast.

I smirk at the thought and decide to tease him some more as I draw the mushroom-shaped head between my lips, flicking the piercing from side to side to torment him further.

A deep, dark groan rumbles from him and the vibration is too much for me—he wins.

The orgasm is short and sharp, leaving me wanting more, with my pussy clasping hungrily at nothing as it craves the sensation of fullness I know only he can truly give me.

He urges me onto my back, sliding me down so that I'm resting on the mattress this time, except we're lying sideways on the bed—a better angle for the camera.

That he moved me, period, tells me that he's been looking at the position of the phone and he's thinking about what he wants to see in the future.

The prospect of that has me strumming a finger over my clit before I pump it into me.

"Ah, baby, that pussy's so fucking hungry for me, isn't it?"

My head rolls. "You know it is. I want your dick, Cole. Give it to me." I glower at him when his dark laughter fills the space between us. "*Now.*"

His smirk is wholly satisfied, the epitome of smug, but I can't get mad at him, not when he's in possession of what I want the most.

I don't even have the chance to squeak as he maneuvers me onto my front, flipping me over like I'm a damn pancake. That's when he grabs me by the knees and 'encourages' me to spread my legs by maneuvering me around as if I'm a doll.

Still, I wriggle my butt for the camera, hissing when he slaps it. Then, the bed shakes as he surges upright.

I don't have long to figure out what he's doing because he crouches behind me, bends low and proves that his stamina is ten-out-of-ten strong because he pulls my ass cheeks wider so that the camera gets to see every inch of my slit, then he tunnels his dick between my folds until the tip prods my entrance.

My back bows when his thickness starts to invade me.

I've never been in this position with him before and it's uniquely terrifying because I already struggle to take his dick, but this is even worse and yet, simultaneously, a thousand times better.

Groaning when he starts to fill me, I try to relax, *try to* because it's impossible.

"You're so fucking thick," I sob into the sheets, my fingers dragging and tugging against the fabric for some semblance of a hold on them.

"Open up for me, baby. Look at this pretty little slit choking on me." He starts to thumb my clit. "I can't get over how fucking beautifully you take me, Mia.

"I want to watch this when I'm on the road and I want to jack off to the memory of sliding into you because no one welcomes me home like you do. This cunt is mine, do you hear me? No one can fill you like I do."

"Cole," I moan.

"Say it, Mia." His thumb slides into my already straining hole, but he presses down and, somehow, it lets him thrust another inch into me.

I shriek at the crazy fullness then whimper. "No one fills me like you do!"

"That's right, babe. This pussy's mine, isn't it?"

"It is," I sob.

"It knows who owns it."

I mewl as he tunnels deeper into me.

"Say it! Tell me who owns your pussy."

A deep groan bursts from my very soul. "*You* do!"

That's when he pushes in, impaling me on him as he drags the tender folds of my pussy apart in the best way possible.

My clit bears the strain as he starts to thrust into me, barely pulling out, keeping me nice and full. Then, he doubles down on his maneuvering—I can feel spit plop on my asshole, and simultaneously, his thumbs do their damage.

One pops into my ass.

The other rubs my clit.

Ordinarily, I'd smack his hand for going near my butt—anything anal isn't my thing. This time, I scream at the triple attack and bite on my sheets as he fucks me into oblivion.

My eyelids flutter as if I'm in overload, and he seems to know because his thumbs make more mischief—the one strumming my clit moves faster, and the other adds pressure to his dick, making me feel even fuller than before.

"Maybe I should shove that wolf's dildo up here too. Really stuff all your holes. Or maybe I won't. Maybe I won't let you ever use a dildo again because if you need to get off, I'm the one who's going to do it.

"You can sit on my face or my cock, baby, but I'm the one who owns your pleasure. I'm the one who was put on this fucking earth to get *you* off. Do you hear me?"

"Cole!" I scream as he starts to pound into me, harder than before.

"Tell me you won't use a dildo again."

"I won't. I won't. Only your cock—"

"That's right. Nothing but the best for this pretty pussy."

That's when the overload triggers my meltdown.

Lights flicker behind my eyes as I sob through an orgasm worthy of a nuclear blast.

He bites off a curse and I swear to fuck, I can feel him pump me full of his cum.

I shudder and jerk, utterly overwhelmed by his attentions as he drives me to the outer edges of sanity.

Finally, my pussy is granted some semblance of relief—he pulls out.

But with it, I can feel his seed slide out, running free. Until it collides with his tongue. I shudder as he thrusts it into me, keeping him inside me as long as he can.

Slowly, I sag into the mattress until he's finished, then he flips me over, settles on top of me, and lets our mouths collide.

My eyes flutter open at the taste of us both, but that's when his head tilts to the side and I know he's staring straight at the camera.

I stick my tongue out, letting him fuck it and suck on it and lick it so future Cole gets the full show, and then and only then does he curl me onto my side and draw me deeper into his hold.

"You don't want to turn off the camera?" I mumble, utterly wrecked.

My pussy is too.

Fuck, it's going to hurt to walk tomorrow.

"I wanna see this on the road. Want to remember what I'm coming home to."

His words hit me hard. I clench my eyes as I turn my face into his chest, trying not to panic at how badly I want him to mean that.

How desperately I want to be that for him—his home.

Forever.

His future.

When he rolls us onto our sides, his hand stroking my hair, I know that we're both on the same page—we both want that.

The time for deliberating over whether there's more between us than friends with benefits is in the past.

The waiting game is over.

I shiver at the thought, unable to believe I've taken that crazy step of falling for him, of *trusting* him enough to let myself be vulnerable…

Because, after all, to love is to open yourself up to the deepest of hurts and I've already been hurt so much in my life that I don't know if I can handle *him* hurting me too.

So, even though the words are on the tip of my tongue, the feelings dominating my heart, I don't say them.

Not because I don't feel them, but simply put, I still don't *dare* say them.

Not yet.

To say them out loud is for them to be real.

And for a little while longer, I want to exist in this cocoon that scents of us, where I feel safe. Replete. Happy.

For the first time in too long.

Until Curtis decides to live up to his name that is.

The demon who possesses him encourages Curtis to bound out from under the bed and swipe Cole's ass before darting away with the speed of a rally car.

The best part?

It's caught on camera.

WEEK SIX

CHAPTER 40
COLE

EARLY THE FOLLOWING WEEK

Jolene - Dolly Parton
&
Him & I - G-Eazy with Halsey

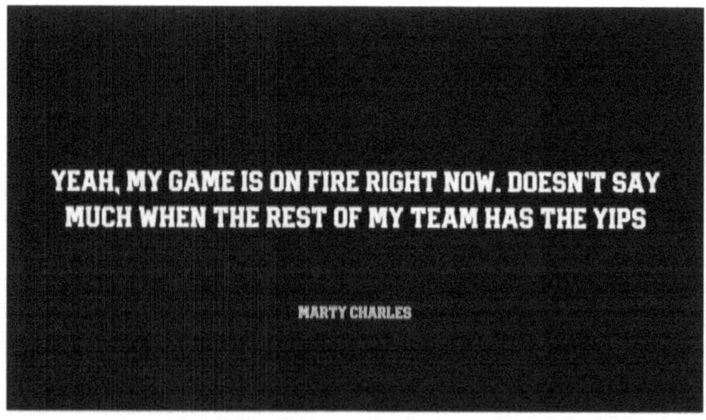

"YOU'RE MAKING me look bad, Cole."

"Fuck off, Callan," I retort around a yawn. "I didn't play that shitty tonight."

"What's with you and Colt—"

"What about Colt?"

"He's... been grumpier than usual. Think some chick rejected him. Not sure why he cares. They all want him.

"Remember when that model followed him here from Saskatoon and he had Mrs. Abelman get rid of her because she stuck around worse than cow shit on a boot?"

My smirk blossoms of its own accord. "Yeah, I remember." Poltergeist Abelman would give Morticia Addams the heeby jeebies—you'd have to be an idiot to get on the wrong side of her. "That was fucking awesome. Who was this broad?"

"Mum asked that too. You're both nosy."

I snicker. "I spoke to her last night. She never mentioned Colt being down."

"I called her before I rang you. Anyway, Colt hasn't said. He looks… sad.

"Wonder why things didn't work out. It's not as if Colt's cruel. He's nothing like Pops. I bet he'd make a great partner."

I yawn. "Tell him that. He'll feel better about himself."

"As if *Colt* has esteem issues." The smattering of hero worship in that statement has me grinning to myself.

Seeing that we're approaching Chuck's, I add, "Everyone, even Colt, has self-esteem issues. Anyway, I gotta go, little bro. I'm sorry that my game performance embarrassed you. I'll *endeavor* to do better."

His tone is sanctimonious. "I should hope so. Speak later, Cole."

Tired doesn't describe my fatigue when we pull up outside the bar, but I said I'd come for Mia after the team returned to the city and that I'd bring her home with me—definitely no hardship. Been thinking about her most of the damn day anyway.

The lights are still on in the bar, though, when we get there, so I tell Burrows, "Do you mind waiting?"

"Of course, sir. I'll go find somewhere to park. Text me and I'll get here as soon as traffic allows."

"Thanks, because I could use a beer."

My five minutes on the ice tonight were fucking exhausting.

He nods at me in sympathy as I clamber out of the car. My calf's better, not even that weak, but I got thrown into suicide sprints plus the game, and I want to fall asleep but my adrenaline is still pumping so I could do a hundred jumping jacks—it's weird.

When I make it to Chuck's, I tap on the door, knowing it's closed for renovations.

I see Mia through the window, her hands on her hips as she surveys the walls in front of her.

At my knock, her head whips to the side and her smile is like feeling the sun on my bones after a long, cold winter up in Pigeon Creek.

I've read a lot of books that talk about this feeling, but I never thought I'd get to experience it. I enjoyed reading how not every relationship ended up like my parents'. They were why I started on the romance books.

It's strange to think I'm living a story from one.

Well, I will be.

Once Gracie knows the truth.

And she will.

Because I'm not letting Mia go.

I can't.

Unaware of my thoughts, Mia scrabbles at the lock to let me in and her arms slide around me in a welcome home that fills my metaphoric cup. "You did great!"

I huff out a laugh. "Now I know you're trying to make me feel good."

Her lips twitch. "You were great for the five minutes you played. How's the calf?"

"It's fine," I assure her, sliding my arm around her waist. "Honestly."

"You promise?"

"I promise. I wouldn't have played otherwise. Gracie grilled me yesterday and again pregame about it."

"So, she didn't believe you either?"

I chuckle. "Nah. But she's naturally suspicious. I'm starting to see how you two got along so well."

Her nose crinkles as she pats my abs, but she guides me in like I need holding up. Only then does she dart back to the door to lock it.

That's when I realize she's listening to country music.

I want nothing more than to sit on a stool and molder away there, but when she returns to my side, I snag her hand and pull her against my chest.

I have no idea what the song is but it's depressing and perfect for my two-step waddle.

"I'll get you dirty!" she chides with a laugh.

"You can get me clean later."

Her head bumps my chin as she tucks it there while I hold her. "You remembered," she says on a sigh.

That her dad used to dance with her mom around the kitchen every night?

Yes, I did.

Her sigh is happy.

This song is… *not*.

"Aren't there happy songs?"

"Sure. But I like the sad ones and you can't say anything. Taylor Swift is the queen of break-up songs."

I pshaw but don't argue, just hold her.

It feels too fucking good to even think about letting her go.

When the song comes to an end, I murmur, "Want to start a new tradition?"

Her smile is soft and warm and filled with tenderness when she looks at me. "Nah. That was their tradition." She runs her knuckles along my jaw. "We need to make our own. Want a beer?"

"You read my mind." Perching on a stool and refusing to admit that it feels good to get off my feet, I take a look around. "You've done a lot more than I expected."

"Jarvis and Beanpole came over earlier to help."

"Trust you to want to paint on the day I'm out of state," I grumble. "I'm good at painting too."

"You can always help tomorrow."

"Damn straight."

It's not the first time I've been in Chuck's, but I can tell that a lick of paint was exactly what was needed. It's still a dive, but it's more respectable than the pit it was.

"I saw that video hit nine hundred thousand views. Way to go, baby."

She beams at me. "Another one started to take off too."

"The baseball one?"

"Yeah. Jarvis made that. Which is funny seeing as he hates baseball. We get this place looking nice, maybe there'll be an uptick of clients. I'm thinking it'll be done tomorrow. We just need to clean the memorabilia as best we can."

I hear the pop and hiss of a bottle being opened and take a deep sip once she passes it to me.

Sliding into my pocket, I find a twenty. "Keep the change."

"You're cute," she drawls, and I side-eye her when she nuzzles her nose against mine and tucks the twenty into my belt.

"It's tough being me."

"Love the jacket, by the way."

I smile at her. "It's neat, huh?"

She pecks my cheek. "Yup. You look like a sexy zebra."

"Gagné said I was making Bret Hart feel bad about his wardrobe choices." My lips form a pout.

"Who's he?"

Unsurprised she doesn't know the old-school wrestler, I mumble, "Never mind. Zebras are in this year."

"Did they ever go out of fashion?"

I click my fingers in agreement. "This is why I like you."

"You're easily pleased," she teases with a small grin. "I noticed that you go whackier with the clothes when you're tired."

I blink at her. "Nah."

Her shoulder hitches. "Could be wrong."

As my mind gets to work on whether or not she's right, I decide I don't want an answer and, instead, shift tacks. "Where's the memorabilia?"

"Back office. There's a lot of stuff. I grabbed it and dumped it on the desk. I need to dust it. We never touched it for fear it'd fall apart."

"I'm starting to see why Chuck had to bribe the health inspector."

She snorts.

"Mind if I check it out?"

"It's a mess, but sure. I need to clean up some of the brushes, then I'll be with you. The walls made them dirtier than the paint did." She steps over to the decorator's table, where she's got a bottle of paint thinner waiting for her to pour into a bucket.

As she plops the brushes into the liquid, I check out the signed Gretzky jersey on the countertop before heading for the back office, scanning the collection of arcade games as I go.

There's a *Bad Dudes* that has me smiling fondly as I think back to the times we used to hang out at the arcade when I was billeting with the Bukowskis. But the four-slot Neo Geo has me arching a brow—Chuck liked some niche shit.

A belief that's confirmed when I see the state of the office. "Wow, you weren't fucking kidding!"

"About it being dirty?" she hollers.

"No, about dumping and running."

There's a shit ton more stuff than I expected. The desk is full of it and it's heaped up in a pile that promises a memorabilia landslide.

That reminds me: "I forgot to bring it with me but in the car, I got Kinnock from Chicago to sign his helmet."

"Oh! Thank you!" she shouts. "You didn't have to do that."

I roll my eyes. "Yeah, of course, I didn't."

Seeing as she's figured out I'm lying about not being able to balance on the ice, though my spinning momentum *is* lacking, I have to do something to help her, and if that means scalping signed memorabilia from old teammates, then that's what I'll do.

No way in hell I can cope with—

I push a forceful brake on that thought.

She'll do what she has to do.

She's a responsible adult.

She can lead her life how she wants.

She has bills to pay, a bar to run, and staff who need roofs over their heads.

Even if I hate every fucking second of it.

So long as I'm along for the ride with her, that's all that matters.

Jealousy is new to me. Much as it is for her. But I have a plan.

Once Gracie knows about us, Chuck's will be my hangout. I'll drag some of the others down here too. Greco—he hates Liam. He'll come here to stick it to the captain.

Because Gracie will eventually accept Mia and my payback will be as bad as Prometheus's, but Liam? Nah. Forgiveness will be a long time coming.

She's worth it though.

Plan in place to get this bar ticking over through fans showing up to catch Stars having a drink here, I nose through the pieces on the table. Unfortunately, it's like a game of Jenga. One wrong move and everything'll nose-dive.

Carefully, I pull the tangle apart and lay it on the floor so that she'll be able to access it better later.

"Man, you have a Grey Junger signed bat?!"

"Yup. That was a part of Chuck's hoard." Her head dips around the door. "There are a couple of neat bats. Chuck had a thing about collecting 'em. He got real excited when he set them on the wall."

"You could have sold this for twenty grand."

"Wow. The value must have increased a lot since he bought it."

Something in her tone has me clearing my throat. "Yeah. Maybe."

"You… You're sure it's worth that much?"

I think about the birthday gift I got Colt this year—a signed Babe Ruth 1946 American League baseball that cost over fifteen grand. "I'm sure."

Sure that Chuck was a douche.

"I guess it wouldn't be much of a sports bar without memorabilia on the wall."

"It's practically two months' payments, Mia."

"Chuck said the collection was mostly nostalgic."

Chuck was an idiot.

"He was wrong."

Even dirty, this shit is worth a fortune.

Her smile is better than a leg massage after bag skating. "If the time comes and turnover doesn't pick up, then I know what to sell first, I guess?"

"Yeah."

She glances at my handiwork. Her expression is nonchalant but she can't hide her hope from me. "Some of this stuff's worth a lot, then?"

I point to an Aaron Judge batting helmet. "That's worth about twelve hundred bucks. Never mind that—" When she frowns, I break off to ask, "What is it?"

"I-I don't understand. I asked him to have it valued. He said because things weren't pristine, they were worthless. How could he get that wrong?"

Because he was a manipulative jerk-off who didn't care about leaving his niece to drown in his debts.

"Maybe he got the wrong person to do the valuation," I try to appease, but I know she's putting one and one together and getting two.

Her sigh is tired. I hate that. "I'm almost done out there."

"Take your time."

I return my attention to Chuck's hoard. Can't deny that there's some cool shit here. The man might have been an arrogant moron who didn't deserve his niece's loyalty, but he had a collector's eye.

Which, of course, is why he didn't want to let it go. You spend a lifetime bringing a collection together, it kills something in you to break it apart.

Just not when you're three-quarters of a mil in debt and know you'll be dumping that inheritance on a woman who loved you…

"Cole?"

"Uh-huh." I nose through a few signed balls. One's in a glass case, but most are plunked on the desk.

"You know I'm grateful, right?"

"For?" I flick through a picture album with signed photos from some of the greats.

"Helping with the hockey memorabilia."

Hearing her proximity, I shoot her a grin. "I saved those fuckers' asses many a time. The least they can do is sign a helmet for me."

"Still… that side of the bar would be empty if it weren't for you. Fourteen grand doesn't buy you much of the new gear and, because of *you*, the walls are full. I wouldn't have been able to do that without you, so thank you."

"You don't have to thank me. I enjoy doing it."

"Oh, yeah, I'm sure."

"Hey, Gracie's starting to think I have kleptomania. It's worth it for that alone. I'm pretty sure she's building up to asking me if I need a session with Liam's shrink."

"Only you'd think that was a good time. You're a strange man, Cole Korhonen."

I wink at her. "*Your* strange man."

She stills. Sucks in a breath. Shoots me a tiny smile that makes every-fucking-thing I'm doing—my disloyalty to Gracie, lying to Liam, living a strange half-life that's shrouded in untruths, shattering a trust that's decades in the making once Mia and I come out in public —worthwhile.

There isn't much I wouldn't do for that smile.

Then, she makes it so much better by whispering dazedly, "*My* strange man," then scuttling back to the bar.

I know she thinks I didn't see her smile but I totally did.

I also know she's aware that I'm not going to take her gratitude.

I'm doing this for both of us.

I need Chuck's to work as much as she does because Mia and charity don't go together like a horse and carriage. She's gotten used to me bringing this stuff back but only because she thinks it's 'free' to me.

If she thought I was paying for anything, she'd lose her shit, and because I'm not an idiot, I make sure that what I get old friends and teammates to sign is their current grody gear.

What she doesn't know is that she needs to buy shares in Febreze because that shit *stinks*.

I don't even realize how much time has passed when I make it to the bottom of the pile on the desk. There, I discover a baseball card binder that has me humming happily.

I used to collect trading cards. I stopped but the boxes are still in my apartment. Only the best ones are in cases displayed on shelves, interspersed with the trophies and crap I've won over the years.

Settling in the recliner that I know Chuck used to sleep in, I rock back, admitting to myself and no one else that my calf is twinging.

As I flip through the pages, Mia yells, "I'm sorry I'm taking so long. I had to clean the baseboards. Give me another ten?"

"Yeah, sure," I shout, quietly content with what I'm doing as I flip through Chuck's collection.

A quick flip and it reveals a full book. My inner child is gleeful at the prospect of finding treasure amid the mass, and that's when I realize this isn't Chuck's.

At least, not her uncle.

There are some *old* cards in here.

My brows lift higher and higher when I see most of Marty Charles's teammates have cards. That they're signed tells me he wasn't afraid to hit them up for signatures like I'm not.

My grin turns goofy at the parallel, but mostly, glee crash-lands deep in my gut because this collection *is* buried treasure.

"Mia!"

"Yeah, babe." The music cuts off for good this time. "Nearly done. I'll be there in a sec."

When I lean down to grab my beer from the floor, that's when the stupid recliner decides that it no longer wants my butt on it. The left armrest literally drops to the floor, knocking over the bottle. The loss of balance almost has me tumbling alongside it, but my desire to save the binder is greater than the desire to spare my ass from plunking on a carpet that saw better days ten years ago.

That's how she finds me—in a puddle of beer and broken bits of spring.

"What the hell are you do— Cole! Are you okay?" She runs toward me, and I can't stop myself from chuckling as I tilt my head up, noticing she turned off the lights in the bar behind her because nothing spotlights her path from the doorway.

"Jesus Christ, Mia. I don't think Chuck's spirit approves of me if his fave recliner is out to kill me."

She tries to haul me up, but I know I'd bring her down with me if I gave her my full weight. Still, the thought's sweet so I let her help me some.

"That chair's a death trap," she excuses.

When I'm on my feet, I grimace at my wet pants. "No shit."

Mia studies the recliner. "Last time, it was the other armrest. I guess I'll have to toss it."

Her sorrowful tone has me curving an arm around her shoulders. "I'm sorry, baby. I didn't realize…"

"How could you have?" she reasons, patting my abs again—that's becoming a signature gesture of hers.

I don't know if she likes touching me or if she needs an excuse to feel me up. Whichever, I'm a happy man.

"Anyway, why did you call me?"

With a half-bow, I wiggle the binder in front of her. "This is gonna save your bacon."

"My bacon, huh? That one of your mom's sayings?"

"Yup. But this is Canadian bacon. Better than US bacon."

"If you say so." She squints at the folder. "What about it? My grandad's collection of cards?"

"Your granddad? Huh. That makes sense."

"What does?"

"Why all of Marty Charles's teammates signed their cards. He must have gotten them autographed for his kid. You can sell these."

She frowns. "Oh, I don't know—"

"What use are they in this binder, Mia?" I demand. "It's not like they're even displayed. They could help lighten your load."

"You think?" Her nose crinkles. "I'm sure they're not even worth that much—"

"Not worth that much?!" I sputter before I drag open the first page and show her. "See this fella here? He was a Yankees pitcher. Ralph Terry was named MVP after they won the 1962 World Series."

"So, his card is worth something?"

"We need to take this to an independent appraiser. I'm telling you—" Something about the corner of one of the cards has me frowning as I lift it to the light. That's when I realize some of the slots are doubled up. "Huh. That must have worked loose from when I fell."

Glancing around the room, I find a roll of paper towel. Determined not to ask why Chuck had that in an office that was also his bedroom, I snag a piece and use it to awkwardly pull out the second card.

When I see the face staring back at me, I blink.

Then, I read the name.

Then, I swallow.

Then, I stagger back, except behind me, there are a bunch of parts from Chuck's recliner so I go down like a lead weight.

Amid that, I hold the trading card to my chest so I don't damage it when, ignoring her shriek of, "Cole! Oh, my god, are you all right?!" I land flat on my ass again.

"Honus Wagner."

I practically breathe the holy name.

"What?!"

As she starts trying to haul me up again, I whimper. "Not what. *WHO.*"

"Huh? I'm Mia Charles, Cole. Remember me? You kinda like me. Did you hit your head? Oh, god, do you have a concussion?"

"Honus. Wagner."

"No. I'm—"

"Mia! I know who you are. I didn't hit my head. This is Honus Wagner's trading card!"

"What about him?"

"What about him?" I shriek. "It's a HONUS FUCKING WAGNER card, Mia. Holy goddamn shit! It's HONUS WAGNER." I realize I'm bouncing on the floor but I don't give a damn. "Don't you know what this is?!"

"A baseball card! Come on, let's get you up. Fuck, if you've made your leg worse, I'm going to cry, do you hear me?"

That has me shaking my head. "I'm not hurt, Mia." Her prodding hands have me growling, "Baby, listen to me. *This* could be the answer to your prayers!"

That earns me a scowl. "Cole, I need you to get up. You're bleeding and I have to—"

"I'm bleeding?" I pass her the card. "Put that somewhere safe! It has to remain in pristine condition."

"For God's sake, screw the damn card, Cole. We need to stop the—"

"MIA! You have to listen to me. This is worth millions of dollars."

"You're lying about hitting your head, aren't you?"

"Why would—"

Both of us fall silent at the sound of glass breaking.

Frozen, we stare at one another until she whispers, "You heard that too, right?"

"It was a window," I confirm.

The sound of more glass breaking shatters through the stillness.

But it's followed by another sound, one I'll never fucking forget.

My hands grab a hold of her arms. "Fire."

Her eyes flare wide. "No! It can't—"

"It is." I jerk my chin at the open doorway where shadows are already starting to flicker in what was once darkness. The glow has commenced. Red and feral. "Look. You can see it. Where's the emergency exit?"

She swallows. "O-Out there."

"Fuck," I hiss as I jump to my feet, adrenaline soaring through me, masking my myriad aches and pains as I make it to the doorway.

The chaos might only have started a few minutes ago, but it's already growing. Surging toward the bar and the table she was using to hold her equipment, drifting over the floor like a snake being charmed, pouncing from oily rag to oily rag that she hadn't picked up yet.

"FUCK," I snarl this time when I see the fire is about to—

I shove away from the doorway as I slam it closed, practically leaping on her as I drag her toward the desk while the fire collides with the bucket she'd used to clean her brushes.

The blast as the fire ignites the paint thinner is a trigger my brain wants to hide from, but I've never been afraid to face my fears.

Even when Betsy was dying, I felt no compunction about jumping into the blaze to save anyone I loved.

The sound of the fire raging, of glass bottles exploding, of the destruction, has Mia tunneling deeper into my arms as I try to figure out our best next move.

"The fire's going to hit the office soon enough." On the lookout for a high window, I find one and point to it. "Do you have a key for that?"

Unlike me, her reactions are dulled. But fire is my natural fucking enemy and we. Will. Not. Burn like my Betsy did.

I snag a hold of her shoulders and shake her. "Mia, answer me. Do you have a key for the window?"

In a daze, she nods, her head whipping toward the door where the sound of the fire gusting grows increasingly louder. I can already feel the temperature spiking, and I know we have to act fast.

In the distance, I hear sirens, which tells me a neighbor or passerby has called 911—thank God. But that could still be too late for us if we don't shift our asses.

"Where's the key, Mia?"

I bark the question again until she jerks in response then tugs at the bottom drawer on the desk.

Because she's moving too slowly, I take over. After tearing through the piles of crap in there, I find a bunch of keys. Only problem? There are about forty. Did Chuck do anything without excess?!

And, no, we do not have that in common.

"Shit," I hiss before I shove them at her. "You need to tell me which is which."

"Y-Yellow upper." She whimpers at yet another explosion, shoulders cowering in terror.

I need to go two lifetimes without seeing her like this.

Another blast rocks the floor.

Ah, shit—the fire must have reached more of the liquor bottles.

I refuse to lose my cool as I search for the 'yellow upper,' which turns out to be a rubber case on the bow of the key.

Correct one in hand, I jump over the broken recliner to reach the window. The key slots in, turns, and lo and behold, it opens too. What, with Chuck's penchant for bribery, I wasn't sure if it'd be jammed shut. Fire code be damned.

The cool air blowing into the office is a danger in and of itself, though.

Returning to her side, I grab the trading card binder, snatch Honus from her hand and tuck him back into a slot for safety, and order, "You hold onto that, Mia, or I'll whoop your butt," before I pick her up bodily and take her across the room.

But my angry words are unnecessary—she clings to the binder like it's a life raft and we're adrift at sea.

If only.

I almost drop her as another burst of flame has the glass front shattering, but I take her to the window and prop her up as I bark, "You need to roll through this."

I help her wiggle past the opening, peering back to check the lay of the land and find that the fire's licking beneath the doorway. Smoke is beginning to rise, black and amorphous.

As I start coughing, she rolls into the alleyway.

With her safe, I concentrate on getting myself out. Seeing as I'm stacked like a brick shithouse, it's not going to be as easy as it was for her.

Knowing I'll have to lever my body through the aperture, I drag the bulk of the recliner to the wall, stand on it, then throw myself through it face-first.

That seems to wake her up from whatever daze she was in because when she notices me struggling, she screams, sobbing as she clings to my jacket and tries to pull me through.

Her panic isn't helping. At all. Not when I'm trying to shove aside memories of the horses screaming in terror, in pain—

For a second, I freeze.

Thrown back to that time.

Tied in place by my father.

Unable to save our beloved horses.

Then, she slaps me.

"COLE. You're going to get those hockey glutes through this window even if you have to scrape off ten layers of dermis to do it," she shouts before screeching, "Do you hear me?"

I shake my head, forcing my brain to work, and with a heave, I start at it again, but fitting a round peg into a rectangular hole was never going to be easy.

Then, the Mia I'm used to makes an appearance.

Mouth tight with resolve, she tosses the baseball card binder onto the ground, uncaring that it's worth millions of dollars, and plunks herself in front of me, arms aloft. "Give me your hands."

"You're not strong enough."

Her growl is like that of a momma bear trying to spare her cubs from a hunter's rifle. "I'm plenty strong."

There's no harm in trying.

I give her my hands and snap, "Give me a countdown."

She nods. "Three, two, one—"

I try to relax, knowing that might help and let her attempt to heave me through.

A scream of exertion escapes her as she drags me a couple inches through the window then, chest heaving, roars, "AGAIN."

The next time, we break off because she starts coughing as the smoke filters through the room and into the night air.

It takes three more attempts until my fucking *ass* is through this godforsaken window.

I swear I'm never going to hear the end of this if she tells anyone.

She's supposed to have the phat ass in this relationship, not me.

Finally, I can scrabble through as a gust of fire hits the polyester rug beneath the recliner and tears through it.

Sweat pours down my face as I hurl us both to the other side of the alley, in time for us to see the fire rage through the office like a starved man.

For a second, both of us sit there and watch the destruction.

Then, she releases a wail as she starts crying.

I close my eyes and curve an arm around her shoulders. "We need to move aside," I rasp hoarsely as she weeps in my embrace. My lips find her temple and, coughing, I whisper, "Thank you for helping me."

More shudders wrack her frame and her hands scrabble at my sweater as she whimpers. "I couldn't lose you. God. No. I need you, Cole. I need you."

I bite the inside of my cheek as her words break off into sobs.

Knowing we have to get away from here, I encourage her to stand.

The adrenaline's still flowing free so I snag the trading card binder then half-carry her down the alley, in time to see the red and white lights flickering in the distance and to hear Burrows shout my name, but it's too late for Chuck's.

Too late for Mia's legacy.

With my head tilted so I can watch the street, I turn her away from the scene and stand there, holding her, until the first responders find us.

CHAPTER 41
MIA

It's Been Awhile - Staind

"I DIDN'T DO THIS," I snap as the officer stares at me with a dubious frown.

They're already pissed that Cole brought me to his apartment and that we didn't hang around at the scene, but after I saw the state of Chuck's, something imploded inside of me—I haven't been able to stop crying since.

It didn't help that Jason was standing in the crowd that gathered around the bar—sporting a smug smile.

Not that the cops believe me.

Assholes.

As for Jason, I wish I'd done more than knee him in the balls that night I kicked him out of Chuck's permanently.

Dear God, he's crazier than any of us thought if he could do this.

We'd always joked about him taking one too many hits to the head during his football career, but *this…*?

Cole, at my side, bites off, "I told you that someone broke a window. Then, there was more glass shattering and the fire started. Mia was with me the whole time. If you think this was for insurance fraud, then you need to check the CCTV footage in the area because that'll prove what I'm saying."

"This Jason Griggs' character was standing in the crowd, you say?"

Why does Officer Adamson sound so incredulous?

I can't believe this is happening.

I know what we're saying sounds crazy, but he's in the NYPD. Surely he's used to crazier midweek nights than we are?!

My chest starts to feel tight.

Really tight.

Until I can't breathe.

That's when I start coughing.

The combination has me staggering back into the wall, sinking slowly as everything closes in on me—vision narrowing, ears focusing on the deafening whoosh of blood, throat tight as if oxygen is too dense for me to suck in.

"Mia!" Cole cries, running to my side and crouching next to me. "See what you did, officers?"

His snarl has me glancing at him, focusing on him—my light at the end of the tunnel.

"That's it, baby," he croons, exaggeratedly inhaling and exhaling until

I'm following him, my tunnel vision beginning to widen some as I look at his beautiful, concerned, furious-on-my-behalf face.

An age later, as my breathing normalizes and my panic's chokehold on me lessens, he growls at Officer Brownhill, "Look, she had nothing to do with this—"

"We're asking routine questions, sir," is the penpusher's retort—even in my state, I notice that he calls Cole 'sir' but never calls me 'ma'am.'

These two asswipes are inches away from fangirling.

"These don't seem routine to me. Shouldn't you give her a number or something so she can contact her insurance?"

The officers share a look and I whisper, "I can't believe they think it's insurance fraud."

"Because that's smart, isn't it? She's dating an NHL player and you think she wouldn't hit me up for money instead of pulling a fraudulent stunt that could get her ass in jail," Cole snarks. "Look, I think it's best if you come back tomorrow. We're both overwrought after surviving an *arson* attack."

The officers share another glance but nod and make a retreat—only because he is who he is.

I read that loud and clear without even having the energy to lift my head and study their expressions.

Cole guides them from his apartment, leaving me sequestered in his kitchen, still in the corner.

It's only once I'm alone that reality hits.

Chuck's is gone.

Forever.

It's not even a case of rebuilding.

There's nothing left.

And if it weren't for Cole, the cops would probably have arrested me for insurance fraud.

My mouth trembles as I cover my face, well aware that my cheeks are sticky with tears and raw from how much I've cried since the blast.

The blast.

The legacy is no more.

I'm the one who ended the line.

Me.

I promised Chuck that I'd keep it going, but here I am, the owner of a bunch of rubble and ash.

I jerk when I see Cole kneel in front of me. His face is covered in soot that he's swiped away with a towel, but microparticles still make him look dirty.

My mind automatically focuses on how I could have lost him tonight.

We barely got him out of that damn window in time, and watching him cough as the EMTs insisted he use an oxygen mask hurt *me*.

The man is a force of nature and *I* brought him into this.

It's the concern in his eyes that reaches out to me through my misery, however. That concern is for me when this is all my fault. I don't deserve it *or* him.

Reaching out with both hands, I watch Cole take them in his and close my eyes as he squeezes my fingers.

"I'm so sorry I got you involved in this."

His frown makes an appearance. "You didn't. It's not like you wanted it to happen, honey.

"Even if you *had* planned the fire for the insurance, you'd never have intended for us to get hurt—"

"Is that what you think?" I drag my hands from his. "Because of what I did to Gracie?!" That last part comes out as more of a shriek. "You think I'm that desperate I'd—"

"Mia," he snarls, his interruption reassuringly immediate and wonderfully aggravated. "You fucked up with Gracie but you're not the devil incarnate, for God's sake.

"So, what, you sucked as a friend. It doesn't mean you're a horrific person. If Gracie didn't have an inferiority complex, she'd have made you pay for what you did and, eventually, you'd have earned her forgiveness.

"I love her like a sister but she's not perfect. She cut out a good friend because she was blinded by her own issues. How can we make up for our actions if we're not given the opportunity to?"

"I don't deserve a second chance," I mumble miserably.

"You didn't kill someone," he barks. "By your logic, she's right to cut me from her life too. Because I dared fall for someone she doesn't approve of! But that's the difference here. If she even tries that bullshit with me, I'll be in her face until she pranks me to get over her snit.

"Look, I already told you that I know you're like my brother Colt." He swipes a hand through his sweaty hair. "You'll ruin yourself financially to save a dumb plot of land—whether it's in Midtown or Pigeon Creek.

"You're too stubborn by half to pull a stunt like this. Never mind the fact you're not that dumb. You didn't see your reaction once the fire took life. You were terrified—not relieved. You were as surprised as I was."

His growled words make me shudder as I reach for his hands again. "I'd never do anything to hurt you."

"And you didn't." He tightens his grip on my fingers. "That fucker, Griggs, did. I wish you'd told me about him. Why didn't you?"

"Not your circus, not your monkeys."

He pins me with a hard stare. "We both know that's bullshit. You're totally my monkey."

Sniffling, I croak out a soggy laugh as I raise our joined hands to swipe at my own dirty cheeks. The tail end of my laughter is chesty from smoke inhalation and I notice his gaze darkens with concern.

"I lost it all, Cole."

"*You* didn't do anything," he dismisses. "That asshole is the one who took it away from you. This is not your fault and it's nothing you could have prevented or stopped. This is… *life*, honey. It blows. And I'm so fucking sorry, but you can't blame yourself.

"Not that I know why I'm telling you this because you'll blame yourself anyway. You're so like Colt, it's unreal. Everything's always his fault and his responsibility," he rambles on, but it's oddly soothing. "Like, I think the dude would take the blame for global warming if he could—"

A waterlogged chuckle escapes me. "I promise I'm not that bad."

His grin is pure Cole. "I'm relieved to hear it—"

Pounding sounds at the door.

My head whips toward the entrance hall.

"Hey, it's okay," he soothes.

"I didn't do it, Cole, I swear! What if they're back to take me in for questioning? They might want to arrest me!"

"Baby, I'd be five minutes behind you with one of the best lawyers in

Manhattan to represent you. If it is them, don't say a word until the lawyer gets there—"

"YOU OPEN THIS GODDAMN DOOR, COLE KORHONEN!"

His eyes flare wide as he gulps. "Worse than Lady Justice, it's Gracie Bukowski."

My nerves settle some, but not a lot. He's right—I've seen Gracie armed with a bat. You have to be swift to avoid her swing.

"Cole!"

Not Gracie that time, a guy.

"She dragged Liam into this." Harrumphing, he gives my fingers a final squeeze before getting to his feet. "Coming," he hollers, but the pounding continues.

"What I want to know is why the last person to hear about you and Mia Charles hooking up is *me*," Gracie snarls as the click of the door sounds. "Because, apparently, the entire city knows."

"Ah, shit. Really? I thought I got us away quick enough."

"Which part are you feeling bad about?"

"Well, both. Or, huh. All three? No, there are four things you're pissed about, right?"

"I'm pissed about a lot," she agrees, her voice calming.

Danger signs flash in my peripheral vision as I burrow my head against my knees.

Gracie's like a storm, after all. The calmer she is, the more dangerous the aftermath.

"What. The. Fuck. Were. You. Thinking?"

"I told you to stop seeing her, dude," the guy, Liam, mutters.

"Don't get me started on you! You should have told me!"

"I told him to stop seeing her! I watched him text her, dammit. I got him to cut ties. There wasn't much else I could do!"

"Apart from fucking telling me. Instead, I had to get a call from your driver that you and *Ms. Charles* were safely in your apartment after a nasty blast at the 'establishment' she runs."

Gracie says all that in such a way that I know she's mimicking Burrows verbatim.

"Burrows tattled on me?" Cole grouses.

"I'm your contact in case of emergency! Of course he's going to tell me that you defied death in a fucking fire! Look at the state of you. If that bitch had anything to do with—"

"Gracie, you shut your damn mouth. I'm used to you being a little bit a lot but you need to chill out. Mia had nothing to do with this. I've had enough of people accusing her of shit that she didn't do."

"You have no idea what she did to me."

"Yes, I do. How do you think Liam got me to cut ties with her? He told me and I fucking *shunned* her. We're talking *Game of Thrones* level shit here—"

"I didn't get a news highlight of some *rando* walking down the street naked and getting cussed at!"

"And is that what it'd take for her to apologize and for you to accept it? Jesus Christ, Gracie, listen to yourself! What she did was fucking wrong, but did you ever ask why she did it? Did you ever let her try to earn your forgiveness?"

"No, and don't you dare excuse her! She ruined my life and she didn't even care—"

I burrow my face deeper into my arms.

"If you knew how much she cared, you'd cry! And *ruined your life*? Could you be any more dramatic, Gracie?"

"You can't—"

"Shut—"

"YOU TWO," Liam roars. "If you're not going to listen to one another, Gracie, I'm dragging you back upstairs. At least let the other finish talking!"

Gracie sucks in a breath whereas Cole expels one.

"This could have been insurance fraud. The Charles are capable of anything."

A sob shudders through me at her condemnation—I deserve it. I know I do, so I stay silent and don't bother defending myself.

"It wasn't insurance fraud. I was with her when it happened!"

"Chuck could have organized it. You'd be there as a witness that she had nothing to do with the fire and he could have brought home the payout."

"Fuck, Gracie, she loved that place. It was her legacy. Why would she betray you to save it, only to let it burn down to the ground? Anyway, Chuck's dead."

"Chuck's *dead*?"

"He died earlier this year," he confirms softly.

There's blessed silence for a couple moments until she mutters, "Well, damn."

I hear footsteps but I don't look up. I hear the scraping of a stool. I hear more footsteps, heavier ones, masculine ones, then Cole sighs. "I'm sorry I hid this from you, Gracie."

"Hid this? More like you lied to me." Her tone is less virulent than before.

But it doesn't surprise me—one of the reasons that what Chuck and I did hurt her so badly was because she cared about us.

"Yeah, I did. If it's any consolation, I love her."

Gracie doesn't hear my gasp because it's covered by her own.

Cole shoots me a soft glance, and with our eyes locked, I whisper, "We shouldn't... It's too soon to say it out loud."

"Too soon? Ha! I loved you before you had to drag me out of that window tonight, Mia, and now, I'm in love with your biceps—"

Gracie's expression is oddly blank as she leans on the stool to stare over the counter at where I'm sitting. I can feel her attention but I'm focused on Cole: his declaration, his proud-as-a-peacock expression.

Not a single damn part of him is ashamed of his feelings for me. With Gracie as a witness, somehow, it makes the next breath I take that much easier to inhale.

This is happening.

Fast or not, he loves me.

Fast or not, I love him.

"I love you too," I croak—hey, it might be quiet, but it's out loud.

"What do you mean she had to drag you out of a window?" Liam inquires bemusedly, completely unaware that the ground beneath my feet quaked.

"We were stuck in Chuck's office—"

Gracie gulps. "You guys escaped through the window that leads into the side alley?"

I nod before I rock my head back. "He couldn't get out."

Liam snorts but Gracie elbows him in the side. "Liam!"

"What? I told him his ass was getting bigger. And he's here. It's not like he's in danger anymore."

Cole huffs. "My woman appreciates my bubble butt."

"You're the one who can't get any pants to fit," Liam snipes.

My brow puckers. "You get those jeans tailored to you?"

His sheepish grin is answer enough.

"You saved him?" Gracie breathes.

"She did." Eyes flickering between us, he clearly sees a way to right all the wrongs I made.

But, I won't let him take that route.

"Even though it's far too soon, I love him. I wasn't about to leave him until the fire department showed up."

"Your guns are gonna ache tomorrow." Liam's gaze darts between us, though Gracie's at the center of his focus. "I guess you're the reason he's been gaining weight?"

Cole stacks his hands on his hips. "I am standing here, you know?"

"He hasn't put on that much!"

"Twenty pounds," Gracie tacks on, her expression contemplative as she maintains that hyperfocused stare.

My brows lift but he shrugs. "Is a man not allowed to be happy? Anyway, it's mostly muscle."

"And, apparently, it's all centered in your ass," Liam crows.

Gracie elbows him again. "Shut up. We could have lost him tonight if it weren't for Mia." I can see she's having a hard time reconciling what she perceives me to be with that.

Even Liam's smirk fades at her reasoning.

"The firefighters would have saved him."

I think.

The idea that they might not have has me freezing in place.

My lungs feel like they're seizing as anxiety crawls over me. Something that only takes a deeper hold when the memory of the fire meeting Chuck's ancient rug flashes before my eyes.

"Mia?"

Cole's concerned tone snaps me back, but it doesn't stop me from rubbing my arms where goose bumps have gained ground.

"I wasn't about to risk waiting for the firefighters."

I'd have figured out how to tear off the goddamn window frame if need be.

"Because you love me," Cole preens, strutting over to me and dropping to my side as he nuzzles me deeper into the corner so I literally have no room.

Instead of feeling suffocated, I feel surrounded. In a good way.

I rest my head on his shoulder. "I do, even if it's madness."

"It's not madness. I'm awesome."

"You have a too-high opinion of yourself," Liam chides.

"He's awesome," Gracie agrees, ignoring her fiancé. Then, right at me, she spits, "Too good for you."

Each word's like a knife to the heart.

"Gracie, don't."

I can't cry anymore so I nod at her. "I know."

"Mia! You're *everything*. Don't you listen to her."

His defense of me has me shielding my face with my fingers.

I don't deserve him—she's right.

There has to be a reason why the only people I can keep in my life are staff or clients.

Gracie's lips pucker. "Will you guys leave the room? I want to talk to her."

"No, she's been through hell tonight. She doesn't need to get shit on by you."

Honestly, tonight couldn't get much worse so there's no bullet to even bite. I want to get this over with.

"I'll talk to her."

"Mia—"

"Please."

He heaves a sigh but the look we share has him grousing, "Shout out if she gets nasty."

"Jesus Christ, Cole. What is this? Middle school?" Gracie mumbles as he clambers to his feet.

That has him sniffing. "If the vibe fits…"

She rolls her eyes as Liam joins Cole when they leave the kitchen. Immediately, they're bickering.

"…asshole. Should have left—"

"You don't know her!"

"—Gracie is—"

"—she's wonderful. Kind. Generous. Her—"

To that soundtrack, Gracie steps toward me.

Like there's nothing unusual about my position, she takes a seat beside me. "Why are you on the floor?"

"Panic attack." I cup my elbows as I hug myself. "The cops accused me of insurance fraud. I freaked out."

She grunts.

"I didn't do it!" I can hear her condemnation in that harsh susurration. "You know what that bar meant to me. It's all gone, Gracie. Every filthy counter, each dust-stained item of memorabilia, all the battered arcade games…" A soft sniffle escapes me. "I can't believe I'm the one who lost Chuck's."

She purses her lips. "I didn't expect to ever see you again."

"Why would you? We deserved to be cut out." I stare at my knees. "For what it's worth, I'm sorry."

"It's worth nothing."

"I figured as much, but I wanted you to know anyway. I regret it. I never thought I was the kind of person who could do… that, never mind to someone I cared for deeply, but you live and learn things about yourself along the journey. Some good, some bad."

"If it weren't for Liam, you could have derailed my whole life."

"I'm sorry."

"He gave me a job and that saw me through my final year of school—"

"I'm sorry."

"You brought the whole city's eyes on me—"

"I'm sorry."

"It's not enough. You don't understand what you did!"

"I do!" I cry, for the first time raising my voice. "I know I let you down. I know we treated you like family and we sold you out. I know that we lied. I know that we hurt you. I know, I know, I know!" I twist on the floor to stare at her. "*I hate myself*, Gracie. When I tell you that Cole is wonderful, he really is. I love him. I-I can feel it. Here." I press a hand to my chest, right above my heart. "I never expected that, but even more, I know I don't deserve that. If I can do what I did to *you*, what could I do to him?"

She frowns at me. "That's illogical."

"Is it? I already don't recognize myself in the mirror, Gracie." I dig my fingers into my eyes. "But I was scared. We were backed into a corner and it…

"There are no excuses. I know that. I accept that. It's why I never pushed things past sending you some texts. It's not because I didn't care, but because I know I'm not worthy of your friendship.

"I'm not even sure if I'm worthy of Cole's love."

She's silent for a minute. "That's a tad harsh, isn't it?"

A scoff bursts from me. "Not as harsh as what I did to you. And didn't you tell me I wasn't good enough for him?"

Her mouth flatlines. "Whose idea was it?"

"Does it matter?"

"I'm the one who gets to ask the questions. You're the one who gets to answer them."

I release a heavy exhalation. "Chuck's."

"Why?"

"Did you notice that last year I'd been paying cash for our alcohol deliveries?"

"I did."

"That's because he'd run up such a high debt that they refused to drop off orders anymore without cash on delivery.

"But we weren't paying off our debt, and they called it in. No alcohol, no bar. No bar, no money. No Chuck's. Everyone on the staff would have been unemployed."

"I knew his accounting system was a dud, but I didn't realize—"

"Me either. I'm in debt up to my eyeballs, Gracie. Nearly a million dollars with his medical bills."

She blanches. "Fuck."

"Yeah. Fuck. I'm not with Cole for his money. He'll tell you himself that I won't take anything from him apart from coffee and food."

"It did occur to me to think that."

"And I deserve it."

She's quiet a moment, then: "I don't understand you."

"Me either."

"No. You were like me. Boisterous and rowdy. What the fuck's happened to you?"

"Nothing was the same once you left. E-Everything changed. Even Chuck… It was why he started going downhill. It's a hard thing to accept about yourself—the depths you'll go to when backed into a corner.

"Then, he died, and I've been consumed by his loss but also the state of things he left me to deal with." I rub my eyes. "I'm tired, Gracie. I don't have it in me to be boisterous and rowdy. The only highlights of my days are when Cole bounces in. That's the only time I feel like *me* again."

"He does bounce, doesn't he?"

My smile is small but there nonetheless. "Probably because of his bubble butt."

"You really had to squeeze him through?"

"Yeah. He got lodged in. I was so fucking scared, Gracie. It was…"

When my cell buzzes, I drag it out of my pants in case it's the cops or an insurance adjuster. My brows lift at the message from Camille at the stables.

> Camille: I heard about the fire at your bar. Are you okay?

> Me: How do you know about Chuck's?

> Camille: Cole talks about you. A LOT.

> Me: Ugh, sorry about that.

> Camille: Don't be. I'm glad you're safe. You are, right?

> Me: We are. Cole was with me. We inhaled some smoke but the EMTs sent us home and told us to get checked out if we had any breathing issues.

> Me: He'll need a physical. I doubt his GM would let him play without one.

"Damn straight."

Unsurprisingly, Gracie's reading the chat over my shoulder.

> Camille: If you guys need anything, then I'm only a call away.

> Me: Thanks, Camille. I never expected you to reach out so I appreciate that.

> Camille: Hope to see you around the stables!

"Who's this Camille chick? What stables?"

I don't tell her that she's nosy—I already knew that.

"Cole rides at the ones she owns. The Camille O'Donnelly Foundation."

She blinks then repeats, "Camille O'Donnelly?"

I shrug.

"Small world. The O'Donnellys are Liam's cousins."

Dismissing that, I fidget with my phone. "We were waiting. We gave each other eight weeks—"

"Eight weeks?"

"To make sure we wanted to date one another before he confessed to you who I was." Though her eyes widen, I continue, "You matter to him, Gracie. Please, don't punish him for wanting to be with me."

"What week is this?"

"The last day of the sixth one. I knew I wasn't going anywhere by the fourth week. I-I didn't think love could be like this but... he makes me happy. Whether I deserve that or not, he does."

"Everyone deserves to be happy."

"Even traitors?"

Her sigh is long-suffering. "Even traitors."

"I was going to fight for him. If you'd have... Well, I don't know. But I'd have fought."

"Cole deserves that."

"He does."

"How did you even meet?"

"He hired me to be his figure-skating coach. The rink he uses for private practice, one of the girls on the staff always recommends me because I helped her sister in the early days of her career." A soft smile kicks up the corner of my mouth. "She's heading to the Nationals next year. She outgrew me."

Story of my life.

Gracie frowns. "You look nostalgic."

I shrug. "I am. That could've been me but it wasn't my path."

"Why wasn't it? You skated competitively for a while, right?"

"My parents died and I lost the heart for competing, but I like helping other people follow their dreams."

A breath gusts from her.

"I-I don't expect you to forgive me."

"Good thing because I don't. Might not for a long time. But for Cole, I can push that aside to be… *cordial* to you.

"We're family. He comes to my parents' place for Thanksgiving and Christmas. We're all up in each other's business. Cutting you out cuts him out and I'm not willing to allow that to happen, so I'll put up with *this* and we can deal pleasantly with one another."

Hope flutters inside me. "We can?"

"Yeah. On one condition."

I still. "What condition?"

"That when I call on you for a favor, you say yes."

Okay, so that's unexpected. "Fine."

Gracie arches a brow. "That was easy enough."

"I know that we'll never be as close as we were, Gracie, but whatever you need from me, I'm here."

She hums then, after straightening to her feet, pats my knee. "Thank you for saving him."

"You don't have to thank me." The words make my already leaking eyes leak some more. "I love him."

Another hum. "You should rest."

With that, she makes her departure.

As I watch her go, my shoulders sag.

'Being cordial' with one another is more than I thought to ask for but I'm still sad. I lost one of the best friends on God's green earth through my own actions. *But,* she didn't say she'd never forgive me so not all hope is lost.

With a heart that's oddly heavy *and* light, I get to my feet too and stride over to the kitchen cabinet that houses glasses before I head to the fridge for some cold water. Lifting the glass to my forehead, I let it cool me down before I take a deep sip.

That's when I see it.

The binder.

Pursing my lips, I pull out the first page of cards from their slots.

Not all of them are doubled up, but a few are.

Some even have notes on the back.

Asshole.

Stinks of wet rags.

Got his wife to screw the coach so he'd be pitcher.

He beat my record.

Apparently, that deserves the same condemnation as the rest.

Though the messages aren't exactly *nice,* my fingers smooth over the words.

My great-granddaddy's scrawl...

Maybe the OG Chuck hijacked his kid's trading cards, or maybe they *did* belong to my great-granddaddy and not his son?

A soft smile curves my lips as I turn them over. I don't recognize the names, but then, baseball isn't my sport. It was my family's, and what little I know, I picked up by osmosis or by accident as it's never been intentional.

I've no idea why Honus Wagner's card was hidden, especially when he played in a bygone era, but who am I to question why?

Hell knows if he was an inveterate gambler—maybe he was trying to hide it from his bookies?

Heavy footsteps sound down the hallway and when Cole spies what I'm doing, he gasps. "MIA! Why aren't you wearing gloves?"

My smile deepens at his horror. "Come and look at the messages on the back."

His outraged scowl comes along for the ride as he stands beside me, then it lessens as he barks out a laugh. "Your great-granddaddy was as sassy as you." He studies the faces. "I know my cards, Mia. Trust me when I say you've got over ten million bucks' worth of trading cards here, baby, because your provenance is solid platinum."

"In my dreams."

A growl escapes him as he drags out his cell phone, then after a couple minutes, he shoves it under my nose. "Look at that. It's the exact same card. I'd know because I tried to buy it last time one was on sale."

My heart almost freezes in my chest as I stare at the confirmation of a bid on a lot by an auction house. "You were going to spend five million on a piece of paper?!"

"Colt loves baseball. He deserved it." Sniffing, he wiggles his cell. "But see what I mean? You don't have to worry about money anymore, baby. Your great-granddaddy has you all set up."

My hands shake as I back away from the priceless card collection. "That won't help convince the police that I didn't start the fire."

"CCTV will do that. And if it doesn't, then we'll lie about when we found these cards."

"We can't do that!"

"Sure we can." He tugs me into a hug. "But that's a worst-case scenario. We'll deal with that as it comes.

"Tomorrow, I'll get a lawyer in if they can't use their eyes to see it for what it was—arson."

His hand smoothes over my hair, stroking it as he draws me ever deeper into his hold. "What did Gracie say? She'd better have been nice to you."

"She was candid," I mumble, still trying to get over the binder plunked on his counter being so valuable. "Did she... Will she..."

"Is she holding a grudge against me? Hell, yeah. I've got one massive dose of payback incoming. But it's worth it. *You* are worth it."

"Am I?" I breathe.

"I already told you that you are, but I'll tell you a thousand times if that's what it takes for you to believe me." He leans back so he can tilt my chin up. "I love you, Mia. For you. Because of who you are. Because of what you are. I love your heart. I love your mind. I love your ass—" He grins as I slap his arm. "—and I love your strength. No matter what, I know we can get through anything because of that strength. You're a fighter, Mia. Never forget that."

"I'm a survivor."

"Aren't we all?"

"I love that you think purple and green are a great color combination. I love that when you burst into a room, you bring the energy of a thousand lightbulbs popping on at the same time. I love that you make me laugh. But more than that, I love your kindness. I love that you're so open. I love your bizarre taste in books.

"I love that when I'm with you, the buzzing in my ears fades to nothing because you take all my focus. I love me when I'm with you. I'm stronger. I'm less afraid—"

His mouth presses against mine. "I love me when I'm with you too. You raise me up, baby. Just like how they say in my *bizarre* books."

Despite the fact that I'm on the brink of yet more tears, laughter explodes from me. "You and your romance novels."

"I'll make a believer out of you. One day."

I cup his chin. "I think you did that when I skated onto the ice and you patted me on the shoulder like I was a dog."

His nose crinkles before his expression brightens. "Hey, you know what this means, don't you?"

"Once your calf is 100%, you can stop faking sucking on the ice and we can take a shot at that gold-medal-award-winning routine you want to reenact?"

His eyes gleam. "Exactly."

I lean up on tiptoes to press a kiss to his lips. "Never change, Cole."

"I won't, baby. You're stuck with me."

The words settle deep in my soul.

Unlocking something in me I didn't realize was tightly fastened.

My arms slip around his waist and I huddle into him.

I could have lost this man tonight. Instead, he's here. *We're* here. We have Gracie's blessing, **ish**, and my debts are potentially covered. Chuck's is gone, but it's a place, not a person. Places can be fixed. Things can be bought.

Death is the only permanent part of life, and Cole and I are beautifully alive.

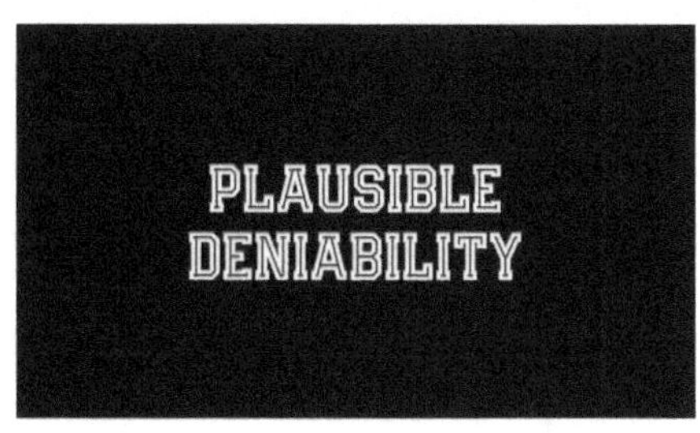

Liam: This message is not Gracie-approved.

Matt: Oooh, I'm all ears.

Gray: Isn't that why Cole nicknamed this chat 'Plausible Deniability' lol

Cole: Ah, fuck.

Liam: The billet brothers hereby declare war on Cole.

Gray: We do?

Matt: Why?

Liam: He's dating Gracie's archenemy.

Cole: Fuck off! I'm not dating her archenemy. I'm in love!

Cole: TBH, I'm surprised I got away with it as long as I did so it's your fault that you didn't notice my heart had been stolen by a sexy imp with a heart of gold.

Liam: You're in love with her archenemy, then.

Matt: You're in love?!

Gray: You have been kinda quiet, Liam. Not been meddling as per usual.

Gray: Everything okay? I just thought you were happy with Gracie. Ya know, deep into the honeymoon period

Liam: I'm not important. I am happy.

Liam: Our so-called bro IS the problem.

Cole: Gracie gave us a pass. You have to as well.

Liam: I don't have to do dick.

Liam: You weren't the one who had to deal with the aftermath of those fuckers betraying her!

Cole: I know I wasn't. I won't make excuses for what Mia did. But I love her. She loves me.

Liam: You betrayed Gracie too.

Matt: Whoa. That's fighting talk, Liam.

Liam: Sure it is. The chick who went on live TV and said that the Bukowskis regularly drank at that bar where Gracie used to work… that's the broad Cole's with.

Gray: Jesus Christ, Cole.

Matt: Why would you do that to Gracie?

Cole: It wasn't intentional! We met by chance.

Gray: Wait. Is that the chick you were getting all lyrical about? I wondered why I hadn't heard from you in ages.

Cole: Because when I found out what she'd done to Gracie, I cut her out. Cold turkey.

Gray: What went wrong then?

Cole: I met her again.

Cole: I fell in love with her.

Cole: I'm IN love with her.

Cole: I won't apologize for that.

Matt: To be fair, Liam, we didn't give you any shit for falling in love with our sister.

Liam: Excuse you? Plenty of shit was given

Gray: We could have given you more.

Gray: If Cole loves her, then, bro, what do you expect us to do?

Matt: Does she love him too?

Liam: She says so.

Liam: I won't let you hurt Gracie, Cole!

Cole: I never thought I'd hurt her. It wasn't my intention. But my falling in love is separate from causing her pain.

Cole: I love Gracie. She's my sister. I was going to come clean about this but we were waiting to see if it was worth it.

Gray: What do you mean?

Cole: We said that we'd make a decision after eight weeks to bring this up with Gracie. But that there was no point if it was only chemistry keeping us together.

Gray: Sounds plausible.

Matt: It's been eight weeks?

Cole: No. There was a fire tonight and it brought things to a head.

Gray: Jesus Christ! Are you okay?!

Matt: A fire?!! What happened?

Matt: Talk about burying the damn lede, Liam!

Cole: She saved my ass, guys. Literally. Got me through this tiny window. I don't know how she did it, but I can confirm my butt is bruised like fuck. It's one of those friction bruises too, so I look like I have a bunch of hickeys down there.

Matt: TMI, dude

Gray: Lol. Only you, Cole

Gray: But... she saved you?

Liam: By her own admission, the firefighters would have gotten to you in time.

Cole: She's being modest. The room was engulfed in flames moments after she helped me escape. Like an idiot, I panicked and tried to go through the only window face-first. FML. There'd have been Cole BBQ served tonight if it weren't for Mia.

Cole: We're lucky. I'M lucky—she saved me.

Cole: If you can't forgive her for what she did to Gracie, that's fine. She knows she did wrong, and she'll make amends however Gracie needs her to. But I love her. So you need to cut her some slack.

Matt: Cole's got a point, Liam

Gray: You need to let the girl prove herself.

Liam: I don't have to do dick!

Gray: Sure you do. That's what family does, no?

Liam: Ah, fuck.

Cole: She's good people, Liam.

Liam: Good people don't betray friends.

Gray: They don't, but are we really going to condemn her for life without giving her a chance to make up for what she did?

Gray: Gracie's so cut and dry with this stuff. One strike and you're out. But that's not how it should always be. People change.

Liam: When did you turn into Maury?

Matt: Don't be a baby because you know he's talking sense.

Matt: I think I speak for Gray and me, Cole, when I say we'll keep an open mind. But if we think she's in any way false or unworthy of you, we'll be the first to tell you.

Gray: We will.

Cole: That's all I ask.

Gray: Liam, do you think that's fair?

Liam: Tabarnak.

Liam: I guess so.

Gray: Anyway, your heart's not in it. If you really wanted to fuck Cole up, you'd have brought Trent, Noah, and Kow in on this war.

Matt: Yeah, they're trying to make up for years of sucking as brothers lol so you know they'd have fun torturing Cole if they knew the truth.

Cole: Please, guys, stop helping me

Matt: You're a big boy, Cole. You can take it. :P

Cole: :/

CHAPTER 42
MIA

LAWYERS MIGHT BE SHARKS BUT ALWAYS PAY
THEIR BILLS. YOU NEVER KNOW WHEN YOU NEED ONE
IN YOUR CORNER

MARTY CHARLES

I'M TOO busy panicking to even see the hand that settles in front of my face until Cole clucks his tongue. "Baby."

I jerk backward and stare with wide eyes at the woman in front of me who introduces herself as: "Rachel Laker."

"This is your lawyer, Mia," Cole assures me as my eyes grow ever wider.

"Call me Rachel," she asserts.

I cast a glance between the two of them and blurt out, "I didn't do this."

Rachel shrugs. "Whether you did or didn't, I'm damn good at what I do."

"Aren't you supposed to believe that your clients are innocent?"

Her smile makes an appearance—it reminds me of a shark who's found itself at a comedy club. "Thankfully, no."

"But I really didn't do it," I whisper miserably, shaking fingers swiping at my already-leaking eyes.

God, I'm such a mess.

"She had no need to," Cole inserts, shoving the card binder that he's been clutching to his chest as if it's a newborn baby at her. "This is worth millions, Rachel."

She accepts the binder and her brow lifts as she starts to flip through the pages. "Even I recognize some of these names. It belongs to you, Mia?"

I swallow. "It's been in the family for decades. Since my great-granddaddy played professional baseball."

"You heard of Marty Charles, Rachel?"

Her lips quirk at the corner. "Who hasn't? Didn't he say, 'A coffin doesn't come with a bank account?'"

"Sage words from an inveterate gambler who lost everything, *twice,* before he hit forty-five," I mutter, quite capable of being disapproving even in my current state of freak-out.

Rachel hums then gets right to business. "I spoke with the sergeant on duty. They think this is insurance fraud."

"But it isn't," I whisper. "I don't even know if there *is* insurance on the damn bar, never mind for how much."

Her brows lift even higher than before. "Is there a reason for that?"

"Her uncle owned the bar and she inherited it."

"If it doesn't land in my mailbox, it's a payment I don't have to worry about. Yet."

"So, you're in debt?"

"Mountains of it. But I have a debt consolidation loan and I'm paying it off. I also have enough savings to cover the loan for at least three more months."

She takes a seat by my side. "Why not sell the trading cards? The Yogi Berra one has to cover most of your debts on its own."

Before I can answer, Cole does for me: "She's sentimental."

Her eyes narrow at his interruption. Then, she flicks a glance between the pair of us. "You do know that you won't be allowed into the interview room, Cole?"

He harrumphs.

"I didn't do it," I repeat.

"And clearly, Cole doesn't want you to go to jail whether you did or didn't because he wouldn't have acquired my services."

The cost of her shoes alone tells me that Cole brought in the big guns.

Turning to him, I ask, "Do you believe I wasn't behind the fire?"

"I do," he promises. "But that doesn't mean I have faith in the US criminal justice system either. I'm protecting you from incompetence. Let's nip this in the bud before it can sprout stinging nettles."

"Another of your mom's sayings?" I ask him softly.

He shoots me a smile. "Yup. Rachel's the best at what she does, Mia. She'll make sure this is the last interview you have to attend."

His faith in the other woman, in the fact that I didn't do this, makes the tension in my shoulders settle down some. His hand smoothes up my arm until it finds the back of my neck. His warmth eases even more of the tension away, making it that smidgen easier to breathe.

"Do you have a reason to think someone could do this to you, Mia? An enemy?"

"The cops didn't believe me when I brought this up."

"I'm not the cops," is her simple reply to my mumbled retort.

"They wish they were on her pay grade," Cole adds cheerfully.

With shoes like hers, I wish I were too.

"There was a long-term patron that I banned from the bar—"

"Why?" she interrupts.

"My uncle was a lot more permissive than I am as the licensee. He was aggressive to staff, a bully, and he didn't know how to keep his hands off the female servers."

"Your uncle allowed that?"

"I think he thought it was funny."

"Chuck was such an asshole," Cole mutters.

Wishing I could argue with that, I sigh. "He was old-fashioned. When a mutual friend of ours used to work for him, we had a not-so-funny running joke that we'd hammer Jason in the head with one of Chuck's baseball bats. It kept him in line until Chuck passed away, then he started being… weird."

"Weird, how?"

"Less sexually aggressive. Well, physically. But he started being more suggestive."

"Verbally?"

"Yes. All round, he was more of a bully. Once, I saw him denigrating a male staff member and I gave him a warning that I wouldn't take that from him anymore. The next time he tried it, I banned him. I guess I pricked his ego."

"No offense, Mia, but it's a major upgrade from bully to arsonist."

"I saw him in the crowd."

"That's why you think it's him?"

"It's the only reason I think it's him. I have no idea why anyone would want to do this if it's *not* him."

Rachel flicks a look at Cole. "And that's why I'm here."

His nod is small.

Even I can see this doesn't look good.

Especially without the trading card collection as backup.

I could have arranged this beforehand. Could have even—

He seems to sense that I'm spiraling because he pulls me into him so that our foreheads are resting atop one another. "You didn't do this. You're a fighter. You were fighting for Chuck's. Rachel is only here because *I'm* fighting for you. Do you hear me?"

"I do," I whisper, but I'm not given the opportunity to say anything else because Officer Brownhill makes an appearance.

He was a jerk to me last night, but he withdraws a bundle from under his arm and shoves it at me. "We were collecting evidence and came across this."

I gape at the signed Gretzky jersey. "How did this survive?!"

"Gretzky's always been a miracle worker," Brownhill mutters.

"Thank you so much," I whisper, eyes filling with tears as I unfold it, relieved for Jarvis's sake that it wasn't destroyed.

Though the frame obviously didn't make it, it's pretty much intact—only a very strong scent of smoke lingers in the fabric.

The next few minutes drift by in a blur as, leaving the jersey with a drooling Cole, I'm guided into an interview room by a new face, Detective Garcia, and reminded of my rights.

"I'd like to know why my client has been brought in for questioning as if she's some kind of criminal when she's clearly a victim of arson," is Rachel's initial sally.

The offensive start tells me how she's going to tackle this interview and it makes the butterflies in my stomach settle down some.

With that one statement, I know that Cole's right—Garcia wishes he were on Rachel's pay grade.

"The same could be said for why your victim has hired a known criminal defense attorney such as yourself, Ms. Laker."

"Hiring a defense council isn't a privilege, officer," Rachel practically purrs. "My tab is being picked up by her boyfriend. The NHL player… You might have heard of Mr. Korhonen."

"Just because she's dating a wealthy man doesn't mean she's incapable of committing a crime."

"Perhaps not, but it would make more sense for her to ask her wealthy boyfriend for a loan than to commit insurance fraud, wouldn't you think?" Her brow arches and scorn etches its way into her expression. "It's a ridiculous premise, in fact. If you look into my client's bank account, you'll find savings that cover her outgoings, enough to make even a simple mind question her motive behind setting fire to a bar that's been in the family for generations."

Though I blink at her words, I keep my gaze locked on the cuff of the Stars' hoodie Cole swathed me in earlier when we got the call from the cops. It's ten times too big, but it smells of him and laundry detergent and it covers me better than a blanket—I feel like I'm wearing one of his hugs.

He, of course, loves it because it's got his name and number on it.

That's when I realize I'm as bad as Betsy!

"—and why would someone commit arson if there was—"

Before Garcia can finish that sentence, Rachel inserts, "Isn't that your job, detective? To figure out the means, motive, and opportunity behind a crime before unfairly accusing an innocent victim of committing arson and insurance fraud on a bar that has been a part of her family for decades?" Rachel taps her nails against the table. "I'm curious as to why you haven't investigated Ms. Charles's statement. Or was it easier to look no further than a woman trying to make her own path in the world?"

Garcia rolls his eyes. "Oh, yes, this random man in a crowd who held a grudge against her. Because that makes sense."

"It makes more sense than *her* doing it."

"Jason isn't well," I insert, earning myself a glower from Rachel.

Garcia demands, "Could you explain what you mean by that?"

I tap my temple, cowering as Rachel's scowl darkens. "Everyone in the bar knows that he used to play college ball and was supposed to get drafted to the NFL until he got hit on the head too many times.

"He's always been aggressive. Me throwing him out, humiliating him in front of his cronies, maybe it tipped him over the edge?"

"How did you humiliate him?"

"I kneed him in the balls," I mutter.

"You have no other known enemies?"

Rachel murmurs, "You don't have to answer that."

Contemplating the question, I slowly shake my head. "No one that'd dislike me enough to destroy the bar." I swipe a hand over my eyes. "Everything went up in the flames. A single jersey is all that survived.

"My uncle was beloved. Even if I'm not, it's a big leap and I can only imagine that Jason has lost the damn plot. But he's a macho man. I-I guess I should have expected retaliation." My mouth twists into a grimace as I accept that I did expect it. Subconsciously. "I figured it'd be in a different way."

"Different how?"

"I thought he might have cornered me one night. Might try to hurt me. Physically." I fiddle with my cuff. "Maybe sexually. I never left the place alone. I was either heading out with one of my staff or Cole came to pick me up."

Silence fills the small room until Rachel breaks it with: "And there you have it, detective. My client was taking steps to protect herself from this man who she clearly felt threatened by. So unless you have any real evidence against her, which we all know you don't, you need to either arrest her or leave her alone."

Garcia studies me for so long that nerves crawl up my spine, making me feel like ants are roaming the expanse. Then, at long last, he states, "You're free to go, Ms. Charles. We'll let you know of any updates."

"No, you'll let *me* know," Rachel retorts.

Garcia concedes that with a nod as his chair scrapes back and he clambers to his feet to guide us from the room.

When the door opens and we're led into a short hall, Cole strides over to me.

In less than ten seconds, I'm wrapped up in his arms and finally, I feel safe again.

Sagging into him, I hear him and Rachel converse over the top of my head about how either her paralegal, Susanne, or her executive assistant, Parker, will keep him regularly updated, but I'm too busy focusing on how differently that would have gone if he hadn't brought Rachel in.

It's only when we're in his car on the ride home that I press myself deeper into his side, entwine our hands, and whisper, "You put book boyfriends to shame."

He stills. Considers my words. Then, he surprises me by not gloating. Instead, he presses a kiss to my forehead. "You make it easy, Mia."

Dionne: The bar was on fire?!

Larry: What the fuck

Beanpole: No way!

Jarvis: Mia? Are you okay? I tried calling but you didn't pick up.

Dionne: I can't believe this!

Two hours later
Jarvis: Mia?

Four hours later
Beanpole: You're scaring us, Mia

Eight hours later
Jarvis: I saw the feature on the news. You're being investigated for insurance fraud?

Thirty minutes later
Mia: I'm sorry I didn't message you last night. Things were

Mia: A lot.

Mia: The cops have been a real pain in the ass.

Mia: I wanted to let you know that I'll be working on rebuilding the bar.

Dionne: I'm so sorry for what happened!

Jarvis: Are you all right?

Mia: I'm fine. Cole and I were caught in it but we got out with some smoke inhalation.

Beanpole: Holy crap. You were caught in it?

Larry: That's insane

Jarvis: Was it faulty wiring or don't they know yet?

Mia: No. Jason started the fire.

Jarvis: JASON?

Dionne: I always knew he was a bad egg. That jackass!

Beanpole: If I see him around, he's due a meeting with my fists.

Mia: No! Leave it. The police are investigating.

Mia: But I wanted to let you guys know that I'll be rebuilding Chuck's and until then, I'll be covering all your wages. I know it doesn't help with the tips you'd be missing, so I'll be upping your rates to $20 an hour

Jarvis: :O You can't do that! How will you afford it?!

Dionne: Jarvis is right! You can't afford to pay us that, honey. Don't worry, we'll get other jobs.

Mia: No, I wouldn't offer if I couldn't cover it.

Mia: Chuck got the best insurance coverage, surprisingly, so it'll pay for the rebuild.

Mia: Plus, I found a family heirloom that Cole says is worth a lot of money. That will help once I can sell it :)

Mia: I understand if you guys need to get jobs in the interim, but I hope that when Chuck's is back in business, you'll return <3

Jarvis: Of course we will!

Dionne: For sure! If you don't mind about the salary, then I might stay at home for a little while. My mom's been sick and could use some help around the house.

Beanpole: You're stuck with us, ain't she, Larry?

Larry: She is, yep. You hurt, Mia? I'm pretty sure Chuck is rolling in his grave at what went down last night

Mia: No, I'm not hurt but I've been better, Larry, and I'm getting there.

Mia: I'll keep you guys in the loop, okay? But until then, I'll deposit the wages into your accounts.

Mia: Thank you for giving a shit, guys

Larry: Girl, of course

Jarvis: For sure!!!!

Dionne: How could you even think we didn't?

Beanpole: I'm kinda mad at you for not realizing that we're a family of misfits!!

Mia: You make me feel a lot less alone and that's something I can't thank you enough for <3

Mia: Speak soon xoxo

Mia: Oh, and hey, @Jarvis. It's a miracle! But your Gretzky jersey survived. The next time we meet up, I'll bring it with me for you

Jarvis: I always knew Gretzky was the second coming

CHAPTER 43
COLE

willow - Taylor Swift

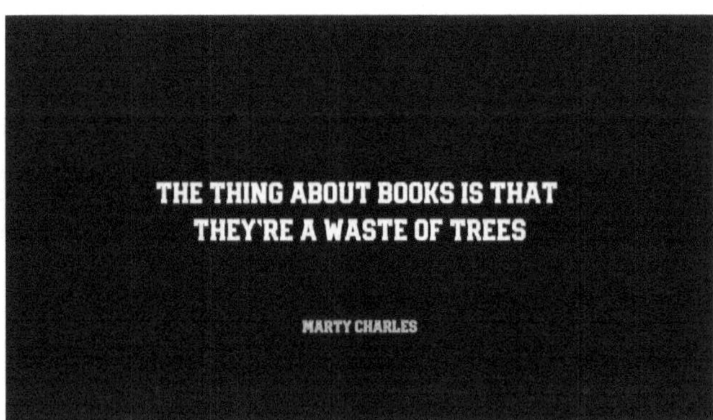

ALL'S QUIET when I make it into my living room.

Oddly quiet.

I've gotten used to the chaos of multiple cats infuriated over their territory changing.

Curtis and Cubert have even joined forces to cause mass destruction of the interior decorating kind—it's fortunate that things are *things* to me.

Well, aside from baseball cards and my trophies.

If they somehow managed to wreak havoc in my trophy room, I'd probably need Liam's shrink more than he does.

I peep my head around the corner, wondering if Mia headed out when I was in the shower. The last I heard was her trying to get off the phone with Garry, Walt, Robbie, and Biff—Chuck's cronies—who were checking up on her en masse while trying to score free tickets to my next game.

Easy to see why they were pals with Chuck.

I don't find her in the living room, but I learn she didn't go out when I stride toward my bedroom.

Where she's reading.

A gleam appears in my eyes when I see it's one of my favorite Omegaverse titles—I hand-bound that goddamn book for her and she rolled her eyes at it.

But she's not rolling her eyes anymore.

Oh, no.

Suddenly, the hours of work on that fucking book are worthwhile because my beautiful, dirty girl has her hand between her thighs.

Soft sounds of pleasure escape her as she reads one of the many, many sex scenes in the book, and I take a step back.

Two.

Quietly.

Then, I retreat to my office where a bunch of packages arrived this morning. One of which is something I was excited to receive but I had to stick with my routine or I'd be screwed for the rest of the day—it's game night, after all.

Derailing with sex is okay, but opening PR packages… nah.

Still, I toss the ones I don't want aside, looking for the box that has zero branding on it to a suspicious degree.

I *knew* she'd love that Omegaverse stuff and I planned ahead.

Box in hand, I tear into it and come up with the goods.

With a pleased grin, I head to the bathroom to wash the 'item,' then I stare at it and wonder how the fuck I'm supposed to get it on my cock.

Pondering the bright purple and green ring, I drag the opening wider to see if my dick'll even fit in it.

It's stretchy as hell so I think it will...

Ten minutes later, semi-hard from the constriction, I manage to get the motherfucker on.

"This had better be worth it," I grumble to myself, even though I have to admit Cole Jr. has never looked more beautiful.

Snorting at the thought, I retreat to the bedroom and find her pink-cheeked and breathing heavily.

Her eyes light up at the sight of me, though, and she opens her arms for me. "This book is hot."

"Told you," I tell her smugly before I blow a chef's kiss.

"This is why you dose us up in lube sometimes."

When I have a bottle within reach...

"That and the fact that I have a legendarily large cock to get into your deliciously tight pussy."

Her eyes settle at half-mast. "Get the legend over here, would you? You've got a mess to clear up."

"Why is it my job?"

"Because you introduced me to this," she quips. "How am I supposed to focus, Cole?"

"Well, we've found a way to make you chill out..."

"I'm not feeling very chilled."

This all started with her freaking out about Rachel's staff not having been in touch yet.

I'd made the book at the same time as the Reylo one, but I'd held this back, thinking it might be too much, too soon.

I shouldn't have doubted her.

As I clamber onto the bed, I murmur, "Are you pantsless?"

"Duh."

Flat on my back by this point, I tap my chin. "Come on, baby girl. Take a seat."

She scrambles out from under the sheets without a second thought, revealing...

Ah, shit.

My semi morphs into a painful erection.

My jersey.

No panties.

And she was jilling off while reading one of my favorite books.

Before she settles her knees on either side of my face, I stare at her and rasp, "If I didn't love you already, I do now."

A small smile curves her lips. "I've pleased my… Alpha?"

Oh, fuck.

I swallow. "Very much… Omega."

She shivers as she lowers herself onto me, and I take a deep sniff of her pussy that has her shrieking with laughter and bobbing onto her knees again. "Cole."

My grin is wider than the Cheshire cat's. "What? They sniff and scent mark!"

Mia bites her lip. "I should shower first."

"You showered this morning."

"Yeah, but—"

I cluck my tongue, grab a firm hold of her ass, and drag her onto my mouth. I stop with the teasing because I can sense genuine self-consciousness behind the words and decide to take her mind off things by the simplest route.

She's wet too—slippery and juicy and so fucking devourable that I want to eat her until the end of time.

As the tip of my tongue tunnels through her folds, I flick her clit a couple times before thrusting into her slit, circling the hole that takes me beautifully, and, in between licks, I murmur, "I love your scent. I fucking love this pussy that welcomes me in. I love how you taste and what you do to me—"

"Cole," she moans.

I smirk against her slit then suck on her clit until she's wriggling, riding me, going as far as to surge high enough to rub most of her cunt on my face.

Now that she's forgotten about being nervous, she's lost to this chaos, and I'd have her no other way.

When she starts to drag off the jersey, I only know because I'm gusted with a wave of air that's scented by our mutual soaps. I slide my hands along her back from below. My nails may be short but they're blunt enough to rake down her spine. She shudders in response then flops forward as I get to work.

Only stopping when she's screaming my name this time, on the cusp of release, do I flip us over. Ignoring her distressed cries, I settle between her thighs so she doesn't get the chance to see my dick.

When I'm looming above her, I find her mouth with my own and thrust my tongue into her so she can taste herself. "You're better than maple syrup, Mia," I retreat to rumble. "Do you know how sacrilegious that is for a Canadian to say?"

A dopey laugh escapes her.

For a second, we stay like that, my dick settled against her pussy, my weight on her, me covering her, shielding her, blanketing her…

There is nowhere else I'd rather be than here.

Forever.

It's a stupid time to ask this of her, but… "Move in with me."

Her eyes pop open. Wide. Enough that I know I've ended her buzz. "What?"

"You heard me."

"You don't have to…"

"I know I don't. I want to."

"I-I thought the cats were driving you crazy."

"They are," I dismiss. "In a good way."

"This was supposed to be temporary," she whispers, rubbing her fingers over the now-damp line of my jaw.

Angling into her touch, I hum.

"Cole?"

"What?"

"It was only supposed to be until this situation with the cops was dealt with." She bites her lip. "And I stopped waking up crying."

I could strangle Jason Griggs.

I've had a couple shit nightmares myself, but every time I wake up to find her sobbing in my arms, the urge to kill Griggs renews itself.

"I know."

"And?"

"And I had no intention of letting you move out, then I realized I should warn you about that."

She pins me with a look. "What? You were never going to let me leave?"

"No one can make you do anything you don't want to, Mia," I point out, letting my nose rub hers. "I was going to make you so happy that you forgot about leaving."

"What changed?"

"I remembered that I hate miscommunication."

A chuckle bursts from her. "Yeah, it's, like, your least favorite trope."

I squint at her. "Are you mocking me?"

"Hell to the yeah." But her fingers stroke through my hair, sliding along the curve of my scalp, nails raking down in a way that makes my freakin' spine tingle.

"Think about it, okay? You're already mostly moved in."

"I'm really not. I brought the cats and enough stuff with me to last a couple more days..."

"We can get a U-Haul."

Her lips twitch. "Don't pretend like you've ever moved in your life."

"I've moved plenty."

"And paid a bunch of movers to do it for you."

"Perks of the idle rich. You could be one too." I wink at her. "Come on. We're great together. Gracie knows. Most of the city as well. There's nothing to stop us."

"Aside from an arrest warrant."

"We're not exactly crossing state lines, babe. Anyway, you're not going to be arrested. Do you know how much Rachel charges? Her rates are practically extortion, but she's damn good at what she does."

Talk of her arrest has my dick deflating, which is the opposite of comfortable with the damn cock ring on—the sacrifices I make for this woman. *Honestly.*

"You never told me how you met her."

"She manages some charitable foundations and invited me to a gala for one when I was in Jersey. We got to talking and I learned that she's a shark so I always kept a hold of her number."

"You're not just a pretty face, are you, Cole?"

"She thinks I'm pretty," I declare to the room, which has her snickering. *And* snorting when I flutter my lashes at her.

Her fingers tug at my hair this time. "You really mean it?"

"I really mean it."

"Thought you liked my apartment?"

"I do. But if you're going to keep finding cats, we need to prepare."

Her smile is incandescent. "I love you, Cole."

"Ah, but will you move in with me?"

Eyes gleaming, she nods. "I will."

Exhilaration swirls inside me. Better than a Cup win.

I press my mouth to hers and devour her, savoring her taste, the rightness of this, how much I goddamn want her, how much I need her, *love* her.

Pushing my forehead onto hers, I rasp, "I never expected to have this."

"To have what?"

"This. Us." I kiss her softly. "Thank you for coming into my life."

She melts beneath me. "You don't have to thank me for that. If anything, I feel the same."

"Even though I make you read romance?"

Her smile widens. "If you keep giving me stuff like this, it's more research than hard work."

She hitches her legs high on my hips and arches against me. Barely any wriggling from her has my dick hardening, and that's when I start to worry about how damn long I'm supposed to have this cock ring on…

Before my brain can process that, she slips her hand between us and slots the tip to her gate.

"Do I even want to know why you're wearing a cock ring?" she mumbles against my mouth.

I shake my head instead of answering, groaning as the relief of being back inside her overwhelms me, overtakes me, in fact. Overshadows everything as I'm welcomed in the only place I want to be.

As I rock into her, I press my elbows to the bed on either side of her head and make love to her.

Low.

Slow.

Passionate.

Loaded with the feelings I have for her.

I've waited a lifetime for my book girlfriend, after all.

I've found my Mia.

I snag a hold of her knees and butterfly them to the bed. Using them as leverage, I ride her faster, watching as she flutters her fingers over her clit, gaze locked on mine as she begins the climb to her orgasm.

When her pussy starts to tighten around me, I'm so close to exploding that I'm relieved for the cock ring—even if my dick does drop off tonight.

Her eyes close. For the first time, we lose that connection. Then, her throat arches as she rocks her head and lets out a deep moan.

I take that as my cue.

I shove into her, going that much deeper, and she squeaks beneath me, mouth forming a perfect 'O.'

"Ohmygod," she sobs.

I find her mouth and thrust my tongue against hers, only pulling back to rumble, "Take my knot like a good little Omega."

Her eyes pop open again and she stares at me blindly as her nails dig into my shoulders, clinging and clutching at me as her hips buck against the new thickness while her cunt struggles to take it all.

That's when I let loose.

"Such a perfect, perfect girl. Taking everything I have to give. Can you feel my cum?" I rasp through the exquisite torture of an orgasm with this fucking ring on. "I'm filling you with me, Mia. You're mine. Mine. Only mine."

Exploding around me, she moans long and low.

"This pussy was made for my cock." I nip her bottom lip, hard enough to mark, testing the resilience with my teeth.

"Your dick was made for my cunt," she counters.

I shift back only to whisper, "Knew I'd get you to admit that."

When she gawks at me vacantly, I smirk at her, smug to the last, then press a kiss to the tip of her nose before I find her ear and whisper, "Who do you belong to?"

Her throat bobs. "You."
"Just as I belong to you…"
She nods, but her eyes are teary.
"Always," I murmur, softly kissing her.
"Always."

OVERTIME

WIFE OF NEW YORK STARS' RUBEN KERRIGAN DIES

BY MACK FINNEGAN

Lacey Kerrigan, wife of Ruben, passed away yesterday. The circumstances behind her death have yet to be made public, but there'd been long-held speculation that there was an illness in the family when Ruben took FMLA.

Lacey leaves behind a husband and a daughter, friends as well as an extended family.

Outpourings of sympathy have already flooded social media, and we here at PSN would like to offer our sincerest condolences to Ruben and London at this sad time.

CHAPTER 44
MIA

In The End - Tommee Profitt feat. Fleurie, Jung Youth

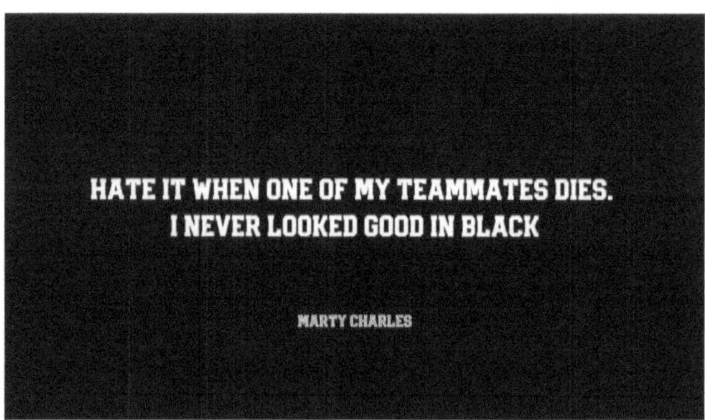

MY HAND TIGHTENS in Cole's as we walk away from the burial site where Lacey Kerrigan was laid to rest.

Quite unintentionally, this was my first public outing as Cole's girl-friend and the press have been horrifyingly rabid.

I only decided to come because Cole, upon learning the news of

Lacey's passing, had looked so damn sad that I didn't want him to deal with this by himself.

When he stops in front of the grieving husband, Cole gently rubs his shoulder and softly pats the back of the baby in Ruben's arms. "I'm so sorry, Ruben. I wish you and London had gotten more time with her."

He stares blindly at Cole, then his features crumple and he lifts his hand to shield his expression. Those puffy eyes tell a tale of their own. "Me fucking too." There's a slight hesitation. Then, he adds, "Cole."

"Did you manage to figure out how things are going to…"

He breaks off but Ruben seems to know what he's talking about. "Yeah. Thank you. For suggesting the leave. At least I was there with her. Focused on her. Not thinking about fucking hockey at the end."

"Anything I can do—"

"—*we* can do," I correct.

Cole nods and shoots me a grateful smile. "—let us know."

"Thanks. I appreciate the offer." Ruben swallows. "It's…" His breath stutters in and out. "…really hard."

The understatement has me shifting closer to him. "It's so easy to want to give up, Ruben. But London's the reason you have to keep going."

"I don't even know how to keep myself in line, never mind her." He closes his eyes. "I want to go to sleep and wake up. This has to be a bad dream." The sob that's torn from him is so much worse because London has no idea what's going on. She's gurgling and happy and lost to her surroundings.

Maybe that's why I start crying too.

This guy doesn't even know my name, but it doesn't stop me from lifting an arm and holding him as best I can.

Cole moves into his other side and draws Ruben into a group hug.

"I wish there were something we could do to make this better," I whisper rawly. "But we're here for you. I swear. Anything you need—"

Ruben sags against Cole, who takes his weight. "My old man told me to grow a pair. I—"

"You don't listen to him," I grind out.

"Ignore that jerk," Cole agrees, clapping Ruben's back. "You take whatever time you need to get through this. We're waiting for you on the other side, you hear me?"

Slowly, we shift aside, letting him straighten of his own accord without erasing our support.

"T-Thanks," he rasps, leaning his head against London's. "I can't tell you how much I appreciate that."

Gently, I stroke a finger over London's cheek before Cole tugs on my other hand and encourages us to shuffle forward. As soon as we do, there's a veritable firestorm of camera flashes.

When we make it into the car, finally free from the press as Burrows puts the pedal to the metal, I ask, "Would you do something for me?"

"Sure. What is it?"

"I made an appointment at a tattoo parlor before I knew we'd be attending Lacey Kerrigan's funeral… Would you come with me?"

His smile is sad. "Yeah. Why not?"

I squeeze his fingers for the ten millionth time today and settle in for the ride after I call out, "Burrows, can you take us to Indiana Ink in Verona, please?"

"Of course, Mia."

The leather seat squeaks as Cole turns to me. "You know Indy?"

"Yeah. She does all my ink." My brows lift. "Take it you know her too?"

"Of course. She did my back piece, plus this one." He points to his forearm where there are layers of inked feathers decorating it beneath his expensive sports coat. "How didn't I know yours were by her?"

"Is that a rhetorical question?"

He pulls a face. "I was supposed to see her earlier this year but things got messy."

"Messy… Understatement. Well, you can make one today," I chirp. "Orrrr… I know she'll let you double up with me."

"What kind of ink are you getting?"

"Gotta commemorate Betsy becoming a part of the fam."

"You have a good heart, Mia."

"Hush."

"No. You do. I'm honored to take up a good chunk of its real estate."

I snicker. "That's a weird way of phrasing it."

"Is it? You still look freaked out when I tell you I love you."

"I don't freak out," I mumble.

"Sure you do."

"Don't."

"Do."

Burrows clears his throat, drawing us from our bickering.

Cole smirks at me, more like his normal self, and I roll my eyes.

"What are you getting?"

"You know she specializes in mandalas?"

"Yep."

"I want a cat-shaped one."

"Cool."

"You going to get some ink?"

He purses his lips. "Yeah. But I don't know if she can do it. So I'll ask her first before I get my heart set on it."

Nodding my understanding, I sit back for the ride, relieved that I broke his sorrowful mood.

I know how grief can settle on someone. He didn't have to meet Lacey for him to feel his teammate's pain.

That's something I'm coming to learn about professional hockey players—they have odd dynamics but they consider themselves family.

Apparently, that's how I came to possess a bunch of memorabilia from other teams. Cole guilt-tripped them into signing their uniforms for me.

I bite my lip at the thought of all that going up in smoke. The only saving grace, of course, is that I didn't get charged for insurance fraud.

Jason Griggs was recently arrested for arson. Not only that, but his dumb ass created a Frankenstein cash app account that he used to steer suspicion onto me. He wanted it to look as if I'd paid him to start the fire. Thank God his plan was riddled with holes because that finally made the police take note.

Now, his lawyer is trying to blame brain damage from his football career, *thirty years ago,* for his actions.

We always knew he had aggression issues, but to set fire to Chuck's *then* tack on a conspiracy charge is a whole other level of crazy.

I can't help but feel lucky he decided to target the bar and not *me.*

Especially with how he was becoming more and more aggressive in his manner.

"Hey, where'd you go?"

I blink at him. "Nowhere."

"Were you thinking about that jackass again?"

I hitch a shoulder. "Just grateful that he targeted Chuck's and not me."

His mouth rounds and he shudders. "Fuck, I never thought of it that way."

Nuzzling into his side, both of us fall silent as we ride toward Verona.

By the time we arrive, Cole's tugging me deeper into his hold as if he's retroactively protecting me from an already incarcerated threat.

I don't argue—it feels good to be so close to him.

"Hey, babe," Indy greets as we walk through the door. Then, her brow lifts when she sees Cole. "Long time no see, douche canoe. I thought you went to Ricki in Manhattan to get the rest of that back piece done."

Her sniff tells us what she thinks about *that*.

"As if I'd dare," he declares, lifting his free hand to his heart.

My lips curve at his antics—honestly, he's so melodramatic, it should be exhausting. Instead, I've never smiled as much in my life.

"Yeah, you'd dare all right, Mr. Korhonen." Her gaze cuts between us. "You shacked up with this doofus, Mia?"

I grab a tighter grip of his arm. "He's *my* doofus, Indy, so be nice."

She clucks her tongue as Cole cries, "Hey!" When I peek up at him, he's pouting, and I have to kiss that pout. It's a biological imperative.

"More pussycats found you, chick?" Indy asks.

"One more. Betsy." I tug on his hand. "Can you fit Cole in? He wants some commemorative ink too."

She narrows her eyes at him. "Only if you book time in for that back piece. It's glorious and I don't want anyone else fucking it up. If they do, it'll be wasted, and don't make me waste my art on you, Korhonen, or you'll suffer the consequences."

He mock-shudders. "Sounds like an offer I can't refuse."

She hums. "I know you too well. You're lucky my schedule is light today."

Ten minutes later, she's busy drawing my mandala while Cole explains what he wants.

When I listen to his request, I bite my lip.

I know he never forgot Betsy, but he didn't let go of the memory of her passing either. I'm not sure whether it's the kitten, surviving another fire, or because he feels loved, but several hours later, with both of us stinging in places thanks to our new ink, I can't help but study his and smile.

A beautiful rendition of Betsy is posed, mid-canter, on his ribs. Atop her saddle, there's Betsy the kitten, perched like a queen, a small crown tilted on her ears that matches the larger one sitting on Betsy the horse's head.

It's both nuts and beautiful—which sums up Cole entirely.

Which is when it makes sense—*Queen Elizabeth.*

"You named your horse after a queen?" I demand when I see the final piece.

"Only kings get to ride queens, babe." He raises my knuckles to his mouth and presses a kiss to them. "Which makes you Queen Mia."

My lips quirk into a grin as he bows over my hand like a courtier of old. "You're ridiculous."

"And you love me for it, *KillerCatQueen.*"

He's not wrong…

Cole: Ruben, we all wanted to tell you how fucking sorry we are about Lacey

Liam: Yeah, man. It was hard at the funeral with the press hovering around us, but I wanted to loop you in on some of the stuff Gracie is putting in place for you

Cole: Gracie rocks, Ruben.

Liam: She's got you this nanny that'll travel with us so that London can come along when we're on the road

Jude: Not that we're pushing you to come back or anything

Liam: No! Of course not. But like, I know that hockey got me through some shit times, and maybe it'll help you?

Liam: Anyway, that's not it.

Liam: Gracie's on the warpath.

Liam: Keep telling her she's deferring her grief… You can imagine how that turned out for me.

Cole: G's arranged for a food fest to come to you.

Jude: Mercy will be over, Ruben, with a bunch of lasagna and casserole dishes so that you don't have to worry about food

Cole: Mia will be by to help clean as well if you need?

Liam: There'll be a nanny on staff at the rink for London during practices too

Cole: Ruben?

Liam: We'll leave you in peace, dude. But we're here. Let the ladies in because otherwise, I feel like your doorman will go nuts trying to stop them from storming the barricade

Cole: Lol. You know it.

Liam: We're here for you

Jude: All of us

Jude: Even if Cole isn't an A yet lol

Cole: I'm an A in spirit

Liam: An A-hole lol

Fourteen hours later
Ruben: ...

Cole: How was the lasagna?

Ruben: Good

Jude: How're you doing?

Ruben: Feel like I'm dying

Ruben: London gets me out of bed every day

Ruben: But the lasagna made me eat so that's something

Liam: Hey! That's great

Liam: You ever need to talk, we're here.

CHAPTER 45
MIA

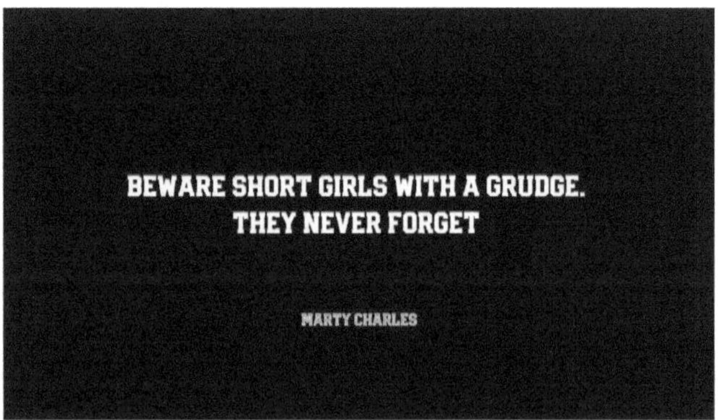

WHEN A KNOCK SOUNDS at the door, I draw my head out of the closet where I'm attempting to store my clothes.

I didn't take into account how much Cole has.

"Emptied a quarter out for me, my ass." I stomp over to the door, dragging it open without checking who's on the other side first. "What?"

Gracie merely arches a brow at me. "Stressed?"

It's hard to stop myself from bristling.

I don't know if we'll ever get to a place where I don't feel that way around her—she looks at me like she still thinks I'm a traitor, and I still can't believe I betrayed her.

It doesn't make for a comfortable interaction.

"Cole has too many clothes."

"He told me you were moving in today." She peers over my shoulder. "I didn't even know he liked cats."

"Well, he might not, but he doesn't hate mine." I hitch a shoulder. "He's at the stadium."

"I know. That's why I'm here."

Immediately, I tense. "What do you want?"

"I heard something through the grapevine."

"About?"

"Your mom?"

Inside, I can feel myself close down. "What about her?"

"She was murdered."

"Did Cole tell you?"

"No. I read about it on this damn blog that knows way too much about the team." She pauses. "I've no idea who her source is or I'd have stamped it out." Her sniff tells me that the 'stamping out' would be hella painful. "Is it true?"

My fingers tighten on the door. "Yes."

"Why didn't you tell me?"

"I didn't want to."

Gracie's eyes narrow. Relief filters through me as she hitches a shoulder, but it's swiftly replaced with dread. "It's time to call in that favor…"

BUKOWSKI CONTINUES WITH BOLD MOVES AND BRINGS ELLISON TO THE BIG APPLE.

BY MACK FINNEGAN

Stars acquire Matt Ellison in a three-way trade, which sees Roger Davies heading to Winnipeg. The Rebels sent Rob Smith to Boston, while the Bulldogs will also get the Stars' second-round pick in next year's entry draft.

New York Stars' fans had this to say:

"Hockey's a man's sport and Bukowski's proving it. She's too damn soft *but* she's got great connections. I can't deny that." John F, Staten Island, NY.

"I think she's too cautious. I couldn't help but notice the Stars have more players wearing neck guards than any other team in the

NHL. Some women just have to control everything. I'm not a fan." Harry D, Bronxville, NY.

"I'm so excited to have Matt Ellison on board! Everyone knows he'd only come back to New York for this GM. His season with the Liberties didn't exactly end well last time. I'm so excited for what's coming! Go, Stars!" Gerry J, White Plains, NY.

Heads Will Roll - Yeah Yeah Yeahs

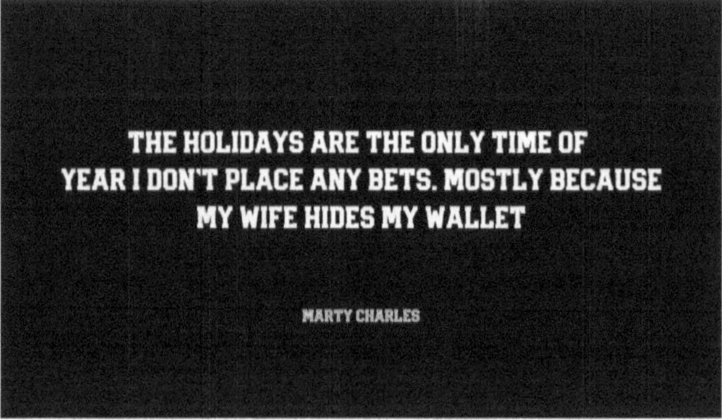

"WHAT DID you do with them, Gracie? If you've thrown them out—"

"I didn't do anything with them, per se," is her serene retort.

Matt, who's off his feet as he's just had meniscus surgery, snorts. "That means her fingerprints are all over the scene of the crime."

"Which so happens to be my closet!"

"Let's face it, that was already a crime against nature," Liam answers unapologetically, his smile smug.

"You know this defense of Gracie was cute and all in the beginning," I snipe, "but it's getting pretty fucking old. Do you know how much my wardrobe was *worth*? And now I have to wear this shit!"

Hanna frowns. "You look very nice, dear."

"I look like I got dressed at Saks!"

"That bad thing?" Fryd inquires as he scoops a massive amount of mashed potatoes onto his plate.

"Yes, Fryd. It's a terrible thing."

"Why no purple today?"

"Because your daughter stole my clothes."

Fryd squints at me. "Deserve it?"

"No, Fryd, I didn't damn well deserve to have my clothes stolen and replaced with this crap. I never agreed to that. I consented to a time-out but not to this travesty."

I'm *beige*.

It's horrific.

Gracie preens. "Your clothes are Pirenzi-approved."

A shocked gasp escapes me. "You colluded with my agent *and* my girlfriend to steal my clothes?"

Trent breaks in, "Pass the yams, Mom."

"Your agent is banging."

I glower at Kow. "She's a she-devil."

"You can bang demons."

Fryd grumbles, "Demons for hell."

"Or bed," Kow mutters with an unrepentant grin at me. Unrepentant because I've already been bitching at my billet bros about the sponsorships she's trying to hitch me up to.

I asked for *green* so she wants me to be the front of the Canadian Cranberry Committee, for fuck's sake.

I'm tempted to sign the contract because I know she was trying to hem me in with this deal—

Huh.

Eureka.

"She's single," I inform Kow with a bland smile.

If two hellspawn belong together, it's Kow and Pirenzi.

"She is?" He clucks his tongue. "Interesting."

"Cole, dear, do we have to discuss this today?" Hanna chides as she starts handing dishes down the table. "It's Christmas, after all. You're wearing very nice clothes and—"

Aghast, I sputter, "That's not the point, Hanna!"

Mia clears her throat. "I do miss the purple and green combo."

"See?" I press a kiss to her temple. "Glad someone's got my wardrobe interests in mind."

Ollie, Fryd and Hanna's newly adopted son, snickers. "Purple and green don't go together."

"Everyone's a critic. Gracie, come on! When are you going to give them back to me?"

"Not until you learn a lesson."

"I learned my lesson!"

"I disagree. Anyway, we've got a charity ball in the new year. I don't want you showing up looking like the Joker. It'll kickstart this season's outreach program."

"Wow, that's next February, isn't it?" Liam mutters.

Even *he* is surprised at how long my punishment is going to last.

But Gracie's turning despotic since she became GM. She even threatened to never make us pierogi again if we didn't start wearing neck guards.

Cruel woman.

Even on the ice, she's dictating my wardrobe choices.

"I'm not talking to Gracie either. What the fuck did you send Davies to the Peg for?"

She smirks at Kow. "You're welcome."

A soft hand squeezes my thigh, and I turn to Mia.

The circumstances of Gracie's 'favor' make it hard to be mad at her. It didn't escape my notice that G tried to have her betray me too…

The only flaw in my sister-from-another-mister's plan?

Mia's panic attacks.

When Gracie put in the request, Mia broke down and only I could get her out of it. Then I had to *agree* to being fucking pranked.

Honestly, it's a sad state of affairs when a man has to willingly agree to lose his clothes as part of a peacekeeping operation.

But it was only supposed to be a time-out. And nothing about the amount of beige I'm wearing is that.

"I know what this is about." I wag a finger at my sister. "*Game of Thrones*."

She smiles at me smugly. "Be grateful I don't have you walking around naked, hmm?"

"I'd prefer to be naked than wear this crap anymore!"

Oren cuts into his turkey. "Why don't you buy something else to wear?"

"Because my closet was carefully curated over decades, Oren. That's why."

"More like it's your tickle trunk," Kow jeers.

"I like Mr. Dressup," Fryd states. "They stop make shows like this no more."

"Hey, but you're bigger now," Matt points out. "Surely half of that stuff didn't fit."

"It's the principle!"

"Yes, dear," Hanna agrees.

"I know a great Salvation Army thrift store over in the Bronx," Ollie chimes in.

I stare around the table, finding no one willing to give me sympathy until I'm left with only one fate—to dig into Hanna's beautiful food with a pout.

But it's amid the chaos as Hanna serves dessert that Mia whispers in my ear, "We can cook up our own revenge?"

The words give me pause. Then I stare at her. "I love how your mind works."

Cole: Hey Kyle. Could you do me a favor?

Lewis: What's up?

Cole: I need some help

Lewis: With?

Cole: I have some private ice time booked tomorrow… We can talk there.

Lewis: Sure thing. You got me curious

Cole: I'll send you a link to the rink

Lewis: Cool

CHAPTER 47
COLE

Happy - Pharrell Williams

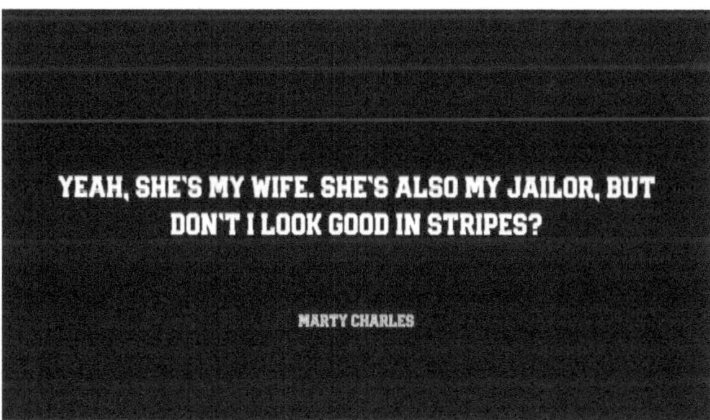

WHEN THE PUCK DROPS, my adrenaline surges.

I've always loved my job, but since Mia and I started dating, something's shifted inside me.

It's as if my happiness is amplifying everything that I love doing.

And what makes this rock all the harder?

My girl's in the friends and family box, an actual PAL, cheering along as she wears *my* number and she **still** sent me porn with an '*xo*' before the game.

Could life get any fucking better?

Wait, it could—Hanna, Fryd, and Ollie are still in NYC after helping Matt with his move. All four of them are sitting behind our bench.

I'm floating on cloud 9, I swear.

Like she's a magnet, I take note of that one 'fan' in the crowd who attends every game in the opposing team's jersey, but I won't let her fuck with our mojo.

When Gagné trips a forward, I watch as the linesman sends him to the sin bin. There are some boos and hisses in the stands, but he shrugs as he skates over to the penalty box.

Liam lines up for the face-off, snatches the puck, and slices it toward Lewis who's promptly surrounded by a couple Lumberjacks. Feeling the hit coming, he spots me in front of the crease, allowing me to one-time it between the goalie's legs.

After Lewis wins the face-off at the start of the second period, McIsaac intercepts the puck and passes it to Liam, who's waiting by the blue line, ready to lead us into the Lumberjacks' zone. I fly in and rush to position myself as a screen in front of their goalie. Liam takes a shot and with my stick, I tip it into the net.

Talk about being in the right place at the right time.

That's when a song blares on the speakers and I grin as I high-five Liam and Lewis, who converge on me to celebrate.

I may or may not do a little boogie to the beat of the song, which has Liam shoving me away with a laugh and Lewis grinning at me.

We line up for face-off at center ice, and this time, it's like I can do no fucking wrong.

The puck and I seem to be in silent agreement that it needs to remain glued to my stick until I decide to shoot it into the goal.

As "Happy" by Pharrell Williams continues to play after I score, I wink at the Lumberjacks' forward as the puck drops, not about to be disheartened by his dour mood. Especially as the rest of the game goes our way too.

Somehow, it's only fitting that Lewis, Liam, and I are the three stars. Because I rocked the most tonight, I skate on first, laughing when "Happy" blares on again.

I give the crowd a show as I move over to the boards to hand my stick to one of the kids in the audience. Liam skates on next, followed by Lewis.

Once Lewis has passed out his stick, I skate toward center ice and beckon them over.

Liam, accustomed to my antics, rolls his eyes at me but traipses onward. Lewis shrugs and does the same.

As soon as we're all together, it's like it's freakin' fate.

The chorus hits.

I spin.

Laughing, Lewis spins with me, calling out, "Liam! Come on, bro, you gotta join in!"

Liam, grumbling under his breath, does as well.

All three of us turning pirouettes on the ice has the crowd cheering like lunatics, and ten thousand cameras flash in response.

NEW YORK STARS WIN 5-3 AGAINST NEW JERSEY BLUE DEMONS

BY MACK FINNEGAN

In the last game of this calendar year, Cole Korhonen came face-to-face with his former team once again and declared war on them in a brutal match that saw him score his third hat trick of the season, with Donnghal completing the score. It's the season of goodwill to all men. All men apart from the New Jersey Blue Demons.

Hilariously, the crowd was ready this time for the Saskatoon native to bring those goals home—instead of hats, they tossed a variety of pink and red items onto the ice. Anything from bras to fabric scraps and dishcloths or towels.

His style, or lack thereof according to some, is shaking the city to its core.

Known for his love of all things pink, Korhonen was celebrated by the crowd for his hat tricks in a style he must surely approve of!

With Korhonen, Donnghal, and Lewis heading onto the ice as the game's three stars, one has to wonder if their new team celly has gone down as well in the locker room as it has across the world—footage of the three spinning forwards has entertained audiences far and wide since their first 'display' two nights ago.

Figure-skating coaches/schools have announced record-breaking sign-ups as a result.

Word is that the left winger who, for the majority of his career and despite his formidable talent on ice, consistently struggles with his edge work, has been receiving private tutelage from his girl-friend, Mia Charles.

One-time state champion, Charles, currently offers lessons in New Jersey—Korhonen's old stomping grounds.

Cole: Hey

Liam: What?

Cole: I know you're not mad at me still.

Liam: Says who?

Cole: Me

Liam: What do you want?

Cole: ...you're making me feel bad.

Liam: GOOD

Cole: You have to be nice to me now that Gracie's punishing me

Liam: We do function as individuals, Cole.

Liam: Meaning she can be fine with you dating Mia and I can be pissed.

Cole: Dude, you're not still mad at me.

Liam: Sure I am.

Cole: Lies

Cole: What's got your boxer briefs in a bunch?

Liam: Nothing. It doesn't matter

Liam: You're right though. I'm over you dating Mia.

Cole: You are?!

Liam: Yeah. Seeing you together at the Bukowskis made me realize this was serious. There's nothing I wouldn't have done to be with Gracie, so I get it.

Liam: I'm just giving you shit.

Cole: Ah, that's all right then.

Cole: Seriously, though, you okay?

Liam: Yeah. I just got selected for the All-Star game.

Cole: Like that's come as a surprise lol. (Go you, bro.)

Cole: I'm going to propose

Liam: Wow! Already?

Cole: When you know, you know…

Liam: Ain't that the truth

Cole: I'm gonna take her to meet the fam in Pigeon Creek

Liam: Lemme guess. You want me to catsit?

Cole: :/ Would you mind? I'd really appreciate it. It'll be Betsy's first time without us.

Liam: This is what the Twilight Zone feels like lol

Liam: Yeah, I'll check on them. Make sure you stock your fridge with kombucha because I'm going to drink you out of house and home

Cole: That's fine. I can handle your boring snacks. Just don't get cum on my sofa

Cole: A man's sofa is sacrosanct. Only his cum should be on his sofa

Liam: Note to self: do not use Cole's soft furnishings.

Liam: Got it.

Cole: Dude, I need a favor, @Callan

Callan: What?

Cole: First, I gotta tell you something.

Callan: Do you have to be so pedantic? When I was finally brought into this damn chat, I expected to have a lot more fun.

Callan: You guys are fucking boring.

Cody: That stings, little bro. Really stings.

Callan: Like I care. Be more interesting.

Cody: Sir, yes, sir.

Cole: I may or may not be dating someone

Colton: Everyone knows that.

Callan: Yes. Everyone.

Cole: Kinda meant to tell you first.

Cole: Then, you know, didn't.

Callan: I'm well aware that you suck.

Callan: Do you think you're in a position to ask for favors?

Cole: It's important.

Cole: And I need your brain.

Callan: For?

Cole: Gonna propose to Mia.

Callan: You definitely have some fucking nerve.

Callan: You gonna marry Mia for real?

Cole: If she'll have me.

Cole: She'll be safe with me. I swear.

Cody: Why do I feel like I'm getting half a conversation here?

Colton: Let the babies of the family have their secrets lol.

Cole: Fuck off

Callan: What favor do you need?

Cody: Wait, why is Callan the only one you're asking? We should all help with this engagement shit. Make it a real family affair.

Cole: What? You in the country?

Cody: I could be for this.

Colton: I can't get you back here for Thanksgiving, but you'll come for a proposal that'll likely suck because Cole does?

Cole: HEY!

Cody: What's there to do on Thanksgiving apart from eat? I'll stick to the barracks for that.

Callan: It's like you guys try to blow

Cody: Lemme tell you, little bro, there's a big world out there.

Callan: That you think this is news to me is worrisome.

Cole: Can we get back to the situation at hand?!

Callan: What do you want me to do?

Colton: What do you want US to do?

Colton: Cody's right. We should all get involved here.

Cole: Ah, fuck.

Callan: You don't have to. I can handle it. I'm emotionally more mature than Cole anyway.

Cole: Thanks, Callan. Thanks.

Cody: BURN

Colton: Hehe.

Colton: But no. Let's torment him en masse. He deserves it. Not sure what for, but he'll have done something.

Callan: You're not wrong.

Cole: FML.

Cole: Okay, some of us don't have ALL day to get railed on by their brothers, so...

Cole: It's like this...

CHAPTER 48
MIA

Welcome Home, Son - Radical Face

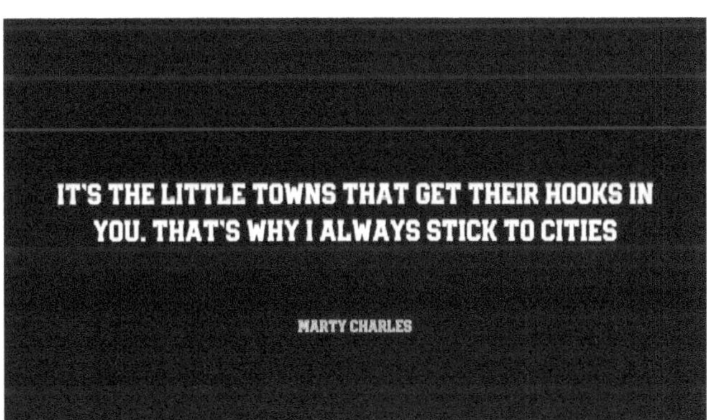

I SWEAR, since Cole came into my life, left is right and up is down.

When we travel via private jet to Canada, it's already an out-of-world experience, but as cool as that is, what's even better is flying over land that's belonged to his family for generations.

It's clear that he's used to it—not the money but the standing that gives him all these privileges. While he's cocky, he's not arrogant. It's more that he takes it for granted.

Still, I can tell he likes watching me experience it. That's why I love him—he doesn't shame me for having grown up with less, simply enjoys giving me more.

With a run of home games in New York, Cole decided to 'commute' via private jet. See what I mean? Privileged. But we get to spend a few days (my birthday included) in Canada which, for a noob, is awesome.

Pigeon Creek is cute as hell.

It belongs in a Canadian Hallmark movie.

It's quaint and charming and I don't understand why he doesn't like coming home—I'd live here in a heartbeat.

Then, his father returns and suddenly, I get it.

Clyde's creepy as well as cruel. He treats his sons like dirt and while Lindsay fights back now, where before I know she didn't, it's easy to see how their relationship would have such an impact on Cole.

Clyde's attitude stinks.

Especially toward me.

He's got more arms than an octopus and leers at me every chance he gets.

His mother, on the other hand, has been so kind and welcoming to me.

His brothers are wonderful too. Not that I've seen much of Callan, for obvious reasons. But he's still sweet and I love the banter they all have with one another—it makes me wish I'd come from a big family.

It's a damn shame that the prospect of running into his father keeps Cole out of the country.

"Are you cold?"

"Huh?"

"You shuddered." Wrapping an arm around my shoulders, he hauls me into his side. "I'll warm you up if you want."

"I can't handle that amount of heat and neither can Pigeon Creek."

He smacks a kiss on my temple. "It's what the place needs. Might liven it up."

I stare around the picture-perfect town and shake my head. "We both see something different."

"What do you mean?"

"I mean this place is adorable."

"No way. It's a dive."

"A dive?!" I shriek, twisting to gawk at him. "It's gorgeous."

"It's old-fashioned."

"Cute."

"Boring."

"Quaint."

"Slower than frozen maple syrup! It's a backwater, babe. You don't have to be polite because you're afraid of hurting my feelings."

I blink at him. "I'm not being polite. Your perspective's skewed. I do have a question though.

"Hit me with it."

"Where are the pigeons?"

"The pigeons?"

"Yeah. You know, the birds!"

"What birds?"

"It's named after pigeons!"

"No, it's not."

"It is!"

"It's not." He snorts. "Pigeon was this old fucker who conquered something or other."

"Informative."

"I don't remember what he did. Killed someone, colonized something. You know the drill. He was a piece of shit who didn't deserve to have a town named after him. *But*, there's some satisfaction in knowing all he amounted to was you thinking his town was about birds."

His smugness deserves a kiss. As well as a shove.

"Hey! What's that for?"

"Being annoying and cute at the same time."

That makes him smugger!

He starts us walking again, leading us past the tiny 'Pigeon Creek Herald' offices to the not-so-tiny 'Cole Korhonen' rink and onto a tinier bakery—Harold's Baked Goods—where I get proof that Cole's a legend in town.

The customers both gawk at him and whisper around him. He's so used to it, though, that he doesn't appear to notice.

As he buys us some water, hot chocolate, and a couple pies he calls butter tarts from a guy called Harry who's limping around with a cane yet moves faster than Cole when he's on the ice, he asks, "Skewed in what way?"

I don't answer until I've guzzled half my bottle of water. Not because I'm drinking, but because I'm thinking.

"Your father's tainted your memories of the town because you didn't enjoy your childhood growing up here. But that's not Pigeon Creek's fault." Whipped cream gets caught around his mouth so I press kisses where it landed and scoop it up with my tongue. "I like it here," I inform him. "Not because it made you into the man I love, but because it's sweet and I haven't had a lot of that in my life. I always traveled to the bigger cities in New York State for competitions. We never went to small towns, so cities are all I've ever known and the people are different. The atmosphere is too."

Though most of him softened—except for one part—when I started licking the cream from his mouth, he stares out of the bakery's picture window and onto Main Street like he's never seen it before.

"I guess it's…" He clears his throat. "What did you call it? *Quaint.*"

I smile. "It really is."

His gaze drifts to me. "You wouldn't mind visiting again?"

Tugging on his hand, I tell him, "I'd love to."

His grin makes a reappearance, but it's softer this time. Gentler. Then, he looks back onto the town with a frown—as if it's a puzzle he can't solve.

Maybe, given time, I can help him out with that.

New York's always been my home, but I'm not blind to its flaws or faults. As I know Pigeon Creek will have many, I'm also aware that Clyde's wrecked Cole's memories of home and that's not fair.

As we leave the bakery, Cole lets me tug us around Pigeon Creek as I explore the small stores and doesn't even complain when I drag him into the museum. Part of it's for me, but it's also for him.

We can learn about his hometown together while he unravels the knots that childhood trauma left behind.

And even though I've known we're serious about one another, it's this visit to the tiny town that birthed him that makes me realize *how* serious.

Love is one thing, but it's flighty. A butterfly you can't catch. An ethereal emotion that exists without a foundation and is expected to weather any storm.

This is different.

It feels like we're building that aforementioned foundation.

One brick at a time.

And maybe, someday in the future, that'll bring us back here, to Pigeon Creek.

I told you so...

BLOG

A LITTLE BIRD told me that Jude Gagné's recent injuries might not be hockey-related *and* that there is a divorce in the cards…

Yes, dear reader, you heard it here first.

It appears Jude might be a member of some illicit fight club. How illicit, I'm not sure. *Yet.*

Watch this space…

If I Ain't Got You - Kaliz Ash

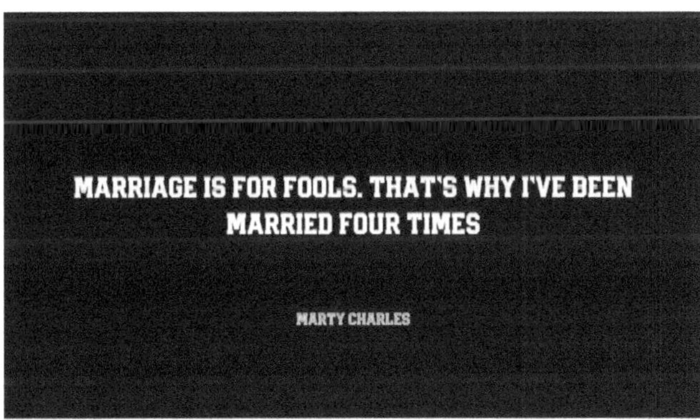

"WOW," she breathes as she stands on the veranda in a part of the house I haven't shown her yet—my folks' wing—peering onto the prairies. "I didn't realize… How is it so big? I saw it from up in the air, but this is—"

Because she's speechless, I chuckle. "We make everything big in Pigeon Creek. Haven't you realized that yet?"

I check my phone for a message from Jude but the asswipe hasn't gotten back to me about this divorce bullshit that's hit the press.

"Lies. Aside from you and your brothers," she teases with a laugh.

Shuffling behind her, taking a second to admire my jersey on her, I press my hands to her hips. "I love this on you."

Her grin lights up my heart. "Why do you think I wear it?"

"If I could get away with it, I wouldn't let you wear anything else."

She rolls her eyes but the sparkle in them makes the love I feel for her settle in my very soul.

We met when that sparkle had been extinguished by life, so I consider it my duty to make sure it's there.

Every day.

For eternity.

When she rests her arms around my waist and nuzzles her face into my throat, I ask, "You okay, baby?"

Her sigh is… happy. "I'm glad we came."

"I figured Mum would make us a shepherd's pie and would serve Deep N' Delicious cake and it'd be your new favorite birthday meal. No balloons but—"

She nudges me. "We make our own traditions, remember?"

My mouth quirks at the edges. "Sure do."

"Waking up with you at my side on my birthday felt *good*."

"You're not alone anymore." I hold her tighter, needing her to know she'll never have to feel that way again.

"No. But, I don't mean that. I miss them, don't get me wrong. My heart just felt… I got it. Why Dad wouldn't want to be without Mom and, for the first time, I—"

"You're glad they're together even if you wish they were able to celebrate with us," I slot in.

"Yeah."

I kiss her cheek, taking note of her breathing—she's not panicking. This conversation hasn't triggered an episode. This is a wound that'll never heal but if we can make it scab over, I'll be happy. "They *are* here with us, baby. We have to believe that."

She clears her throat and her tone chirps up as she declares, "That Deep N' Delicious cake for breakfast while hanging out with your mom sounds like a great new tradition to me.

"I didn't expect to meet her so I'm glad that I did. Why does that cake taste like she made it from scratch?"

"McCain calls it a recipe, but I call it magic crack. Gotta admit, though, I didn't expect you to fall in love with my hometown from h—"

"Don't say it!" she warns. "Pigeon Creek is not hell."

Her defense of this place makes something weird happen inside my chest. It's kinda squelchy. A bit gross. But ultimately, good.

They never mention shit like this in the romance books.

It's all orgasms and smiles and happily ever afters—those fucking genius authors never talk about squelchy organs and a strange urge to sing at inopportune moments because you can't contain your joy.

I should probably sue.

"I thought she'd hate me."

"Who?"

"Aren't you paying attention? Your mother!"

"Oh."

I'd looped her in on the convo I'd had with Mum about her this summer.

To be fair, I'd kind of expected Mum to give her shit too, but she didn't. After I shared what really went down, she's given Mia the benefit of the doubt and they appear to get along well with one another.

It doesn't escape my attention that she's not as glad to have met my father.

Considering he's been a fucking creep every time they've interacted over dinner these past few days, I can't blame her.

"Nah. You make—" Her favorite son's organs squelchy. "—me happy. How could she hate you?"

"Easily," she drawls.

I stroke my fingers over my number on her back. "Impossible. You're too sweet to hate."

"Only in your eyes."

"To be fair, mine are the ones that matter the most."

"Your ego, I swear," she grumbles.

"Pigeon Creek made that plenty big too." When she snickers, I whisper in her ear, "If we were alone, I'd fuck you out here."

She swallows. Audibly.

I smirk. Silently.

"I wouldn't say no."

"Good to know," I joke. "You got me thinking. In the future, I might want to build something—" I turn us so that she can see where I'm pointing. "—on the west of the acreage. You'll get the same vista but the sun sets over there and I know how much you love that. Plus, I'd get a hot tub…"

"I like the way your mind works."

"We're on the same wavelength."

"I didn't think you'd want to live here again, I mean, from what you said about the town."

Sliding my arms around her waist, I scan the panoramic view ahead of me. Thousands of acres of Korhonen territory that have belonged to us for generations…

"Maybe seeing you fight for Chuck's inspired me." I graze my lips over her temple before I settle my chin on the crown of her head. "And watching how much you appreciated Pigeon Creek definitely got the cogs whirring. You were right—I do need to dissociate a dislike for my father with a dislike for my land."

She rests her hands on top of mine. "There's no place like home."

"Home doesn't always have to be a place though."

Mia stiffens a little before she sags into me. "No. It doesn't."

A smile curves my lips—damn straight, we're on the same page.

"For example, if you came out here with me, then I wouldn't even miss the city."

"No, I wouldn't miss it either. I do want to rebuild Chuck's though, Cole."

"Of course. Once the insurance coughs up the dough." That insurance was the only thing Chuck did right—it'll cover the rebuild and more. "I… Maybe it's a nice place to raise kids, you know?"

Her eyes widen. "Yeah, I can see that."

"I think we need to make it a real hockey hangout."

"Huh? Pigeon Creek?"

"No. Chuck's," I correct with a snort. "I can bring friends down and we can put the bar on the map."

Her cheeks flush which, considering the temperature, is a miracle. "You don't have to do that."

"Sure I do." I kiss the tip of her nose. "We're a team, aren't we?"

She immediately softens. "Yeah, we are."

"Anyway, I pull a mean draft."

"I bet it's all foam and no beer."

"I'm wounded."

"Not as much as my bank balance would be if I left you in charge of the bar."

Grinning because she gets my bullshit and bats it outta the park like always, I drift my lips over her cheek and down to her jaw. "With how much publicity you've attracted recently and the auction all arranged, I think your accounts will be fine. FedeLoans sucks for not giving you the option to buy out the debt consolidation loan though."

A soft moan escapes her as my hand settles on her stomach—beneath my jersey. "I-It's fine. I can afford the monthly installments now."

"Just in coaching classes alone seeing as your dance card's full." She's always had other students, but she'll be slammed when we're back in the city. "I liked being the teacher's pet, though."

Her laughter is breathy. "You'll always be that, baby."

After the fire and the stress of the past year, she agreed to take a few days' vacation when I nagged her. She was ready to get to work as soon as the calls came in from that shout-out in PSN News, but I stopped her.

Not only does she deserve a damn break, but my games aside, I wanted to spend some quality time with her before the madness of the upcoming year starts.

We're going whole hog for the Cup, and she's not only rebuilding Chuck's but has her coaching too.

As I nuzzle her throat, moving up to her ear, I whisper, "Wanna make a memory?"

She squirms against me, proving that she can speak 'Cole' fluently. "You said we shouldn't."

"I changed my mind."

"Someone might see."

"Naw."

"You sure?"

I think about Poltergeist Abelman who sees all and knows all of the transgressions that occur under this roof...

"Positive."

She arches her neck, exposing the sinews of her throat to me. As I kiss and lick there, fluttering my tongue over her agitated pulse, I unfasten the fly of her jeans.

Slipping a hand inside, I trace my fingers over her panty-covered pussy and find the crotch.

"I like this home—" I tap her slit. "—better than this one."

A laugh hiccups from her as my fingertips delve under the fabric and rub her clit. "Don't be sweet."

"I'll be dirty," I vow, abandoning her pussy and running my nose down the front of her sweater where I rub one of her nipples with it before moving lower. Tugging on her jeans, I draw the waistband over her hips and lodge it around her upper thighs.

I nudge her feet wider apart. "I wanna taste you, baby."

"Knock yourself out," she breathes when I drop to the ground in front of her and drag her panties down next.

"You wet for me, Mia?"

"You should find out for yourself."

"With my tongue?"

"I think that'd be a great choice." She peers around guiltily then, like the good little exhibitionist she is, frees herself from my hold to strip out of her pants.

"God, I love you," I praise in delight.

"Hurry! It's cold out here!"

No shit—she's braver than I am.

Mia leans on the rail and hitches one foot to the middle spoke so that she can womanspread.

Behind her, there's my land.

Above her, there's nothing but the sun and the sky.

There is literally nowhere else on this earth I could imagine as being my favorite place other than *here*, right now.

"You only gonna look at it?" she grumbles but takes the situation into her own hands. Her fingers find her clit and she rocks her hips as she strokes it. "I'll do it myself."

"You think that's a threat?" I retort, amused by the thought. "I love watching you touch yourself. You're so fucking beautiful and so goddamn filthy."

Shifting forward, I nip at her fingers before I take one into my mouth. I hear her breath hitch so I suck harder, then I let my tongue trace along its length before I ninja her and delve between her folds.

Her yelp is delicious. But not as tasty as her cunt.

Fuck, she's better than pineapple on pizza.

That's saying something.

I suck on her clit, giving her some good, solid pressure. I know I'm hitting the spot because her hands tug on my hair as if it's a controller. I continue like that until she's rocking her hips, then I move lower, sliding my tongue inside her pussy and using my nose to rub her clit.

She thrusts against me, riding my face, moaning and whimpering as her breathing joins the chorus. She's all I can hear and all I can feel.

She's so perfect, I can't stand it.

I thrust my tongue into her faster, faster, wishing it were my cock but also glad to give her this. To give *me* this. A better memory in this house. One that I don't want to forget.

The flat of my tongue slips higher this time as I swoop it over her entirety. She squirms against me and completes my mission:

"Oh, Cole. Cole. Cole. God, I love you. Your tongue. Honestly. The best. No tongue like it. Faster. Ummmm. Yeaaahh. God. Like that. Harder. Fuck. Yes. More. Co—le. No. Don't slow down," she whines when I tease her. "THAT'sss it!!!!!!!"

I can see the exclamation marks like her finger got jammed on the keyboard.

From below, I watch her bite her hand so hard, it's a miracle she doesn't bleed as she wails through her release, hips still rocking as she rides my face, eking out every ounce of pleasure.

Just like she was born to do.

"Oh, my god," she cries when I continue eating her out, savoring her juices and settling in for part two, but that's when my phone rings.

Callan's notification tone.

That little pussyblocker!

Kissing her clit, I give her a nuzzle with my nose then mumble, "I have something else to show you today but we have to sneak around."

"Huh?" she garbles, staring blindly at me.

"Feel good, baby?"

Her lashes flutter as her head tips back. "Uhhh-huh."

Chuckling to myself, I help her get dressed. 'Help her' because her legs are like limp noodles.

It was harder to get the panties on than to get *her* off, but my fumbling eventually irritates her enough that she pulls on her jeans by herself.

Thank Jesus for that.

When she's dressed, her pupils are still gluttonously dilated. "You said sneaking around."

"I did," I confirm, surprised she heard that much.

"Where?"

"Someplace close."

"Why?"

"Because where we're going isn't technically our land."

"Then, why are we going there?"

"Because no one will stop us."

"Technicalities?"

"You got that right."

As we maneuver through the house, we stop once in my room because she insists I clean my face.

Pouting, I comply, but only because I'll be seeing Callan soon.

After, I drag her outside and into my SUV, and I whack on the heat because it's below freezing outside and she still has to be feeling the chill from being half-naked on the veranda.

But hey, I figured out how to make use of the frigid winter because the McAllister lakes are eight inches thick and that means they're skate-worthy.

Twilight is almost over by the time we make it to the lake in question and it's edging more toward dark.

"This looks like the kind of place you'd go to get killed by an ax murderer."

"You have a wild imagination. The TBR list I'm cultivating for you is obviously working."

She hums as she examines the gloom. "Aren't you the lucky one?"

Unable to stop myself, I cackle then hit the brakes when the lights glint off one of my helper bees.

I say helper bees and I mean my goddamn brothers.

"Just wait here a moment."

"Gladly."

I jump out onto the lakeside and head over to Callan, who's bossing Colton around.

"Not there, Colton. For fuck's sake. How many times do I have to show you this?"

My lips quirk as Colton snipes, "You definitely inherited Pops's people skills."

"I have no patience for morons."

"Meaning you have no patience for Pops, Callan?" Cody drawls.

"Exactly. Colt's just not concentrating and he needs to start before I—"

"Before you what, kiddo?"

I wade into the grumbling. "You manage to get them set up in time?"

"Of course, we did," Cody derides. "Jesus Christ, I earned the Star of Military Valour and my baby brother thinks I can't set up a bunch of candles on a fucking lake."

"This is life or death too, Cody."

"Cole, my man, it truly isn't. Though," he concedes, "Mia's too good for your ass so I guess it is."

"Damn straight."

I shoot Callan a look, well aware of how difficult the past week's been on him.

Before leaving, Colton and Cody wish me their version of good luck:

Colton: "Don't fuck this up."

Cody: "I wouldn't blame her for saying no so be convincing. Mum likes her."

I snag a hold of Callan's arm and keep him back as the others stare at us curiously before jumping on their respective ATVs and taking off for home.

"You all right?" I ask Callan.

"Been better," he mumbles before he mutters in a rush, "You swear you won't tell her that I've seen her naked?"

"I don't feel like humiliating either of you, Callan," I lie because she already knows whose account I stole. I scrub a hand over his head. "Thanks for doing this."

"You're welcome." He tosses a remote at me. "When are you guys going back to NYC again? I'd like to leave my bedroom at some point."

"You're out now, aren't you?"

"Yeah, but this isn't my idea of a good time."

I tut as he slouches off into the darkness. "Hey, you're not going to tell Pops about her past, are you?"

"Why would I? I love her, dude."

That has me blinking at him. "Awkward."

"Yeah, but I'm used to being second best to my brothers. There's no change there."

Before I can answer, he clambers onto the back of his ATV and lights it out of here.

I watch him go then, with a sigh, reach for my phone in my pocket so I can send him a message.

> Me: Second best? You're better than all of
> us, kid.
>
> Me: When you find your one, she'll only have
> eyes for you.
>
> Me: That's how it's supposed to be.
>
> Me: Thanks for your help, Callan. I really
> appreciate it.

I know he won't read that until later, but it's okay—as long as he reads it at some point, I'm fine with that.

When I turn around at the sound of someone clearing their throat, I whisper, "Just give me five."

"It's on your dime, Mr. Korhonen. I'm here until ten PM."

Running back to the SUV, I open the door at the same time as I hit the button on the remote Callan gave me.

Hundreds of lights flare on and start flickering over the width of the lake. At the sight, she releases a happy laugh as she stands on the step beside the footwell to peer over the door.

While she's occupied with that, I grab the skates I dumped in the back seat earlier and pass her her pair. "You ready to skate?"

"I was born ready," she teases. "But you're not wearing the right skates…"

Waggling my regular hockey skates at her, I shoot her a grin. "Sure I am."

With the lights on in the SUV, both of us lace up.

Five minutes later, we stomp over the snowy ground toward the lakeshore.

"You certain this is thick enough?"

"Had Callan measure it."

She tuts. "You're cruel."

"Hardly. He was glad to get out of the house."

As I slide onto the ice through a thin pathway that Callan left free from candles, I hold out my hand for her to take.

Laughing, she mocks, "You only know the first two minutes of the routine, and most of that's on your knees. You'd have learned more if you'd stopped being a jackass on the ice sooner. I still can't believe I fell for that."

"Hey, it's better than nothing. And if it's any consolation, I can't believe you fell for it either."

She chuckles, but in the very center of the frozen lake, we come to a standstill, and as the legends themselves did because a free dance is only supposed to last four minutes and their song was four minutes and eighteen seconds, both of us kneel.

Because that's the cue, the lone violinist plays Ravel's *Boléro*.

She jolts, her head whipping to the side, but I snag her hand, squeeze it, then encourage her to move with me.

We start with our heads barely touching, cheek to opposite cheek. Then, as the music ripples through the air, we begin to sway.

I've never been much of a dancer, but for her, I want to be the best so I may have practiced this without her and with a lot of help from Lewis.

I'll never live it down but fuck it, she's worth it.

In the darkness, with the candles illuminating our path, she watches me move to the beat, arms floating as we drift from side to side, focus locked on one another.

Then, we make half circles on our knees, only stopping until our chins almost brush.

Except, with us, they do. We stagger that move so our lips can touch.

Then, I slide one leg wide for balance while she remains high on her knees. My arms scoop down, one sliding beneath her breasts, the other pressing against her calves which she pins together. Her arms soar as she points them at the sky.

I lift her until she's in an aerial swan dive and stay kneeling on the ice, tilting her until she's standing in front of me.

She lowers her arms to her hips, waiting for my hand to collide with hers for a moment before I release her. Spinning around me, she outstretches her fingers in a playful plea for me to join her, feet weaving in and out effortlessly. Then, both her hands return to mine over my head.

With that, I lift her into the air again. One of her legs kicks up until the other joins it. She returns to that swan dive position of before but this time, she rolls down my front like a kid tumbling over a snow-laden hill, landing on my knees, her skates not even skimming the ice until she's ready for the picks to dig in deep.

That's when I boost her into a standing position and both of us raise our hands to the sky this time.

She spins around to face me, skating in a circle while I pivot on one knee, following her, barely remembering to keep my damn leg up.

This figure-skating shit is fucking hard.

That's when I scoop my leg in and push off so we're both vertical.

We separate to spin on our own before she collides with me in a controlled explosive motion once more. Leaning backward until we tilt into one another, we weave some fancy footwork that has us floating forward until the pair of us skate wide, our knees facing outward, mirror images of one another.

My hands cup her waist as we duck low and skim the ice.

From a crouch, we extend into an arabesque, and that's when she lets go of me and I do a full circle on my own. Lifting my leg, I hold it at a right angle, then I spin.

And I spin.

And I fucking spin.

Hooting as I complete a full spin twice over, I immediately drop to my knees.

She shrieks at the sight but I drawl, "Your lack of confidence in me is hurtful."

"Jerkface!"

Snow sprays me as she skids to a halt in front of me.

Exactly where I want her.

"What did you fall for?"

I dig in my pocket, beam a grin up at her, then, as I pop the lid on the velvet box, ask her, "Mia Charles, will you be my wife?"

She gapes at the ring then lets out a sob before hurling herself at me.

"Is that a yes?" I croak as she practically chokes me with how hard she squeezes.

Mia jerks back, plunks a kiss on my lips, then growls, "It's a hell yes."

A HONUS WAGNER TRADING CARD HITS RECORD-BREAKING HIGH BID IN ONE-OF-A-KIND AUCTION

BY MACK FINNEGAN

A rare trading card of Honus Wagner went up for auction yesterday, one lot amid a dedicated sale for a single collection of rare trading cards that recently came onto the market.

The last sale of a Wagner card reached $6,600,569, but yesterday's lot topped seven million from an anonymous buyer.

The original owner of the trading cards is Marty Charles's great-granddaughter.

The record-breaking World Series winner apparently started the collection for his son, but it appears he used it as a secret journal with some cards annotated with his personal opinion of specific players.

Between fifty and two hundred copies were said to have been

made of the unique 'Honus Wagner' trading card, with only a handful still surviving.

Ms. Charles, the owner of Chuck's, a bar in Midtown that was recently destroyed in a fire believed to be arson, now belongs in a different tax bracket thanks to the auction that saw her become a millionaire eleven times over because of the other unique cards amid the collection.

'Chuck's' social media account, in light of recent events, has received a wave of publicity with Charles's alleged fiancé and New York Star player, Cole Korhonen, discussing the history of the vintage cards as well as Charles herself sharing anecdotes of her great-grandfather and his opinions on baseball legends.

ONE DAY, I CAME ACROSS AN IDOL'S TRADING CARD.
I TOOK A BEATING TO KEEP IT WHEN MY LOAN SHARK
CALLED IN HIS DEBT.
WORST BEATING OF MY LIFE. BUT MY KID...
GOTTA LEAVE HIM WITH SOMETHING BESIDES LOAN
SHARKS WHO ARE LIKE UNCLES TO HIM
MARTY CHARLES

KillerCatQueen7: Hey, handsome

GretzkyWannabe42: I'm afraid I can't talk to you anymore, queen.

KillerCatQueen7: *pouts* Why not?

GretzkyWannabe42: I'm taken, and my future wife's going to be my sugar momma so I can't rock the boat.

KillerCatQueen7: Ugh, but you were my sugar daddy first!

GretzkyWannabe42: You cleaned me out. What can I say?

KillerCatQueen7: :P

KillerCatQueen7: Lunch's on me?

GretzkyWannabe42: I'm cheap so, yeah. Hawaiian pizza?

KillerCatQueen7: What else, handsome?

GretzkyWannabe42: You know what I noticed recently?

KillerCatQueen7: I dread to think

GretzkyWannabe42: You stopped drinking half a bottle of water before you eat...

KillerCatQueen7: Not just a pretty face.

KillerCatQueen7: Don't need to worry so much about feeling full anymore.

KillerCatQueen7: I'll pick the pizza up on the way home from the rink.

GretzkyWannabe42: I'd say that if I had it my way, you'd never have to skip a meal again (yeah, I'm onto you) but you're my sugar momma now so maybe you're the one who needs to watch my macros ^^

KillerCatQueen7: Oh, I'm watching. Who's the one who brought up food today?!

GretzkyWannabe42: You're right. This sugar baby feels loved <3

GretzkyWannabe42: I'll be back in an hour. Just in the whirlpool.

KillerCatQueen7: Reading smut stuff?

GretzkyWannabe42: Getting inspiration for later.

KillerCatQueen7: :P

KillerCatQueen7: You gonna beat Chicago tonight?

GretzkyWannabe42: Damn straight.

KillerCatQueen7: Do you know you never told me which Taylor Swift song you listen to during your pregame ritual?

GretzkyWannabe42: It changed after I met you

KillerCatQueen7: o.O From what?

GretzkyWannabe42: Used to be "Shake It Off"

GretzkyWannabe42: When you were playing fast and loose with my heart, "Blank Space"

GretzkyWannabe42: Now, it's "willow." It's about falling in love with someone from the very beginning. Why wouldn't that pump me up to go and bring you back the Cup, baby?

KillerCatQueen7: I love you (even if you don't win the Stanley trophy OR beat Chicago later)

GretzkyWannabe42: I love you too :* (Heresy. I'll win it on purpose now. And it's a CUP, babe.)

GretzkyWannabe42: Think we should change our usernames?

KillerCatQueen7: Nah.

GretzkyWannabe42: Admit it. I'm turning you into a romantic.

KillerCatQueen7: ;)

KillerCatQueen7: Maybe <3

CHAPTER 50
MATT

"WHO'S the chick next to the bench?"

Liam, who's midway through a protein shake, blinks at me. "What chick?"

"He means that chick who always wears the other team's jersey," McIsaac complains. "The one who sits rink side."

My brows lift. "Why does she do that?"

"No idea," Liam dismisses, obviously uninterested in the woman's reasoning. "Why did you ask? She shout something at you? She does that sometimes."

"Please tell me it was worthy of getting her tossed from the game?" McIsaac asks, tone hopeful.

I scratch my chin. "She was wearing my jersey."

"Doubtful. She always wears the opposing team's—"

"Exactly. She wore a Bulldogs' jersey. With my name on it."

"So?" Liam finishes off his shake.

"So? Have you seen her?"

"Yeah. Many times."

I huff. "You've got Gracie tunnel vision. Isn't she banging, Lewis?"

Lewis raises his hands. "Don't bring me into this."

"You'll fuck anything that moves but—"

"She comes to every game and cheers for the other team, dude. She's a traitor. I don't fuck traitors."

"That's harsh," I defend.

Cole snorts. "What's it to you?"

"That's my future wife you're talking about." I huff as I fold my arms across my chest.

The teammates around us pause in their ministrations to gawk at me.

I shoot them a smug smile.

"Your future wife?" Lewis repeats with a hoot.

"Since when are you getting married?" Cole demands.

"Why did you ask who she was if you've never met her before?" Liam counters. "And how is a stranger your future wife?"

I hitch a shoulder. "I may have never met her before but that doesn't mean dick."

"I'm confused." McIsaac rubs his temple.

"Doesn't take much," Gagné retorts with a chuckle before shooting me a measured look. "Fifty says she turns you down."

"His proposal?" Cole drawls. "Or when he asks her out the first time?"

Gagné smirks. "Both."

"I'm a patient man. I'll make her mine before we raise the Cup." Spitting into my fist, I hold out my hand for him to shake. "Game on."

The preorder for Matt's story is now live!
www.books2read.com/GameOnGAMazurke

———

The preorder for Colton's story is now live!
https://books2read.com/PigeonCreekOneGAMazurke

———

You can read a bonus scene for Cole & Mia here:
https://dl.bookfunnel.com/156dz333vq

MEET THE CAST

YOU MAY HAVE COME across some characters that you recognize from other titles of mine...

Liam Donnghal and Gracie Bukowski - Captain and GM of the New York Stars

Finn and Aoife O'Grady - Owners of the bakery where Cole takes Mia on their first date. (Liam's family.)

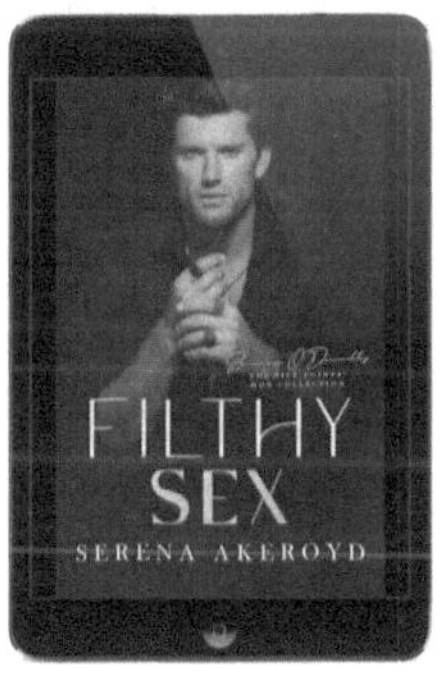

Camille O'Donnelly - owner of the stables (Brennan is her husband and is Liam's family.)

Rachel Laker - Mia's attorney

Cruz - Indy's partner - Cole and Mia's tattoo artist

BONUS SCENE & AUTHOR NOTE

THANK you so much for reading WAITING GAME!

I hope you're excited for Matt's story!

This book resonated with me in so many ways, especially Cole's grief for Betsy. Having lost my Betsy, I understand his pain and hope, that one day, the right creature comes along and will permit me to open my heart to that kind of love again.

Don't forget - the moment WAITING GAME hits 500 reviews, I'll be dropping a bonus scene in my Diva reader group!

You can join here:

www.facebook.com/groups/serenaakeroydsdivas

There's also a bonus scene if you join my newsletter!

www.serenaakeroyd.com/newsletter

Much love and thanks for reading,

Gem

Xo

CONNECT WITH G. A. MAZURKE

For the latest updates, be sure to check out my website!
But if you'd like to hang out with me and get to know me better, then I'd love to see you in my Diva reader's group where you can find out all the gossip on new releases as and when they happen. You can join here: www.facebook.com/groups/SerenaAkeroydsDivas. Or you can always PM or email me. I love to hear from you guys: gamazurke@gmail.com.

ABOUT THE AUTHOR

G. A. Mazurke is the crazy lady behind Serena Akeroyd, crafter of smexy heroes you just wanna lick. While Serena has us expecting dark romance with lots of twists and turns … G. A. is her more mainstream/contemporary personality.

She explores her sweeter side while keeping the sexy we love, where the women fall hard but the men fall harder.

Some of G. A.'s books will cross over into Serena's universes… so expect a cameo or two from beloved characters, while discovering new bands of brothers, with the banter, the laughs and the tears you are used to.